BURNING
IIIIIJUSTICE

BURNING ⫽⫽⫽JUSTICE

TEE O'FALLON

Entangled Publishing, LLC
644 Shrewsbury Commons Ave., STE 181
Shrewsbury, PA 17361
Visit our website at www.entangledpublishing.com.

Amara is an imprint of Entangled Publishing, LLC.

Edited by Heather Howland and Robin Haseltine
Cover design by LJ Anderson, Mayhem Cover Creations
Cover art by innervision/Depositphotos,
curaphotography/Depositphotos,
mcornelius/Depositphotos
Interior design by Toni Kerr

Print ISBN 978-1-64937-339-7
ebook ISBN 978-1-64937-340-3

Manufactured in the United States of America

First Edition September 2023

ALSO BY TEE O'FALLON

To Custer, the most fun-loving, beautiful Chesapeake Bay Retriever I ever met. You were taken from your family far too soon. Would that you could have lived forever on this earth. Forever you remain in our hearts. We miss you.

To Steve—Custer's dad and the best partner a girl could ask for.

CHAPTER ONE

Bright orange-and-yellow flames licked at the night sky as if they were alive, consuming the warehouse and everything in it like a starved animal. Which it was.

Fire is irrational. It destroys that which feeds it.

Tonight, it was a hungry beast.

Over the roar of the blaze, firefighters trained hoses on the structure, starting to get it under control. Eerie creaking rent the air as corrugated metal walls began to bend and buckle. Thick, black smoke seeped from the four loading bay doors and billowed through the collapsed roof. Every so often, glowing embers drifted upward, reminding Brett Tanner of the fireflies he and his brothers used to catch when they were kids.

Even fifty yards away, standing on the edge of the road behind the guardrail and well behind the safety perimeter, Brett felt the intense heat. It was like standing outside in the hot Denver sun in the middle of summer. Sweat trickled down his temples and his back, adhering his polo shirt to his body as if it was glued on. Whether it was from actual pain or repressed memories, the burned skin on his forearm and back tingled and stung.

When the wind shifted, bringing with it the acrid smell of smoke, he tugged on his dog's leash and backed them both farther away. The warehouse contained not only wood and tools but all kinds of building supplies. The air had a pungent chemical odor, telling him the fire had finally reached the solvents—ignitable liquids that acted as accelerants.

The hackles on his neck went vertical. Those smells—smoke laced with chemicals and burning foam—never failed to hurl him back in time to two other fires, ones he kept reliving over and over again.

As night terrors.

Though it had been twenty-five years ago, he remembered everything about the fire when he was eleven years old. *He'd* gotten out alive. His two best friends hadn't.

A house fire a year ago that had killed two teenagers and left him badly burned kickstarted his guilt all over again.

Since then, Brett had been hunting the arsonist he believed was responsible for torching that house. In the process, he'd discovered another arsonist, this one lighting up dumpsters, and now this warehouse. The PD called him anytime there was a fire of questionable origin. Like tonight.

Blaze, his ATF K-9, snorted, and Brett turned to find Sergeant Danny Lopez heading their way. Behind Danny, red-and-blue strobes flashed from police units blocking the road in both directions. One unit moved to the side of the road, and more fire trucks rolled past the barricade, their air brakes hissing as they came to a stop.

Behind the warehouse were several hundred yards of wide open, grassy field edged with thick stands of ponderosa pines and aspen trees. Two scorched industrial dumpsters sat off to the side of the asphalt parking lot, ones that had been deliberately torched only a few days ago. Way too much coincidence in Brett's book.

The gold badge on Danny's uniform glinted in the flickering light. "Might take a while to knock this one down."

"Looks like." Judging by the staccato of loud pops and mini explosions now coming from one side of the building, the flames had just hit more cans of solvents and strippers. "Thanks for the call."

"You got it."

A woman standing about a hundred feet away snapped images on her cell phone. She stuffed the phone in one of the back pockets of her jeans, then tugged a small pad from the other.

"Who's that?" Brett tipped his head in her direction. "Reporter?"

Danny shook his head. "Gemma Scott. NICB. She got here before you did."

Interesting. Considering he'd hauled ass from Lakewood doing over ninety down I-25 to get here. Maybe she lived in the area. Or she had an inside source.

"Catch you later," Brett said. "C'mon, boy."

Thinking he was about to go to work, Blaze happily fell in step beside him, flicking his tail back and forth as they walked over to the NICB investigator.

In his ten years with the ATF, Brett had encountered agents of the National Insurance Crime Bureau several times before. They were the intermediary between the insurance industry, law enforcement, and the prosecutors' offices. If insurance fraud was suspected, NICB occasionally referred cases to the local PD. Depending on the circumstances, and if arson was suspected, they reached out to the ATF. But he'd never heard of Gemma Scott, and no one in his office had ever mentioned her.

However, since this was the second warehouse fire in the Springs in as many weeks *and* at the same warehouse, it didn't surprise him that NICB had sent one of their people.

Brett was convinced this was the work of the same arsonist who'd been setting the dumpster fires all over town, including the ones right behind this very warehouse. Unlike the fire a year ago that had burned him and killed those teens, at least these fires hadn't killed anyone.

As he and Blaze drew nearer, Brett thought the woman looked familiar but didn't think they'd ever worked together. Ms. Gemma Scott wasn't someone he'd be likely to forget.

At about five-one, she was petite. Thick red hair that fell to between her shoulder blades glowed like hot coals in the firelight. She was dressed in jeans, work boots, and a long-sleeve white shirt rolled up to her elbows. Apparently hearing his and Blaze's approach, she stopped jotting in her pad and looked up.

Brett held out his hand. "ATF Special Agent Brett Tanner."

For a moment, she hesitated as her gaze dipped to the badge and gun on his belt, then she took his hand in an unexpectedly firm handshake. Not manly, just confident. "Gemma Scott. NICB. And this is?" She smiled at his dog.

Gemma was an attractive woman, but when she smiled, she was pretty. *Really* pretty. Not for the first time, he could swear he knew her but couldn't place where or when they might have crossed paths.

"This is my partner, Blaze. Blaze, shake hands with the lady."

His dog sat, then held up his paw and cracked his jaws as if he were smiling back.

Gemma leaned over and shook Blaze's paw. "Nice to meet you, Blaze. He's a big one. What is he, a Chessie?"

"You know your dogs." Most people didn't know what a Chesapeake Bay Retriever was. Given his eighty-five-pound muscular body, Blaze was usually mistaken for a Labrador mix on steroids. "You sure got here fast," he said, still wondering if Gemma had an inside source.

"The owner's son, Logan Hicks, called me." She pointed to where a man stood talking to the fire chief. "This is the second fire they've had here in the last two weeks."

"I know," he answered, casting another glance at Hicks. There was always the possibility this fire was set by the owners themselves, who stupidly thought they could burn down their own building and collect on hefty insurance claims.

"And who called *you*?" Her brows rose for an instant, then quickly lowered. "I didn't refer this case to you. In fact, I haven't referred it to *anyone*." Her words held an unconcealed note of suspicion, as if she wasn't thrilled by him being here.

"The PD called me. I've been investigating the arsonist who's been torching all the dumpsters down here." In Colorado, anything south of Denver and the I-25/C-470 interchange was referred to as "down here."

Gemma subtly shook her head. "I think you're on

the wrong track. I don't think the dumpster arsonist you're looking for set this fire. This is either insurance fraud—and I really don't think it is—or something else."

"Something else? Mind sharing?"

Eyes that he thought were hazel—but he couldn't be sure in the dim, hazy light—studied him intently for a long moment. "This company, Frodo Building Supply, is doing very well. With Colorado's housing boom, real estate prices everywhere are through the roof, and the building industry is skyrocketing. Not only is Frodo in the black, but the owner, Robert Hicks, is planning on his son taking over the business when he retires." Again, she pointed to Logan Hicks. "They have no reason to burn down their own warehouse. And before the first warehouse fire last week, they'd never filed an insurance claim. They've been cooperating fully with the claims adjusters and now *this* happens."

"So you do agree that it's arson."

"Of course." Brett could swear she rolled her eyes at him. "Two fires at the same warehouse in two weeks? But again, not the arsonist *you're* looking for."

Brett chuckled. "The dumpsters next to this building were torched a few days ago. Where arson is concerned, I don't believe in coincidences." Like the fact that Torrance Lane, the location of the fire that killed those kids a year ago, was barely three blocks from where they were standing.

"I think that's exactly what you've got here. A coincidence." She planted one fist on her hip. "These warehouse fires don't fit the same pattern as your guy. This warehouse was hit twice. This is personal.

Whoever torched all those dumpsters did *not* set this warehouse fire. I think whoever *did* set this fire may also be responsible for other house fires around Colorado in the last few years."

That pinged Brett's radar. While eventually deemed accidental, the Torrance Lane fire had, in Brett's estimation, been suspicious in nature. "I don't see the link between these warehouse fires and house fires."

"You wouldn't," she said with no small amount of exasperation. "I, however, would, because I have direct access to something you don't, the ISO—Insurance Services Office—database. And I found something. I—"

Brett held up his hand.

Movement. A shadow thirty feet away, barely visible in the field behind her. He continued watching, waiting. It could have been a small tree he hadn't noticed in the middle of the field.

But the tree began to move.

"Are you even listening?" Gemma made a *hmph*-ing sound. "Right. I didn't think so."

"Let's go!" Brett and Blaze leaped over the guard rail, then took off at a dead run. Whatever was out there wasn't a deer or a bear. It was human, and it was running away.

Brett's heart pumped faster as he raced through the parking lot, trying to keep his eyes on the location where he'd last seen the shadow. Given that he usually ran at least seven miles every day, he was in good shape, yet Blaze loped easily beside him, forced to go at Brett's relatively slow pace.

They dodged a glowing piece of the building that

had become airborne. Blaze jumped as the debris landed next to them and exploded in a fiery burst of embers. When they reached the field on the other side of the building, Brett halted his dog and tugged a small, powerful, tactical flashlight from his belt. Breathing hard, he punched on the light, cutting through the darkness, but saw nothing in the field.

He unclipped Blaze's leash and pointed. "Seek!"

His dog took off, his golden-brown coat visible for a few seconds before Brett lost sight of him. Blaze wasn't cross trained as a patrol dog, but if this runner had come into contact with so much as a drop of accelerant, Blaze could track him.

Brett raced after Blaze, pounding over the hard-pack terrain, his boots crunching on the dry grass. He couldn't see his dog anywhere and stopped to swing the flashlight beam left and right in a broader arc.

Panting hard, he tried to slow his breathing to listen. A piercing cry drifted on the wind, and he aimed the beam toward the sound and took off running again. Eventually, his flashlight hit on Blaze's coat.

Blaze sat, his big body trembling. A man on the ground scrambled backward on his elbows. Blaze was by no means an attack dog, but anyone with half a brain would be intimidated by his size. That didn't stop Blaze from eyeing the suspect with the same intensity he'd afford a strip of bacon.

With his free hand, Brett drew his weapon, aiming in on the suspect. He shined the light into the guy's face, blinding him and forcing him to fling his hands in front of his eyes.

"Police. Don't move!" He focused the light on the suspect's hands, checking them for weapons, but there were none. "Roll onto your stomach! Do it now!"

The man complied, mumbling, "Just keep the dog off me."

Brett stuck the end of the flashlight in his mouth and holstered. He grabbed a set of handcuffs from the back of his belt. In seconds, he had the guy cuffed, then patted him down for weapons.

The guy was more of a kid, really. Tall and lanky, covered in soot and smelling like smoke and some kind of accelerant. Probably what Blaze had hit on so quickly. No guns or knives that he could feel. He pulled several items from the guy's pants pockets. Two small butane lighters and a box of matches.

"I didn't do it," the kid shouted. "I swear it. I *didn't* set this fire."

Yeah, right. The evidence in his pockets said otherwise.

Behind him, boots pounded over the hard earth. Another flashlight beam bobbed closer.

"Brett, you good?" Danny asked between breaths as his light landed on Brett's prisoner.

No longer needing it, he took the flashlight from his mouth, clicked it off and stuck it back in his belt. "Yeah, I'm good," he called over his shoulder, then slipped Blaze a freeze-dried liver treat as a reward. "What's your name?" He hadn't found a wallet or any other form of ID. "What's your *name*?" he repeated more firmly when the kid didn't respond.

"Gavin."

"Gavin *what*?" Again, no immediate response. "You're going to be lying here face down in the grass for a long time if you don't tell me your full name."

Gavin exhaled on a groan. "Aldrich."

"Well, Gavin Aldrich. Are you willing to talk to me?" If so, Brett would read him his rights and get straight to the point.

"Yeah. I didn't do it," he repeated. "I didn't set this fire."

The possibility that he was telling the truth was about as likely as Blaze standing up on his hind legs, saluting the American flag, and singing "The Star-Spangled Banner." Then again... His dog actually did salute, and he did like talking back to the TV.

He hauled Aldrich into a sitting position, then read the kid his rights, grateful for Danny's presence as a witness. Whatever else Aldrich admitted to, Brett didn't want to risk losing it on a technicality.

"Well?" Brett prodded. "You said you were willing to talk, so talk. Why'd you torch this warehouse?"

Aldrich's mouth opened, then snapped shut. His lips compressed into a tight line. The kid looked away, his lower lip trembling. Seemed like the moment of cooperation was now null and void. Whatever was going on, he'd get it out of the kid sooner or later. Nothing like a night in jail to loosen lips.

"Let's go." Brett grabbed Aldrich's elbow and helped him to stand.

Surprisingly, by the time they returned to the warehouse parking lot, the fire was nearly out, which was a good thing. The priorities and necessities of fire suppression could inadvertently destroy or conceal evidence, and Brett wanted to get Blaze in there ASAP.

As they drew nearer, a firefighter approached them. "The fire's still burning on one side of the ware-house, but we found something you need to see." The firefighter—S. Downing, according to his coat name tag—hitched his head toward the side of the building that was no longer on fire.

Gemma appeared behind them, holding up her credentials. "I'm coming with you."

Downing looked at her, then gave a slight shake of his head. "I don't think that's a good idea. It's still dangerous in there. It's—"

"Yeah, yeah, yeah." This time, Brett was sure Gemma rolled her eyes. "The fire might restart. We could be electrocuted by downed power lines. Residual particulate inhalation. Structural weakness could cause the rest of the building to collapse on our heads. I'm aware."

"Apparently so." Downing cleared his throat. "My mistake."

Brett did his best to contain a snort. The lady might be small in stature, but she had balls, and she knew her fire scenes.

"No problem," Gemma replied as she began tapping the tip of her boot on the asphalt. "Let's go. Time's a-wasting."

"I've got him." Danny grinned, obviously amused by the ballsy exchange as he took custody of Gavin Aldrich. "I'll put him in my car."

"Thanks." To the firefighter, he said, "Give me a minute."

Brett and Blaze jogged back to his SUV, where he grabbed pairs of vinyl and unused, virgin leather gloves, along with a few evidence bags he stuffed into a thigh pocket. "Show me," he said when they'd returned to the same firefighter.

They went inside one of the doors that had been

broken open to vent the building. Though the fire was out in this part of the warehouse, firefighters continued spraying water to disperse any remaining vapors. Burned and charred debris lay everywhere, wispy gray tendrils spiraling upward. A multitude of smells permeated the air.

Smoke. Burned rubber. Melted plastic. Chemicals. Smoke was still the dominant scent, but now that they were inside, the chemical odor was stronger, similar to the stench of permanent markers.

Blaze tugged at the leash, his nasal receptors already pinging with accelerant odors even Brett could smell. "Seek."

His dog began sniffing, circling twice, before leading them to the remains of a small sofa plunked in the middle of the smoldering warehouse. Blaze sat, and Brett slipped him another freeze-dried nugget. "Here's the fuel package." He nodded to the sofa. Upholstered furniture was made of metal, wood, natural fibers, and foam padding, most of which were fuel for a fire.

"He must have used these." Downing pointed to a dozen rectangular cans scattered on the floor.

Most of their labels had been burned away. Brett nudged one of them with his foot. Empty. The letters MEK were barely visible. Methyl ethyl ketone.

Brett gripped Blaze's leash tighter. There wasn't a single bullet point on an MEK label or Material Safety Data Sheet that he couldn't recite by heart. Approved usages. Health hazards. Exposure limits. Toxicity. *The label is the law*, but if improperly used, MEK could quickly become RBS. *Really bad shit*.

MEK was a colorless, highly flammable liquid that

smelled like acetone. As a readily available industrial solvent, it was commonly used as a degreaser to remove adhesives and paint and often used in the aircraft refurbishing process to prep the fuselage for repainting.

Brett stared at the cans. Gasoline was the universal accelerant of choice for an arsonist, so why use MEK? Because it was readily available on the warehouse shelves? *Maybe.* Or because the arsonist was familiar with it, knew exactly what kind of damage it would do? Most arsonists found a method they liked, then stuck with it.

MEK had also been the culprit at the Torrance Lane fire. For various reasons Brett disagreed with, arson had been dismissed as the cause. Despite that determination, to this day, he still suspected arson. Since then, he'd followed up on every single fire in Colorado Springs, to the detriment of his personal life and his sanity. Somewhere out there was the missing piece of evidence he was convinced existed to prove that fire was arson. Until he found it, he'd never give up, never stop searching, and never find peace.

"What's with the rope?" Gemma pointed to pieces of singed rope dangling from stacks of burned, blackened lumber. "Trailers?"

"Yeah." Brett nodded. "Fire always tells you where it came from. Before they burned, those pieces of rope probably ran all the way to the sofa. That way, he could be sure the fire would hit whatever was on the shelves."

Telling them whoever set this fire wanted to make sure it destroyed as much of the contents as possible. Maximum destruction. Brett looked around at what little remained of the shelving and warehouse stock. The arsonist had pretty much accomplished his goal.

"This way." Downing went ahead, sidestepping a pile of debris and a row of collapsed metal shelving.

Gemma followed, skirting the same debris, but her shirt caught on a piece of jagged metal sticking out from the damaged shelf. She uttered a soft cry, then started falling. Headfirst.

Brett lunged, wrapping one arm around her waist, then scooping her up against his chest the same way a groom would carry his bride over the threshold. "I've got you."

Her chest heaved against his. She was small and curvy, fitting perfectly in his arms. Somehow, in the midst of all the residual smoke and chemical smells in the air, Brett breathed in something pretty and sweet.

For an infinitely long moment, their gazes met and held. Something seemed to sizzle between them. A spark of electricity.

She pushed at his chest, her hand searing an imprint straight through his shirt to his skin. "Thanks, but um. You can put me down now."

"Uh, right." He released her legs, letting her body slide down his to a standing position.

"Hey, back here." Downing waved them over to a corner of the warehouse, where he pointed to the floor.

Before Brett could identify what the firefighter was pointing to, he smelled it. The sickly scent of burned hair and flesh. The body was charred beyond recognition. No remaining hair or identifiable facial features.

He blew out a breath. This wasn't what he'd been

expecting. The charges had just changed. Drastically.

For this fire, Gavin Aldrich would be charged with arson and now…

Felony murder.

CHAPTER TWO

"Mr. Aldrich," U.S. Magistrate Judge Maritza Tafoya stated, "you are remanded to the Pine Springs Mental Health Treatment Center in Colorado Springs for a preliminary psychiatric assessment. This assessment will determine if you are a danger to others and will be a deciding factor as to whether you enter the correctional system or the mental health system."

Judge Tafoya paused to look at her laptop. "Mr. Aldrich, you are ordered to reappear in court two days from now."

"Your Honor." Aldrich's public defender, a man in his late forties and wearing glasses, stood. "I assure you my client is *not* a danger to others. He and another homeless man were sleeping in the back of the warehouse. My client managed to get out, but his friend didn't. This was the first person who cared about my client and helped him in a very long time. Mr. Aldrich's background is quite complex. We need more than two days to conduct a comprehensive psychiatric assessment. I'd like to request an adjournment for two months, allowing sufficient time for a thorough evaluation."

"Mr. Manning, I've read the pretrial report." The judge picked up a folder, then put it down. "You have two days, and you're lucky I gave you that. After I read the psychiatric assessment, I'll make my decision." The judge stood.

"All rise," the bailiff said in a monotone voice.

Four rows back from the wood rail separating the prosecutor and defense counsel's tables from the public benches, Gemma stood, noting the judge was already halfway through the door to her chambers before the handful of other people in the room had even made it to their feet. The judge's perfectly manicured, fire-engine-red fingernails contrasted sharply against her black robe.

I can only wish.

She glanced at her short, stubby excuses for fingernails. Between her job and renovating the fixer-upper she'd purchased last year, there wasn't a chance in Hades of her nails ever extending farther than a gnat's body width beyond her fingers before breaking. A pedi, however, was an entirely different matter. Thick, ugly work boots protected her toes that were, at the moment, painted fire-engine red, her big toes additionally adorned with bright orange flames.

Agent Tanner, who'd been seated directly behind the prosecutor, AUSA Deborah Moran, leaned over the rail to speak with the woman, the movement tightening the black polo shirt over his broad shoulders and back, and his khakis, outlining—

She really had to stop ogling the man's ass and quit thinking about how he'd kept her from face planting on the warehouse floor. Talk about a life's-most-embarrassing moment. Yet, as he'd held her, plastered to his chest, and they'd stared into each other's eyes, she'd felt…what? Secure? Safe?

And heat. Definitely heat, which was ridiculous. It was probably only residual heat from the fire.

The only reason she was having these thoughts was because she hadn't been in a relationship—a *real* one, that was—for years, but even she had to admit that at a few inches over six feet, with a seriously well-muscled physique, sandy-blond hair, brown eyes, and a face handsome enough to give Brad Pitt a run for his money, Special Agent Brett Tanner wasn't hard on the eyes. *No siree.*

With that physique, his good looks, and the *Dirty Harry*–size gun and gleaming gold badge on his belt, Tanner could be the hero in an action-adventure movie. AUSA Moran could easily have been cast as the heroine in the same movie.

Assistant U.S. Attorney Moran was fashionably decked out, wearing a tight-fitting purple skirt and jacket suit, perfect makeup, and glittery gold jewelry at her ears and around her neck. In all, she was svelte, blond, and pretty. She'd seemed competent enough during Gavin Aldrich's initial appearance. She laughed at something Brett said, and Gemma could swear the woman batted her eyelashes.

Was that what it really took to get a man's attention? Flirting, chic clothes, and makeup? If so, then she'd be man-less for the rest of her life, because that *so* wasn't her. She could never rock that look. Then again, she couldn't blame the other woman for flirting. Her hormones had been on vacay for so long she couldn't remember when there'd been any reason to put them to good use. That didn't mean they were dysfunctional or dead. *Yet.* Because again…Brad Pitt.

"Agent Tanner? Ms. Moran?" Aldrich's public defender waved Brett and the prosecutor over just as the deputy U.S. Marshals prepared to whisk his client away. Gemma actually felt sorry for Aldrich. Not only was he homeless, but he was also broke and had no family.

She couldn't hear what Manning was saying. After several minutes of listening, the prosecutor's heavily painted lips pursed, and Agent Tanner's brows lowered. Not for the first time since she'd put it together, Gemma wondered if her game plan for this investigation was sound or a huge mistake in the making.

In the four years she'd been an NICB agent, she'd managed to solve all her cases without working with the ATF. During her first year on the job, she'd uncovered a million-dollar fraud case. Another NICB agent, one whom she'd been flirting with for months and wished would ask her out on a date, had generously offered to help her with all the interviews.

Then he'd stabbed her in the back by stealing her casework and presenting it as his own. He'd covered for his actions by lying and saying she'd been screwing up the case when she most definitely hadn't been. As a result, she'd lost out on a promotion and a hefty bonus. More importantly, she'd lost the respect of her colleagues. To avoid being labeled a snitch, which would only have made things worse, she'd opted not to file a complaint. But she'd never forgotten the dire pitfalls of working with a partner.

Since then, she'd worked twice as hard to prove her worth in the industry. To protect herself, working alone had become preferable, so it wasn't like she *wanted* to work with Tanner, let alone share what she'd dug up. Sadly, she had no choice.

Her investigation had reached the point of needing law enforcement resources that she didn't have, starting with grand jury subpoenas and, hopefully, ending with an arrest. Now that a body had been found at the warehouse fire she'd been investigating, the stakes just got raised, and there'd be no getting rid of Tanner, anyway.

Like it or not, mostly *not*, she either convinced him to work with her, or the case would be assigned to another NICB agent. The only plus side to working with Tanner was his dog.

When they were done talking, Agent Tanner held open the rail's gate for the attorneys, then followed them down the aisle running between the rows of benches.

Gemma stood by the aisle, waiting for Agent Tanner and praying she wasn't about to make a colossal mistake.

"Ms. Scott," he acknowledged and kept walking.

"Wait." She hustled to catch up to him just before he pushed through the swinging doors in the back of the courtroom. "Agent Tanner, wait!"

"Sorry," he said over his shoulder. "I'm in a hurry."

When he kept going down the hallway, beelining for the stairwell, she had to jog to keep up with his long strides. He was probably a jock, running a full marathon every morning before work. "Agent Tanner." She grabbed his forearm, forcing him to stop. The skin beneath her fingers was slightly raised and rough.

Tanner towered over her like a ponderosa pine towered over a dandelion. Given that she was only five foot one in her bare feet, that wasn't hard for him—or anyone, for that matter—to do.

Immediately, she released his arm and stepped back. "Sorry." She'd inadvertently grabbed him right on top of a scar. A burn scar, from the looks of it, and not that old. The skin was still pink and uneven, with a tattoo in the shape of an animal she couldn't quite identify. "Can we talk?"

He glanced at his watch. "Walk with me. I need to let my dog out." Not waiting for a response, he pushed on the door to the stairwell and held it open for her to go first.

"Have you talked to Aldrich yet?" she asked, following him down the stairs.

"He has counsel."

"But you'll interview him eventually, right?"

At the bottom of the stairs, he pushed open the door leading to the main level, again holding it open for her. "Probably."

"I want to go with you."

Instead of responding, he frowned, then continued through the lobby, out the main door, and down the steps toward an unmarked silver Expedition parked at the curb in the no-parking zone.

She raced after him, squinting as the hot, eighty-five-degree September air hit her face, the bright sunlight nearly blinding her. Gemma hustled to catch up to him. "I still don't think Gavin Aldrich set those warehouse fires."

Tanner stopped and turned so abruptly, she nearly crashed into his chest. *A seriously muscled chest.* "He was caught running from the scene. My dog hit on him because he smelled of accelerants. Aldrich had matches and butane lighters in his pockets. Am I missing something?"

Gemma ground her teeth. *Geez.* She really hoped this guy wasn't one of those typical macho federal agents who wasn't open to an idea if it wasn't theirs to begin with. If he was, she'd have her work cut out for her.

Working in a world traditionally occupied solely by men was difficult enough. Being vertically challenged amped up the difficulty by a factor of ten. People often saw her as a child, not as a woman who'd aced nearly every test she'd ever taken and had scored borderline genius on that silly psych test.

And one who wouldn't take no for an answer.

He clicked the fob on his keychain, then opened the driver's side door and grabbed a leash from the front seat. Next, he clicked something on his belt, and the rear passenger door popped open. Blaze, Tanner's enormous Chesapeake Bay Retriever, stood inside the kennel, wriggling, eager to get out.

The moment Tanner snapped the leash onto the dog's collar, he jumped out and trotted over.

Tanner tipped his head to her. "Blaze, you remember Gemma, don't you?"

The sight of such a happy, smiling dog momentarily derailed Gemma's intense focus, and she knelt to greet Blaze. "I'm happy to see you again, too."

Blaze responded with a quick lick to her chin, followed by a throaty, yowling jumble of sounds that, if she didn't know was impossible, she'd swear were *herro, Gemma*. She pointed to Blaze and looked up at Tanner. "He did *not* just say my name. Did he?"

He shrugged. "Who knows? He watches a lot of TV. Talks back to the screen."

Okay. A parroting dog.

Tanner tugged Blaze away and led him to a row of shrubs, where he promptly took care of his business.

"I know it looks bad for the kid, but I think you've got it wrong. Dead wrong," Gemma called after him, wincing at the bad choice of words. She followed them to the shrubs. "He doesn't fit the pattern I've been following. I tried to tell you that last night, but you didn't want to hear it."

Tanner stared her down. "I was a little busy chasing down an arsonist."

Gemma craned her neck and glared up at him. To anyone watching, she must look like a chihuahua staring up at a Great Dane. "Aldrich may very well be an arsonist, but I don't think he set that warehouse on fire last night *or* two weeks ago."

Tanner gave her a look she was all too familiar with, the one that said he didn't believe her. "You did say that last night. Okay, I'll bite. Why not?"

All righty, then. Foot. In. The door.

"There've been house fires all over the state for the last few years," she began.

"Statistically speaking, there are hundreds of thousands of house fires *every* year all around the country," Tanner countered.

"True," she agreed. "But not all burn to the ground. Not all of them are total losses. Last year, two different insurance companies requested the NICB look into two fires, because both had insurance policies with heavy riders, and the insurance companies were reluctant to pay out. Both these fires were officially deemed accidental."

"Go on." Tanner led his dog to a shaded area, and Gemma was forced to follow.

"On the surface, maybe they *did* seem accidental. One of the insurance policies included a rider extending coverage on expensive items for over twenty-five thousand dollars. One of the items was an old painting, and another was for a mink coat."

Tanner shook his head. "I'm still not seeing your pattern. It's common knowledge that riders pay out high replacement costs for personal items."

"Agreed." She nodded, encouraged that he seemed to be interested. "Like you, it's my job to investigate anything that could be arson-for-profit. The NICB is funded by insurance companies, so when they ask us to look into something, we do."

"I take it you did?" Tanner sat on a bench and gave her a half smile.

Wow. Great smile. All toothy and white, not that it was relevant or anything.

Blaze lay down on the grass in front of Tanner's long, outstretched legs. The dog had to be over eighty pounds. Big dog for a big man. No way could she see him with a chihuahua.

"I did." Without waiting for an invitation, she plunked down on the bench next to Tanner. "I started looking into all accidental house fires in Colorado in the last four years. Then I narrowed them down to those that were total losses and the ones for which the owners had heavy riders for expensive items."

Tanner raised his brows, looking genuinely interested now. "How many did you find?"

"Twenty-one."

"That's about five houses a year that fit your criteria." Blaze nuzzled his head against Tanner's leg. In an unexpectedly gentle gesture, he leaned down to scratch the dog's ears. He might be all tough-as-nails on the outside, but clearly, he had a soft spot for his dog. Gotta give the man credit for that, at least. "That doesn't sound like an overwhelming amount, and I still don't see the connection to the warehouse fires."

"Bear with me here. I dug deeper and guess what?" She leaned in for effect and got a lungful of Tanner's cologne, a citrusy, woodsy scent mixed with a small amount of smoke. She'd gotten a brief whiff of it during the whole plastered-against-his-chest thing. Guess he hadn't had time to get home and shower after the fire and arresting Gavin Aldrich. *And don't forget the dead body.* "Each of those twenty-one house owners used the same titling company—Kobuk Titling Agency—when the land was sold after the fires."

"Go on," Tanner said, seeming more and more interested by the second.

Gemma reached down to pet Blaze at the same time Tanner did. *Great minds.* Their fingers grazed, and the same unsettling heat she'd felt at the warehouse made itself known. *So much for residual fire heat.* What was with that?

They both jerked back their hands.

"I tried getting in touch with that titling company, but I kept getting their voicemail. I've made a dozen calls in all."

"Where are they located?"

"Alaska. I can't exactly pop in for a quick chat, and the NICB doesn't have any personnel stationed there."

"Again, what's the connection between these house fires and the warehouse fires?"

"Maybe nothing," she admitted. "The first time the warehouse was torched, it was deemed an accident. While you were transporting Aldrich to jail, the local fire investigator pretty much determined those cans of MEK we found were used to set the fire last night. No shock there. But one of those twenty-one house fires on my list was *also* caused"—she hooked her fingers into quotation marks—"'accidentally' by MEK, and it was located practically around the corner from the Frodo Warehouse."

Tanner's jaw went hard. One of his arms—the one with the burn scar—was draped across the top of the bench. The thick muscles in that arm went as rigid as a steel pipe, and Gemma could practically see the antennas shooting up from the top of his head. Eyes she'd thought were brown, but were actually a dark blue, came to life, turning as turbulent as a tornado. "18 Torrance Lane."

"Yes. How did you know?"

"I was there. The night that house burned to the ground…I was there."

· · ·

Saying the address out loud was enough to make the blood pound in Brett's ears and the burned skin on his forearm prickle. Gently, he rubbed the burn that was, at times, still itchy.

As if sensing the change in Brett's demeanor, Blaze lifted his head, pinning him with questioning, golden-brown eyes.

"Okay," he said to Gemma. "You've got my attention." If she'd discovered something about that fire that he wasn't aware of, he sure as heck wanted to hear it.

Her gaze dropped to his arm. "Is that where you were hurt? In that fire?"

He nodded. Luckily, he'd left Blaze in the truck

that night, otherwise he might have gotten killed trying to save Brett's ass. "Two teenagers died in that fire. My injuries are nothing."

This disfigurement was his penance for surviving, not only the fire last year, but the one twenty-five years ago from which he'd escaped unscathed.

Brett swallowed the familiar lump of guilt that always rose in his throat when he thought back to that fire. It should have been him who'd died that day, not them. Any pain he suffered was deserved.

"I remember that fire. Why were you called to that location in the first place? The ATF doesn't normally respond to house fires."

"True that." Again, he nodded. "Mostly, we're called in when the locals have a big investigation but not the dedicated resources to handle all the interviews. We have chemists, engineers, and labs to analyze evidence, but we also get involved if there's a big financial loss, interstate commerce, federal property, non-terrorism related explosives, or"—he paused for effect—"a serial arsonist. As a Certified Fire Investigator, I can also collect evidence and fill in when the local CFI isn't available." Which was exactly what had happened that night.

"I read the ATF's findings in the insurance company's file," Gemma said. "I don't recall seeing you listed as the CFI."

Something that still chapped his ass. "Because I was injured during the fire, they reassigned the case to another agent."

"To maintain impartiality."

"So they said." Tom Willard was a decent enough agent with the same training Brett had received but not the same experience.

For a moment, Gemma didn't say anything, just kept looking at him like he'd grown a third eyeball. "Do you agree with the final report's finding that the fire was accidental?" she asked.

No. Twelve months later, his gut still told him it was arson. He'd reviewed Tom Willard's case file more than a dozen times but found nothing to suggest it was anything but an accident. "The final report said it was."

Gemma twisted her lips. "But you don't think so."

"I didn't say that."

"You were thinking it, though." She leaned in closer. "Weren't you?"

The woman either had ESP or she was able to read him like a book. "It was owned by a flipper and was undergoing extensive renovation. A total gut. There was nothing in it but lumber, supplies, a few tools left behind for the day." And two teenagers smoking weed, their lives callously snuffed out.

If only he had made it to the top of the stairs. If only he'd gotten there sooner.

Brett curled his fingers tighter around Blaze's leash. *If only I could have saved them.*

"And three cans of MEK," Gemma supplied. "That was also in the insurance company investigator's report."

"Yeah." Due to MEK's flammability, that fire had raced out of control before the local fire trucks had even left the station. "After the fact, we learned the house needed a complete plumbing and electrical overhaul. That part of the town is still on septic, and the leach field was shot. It also needed asbestos and lead abatement."

Gemma made a *hmm* sound. "That's a lot of expensive renovation. You'd think that, as a flipper, the guy would have seen all that before he purchased a money pit. Maybe, by the time he did, the only way to cut his losses was to burn down the house and collect on the insurance."

Something Brett had already thought of. *All* the investigating agencies had considered that angle but never found proof.

"What was his name again?" she asked.

"Michael Hawkin of Hawkin Construction." Age forty-two, married, no children, living in Longmont with an office on the northern fringe of Denver proper. "No criminal history. He was vindicated of any wrongdoing."

If Brett was right, Hawkin had gotten away with it. Arson *and* felony murder of those kids.

Gemma arched a brow. "You say that like it tastes bad, and the look on your face says it does."

Shit. Now he was wearing his emotions on his face for all the world to see. The foul taste in his mouth came from knowing someone was guilty of committing a heinous crime and not being able to do a thing about it. "Suspicion doesn't convict, and it doesn't carry any weight. The connection you're trying to make to the warehouse fires and house fires you're investigating is weak."

"True, but it's something, and I want to follow up on that mystery titling company. To do that, I need your help." She swallowed with an audible gulp, as if the word "help" tasted about as bad to her as his inability to charge Michael Hawkin did to him.

She might need his help, but she didn't *want* to need it. "What you need is a grand jury subpoena." Something only law enforcement could get for her.

She shrugged. "Yeah. That, too."

"What does your supervisor say about this case?" Brett asked. "Do you have backing from your own people?" He hoped so, because she'd been right about one thing. She had something he could use—direct access to the NICB's ISO database, one of the largest private databases in the world and containing detailed records of insurance premiums collected and losses paid out, plus lots of other useful intel he couldn't access on his own.

"Let's just say my boss is skeptical. He wants something more concrete."

"And you want to use me to get it," he said flatly. Not that he had a problem with that.

As much as he hoped he'd caught the dumpster arsonist *and* the warehouse arsonist, he couldn't deny that he had doubts. He'd registered that Aldrich said he hadn't set "this" fire, meaning the warehouse fire. Maybe the kid had been telling the truth. Could be the only things he'd set on fire were the dumpsters.

And now, there was Gemma's theory that something else was going on here, something that could connect all the dots right back to the Torrance Lane fire. Her access could give him a shot at digging up the truth once and for all.

She sat back against the bench. "I use you. You use me. It's a match made in heaven."

Or hell, if things went south.

Gemma Scott was intelligent, incredibly perceptive, maybe barking up the wrong tree, and...pretty.

Hard not to miss that, but ignore it he would.

Besides, with a dead body, the last thing he needed or wanted was anyone getting in his way, especially not someone who didn't really want to work with him. But if there was the slightest possibility of proving the Torrance Lane fire was arson, he had to follow the trail, no matter how faint. Working with her could uncover something new, something that chasing after random fires for the last twelve months had failed to accomplish.

Finding new evidence.

Brett tugged out his phone and dialed his RAIC.

"Brett," Resident Agent-in-Charge Lori Olyawule answered. "How's my favorite canine handler?"

"I'm your *only* canine handler." With only forty handlers in the country, canine resources were spread thin. Still, Lori liked him and usually gave him carte blanche to work whatever cases he chose to. The only thing she asked for in return was that he do things by the book and keep her in the loop on his investigations so she wouldn't get blindsided by HQ or the press. After Aldrich had been processed by the U.S. Marshals earlier that morning, Brett had called her. Succinctly, he now recapped where things stood. "I'm interviewing Aldrich the day after tomorrow."

"That was quick," Lori said. "How'd you manage that?"

"I didn't. This is where it gets weird. Aldrich's public defender pulled me aside after his initial appearance. Turns out Aldrich has quite the past." Brett hadn't been given a copy of the Pre-Trial Services report, but AUSA Deborah Moran and the public defender had given him the short, and hardly sweet, highlights. "When Aldrich was fifteen, he set fire to his house, killing his father. His mother had died several years earlier, and that's when Aldrich's father started abusing him. After the fire, Aldrich and his sister went into the system. The sister was adopted. Aldrich wasn't. He spent years in a psychiatric institution before being released at eighteen."

Lori whistled, and Gemma's brows shot to her hairline. Their reactions were the same as his had been when he'd first heard Gavin Aldrich's story. Among other things, the kid was suffering from PTSD, something Brett understood all too well.

If Judge Tafoya sentenced Aldrich into the correctional system, he wouldn't get the help he needed. If he remained under psychiatric care and received proper support, he stood a fighting chance. At this point, things weren't looking too promising.

"I'm putting you on speaker phone," Brett said, doing just that, then holding the phone between them. "I'm with an NICB agent, Gemma Scott. Gemma's got a theory. She thinks this warehouse fire may be connected to the Torrance Lane fire."

"Why's that?" Lori asked.

"I'll let her tell you herself." When he held the phone out, surprise lit Gemma's face, as if she hadn't expected to be asked for her input.

Five minutes later, Brett was impressed by her knowledge of the insurance industry, arson-for-profit investigations, and the articulate way she explained her theory.

When Gemma was done, dead silence came over the phone. "I'll leave it up to you, Brett," Lori said. "If you want to work a joint investigation with the NICB,

I'll back you."

Over the phone, Brett met Gemma's questioning gaze. "I'll let you know," he said, then ended the call.

"When were you planning on telling me about Aldrich's history?" Gemma's hazel eyes glittered with a mix of annoyance and suspicion.

In less than twenty-four hours of knowing her, he pegged her as a woman who not only didn't appreciate being overlooked, but would never back down from a fight. And he liked that.

"I wasn't." He grinned. "Not until I decided to work with you."

CHAPTER THREE

The rich, meaty smell of crispy bacon vied with the scent of raw lumber as Gemma walked through her fixer-upper. She bit into a strip of bacon, chewing while she did a one-eighty in the middle of what would eventually become her living room.

Renovations on her tiny 1906 Victorian in the Eiber section of Lakewood were proceeding at a snail's pace. Considering she had no formal carpentry experience, she'd been doing a darned good job by herself.

She bent down to plug in her compressor, wanting to make sure it was primed and ready to go. Her brain was torn between the arson investigation and the next step in what was fixing to be a five-year renovation.

There were some definite downsides to renovating a house alone, and sometimes she questioned the wisdom of that decision. But in the year since she'd closed on her little Victorian, she'd come to understand it was a way of proving to others that she was competent and should be taken seriously. The only times she'd asked for help were when she'd needed a licensed plumber or electrician. Other than that, working alone was easier. On her house *and* on the job.

The oak floor in the great room was covered with protective sheeting, on top of which were stacks of floor and ceiling molding yet to be installed, along with saws, hammers, and every other carpentry tool of the trade. At one end of the room stood a makeshift workbench comprised of two sawhorses and a sheet of plywood that held a small TV, her chop saw, a framing nailer, and a rolled-up set of original blueprints that were actually blue.

Taking another bite of bacon, she sat on the only piece of furniture in the room — a worn, cracked, leather sofa, half of which was covered in sawdust. She sat on the relatively clean side, letting her gaze wander proudly over the new great room.

To modernize a house that hadn't had any work done since the day it was built, she'd knocked down all the walls between the kitchen, dining and living rooms to create a great room. Demo day had been a blast. Literally. Then, using a jigsaw, she'd crafted wood archways between all the rooms for visual separation. Those archways had been her first real carpentry success story.

Yawning, she took a long sip of morning coffee, a special blend, the recipe for which her mother swore she'd been gifted with by the famous New York City gourmet grocer, Eli Zabar, before her family had pulled up stakes from Brooklyn and moved to Colorado.

Through the dining room archway, the morning sun was just hitting the backyard. There was still so much to be done. Like replacing the wood deck where a herd of termites had taken up residence and hooking up the gas line in the new stone firepit. That would all have to wait.

Sighing heavily, she stood. It was time to get back to the job that paid her instead of the one that ate most of her paycheck. Taking her coffee and swinging by the kitchen for another strip of bacon, she headed into the small room on the main floor that served as both a temporary bedroom and office. Her realtor said this room had been added on sometime in the last thirty years. The only thing needed here was a new coat of paint.

Her laptop, two large-screen monitors, and stacks of notes and manilla folders sat on a table pushed against one wall. Taped to the same wall over the table was a three-by-five-foot map of Colorado dotted with red and blue push pins. Next to the map was a spiderweb diagram organizing the ISO data and any common links between the fires.

The adjacent wall contained rows of labeled four-by-six photos taken by fire marshals at the twenty-one house fires she'd been looking into. The last photo on the bottom row had been taken at the Torrance Lane house fire a year ago in Colorado Springs. Next to it were a few photos she'd taken yesterday at the Frodo warehouse fire.

On the floor in one corner of the room lay her sad excuse for a bed—a queen-size mattress. In the opposite corner, next to her closet, stood an antique oak-and-iron school desk she'd discovered in the garage. On top of the desk sat Jaws. Jaws's not-so-little orange body wriggled, and his fins fluttered as he swam to the top of the tank, eager for his morning meal of high-carb, high-protein, freeze-dried fish flakes.

"Good morning, Jaws." She leaned down and smiled. Considering she was the only NICB agent assigned to the area, travel was an essential part of the job. Having a dog, her creature of preference, was out of the question, so she'd gotten a goldfish, one who'd defied the odds and been with her for two years now. If it weren't for her best friend and next-door neighbor, Bonnie, helping out when Gemma went on travel, she wouldn't even be able to keep a fish as a pet.

When she popped the cap off the plastic bottle of fish food, Jaws's body wriggled faster, and his fish lips opened and closed. She dropped a small pinch of flakes onto the surface. "Bon appetit."

Jaws voraciously began gulping down food, reminding her of precisely why she'd named him after the most famous great white shark ever.

Knocking came from the front door. When Gemma opened the door, a blast of eighty-degree air swirled inside. Brett Tanner stood on her front porch, wearing khakis and a navy-blue polo shirt with the ATF badge embroidered on the front, holding a leather portfolio and looking really…big. And still way too tall and way too handsome.

Gemma swallowed, her mouth having gone just a teensy-weensy bit dry. Adding to his powerful presence was the shiny gold badge and holstered gun on his belt. Like a hammer and screwdriver, albeit deadlier, those were his tools of the trade. That and his dog.

They'd agreed to meet at her "home office" to go over the evidence she'd pulled from the ISO database.

Brett looked over her shoulder into the hot mess that was her home. "Nice place."

She arched a brow. "Funny."

He shook his head. "No, I mean it. Eiber is a great section of Lakewood. Older homes with character are worth fixing up, especially ones with a big lot like yours. Who's doing the work?"

"I am." Gemma expected him to laugh. Surprisingly, he didn't. "What, no sexist comment? Not even a 'Careful, you might get dirty or break a nail wielding all those manly man tools'?"

Brett grinned, revealing even, white teeth. "Nope."

Wow. He really did have a killer smile.

He was probably just keeping all his snide, chauvinistic comments to himself. No doubt he'd show his true colors later. Hopefully, he'd wait until after she'd already sweet-talked those subpoenas out of him. She stepped aside for him to enter. His silver SUV was parked at the curb, windows closed with the engine running. "Is Blaze in there?"

"Yep."

"He can come inside." She waggled her eyebrows. "I've got bacon. If you're a good boy, I might even give *you* some."

"Well, how can a guy and his dog say no to bacon?" Brett went back down the stairs to the Expedition and opened the side door. Blaze leaped from the kennel, looking more gold than brown as the bright sun lit his coat. He loped across her weedy, sad-looking front lawn, then bounded up the stairs to greet her.

"Morning, big guy." When she knelt to give him a hug, he responded with the same yowling version of *herro, Gemma* that he'd verbalized yesterday, making her laugh.

"Now," she said to Blaze, "how about some bacon?" Blaze's big ears lifted, and an expectant snort came from the back of his throat, one that didn't quite sound like *bacon*, but it had an upward lilt to it, as if he were saying: *really*? "That's what I thought." She tapped a finger on his nose. In the canine world, the word "bacon" was universally understood.

Gemma led them into the kitchen to the old electric cooktop where she'd left strips of bacon draining on a rack.

"Two is his limit. Hang on a second." Brett looked around the great room as if he were searching for something. He picked up a half-empty can of paint thinner and set it on the floor. "Blaze. Seek."

The dog walked swiftly around the room, sniffing every corner, every rag, and every tool before sitting directly in front of the can.

"Good boy." He petted Blaze's side. "Now he can have bacon. He's food driven, so he has to earn it."

She gave two strips of bacon to Blaze, who inhaled each of them in one bite, crunching happily, then licking his lips and tracking her hands as she placed two more strips on a piece of paper towel and handed them to Brett. "Coffee?"

"Sure." He accepted the bacon, then looked back into the living room as he bit into a strip and chewed.

She poured coffee into a spare mug, then handed it to him. "Cream or sugar?"

He shook his head. Unlike yesterday, his citrusy, woodsy cologne was smoke-free. Reluctantly, she had to admit he was hot *and* smelled good. But she'd been misled by a handsome face once before and vowed never to let that happen again.

"Did you do the plumbing and electrical, too?" he asked.

"No, I hired licensed contractors for that, but I'm

doing everything else myself. The place was in bad shape when I bought it, lots of rotten wood. That's the only reason I could afford it."

He took a sip of coffee, then walked into the living room. Blaze followed, his nose to the ground, sniffing every corner again before sitting directly in front of the TV on the workbench. "Told you he likes watching TV."

"I thought you were kidding."

"Nope. He's got a TV fetish. Sometimes I feel like a bad parent, letting him watch too much of it." Brett put his nose to the steam rising from his coffee. "This is good. *Really* good."

"Did you ever go to the Great Scott Bagel Deli on Wadsworth? It's just south of Morrison Road."

"All the time."

"That's my family's deli. Get it, Great Scott… This is my mom's special blend. I'm a heavy sleeper, and this is the only way I can wake up in the morning."

For a long moment, he stared at her. "That explains why I thought I'd met you before. Your picture is on the wall behind the deli counter."

Her mouth fell open. She was surprised he'd noticed her picture in the first place, let alone remembered it. "Indeed, it is." Her parents constantly pointed it out to customers they wanted to set her up with on a blind date. Being an observant federal agent, Brett had probably glimpsed it on his own. Good thing that, because not a single one of her parents' attempts at setting her up had ever turned into anything good. Finally, she'd had to put a firmly worded end to their matchmaking.

"Your whole family works at the deli. You didn't

want to join the family business?"

Gemma laughed. "Not even for a hot second. Everyone assumed I would, but it wasn't for me."

"How'd they take it?"

"At first, they were shocked." *Understatement.* "I threw them for another loop by going to California for a business degree, then shocked them again by becoming an insurance investigator. Over time, they finally accepted that making Colorado's best bagels wasn't in the cards for me." She waved her hand to encompass the living room. "But when I bought a fixer-upper and told them I planned to renovate it alone, they were flabbergasted." Why was she going all TMI on him? The man could probably care less about her life journey.

"What made you decide to do the renovation by yourself?" he asked.

Gemma widened her eyes. "You really want to hear why?"

His lips curved into that sexy half smile she'd seen yesterday outside the courthouse. "I wouldn't have asked if I didn't."

She hadn't expected him to be interested in her personal life. Maybe he was just nosy or making small talk. "As the youngest of four kids and the only girl, I grew up kind of coddled. All my brothers could change a flat tire by the time they were sixteen. I couldn't. For years, I didn't even know the difference between a flathead and a Phillips head screwdriver."

"Sounds like you wanted to become independent."

"Yeah." Odd how he barely knew her, yet he already *got* her. Somewhat, anyway.

"Having trouble?" He pointed to a corner of the

42   BURNING JUSTICE

ceiling at one of her failed attempts at creating the intricately coped joints.

"You noticed." Much to her chagrin.

Gemma frowned at the stack of floor and ceiling molding. She really sucked at cutting the molding so it met perfectly in the corners without any gaps. Nothing in a century-old house was straight, level, or plumb, making it that much more difficult.

"My dad was a contractor," Brett said, his hand lovingly stroking her chop saw. The image of his big, strong hands stroking *her* intruded in her brain. *Oh god*. Where had *that* come from? "I used to work with him during summers while I went to college. My specialties were molding and window installation."

He set his coffee on the workbench, then unrolled the set of blueprints, holding the sheets down flat. "An eyebrow window. I don't see one on the front of the house."

She joined him at the workbench, staring longingly at the graceful, curved window that had been drawn into the roofline in the original blueprints. "I don't think it was ever installed, even in 1906 when the house was built. I'd love to put one in." Someday. If her bank account could ever support such an architectural luxury.

"It sure would look great." Brett traced the curved window with his long finger. "Bring the old place back to its original glory."

She dug her hands into her empty pockets, pulling them inside out. "Do you have five grand you can loan me or, better yet, *give* me? Because that's what this window costs, and that's just for the window itself. Installation fees would probably be a couple more grand, and that's a job I'd never try to tackle on my own." Installing a curved window on a roof not only took money but skill she didn't have.

"I see your point." Brett rerolled the drawings. "You do have a nice set of tools, though."

"Thanks. Since I don't have the money to hire a general contractor, my father and brothers made sure I had everything I could possibly need." Except the skills to cope. *In more ways than one.*

Brett picked up a small saw next to her nail gun. "All it takes is a little muscle and a whole lot of practice."

"Easy for you to say." As he set the tool down, Gemma eyed the flexing of said muscles and didn't doubt that he had the strength to handle *any* tool, no matter the size or weight. She also got a better look at his tattoo—a dragon curling up and over from the underside of his forearm. The raised, red burn scars were positioned in such a way as to look like flames shooting from the dragon's mouth.

"You're good at your job, right?" he asked, but it sounded more like a statement, surprising her with the compliment. But was he talking about carpentry or her abilities as an NICB agent? "As an NICB agent," he clarified, as if reading her mind.

Gemma nodded. She *was* good at her job, and she was proud of it. Four years later, most people still underestimated her abilities. *Because I'm a woman working in a man's world.*

"That's because you do it every day," he continued. "Trust me, if you installed molding every day for four summers, you'd be good at that, too."

"I see your point." She dropped her gaze to the

mug in his hand. With all those muscles, he could probably not only install molding like a master carpenter but arm wrestle an alligator and win. Gemma cleared her throat. "Shall we get to work?" Though part of her had actually been enjoying the seamless, easy flow of their conversation.

She led him into her home office and winced inwardly. Clothes were draped over an old armchair and a basket of laundry—including the panties and bras she'd forgotten about—sitting next to the mattress on the floor. Maybe he wouldn't notice.

Her hopes were dashed when she turned around to find Brett in full-on federal agent mode, scanning everything in the room. Including her basket of undies. Blaze strolled in and went directly to the basket, shoving his head into her clothes and snorting.

"Blaze, no!" Brett snapped his fingers.

The dog jerked his head from the basket. Gemma's face and neck heated. Draped over Blaze's big head was a white lacy bra. The dog trotted happily to Brett's side, her bra still dangling over his head. She reached out to snag it, but Brett was faster.

"Here you go." He handed her the bra, an unmistakable glint of humor in his eyes. Clearly, he was trying not to laugh. "Sorry about that. Blaze loves the smell of laundry detergent."

Her bra—the prettiest, most delicate one she owned, which wasn't saying much—looked ridiculous in his big hand. She cleared her throat. "I'll have to remember that for next time." She snatched the bra, then turned to drop it back into the basket and winced again. There would never *be* a next time, because there was no way on earth she would *ever* invite

Brett Tanner into her office again. At least not until it wasn't co-located with her bedroom. "Sorry. I don't have much usable space in the house yet."

Mercifully, his attention was diverted to the fish tank. Unfortunately, so was Blaze's. The dog had his snout pressed to the side of the ten-gallon tank. Jaws wiggled faster than she'd ever seen him, back-fluttering to put more distance between him and the enormous hairy beast on the other side of the glass.

"Sit," Brett said, pointing an admonishing finger at his dog. "We do not eat other people's pets for breakfast. Understood?"

Woof.

Brett leaned down closer to the tank. "That's one big-ass goldfish. How old is it?"

"Two." Jaws had ceased fluttering madly and now floated, staring at Brett. "His name is Jaws." Brett snorted. "He's smiling at you."

He gave her a look of disbelief. "How can you tell?"

"I just can." She pointed at the tank. "See? He's doing it again."

"If you say so." Brett shook his head, then straightened and began examining the map on the opposite wall. "You don't use a mapping app?" he asked.

"I do. I also like to print things out. It's old school, but I find if I tack things to a wall and stand back, I can see things I miss on a computer screen."

Taking her cue, Brett stepped back. "Do the push pins represent your twenty-one house fires?"

She nodded. "Most were a total loss. All but one— the Torrance Lane house—had heavy riders, but they *all* used the same titling company. Kobuk Titling.

That's one of the reasons they popped up in my search."

Brett set his mug on the table and began massaging his sculpted, clean-shaven jaw. The man's face was just as handsome now as it had been with a three a.m. shadow. Not that she was thinking about him that way. "And the official cause of all these fires was accidental."

"Yes." She patted the stack of twenty-one manilla folders next to his mug. "Electrical problems. Gas leak. A spark during the renovation process. A space heater left unattended." She paused when Brett's back stiffened slightly. "You name it. It happened. All officially deemed accidental."

He moved closer to the map, studying it intensely before stepping back again. "There are sixty-four counties in Colorado. Not one of these fires is in the same county. Every county and every township has its own responding fire and police departments located in that county. If your theory is correct, that a single arsonist is behind these fires, this is another reason he's managed to fly under the radar for four years. Unlike what people think, not all government entities talk to each other. I'm guessing you've already thought of this."

"Yes." Gemma nodded, adding, "Or *she*. Don't be sexist and assume the arsonist is a man."

"Me, sexist?" A corner of his mouth lifted as he shook his head. "Wouldn't dream of it. Fact is eighty-eight percent of all arsonists are males, and most are between the ages of eighteen and twenty-nine. But I don't think Gavin Aldrich set any of these fires. Aldrich is a seriously disturbed individual caught running from the scene of a fire and with evidence of setting that fire in his pockets. But this"—he pointed to the map—"isn't the work of a disturbed individual. This is calculated."

"Arson-for-profit," Gemma said, gratified that Brett agreed with her assessment.

Keeping his gaze pinned to the Colorado map, Brett edged backward. He continued staring at the map, his brow furrowing as he squinted.

"What?" Had she missed something? She joined him, her shoulder brushing against his arm when she stood next to him. A ripple of pleasant warmth shot through her at the exact spot their bodies had touched. *This has* got *to stop.*

"Look at the map, the push pins, then squint until they look fuzzy." She did as he suggested. "What do you see?"

"A map with push pins."

He laughed. "There's a rough pattern to the pins. Squint harder."

She did. "It's an irregular circle."

"Maybe." He went back to the map and pressed a finger in the approximate center of a vague geographical focal point.

"Denver County." Then again, Denver County was pretty much at the center of *everything* that happened in Colorado.

Brett moved to another wall, eying her spider diagram. "And all twenty-one sellers used the same titling company. What are the chances of that happening?"

"Statistically, none, I'd say."

"I agree." He pulled some folded papers from his

thigh pocket and handed them to her. "So, I got you these."

She unfolded the pages, and her skin tingled with excitement. The first document was a Rule 6(e) letter issued by AUSA Deborah Moran and requiring Gemma to sign at the bottom before the disclosure to her of grand jury matters would be authorized. According to the letter, a court order had been signed by a judge, allowing Brett to share grand jury evidence with her.

The next document was a federal grand jury subpoena issued to Kobuk Titling Agency in Alaska, requiring them to produce documents relating to any and all houses they titled in Colorado for the last five years, including but not limited to titles, chains of title, title insurance policies, liens, property tax information, and a bevy of other documents commonly handled by titling companies during real estate closings.

Now, her skin not only tingled, but her entire body vibrated with energy. *This guy is good*. She couldn't begin to comprehend how he'd gotten a subpoena so quickly. Barely twenty-four hours had passed since she'd run her arson theory by him. That wasn't what had her feeling like a kid who'd just been handed a golden ticket.

The 6(e) letter addressed to her meant Brett not only thought her theory held merit, but he was including her in his grand jury investigation. She was now part of a team. *His* team.

But I work alone. Things are better that way. No egos to fight with, and most importantly, no one to stab me in the back again.

Now that the moment had actually come, how did she feel about working with him?

Maybe it wouldn't be so bad. After all, he had a dog that could practically talk. How cool was that?

"You okay?" Brett asked, a concerned expression on his face. "You look like you're about to pass out."

"No, I'm fine. I just—" Had the shit shocked out of her.

"I emailed the subpoena to an ATF agent in Alaska. He's on vacation, but he'll serve it as soon as he gets back."

"Great." Awesome, actually. "In the meantime, I think we should go back to—"

"Frodo Warehouse," they said at the same time, reminding her of how in sync her parents were, finishing each other's sentences.

"Let's hit the road," Brett added. He and Blaze headed for the door, and when she didn't immediately follow, he turned. "You coming?"

As much as she appreciated him being receptive to her theory, there was something else she needed to know. "Tell me…" She set her mug on the table and crossed her arms. "When I started running my theory by you yesterday, you didn't buy into it. Then you about-faced and latched on to it like a starved dog that's just been handed a meaty bone." She dipped her gaze to his arm. "Is it because you were burned in that fire? Or is there something else going on here?"

A muscle ticked in his cheek, then he went to the wall plastered with the fire photos and pointed to one taken at the Torrance Lane house fire a year ago— one showing burned cans of MEK. "The only thing you need to know is that if whoever's torching these houses is the same person who killed those teenagers, they won't hesitate to kill again if it suits their purposes. And I won't ever stop hunting them down."

She'd been waiting for the other shoe to drop. Maybe it just had.

Not much frightened Gemma, not investigating ferocious fires or deadly floodwaters powerful enough to wash houses downstream. But the intensity of Brett's warning touched off something deep inside her.

The man was on a mission, and nothing would stand in his way. Maybe not even her.

Memories of getting stabbed in the back by a colleague came back in a whirlwind of frustration, pain, and anguish. Working with someone she didn't know might very well be a mistake.

For now, she'd hope for the best and prepare for the worst.

CHAPTER FOUR

Brett parked in front of Frodo Building Supply's administrative office outside downtown Colorado Springs. Beside him, Gemma flipped through her notes again. They'd barely spoken during the hour ride from Lakewood to the Springs. The woman was all business, and he appreciated that.

"Ready?" He adjusted the AC vents to blow directly through Blaze's kennel window between the two passenger seats.

"Give me a minute. I want to finish reviewing my interview of Logan Hicks after the first fire. I have a copy, if you want to read it." She tugged out another report and handed it to him.

"Thanks." He took the report and five minutes later was up to speed on the first warehouse fire two weeks ago. The report was brief but jam-packed with all the requisite details, better than most federal agents' reports.

As he'd been in her office, again, he was impressed by Gemma's investigative and organizational skills. The data she'd culled from the ISO database, her maps, spiderweb diagrams… Gemma really did know her shit.

The local CFI, Jose Turin, had found no evidence of MEK or any other accelerant as being the root cause of the first warehouse fire. Unlike the recent fire, the first one had spread slowly enough that the local department was able to respond in plenty of time to save the structure and most of its contents. Though not a certainty, the cause had ultimately been deemed a "probable" accident, with the possibility of a short circuit in one of the overhead fluorescent light fixtures, which, Logan Hicks said, occasionally made a popping sound when turned on.

Brett watched Gemma studying her report. She'd worn casual yet professional beige slacks and a green sleeveless blouse that clung to her body, accentuating her petite figure. She'd pulled her hair high and tight in a thick red ponytail that draped over her bare, shapely shoulder. It reminded him of the way his best friend Deck's fiancé, Tori, wore her hair. As it did on Tori, ponytails looked good on Gemma. But he shouldn't be thinking about her in those terms. Working together was reason enough to keep things platonic.

The moment he met someone he liked, he inevitably screwed it up. As soon as things started getting good, it was like someone flicked a switch in his brain. He'd shut down, go cold, and close up. When it came to relationships, either he ended it, or they did. It was better that way. If he stayed, his personal shit would inevitably wind up hurting them.

As Gemma flipped to another page of her report, Brett laughed inwardly. With her perceptive abilities, she'd see through his messed-up life in a heartbeat and kick his ass to the curb lickety-split.

To get his mind off thinking about Gemma in ways he shouldn't, he focused on the report. "Does the warehouse have any security cameras?" He hadn't noticed the other night, but it had been so dark, and the fire may have destroyed the cameras before he'd arrived on scene.

She looked up. "It did yesterday, but not for the fire two weeks ago. After the first fire, the owner installed two cameras, one over the front door and the other on the rear corner looking down on the loading bay. Until the first fire, they never thought it would be necessary."

"If the cams were set up to store footage, maybe we can pull something from the feed." Although in Brett's experience, catching arsonists was never that easy. Far too many arson fires went unsolved. "What about a security system?"

"It never went off. Smoke alarms *or* break-in sensors."

Hmm. "Could be we're looking at a disgruntled employee who knew the security code, but that doesn't explain the smoke alarms not triggering."

"That's what I was thinking." Gemma stuffed the reports back into her portfolio, then twisted in the seat and reached through the kennel window to pet Blaze. She might not have a thing for him, but she definitely had one for Blaze. "We'll be back soon." Brett's dog stuck his head out and sniffed Gemma's ponytail before finally licking her cheek.

Well, she did smell good—like warm milk and honey—something he had noticed when he'd caught her in the warehouse and the second he'd picked her up this morning. That and the fact that she was even prettier than he'd first thought. Stunning, actually. Long, thick red hair with subtle waves. High cheekbones and eyes the color of hazelnuts. No makeup, but she didn't need any. Not with her clear, creamy skin and full, pink lips.

But again, thinking about her in anything other than professional terms was a wasted cause. More like, he and relationships were a wasted cause.

"He likes you," Brett observed. Chesapeake Bay Retrievers weren't known for being overly friendly with strangers, although Blaze was an exception to that rule. He pretty much liked everyone but seemed to have a soft spot for certain people. Like Gemma.

"I think I'm a dog magnet." While Blaze licked her other cheek, she laughed, which only incited him to lick harder.

Apparently so.

After Gemma got out of the Expedition, Brett locked it up, leaving the engine running and the AC kicked on high.

"Since I've already spoken several times with Logan Hicks," she said as they walked to the entrance, "I'll take point on the interview."

"Yes, ma'am." Brett was tempted to throw a salute. NICB Agent Gemma Scott was turning out to be a take-charge kind of woman. Some agents might not appreciate that level of drive or playing second fiddle to someone who wasn't a federal agent. Brett didn't mind. The only thing that mattered was that she knew what she was doing, and he wanted to verify his instinct that she did.

She stopped to glare at him. "You don't need to call me 'ma'am.' We're about the same age, you know?"

Yep, he did know. He was thirty-six and figured she was a couple of years younger. Technically, that made him the senior agent. "Yes, ma—" He grinned when her glare went glacial.

Minutes later, they were shown into Logan Hicks's office. Only it wasn't Logan Hicks sitting behind the desk. This man was much older than the one Gemma had pointed out at the fire.

The man stood and stretched his hand across the desk. To Brett, not Gemma. "I'm Robert Hicks."

Brett shook the man's hand. "Special Agent Tanner. I'm with the ATF, and this is—"

"Glad to see the ATF is finally involved in this," Hicks interrupted. His hand was big, his handshake enthusiastic. "Insurance company people don't have the experience you do."

What Hicks was saying, in a not-too-subtle way, was he'd be deferring to Brett, not Gemma. Her jaw tightened. Yeah, that had gone down about as well as a blast of pepper spray to the face.

"My experience with insurance agents," Brett said, glancing briefly to Gemma, "is they can be a real asset to an investigation." How much of an asset remained to be seen. So far, things were looking promising.

Ignoring Hicks's insult, Gemma stuck out her hand. "I'm Gemma Scott with the NICB. I'm guessing your son already mentioned me to you. I spoke with him about the first warehouse fire."

For a moment, Hicks stared at her hand as if she had leprosy. Holding her ground, she didn't move, forcing a reluctant Hicks into taking it.

"Speaking of Logan," Gemma said, keeping her expression deceptively neutral, "I thought we were meeting with him today."

"He had an unexpected appointment. Something to do with one of his kids." Hicks indicated two chairs in front of his desk. "But he set up the video feed from the new cameras and found something interest-ing."

He turned his monitor around, angling it toward Brett. While he couldn't see the steam shooting from Gemma's ears, Brett knew it was there. Not that he could blame her. Hicks was a horse's ass.

He'd been about to adjust the screen, but she beat him to it.

None too gently, she turned the monitor so they both could see it. "There," she said, smiling sweetly. *Sweet laced with a chaser of vinegar.* "That's better."

You go, girl.

He admired that she wasn't about to let Hicks get away with yet another slight. Brett cleared his throat. He pegged Hicks at about sixty-five and being old-school. Deferring to a woman, apparently, wasn't his style. Hicks threw Gemma a look of annoyance, then hit the return key and came around the desk to stand behind them.

"I'm not very good with all these newfangled gadgets and software." Hicks chuckled. "My son cued up footage from the front door where the security system keypad was located. You might want to take notes, honey." He nodded to the portfolio in Gemma's lap, effectively relegating her to secretary.

No need to have superhuman or canine hearing. The sound of her grinding her teeth was louder than automatic gunfire. This guy was pushing all her but-tons. It was a wonder she didn't smack Hicks over the head with her portfolio. Pressing her lips together tightly, she jerked out a pen. Brett had to give her credit for keeping her cool. He, on the other hand, was on the verge of dumping the small metal trash

can on the floor—the one containing what appeared
to be the remains of someone's breakfast—over
Hicks's head. If there wasn't a risk of losing the man's
cooperation, Brett might just act on his impulse.

To annoy Hicks, Brett tugged a pen and a small
pad from his thigh pocket and flipped it open. "I've
got this." He winked at Gemma, then made a few
notes. When he looked up, she mouthed the words
thank you.

The footage rolled twenty seconds longer. Exterior
lighting illuminated the front door of the warehouse,
but it was dark out and the image was dim. A figure—
male, most likely, judging by the height and
build—came into view wearing a hoodie and a bandana that covered most of his face. The figure looked
in both directions before pulling a key from his pocket and inserting it into the lock on the door.

Brett leaned in closer. "I can't be certain. I think
he's wearing gloves."

Gemma moved closer until her warm, bare shoulder touched his arm, and the bottom of her ponytail
swished over his biceps, caressing it and making his
skin tingle. In a good way. He wondered if she'd felt
anything, too. The sudden flush on her cheeks and the
goose bumps on her shoulder—the one that had
touched his—told him she had.

He cleared his throat, forcing himself to refocus on
the video footage or risk losing all concentration.

The time stamp in the upper right-hand corner of
the screen read two fifteen a.m. When Gemma scribbled on her pad, Brett glanced down to see she'd
already noted the time.

The guy went inside the warehouse, closing the

door behind him.

"The keypad is just inside the door," Hicks said, correcting in an acid tone, "or *was*. He must have known the code, because the alarm never went off and we checked with the alarm company. The system was running fine until the fire."

"Do you recognize him?" Brett asked. Hicks shook his head. "When's the last time you changed the code?"

"Two years ago."

"Did you fire any employees in the last two years?" Brett asked.

"Three."

"Why didn't you change the code after each of these people were fired?" Gemma's hand stilled over the pad.

Hicks shrugged. "It's a nuisance to notify all our employees of the change."

Meaning Hicks was so old school he probably didn't like sending emails.

With his eyes still glued to the closed door of the warehouse, Brett said, "We'd like a copy of those three employees' personnel files."

"Of course." Hicks nodded. "I can have my manager make them." He left the office. A moment later, he bellowed for someone named Shawna.

"Looks like he never changed the locks, either," Gemma said as they both refocused on the monitor. "Too old school."

"Agreed." Not that it was too difficult, but she'd also pegged Hicks the same as he had.

Twenty more minutes rolled by before the warehouse door opened. The same hooded figure carried a can in one hand that he set on the ground. From another pocket, he pulled out a pack of cigarettes that he lit with a small butane lighter, similar to the ones Brett had found in Gavin Aldrich's pocket.

Aldrich hadn't, however, been wearing a hoodie or a bandana around his neck, and he was significantly taller and thinner than this man was.

The tip of the cigarette burned brightly, then the figure tossed the cigarette into the warehouse, grabbed the can, and hauled ass north. They watched until he was out of the camera's range.

Gemma pointed to the screen. "That's interesting. He took the can with him."

"Watch." Brett waited for the inevitable. A loud *boom*, followed by a bright flash inside the warehouse. Smoke began pouring through the open door. "If this really is the same guy who torched this warehouse two weeks ago, I'm thinking the first fire didn't accomplish what he wanted—to burn it to the ground. This time, he made sure of it. He doused everything with MEK, then created an interconnecting trail of accelerant all the way to the door."

"Makes sense." Gemma's eyes lit with understanding. "He needed a safe way to ignite it and still make it out safely. When he tossed in the lit cigarette, he set off the accelerant without having to be inside when the place went up."

"And he left the door open." Again, Brett pointed to the screen. "It could have been an oversight, done in haste to escape, but I don't think that's it. He's got some basic knowledge of the Fire Tetrahedron."

"Heat, fuel, an oxidizing agent—usually oxygen—and a chemical chain reaction that keeps the fire burning," Gemma said. "I'm not a CFI, but the NICB sends all of us to arson investigation classes."

Brett nodded his approval. That would make her that much more valuable to his—correction, *their*—investigation.

Several more minutes passed before the roar of a fire could be heard and flames shot out the front door. They kept watching until the video feed ended, indicating the camera's sensors must have fried.

Hicks returned, carrying three manilla folders that he handed to Brett. "Sorry about the delay. I got hung up talking to a customer."

"No problem." Brett flipped one of the folders open, handing the other two to Gemma to read. "Can you give us a quick rundown on these people, starting with why you fired them?"

Hicks sat behind his desk. "One of them, Marissa Young, was late for work nearly every day. We gave her the opportunity to shape up, but she didn't. The next guy, Stavros Medukin, was a stocking clerk who did his job okay, but he turned out to be a mean sonofabitch and was so rude to everyone, including our own employees, that I had to let him go."

"And the third?" Brett prompted, amused to see Gemma jotting all this down even though he'd offered to take notes. A quick look told him her notes were the exact ones he would have made.

"Johnny Nash. He was a cashier who was arrested for burglary."

Gemma looked up. "What did he steal?"

"Nothing from us. At least, nothing we could prove. He was arrested for a series of house burglaries in the area. We didn't even know he'd been locked up until he missed two days of work and the police came around asking questions about him."

"Did these three fired employees all have keys to the warehouse that burned down?" Gemma asked.

"Yes."

She noted Hicks's response on her pad. "And did you get all the keys back from them?"

"All except the one Nash had. The police said he couldn't make bail, so we never had the chance to get the key back. We read in the *Gazette* that he was convicted of burglary and sent to prison. Until three weeks ago, we hadn't seen him in over a year."

Gemma handed Brett the file marked "Nash, Johnny" in the tab. "What happened three weeks ago?"

"He showed up wanting his old job back. I told him no, not with a burglary record. And while he was in prison, we did our annual inventory accounting and discovered a number of tools and supplies were missing, more than the standard amount that gets lost during the course of business or inventoried incorrectly when it arrives at the warehouse."

"How did he take it when you wouldn't rehire him?" Brett assumed not well.

"The little prick called me a motherfucker." Hicks pointed to his chest. "*He's* the thief, but *I'm* the motherfucker. Young people never hold themselves accountable anymore."

"Sounds like he was angry enough to hold a grudge," Brett said, adding, "We'll look into it. Has Jose Turin contacted you yet?"

"The fire investigator?" Hicks nodded. "I already sent him an inventory of what was in the warehouse and a diagram that he asked for showing exactly where everything was shelved. We lost most of our rarer, more expensive wood. Insurance should cover it. Do you want me to send you a copy of the inventory, too?"

"Yes."

Gemma handed Hicks her business card. "And please forward a copy of this video footage, as well."

Hicks took the card and placed it on his desk. "Do you have a business card, Agent Tanner?"

"I'm currently out," Brett lied. "You can send everything to Agent Scott. We're partners on this case."

A corner of Gemma's mouth lifted.

"We'll be in touch if we have more questions," Brett added, then he and Gemma left Hicks's office.

He led the way outside to the parking lot. "Hicks is still living in the dark ages."

"Dark ages?" Gemma shook her head disgustedly as she opened the passenger door and tossed her portfolio on the seat. "The man is a dinosaur. According to his puny dino-brain, all women should be at home, barefoot and pregnant, and if they actually have the audacity to go out and get a job, the only one they're fit for is a secretary. No offense to secretaries, but it's a stereotype."

"Hicks *is* a dinosaur," Brett said. "He'll never evolve, and he's doomed to extinction. People who hang on to the past are generally afraid of the future." And Hicks was so wrong it wasn't funny. In fact, some of the best agents he'd ever worked with were women, the best shots at the firing range, too.

"I've run into a lot of guys in this business who are dinosaurs," Gemma said. "Maybe not T-Rexes, like

Hicks. More like baby brontosauruses."

Brett nodded. "Agreed. He's not the only T-Rex out there, and there could be more of them before we're done with this case. There's nothing wrong with occasionally letting your partner take point now and then. Besides, the next person we talk to may not appreciate my devastating charm."

Shaking her head, she arched a skeptical brow. "I'll take that under advisement."

Once they'd gotten into the SUV, Brett phoned Sammie Aikens, the Denver Special Ops Task Force intel specialist. While they waited for Sammie to pick up, Blaze's loud snores drifted into the passenger compartment.

Sammie answered after three rings. "Brett, where ya been hiding?"

"The Springs, mostly." He pressed the speakerphone icon. "You're on speaker. I'm working with an NICB investigator, Gemma Scott. We need a few registrations, criminal histories, and backgrounds."

He rattled off the names of the three people Hicks had fired. Within minutes, Sammie came back with, "No criminal histories for Marissa Young or Stavros Medukin, just a few moving violations between the two of them. Young has a red Prius. Five months ago, she reregistered the Prius in Texas and got a Texas DL. Medukin has a white GMC Yukon." Sammie recited the tag numbers for both vehicles.

Probably nothing there, but he and Gemma would at least track down Medukin.

Clicking came through the speaker as Sammie's fingers continued working their magic. "John aka 'Johnny' Nash's last registration is an expired 2006 green Tacoma. He has a record. He did a year for burglary. Prior to that, he was arrested once for arson, but the charges were dismissed."

Arson? Gemma's gaze cut to his. This could *not* be that easy. "Any details on the arson arrest?"

"Give me a sec." More clicking. "He was caught fleeing the scene of a car fire. He had a can of paint stripper with him."

"Can you get me a last known address?" Brett asked.

Gemma's eyes gleamed with the same energy thrumming through his veins.

Because they now had a prime suspect.

CHAPTER FIVE

Sally Nash, Johnny Nash's sister, lived in what could only be described as a dumpy apartment on the third floor of a building that looked like it was about to fall down any second and smelled like rotten eggs.

By the time they reached the third-floor stairwell, Gemma was breathing heavily. Naturally, Brett wasn't. With those long legs and powerful thighs, he could probably jog up the stairs of the Washington Monument and not be out of breath. She reached for the door handle, but Brett got there first.

"I've got this." In a very gentlemanly fashion, he held open the heavy door.

Good looking and *chivalrous.* A dangerous combination. That was, if she were the sort of woman who was attracted to the tall, handsome, hunky type, but she wasn't. Come to think of it, when *had* she last been attracted to a man? *Any* man?

Try two seconds ago. *Brett Tanner. Ugh.* And she couldn't deny how the brief contact with his arm in Hicks's office had made her face heat and her skin tingle. She hadn't noticed any reaction on his part, however, so any tingly feelings in this partnership were one-sided. But she did appreciate his moral support after the interview. More than that, he'd surprised her, because she hadn't expected him to see, let alone understand, just how much Hicks had gotten under her skin.

Filthy wallpaper hung in peeling strips from the

dingy hallway walls. The carpet beneath their boots actually made sucking noises as they walked, and the smell was even worse than the stairwell. Mold, mildew, and an odor that reminded her of dead fish. Gemma made a conscious decision not to breathe through her nose.

Brett knocked three times on the door. A shadow flickered in the gap between the door and the floor, telling them someone stood just on the other side. From inside the apartment, a baby started to cry. Brett held his badge in front of the peephole. A moment later, the door cracked open with the safety chain still in place. A young woman in her mid-twenties held an infant to her shoulder. "What do you want?"

"Ma'am," Brett said, still holding his badge. "Federal agents. We're looking for Johnny Nash."

The woman's eyes flared wide as she focused on the badge, staring at it as if it was the muzzle of a gun. "He-he's not here. What do you want with him?"

"We'd like to speak with him," Brett said in between the baby's wails, which were growing louder by the second. "When do you expect him to come home?"

"Oh, I—" Sally Nash cupped the back of the baby's head, making shushing sounds to calm the child. In between flicking her frightened gaze back and forth between Brett and her baby, Sally's eyes glistened. "I'm sorry, I just can't seem to get her to stop crying."

"Your first?" Gemma asked, instantly feeling sorry for the woman, whose left hand was devoid of a wedding ring. Sally nodded. "You don't have anyone to help you, do you?"

Sally shook her head. Tears spilled from her eyes.

"I'm guessing you haven't gotten much sleep lately, either," Brett said, taking his cue and stuffing his badge into his back pocket.

Again, Sally shook her head, looking even more wary as her gaze dipped to Brett's gun.

"May we come in?" Gemma asked. "Maybe we can help."

Hope flared in Sally's eyes so easily, Gemma could only imagine it had been a long time since anyone had offered. The door closed, followed by the sound of the chain being slid open. The door opened again, and Sally stepped aside.

The apartment was surprisingly clean, but with baby clothes and towels draped over every piece of furniture. Unlike the hallway, the place smelled relatively decent.

"What's her name?" Gemma asked, closing the door behind them. Based on the pink beanie, she assumed the baby was a girl.

"Paige." Sally began pacing the living room, bouncing the baby gently. Still, the baby cried.

To Gemma's shock, Brett held out his arms.

"May I?" he asked Sally. "You look like you could use a break."

She turned slightly, covering the baby's head protectively with her hand. "I don't know."

Gemma rolled her lips inward. "I promise he doesn't bite. He's a big, bad federal agent, but inside, he's as warm and cuddly as a teddy bear." *Doubtful*. Over his shoulder, Brett narrowed his eyes on Gemma. Okay, so maybe she'd overstated the cuddly thing. "It'll give us a chance to talk."

With a mixture of reluctance and gratitude on her face, Sally handed over the baby into Brett's waiting arms. Gemma had thought she'd been in shock before. When Brett began crooning to the still-crying infant and whispering silly sayings as he rocked the baby gently back and forth in his muscular arms, she raised her brows, speechless. The infant's cries weren't quite as loud as before. *Who'da thunk the hunk would be good with babies?*

Gradually, the child quieted more, and Gemma's heart squeezed. Just a tiny bit. There was nothing sexier than a big, strong guy holding a baby as if it was a delicate piece of crystal. Although when she'd watched her brothers do it with *their* newborns, she'd thought it was cute. When Brett did it, the word *sexy* had instantly popped into her head.

"Can we sit down?" Gemma indicated the sofa. Keeping one eye on Brett, whose long index finger was now firmly grasped by the baby, Sally sat. "We're sorry to bother you. We were hoping to speak with your brother. We know he just got out of prison."

Sally's eyes flicked to the right as she twisted her hands together on her lap. "I haven't seen him in, um…" Her hands twisted tighter. "About three weeks, right after he was released."

Can anyone say lying? Gemma caught the subtle shake of Brett's head. He'd picked up on it, too. Amazing—*and* unexpected—how in sync their minds were. And this hadn't been the first time.

"Did he by any chance try to get his old job back with Frodo Building Supply?" Gemma asked, watching Brett gently bounce little Paige in his arms like she weighed no more than a marble.

She nodded. "Yes, but he said they wouldn't hire him again because he was an ex-con."

"Was he angry about that?"

"Very, but he said he knew someone in Denver who would hire him. He said he'd helped someone out with a problem last year before he went to prison, and now they owed him a favor."

"Do you know who that was?"

"Um, no." Sally shook her head, again looking down at her tightly clasped hands. "No. He didn't say."

"Do you know what 'problem' he was referring to?"

"No, I'm sorry."

"Do you know where he's staying or what he's driving?" Brett whispered over the now-smiling baby.

Gemma had been about to ask those same questions.

"No." Sally shook her head. "He wanted to take my car, but I finally had to put my foot down and said no. How did you get her to stop crying?"

Only now did Gemma realize the baby hadn't uttered a single cry in the last few minutes.

"Babies love me." Brett winked. "I'm a baby magnet."

Gemma rolled her eyes, recalling his reference to her saying she was a dog magnet. She pulled two business cards from her portfolio, handing Sally one of them. "This is my card. Please call us if you hear from your brother."

"I—" A fresh flood of tears seeped from her eyes. She opened her mouth again, as if to say something, then closed it and nodded.

Gemma handed her the other card. "This is for Hands of Hope. It's a place that might be able to help you. You should call them."

"Thank you." Sally took the card, then stood and allowed Brett to slide the infant into her arms.

Moments later, they were back in the stinky hallway. As Brett held open the staircase door, he momentarily rested a hand on Gemma's shoulder and smiled. "Good job, partner." When he removed his hand, the warm imprint of his long fingers on her bare skin sent a shiver of awareness through her, this one stronger than what she'd felt in Hicks's office. Along with a surge of happiness.

Although she couldn't be certain whether it was because he'd again referred to her as his partner, or whether it was because of the devastatingly charming smile he gave her as he said it. Or the stupid, silly little flutter that followed low in her belly.

Oh. No. Do not *go down that dangerous path.*

As much as she appreciated that he'd acknowledged her rapport with Sally Nash, they were only working together. That was it. It wasn't as if he actually saw her as a woman. When this case was over, they'd part company. For good. That was the way she wanted things. Back to normal and back to working alone.

At the ground floor stairwell, Brett again held open the door. "Too bad Sally Nash just lied her ass off."

• • •

An hour and a half later, Brett drove them back to the Frodo warehouse. After leaving Sally Nash's apartment, they'd managed to track down Stavros Medukin and crossed him off their list of suspects.

For the last week, the man had been in a hospital following spinal surgery. Marissa Young's landlord said she moved to Texas six months ago. To be thorough, Brett had Sammie Aikens run a residential check on Marissa Young that confirmed she'd moved to Dallas.

Meaning Johnny Nash was still their prime suspect.

"You really were good back there with Nash's sister." Good in ways Brett never could be. With his experience holding his nieces and nephews after they'd been born, the screaming infant he could handle. The distraught, crying woman... Well, let's just say he'd been happy Gemma had stepped in and taken point. "You pegged her the second she opened the door."

Gemma sighed. "Sometimes, all it takes is a little kindness to get through to people."

"True that." Brett grunted as the inevitable memories flashed before his eyes.

He'd been in two fires in his life. While he'd escaped from the first one unhurt physically, on the inside, he'd been left deeply scarred. Part of him always would be, and he'd since learned to accept that and live with it. Back then, however, only the support of his family and the kindness of a neighbor—a Marine recruiter—had kept him from throwing himself in front of a train.

Brett braked at a red light and turned to look at Gemma, seeing her in a new light and suspecting there was far more to the woman than just a hard-ass, tough-shelled investigator. "What's your connection to Hands of Hope?"

"During college, my roommate, Bonnie, got pregnant. She didn't have much family to speak of, and they weren't very supportive. They wanted her to get an abortion. She refused. Hands of Hope was there for her. Now she manages the Denver branch. It's green."

Honking came from the car behind them, and Brett saw the light had changed. He headed them down the road again. "I'd say you've got some kick-ass interviewing skills." Unlike what TV and the movies portrayed, interviewing was *the* most important thing in an investigator's toolbox.

Gemma waved a hand in the air. "I don't know about that. I help Bonnie out at Hands of Hope whenever I can. Between helping her through a difficult time and volunteering, I could understand what Sally was going through."

Brett turned off the road and parked in the warehouse lot next to a red Explorer with the Colorado Springs Fire Department emblem on the door panel. The remains of the warehouse were nothing more than a twisted, burned-out mass of metal. "Sounds like you've got a soft, squishy interior, too."

"Yeah, we're two of a kind." She grimaced, as if she hadn't meant to say that. Or, more accurately, hadn't meant to imply they had anything in common. "Don't spread it around."

"Scout's honor." There was a genuine softness tucked away beneath her tough exterior, and he wondered why she worked so hard to hide it.

Blaze woke with a snort, getting to his feet and

sticking his head through the opening. The moment he caught sight of Gemma, he stretched his neck to sniff her ponytail.

"Hello, Blaze. Nice of you to wake up and join the party." She scratched him behind his ears, and he yawned. "Nice teeth. Does he need to go out?"

"Yes, but wait." Brett dialed the number for his contact at the Colorado Department of Labor and Employment. "Kai," he said when she answered. "It's Brett Tanner. How's your summer going?"

"Oh, you know. Another summer working for the State G. What can I do you for?"

"Can you run an employment check for me?" He pointed to the top folder in Gemma's lap. "Name's John or Johnny Nash." When she opened the folder to Nash's application form, he leaned over and read off Nash's social security number.

"How soon do you need it?"

"ASAP."

"How's tomorrow or the day after? I'm seriously backed up."

"That works. Thanks." Only because they'd be interviewing Gavin Aldrich tomorrow, followed by attending his court hearing, and probably wouldn't have time to track down Nash until after that.

"I'll reach out when I have the info," Kai said, then Brett ended the call.

Gemma closed the folder. "What's that going to do for us? Nash just got out of jail."

He snagged Blaze's leash from the rearview mirror. "It's a long shot, but if he did find work up in Denver like he told his sister, then there should be at least one pay period's worth of records on the guy since he was released."

"You know, you're not half bad at this."

"Gee, thanks." *Wiseass.*

Outside, the faint odor of smoke lingered. Brett popped Blaze's door, then waited at the back of the SUV. His dog knew the drill. Blaze leaped from the kennel, took care of business on a nearby signpost, then loped over and waited for Brett to clip on his leash. The moment he did, Blaze began wagging his tail, the same as he always did right before they went to work.

He handed Gemma a plastic 35mm film container.

"What's this?"

"Latex gloves. Best way to keep them from being contaminated."

"Nifty." She pulled out the gloves and, within seconds, had them on.

He opened his evidence kit, pointing at the hard-sided case. Blaze rose on his hind legs, resting his front paws on the tailgate, and began sniffing the kit.

"What's he doing?" Gemma asked.

"I always have him run over my collection kit to double-check my tools, make sure they're totally clean after the last use."

Blaze gave the kit a good sniffing but didn't alert. When he lowered to the ground, Brett pulled down the door. "Let's go."

For safety reasons, what was left of the roof after the fire had been intentionally knocked down by the fire department so it wouldn't fall on their heads.

"Jose?" he called out.

"That you, Brett?" a voice came back from somewhere inside. Moments later, Jose met them at the door. In his hand was a clipboard with a hand-drawn sketch.

"This is Gemma Scott with the NICB," Brett said, and Gemma shook hands with the older, stocky man. "Take any samples yet?"

Jose shook his head. "Just got done with my sketch. The owner sent over an inventory map. The warehouse was divided into sections. Tools. Chemicals. Wood. The expensive woods—ebony, rosewood, mahogany—were on the far end, the key word being 'were.' Nothing much left but an expensive pile of ash." He pointed to a melted box on the ground by the door. "I found evidence inside that the hardwired connection to the smoke alarms may have been cut, which would explain why the alarm company never received the alert."

"Makes sense," Brett agreed. Especially if a former employee, one who knew the building's layout, had set this fire.

He looked inside the warehouse while Blaze strained at the leash. The first thing that jumped out at him was the burn line of ash leading directly to the door. As he'd surmised, the arsonist had lain down an accelerant-soaked rope right up to the front door where he'd flicked that cigarette before making his escape.

"What's the ash from?" Gemma asked, snapping a shot on her phone.

"More rope remains. Unless you give accelerant something to ignite, once the vapor burns off, there's nothing left to feed the fire."

The smell of smoke was more intense within the shell of the warehouse. The concrete floor was still damp from all the water that had been used to put out the fire. "See that?" He nodded to a shallow puddle.

Gemma snapped another shot. "The rainbow sheen?"

"Exactly. It's everywhere. MEK is only slightly soluble in water." Sure enough, Brett detected occasional whiffs of MEK's acetone-like smell. Even if he hadn't, Blaze sniffed at the puddle, then tried to pull Brett deeper into the building, back to where the burned sofa still sat in the center of the warehouse.

"Why doesn't he sit?" Gemma asked. "I thought he was trained to do that when he alerts on accelerants."

"He's trained to find the *source* of the odor, not the odor itself. He'll keep searching to find the strongest scent, and that will be where the fire started."

"There are more empty cans." Jose led the way, pointing to burned cans on the floor. As with the other ones, most of the labels had been burned off. "This one still has a partial label."

Gemma crouched in front of the can. "MEK. Seems to be this guy's accelerant of choice."

"Looks like," Brett agreed. Despite the discarded cans, samples would have to be taken. Only gas chromatography could confirm the accelerant by comparing it to reference chromatograms of known flammable liquids. "Sometimes we can pull partial prints from scalded or sooty containers, but since he was wearing gloves, it's a moot point."

"Hicks forwarded me the video from the front door camera." Jose tucked the clipboard under his arm. "Is the ATF officially investigating this fire?"

Brett met Gemma's gaze. "This fire may be connected to the Torrance Lane fire."

Jose's brows rose. "No kidding."

"Nope. We've got a suspect we're looking to talk to. If it pans out, I'll keep you posted."

They continued walking past partially melted shelving and remnants of the various inventory that was all but destroyed.

Gemma took more photos with her cell phone, and he appreciated not having to tell her what to do. "Take a look at that." Brett pointed first to a burn pattern on a section of corrugated metal wall that had survived, then to another metal can on the floor.

She snapped another photo. "Burn pattern?"

He nodded. "This is where he threw accelerant on the wall and it dripped down to the floor, making this inverted, cone-shaped rundown pattern."

Occasional creaking had him looking around to verify the walls weren't about to cave in on them.

"Brett?" Gemma touched his arm. Even with gloves on, the light contact was enough to make the hairs on his forearm stand at attention. There was definitely something simmering between them, something that could easily derail his concentration, if he let it. *And lead to disaster, as usual.* "Is that body still here?"

"The coroner removed it. We still don't have an ID. Maybe Aldrich can tell us who he was."

Blaze led them to a rack of lumber, most of it burned beyond what would be considered usable. When Blaze sat, Brett fed him a treat. "Good boy." More burn patterns on the floor and another discarded can. A metal drain ran along the length of the warehouse. Chances were the drain would contain significant quantities of accelerant, washed down there by suppression water.

"Even without lab results," Jose said, "I'm confident making an official statement that the cause of this fire was anything *but* accidental. That video Hicks forwarded is the clincher."

"Revenge is the most common motive for a serial arsonist." Brett quickly recapped Gemma's and his disgruntled employee theory. "If Johnny Nash set this fire, he'd want to stick around to watch his achievement, to gain the satisfaction. When arson is suspected, we usually have someone film onlookers at the scene of a fire."

Gemma scrolled through photos on her phone. "I didn't see anyone that night other than us, fire and police personnel, and Logan Hicks."

"It was dark out. Maybe whoever set the fire was here. Maybe we just didn't see him." Brett tugged Blaze back to the door they'd come in. "I've got an idea."

"Hey, wait!" Gemma called out. "Where are you going?"

"Hunting," he threw back over his shoulder. At the doorway, he set down the evidence kit. "Seek," he said to Blaze, pointing outside.

Sniffing the entire time, Blaze led Brett to the edge of the parking lot. From there, he followed his dog behind the warehouse. When he'd expected Blaze to pick up the same scent trail that had led to the tree line where he'd cuffed Gavin Aldrich, his dog veered off, still heading to the trees but on a path fifty feet to the left.

Behind him, Gemma and Jose followed. He stopped to unhook Blaze's leash, then pointed again. "Seek."

When Blaze took off, Brett started to run, wanting to keep his dog in sight. At the edge of the trees, Blaze sat.

His dog had just alerted.

Brett ran to the trees. In front of his dog's paws was a metal can. Unlike the others in the warehouse, this one wasn't burned. The label was in pristine condition.

MEK. Methyl ethyl ketone.

Sweat dripped down Brett's face and between his shoulder blades. "Good boy." He tugged another treat from his pocket and gave it to Blaze for a job well done. His dog chewed happily, then cracked a smile, panting.

Gemma jogged over. "Oh, wow," she said between breaths. "The missing can—the one he took with him. That's amazing. Good boy, Blaze."

A sense of pride washed over Brett. He imagined this was how his dad felt right after Brett had hit a home run in Little League. "He can scent a drop of gasoline on a golf tee in the middle of a football field."

"Absolutely amazing." She pulled out her phone and took a couple of shots. "But we know he wore gloves, so we probably won't get any prints."

Huffing and puffing, Jose joined them, sweat pouring off him and soaking his shirt.

Something else caught Brett's eye.

Stomped into the ground was a mostly empty pack of cigarettes. Like Gemma had pointed out, they probably wouldn't pull any prints from that, either. That wasn't what had his heart thumping faster.

Next to the pack of cigarettes was a cigarette butt. As dry as things were this time of year, it was a wonder the entire field hadn't caught fire.

"Can you take a shot of that?" He pointed to the butt.

"A shot of wh—" She peered closer. "Oh my god. You were right. He *was* here."

"Watching the whole time," Jose wheezed between breaths.

"He probably thought he was safe out here until Blaze and I raced after Gavin Aldrich. I think he got spooked and ran off."

After Gemma had snapped some shots, Brett tugged an evidence bag from his pocket and collected the butt and the empty cigarette pack, holding them up to the light. "DNA. Johnny Nash has a criminal record for burglary. That's a Class 3 Felony, which means he would have been swabbed for DNA. Those records will be in CODIS." If they were lucky, the Combined DNA Index System maintained by the FBI would spit out a hit.

Adrenaline shot through his system faster than water from a fire hose. If Nash—not Aldrich—really set the warehouse fires, then they were one step closer to nailing him. Once Nash was in custody, Brett would grill him about the Torrance Lane fire. If Nash had set that one, too, not even God could save him.

CHAPTER SIX

Gemma frowned at the pathetic excuse for a closet she'd erected in the corner of her bedroom. Not that it was a closet, really, just a thick piece of wire she'd wound around two nails pounded in the wall. Sometimes she wondered if she even needed a closet at all.

Aside from the occasional slacks, her wardrobe du jour normally consisted of exactly three things: jeans, work boots, and a T-shirt. Not the most flattering attire, but it did the job and saved beaucoup on dry cleaning.

"What do you think, Jaws?" Jaws swam to the surface, his body wriggling, as always, from the effort.

"Yeah, you're right." She tugged the sleeveless blue silk shirt off the hanger and put it on. Next came the beige slacks she'd worn yesterday.

Between interviewing Gavin Aldrich, then going to court, jeans and a T-shirt weren't going to cut it. When Brett had dropped her off last night, even he'd grumbled something about having to wear a suit today.

Gemma slipped into a pair of brown flats, which did absolutely nothing to help her vertically or make her legs look any longer—yeah, that was a pipedream—then went into the bathroom to brush her hair and tie it up in its usual ponytail. She'd bet a case of fish food that the women Brett dated wouldn't dare be caught in public with a ponytail.

Who gives a *schmear*? When she was little, that was what her dad—the bagel king of Brooklyn—had taught her to say instead of *shit*. She really needed to get back to that. Since the day she'd left for college, her vocab had taken a nosedive.

On a whim, she tugged out the elastic tie and let her hair fall freely around her shoulders. Not that she was trying to impress Brett or anything. He was just turning out to be a pleasant surprise. Brett Tanner was not only competent but smart. He knew people, and he knew the job. And he *appreciated* her. That might very well be the best part of their partnership.

She dug deep into the back of a drawer and pulled out a tube of mascara. As she twisted off the cap, bits of black stuff fell into the sink. The brush was completely dry.

"Oh, for Pete's sake." *Makeup? Really?* She twisted the cap back on and threw it in the paint bucket that served as a trash can. "I haven't worn makeup in years." So why had she been about to now?

Vanity? Doubtful. When she left the house, she didn't give a crap what she wore or what she looked like. Her mother had always chastised her for that unfeminine transgression.

Pride? Maybe. She didn't want to look like a slob in front of all those fancy attorneys, like that federal prosecutor with her chic designer clothes and jewelry.

Jewelry. *Ugh.* She didn't own much bling to begin with. Gemma yanked open another drawer and grabbed the tiny gold box in the back. Inside were sapphire studs and the matching pendant her parents had given her as a college graduation gift. Like the suit, she hadn't worn them in years. The last time she'd put them on had been the disastrous blind date her parents had set her up on with one of their customers.

After putting on the jewelry, she glanced at her watch. If she didn't get her butt in gear, she'd be late for her appointment with Brett at the Bagel Deli for coffee and to go over their game plan.

Back in the bedroom, she grabbed the matching beige jacket from a hanger and draped it over her arm. Jaws swam to the side of his bowl, his tiny fins fluttering and holding him in place as he watched her. His mouth gulped open and closed.

"What?" She picked up the jar of fish food. "You think I'm overdressed, don't you?" She uncapped the food and dropped a pinch of flakes into the water. Jaws swam to the surface and began gulping the flakes into his mouth. In seconds, the food was gone.

Gemma's stomach grumbled. Speaking of food, there was an everything bagel with scallion cream cheese and a large coffee with her name on it waiting at the deli. And Brett.

A tiny shaft of...*excitement*? Or was it anticipation spearing low in her belly, creating a tiny flip flop, frighteningly similar to what she'd felt yesterday, when their arms had brushed briefly, and later, when he'd complimented her, touching her shoulder and giving her that killer smile?

She clenched her hand tighter around the fish food jar. *No!* Gemma pointed to the fish tank. "And before you say it, I did *not* get dressed up for *him*. I did *not*. I'm just looking forward to seeing Blaze again."

Done eating, Jaws stared back at her, as if to say: *Yeah, right.*

She spun, snatched up her portfolio and keys, then

stalked out the front door. She'd been hoping to make a quick getaway when Bonnie waved to her from the adjacent driveway. She waddled over, one hand on her protruding belly and the other on the small of her back.

Bonnie was the college roommate Gemma had told Brett about yesterday. Married now, and with her second child about to be born any minute, Bonnie was happier than Gemma had ever seen her.

"Morning, Gem." Bonnie's gaze dipped to take in Gemma's slacks and shoes. "Something I should know?"

"You mean, because I tell you everything?" She glanced at her watch again. The deli was only five minutes away, but she hated being late.

"Well, yes. You look nice today." She grinned. "All gussied up."

"I am not—" *Oh, who am I kidding?* For her, this *was* gussied up. Even Jaws knew something was different this morning. "I'm meeting a colleague for coffee, then we have two appointments at the Denver courthouse."

"Coffee, hmm." Bonnie began massaging her belly. "Oh! There he is again, kicking like mad to make his escape."

As she'd done many times during Bonnie's first pregnancy, Gemma placed a hand on her friend's belly. Sure enough, she felt a quick little jab. "I'd say kickball is going to be his favorite sport." Despite the smile, a sliver of sadness sliced through the joy for her friend.

All three of her brothers were married and had given her parents at least one grandchild apiece.

Having children was something Gemma had secretly hoped for, yet with each passing year, the chance of that happening was getting dimmer and more out of reach.

"Tell me something." A suspicious glow came to Bonnie's eyes. "This colleague wouldn't happen to be a *he*, would he?"

"Yes," she admitted. "But in my line of work, most of my colleagues are."

Bonnie nodded, as if giving Gemma's explanation serious consideration. Then she grinned again. "But I've never seen you get all dolled up for one of them before."

Gemma groaned. For some stupid, pathetically unfathomable reason, she wanted to look nice for Brett. "I have to go or I'll be late." As she got into her pickup, Bonnie's laughter followed her. Both her best friend *and* her goldfish knew she was full of it. Full of *shmear*.

Five minutes later, she pulled into the parking lot outside the Great Scott Bagel Deli. The sign over the shop proudly displayed not only the name, but a replica of the Brooklyn Bridge.

Brett's ATF Expedition was already parked by the side of the deli. When she pulled up next to him, she saw that the driver's seat was empty. A big wet rosette left behind by Blaze's snout graced the kennel window. She got out of the truck, ready to go inside, when she noticed the kennel, too, was empty.

Beneath the shade of trees adjacent to the parking lot, Brett walked Blaze on a leash. Catching sight of her, Blaze's tail began whipping back and forth. Brett waved, started walking toward her, and *wow*.

What was it about a suit that made a man look hot? Or, God help her, was it just *this* man? Because she'd never really given it much thought before. Sure, her father and brothers had looked spiffy in a tux at all their weddings, but this was different.

Gemma swallowed. At eight in the morning, the summer sun blared down on them, so she pretended to shield her eyes when what she was really doing was checking him out.

Dark gray slacks made his legs seem longer and his waist trimmer than when he'd worn his 5.11 Tactical cargo pants. A white dress shirt, with its sleeves rolled up to his elbows, made his shoulders seem broader, more powerful. The hot morning sun glinted off the gold badge clipped to his belt in front of the holstered gun.

So he was good looking. Big whoop. Lots of guys were. The guy she'd gone on a blind date with had been drop-dead, cover-model gorgeous. *And a total dick.* Not that Brett Tanner was anything like that guy, but what had changed in the last three days that she was starting to think about him in a completely different light?

"Morning," he said, smiling. "Give me a sec to put Blaze up in his kennel."

With the SUV's engine running, Brett locked the vehicle, then held open the door to the deli, waiting for Gemma to go in first.

"Thanks." She scooted past, taking extra care not to brush up against all that firm, toned godliness. That didn't keep her from breathing in that awesome, manly aftershave he wore. He smelled better than she did. *No fair.* Should she start wearing perfume? The stuff always made her sneeze.

Gemma expected her family to greet her loudly like they always did when she walked in.

"Brett!" her mother called out.

"Hey, Brett," her oldest brother Chris shouted in his deep baritone.

From the kitchen, Rory and Ben shouted simultaneously, "Yo!"

"Good ta see ya," her father said in his thick Brooklyn accent, rushing out from behind the counter to shake Brett's hand.

What the—? God, did her entire family love this guy? She might as well have been invisible.

"Honey, it's good to see you," her mom finally said, coming from behind the counter to wrap her in a warm hug. Like her dad, her mom's Brooklyn accent hadn't toned down even a scooch in the years since moving to Colorado.

"Hi, Mom." Gemma gave her mother a quick peck on the cheek. The deli *and* her mom smelled like yeast and freshly baked bagels.

"Hey, squirt." Chris winked at her as he slathered cream cheese—schmear—on a poppy seed bagel.

Gemma's brows rose as her mother proceeded to wrap Brett in the same familial bear hug she'd thought was reserved only for family.

"Gemma, dear," her mom said. "This is Brett Tanner, one of our *favorite* customers." Her mom turned to Gemma, batting her eyelashes and winking—the unspoken signal she used to tell Gemma this was a customer she'd wanted to set her up with on another blind date.

Gemma gasped, her mouth remaining open as she

looked from her mother to Brett, then back again. *Oh, no. Just…no!*

Her family didn't realize they'd walked in together.

"Isn't he handsome?" her mother whispered, leaning in. "He's smart and nice, too. Such a gentleman."

To cover for the embarrassment creeping up her spine, she averted her gaze, pretending to be interested in the glass case full of deli meats, cheeses, and half a dozen varieties of flavored schmear.

"You okay?" Brett touched her shoulder.

She cleared her throat. "Uh, yeah." Aside from discovering that Brett was her parents' next pick-of-the-day for her.

Her mother straightened. "You two know each other?"

It seemed like all conversation in the deli ceased, although, in reality, it was probably only her entire family who'd clammed up and frozen in place.

"We're working together on a case," Brett said to her parents.

"Oh," her mother said in a high-pitched voice, then clapped her hands together. "Isn't that nice?"

Was it? Traitorous though it would be, next time, she'd insist they meet for coffee at the Burger King a quarter mile down the road. Anywhere but here.

The air conditioning was cranked high inside the deli. That didn't stop the flush of heat creeping up her neck.

Chris cleared his throat. "What can I get you?"

"Toasted everything with scallion cream cheese and a large coffee," she and Brett said at the same time.

Again, with that pearly white grin. "Great

minds…" Brett winked.

"Add two strips of bacon on the side," Gemma said to her mother.

"For Blaze?" Brett laughed. "You'll spoil him."

Gemma smiled. "All dogs should be spoiled."

"I'll have those right out for you." Her mom bestowed Brett with one of her special smiles.

"Thanks, Mrs. S." To Gemma, Brett said, "After you."

Mrs. S.? That sure did sound like he was one of the "deli gang," that group of special customers—regulars—her parents treasured.

Gemma went directly to the high top farthest from the cash register and deli counter, the one directly over which a TV blared the morning news, muffling their conversation from any prying, meddling, blind-date-fixer-upper ears. Brett pulled out a chair for her, then—typical cop style, she'd come to learn—took the one facing the door. In case any gun-wielding, bagel-thieving hoodlums mistakenly walked in.

Two seconds later, her mother brought over their coffees. "Black." She handed one cup to Brett. "Light with two sugars for my little girl."

"Thanks, Mom."

As her mother walked away, Brett's eyes followed her. "You know she's looking at us over her shoulder. Your entire family is."

"I know." She took a sip of her mom's awesome coffee blend. "I can feel their eyes drilling into my back."

Brett nearly snorted his coffee. "I should probably warn you they tried to set me up with you a few months ago. That's why I thought I recognized you the night of the fire. Every time I come in here, they point to your photo on the wall."

She'd thought her face felt warm before. Now it felt as hot as the inside of a bagel oven. "Sorry about that. I wish they would stop playing matchmaker. It's just that all my brothers are married. I'm their only child who isn't." She liked her independent lifestyle but still harbored a few regrets that she hadn't found anyone to settle down with. Given what had happened four years ago, she'd found it an uphill battle to get close to a guy again.

"Hey, don't worry about it." Brett smiled. "I'm flattered they chose me for you."

The way he'd said that sounded so intimate. At the risk of being even more thoroughly humiliated, Gemma asked the burning question she probably ought to keep to herself. "Why didn't you take them up on it?"

He stared at his coffee a moment too long, telling her all she needed to know.

Because I'm not pretty enough. Not girly enough. And I'm too short.

"I just got out of a relationship," he said, still staring at his coffee. "I basically got dumped, but I deserved it."

She rested her forearms on the table and leaned in. "Why? What did you do?"

"Worked. Too much, I guess." He pried the plastic lid off the cup and took a long sip. "We met right before the Torrance Lane fire. She freaked out when I got hurt."

Gemma shrugged. "Maybe that was her way of showing she cared about you."

He made a reluctant sound of agreement. "Maybe, but my burns were never life-threatening, and she knew it."

"Then there was something else bothering her."

"Yeah. Me." He grunted. "After the fire, I spent most of the time—day *and* night—chasing down leads that I thought would prove that fire was arson. Even when I was home, our relationship was never my priority."

"Sounds like she thought you'd checked out on her."

"I did. It was probably for the best. I wasn't cut out for her, and she wasn't cut out for being the girlfriend of an ATF agent. When she gave me an ultimatum—asked me to quit my job—I walked out the door."

"That's a heavy ask." One she'd never make of someone she loved. It was on the tip of her tongue to pry more into his love life, but it was none of her business. "What made you decide to become an ATF agent?"

"It started in the Marines. I hooked up with ARFF, the Corps' Air Rescue and Firefighting unit."

"ARFF? I'm sure Blaze would appreciate that."

"True that." Brett smiled. "When I mustered out, I'd planned to join the Denver Fire Department. Then something happened."

"What?" She leaned in closer, close enough to determine that, for a guy, his dark blue eyes were beautiful. Like Caribbean waters at night, or so she imagined. Jetting off to the Caribbean was a travel list bucket item.

She jerked back. *Oh jeez.*

"You okay?" he asked.

"Yeah. So, what happened?" *Aside from me being a dork.*

"I fell in love." Brett quickly added, "With dogs."
Ahh.

"A therapy dog helped me through a tough time when I was a kid. When I left the Marines, I decided to work with fires *and* dogs. The ATF canine unit seemed like a natural fit. I had to put my time in as an agent and get certified as a CFI. Then I got partnered with Blaze. He's the ATF's only arson dog in the country. The rest of the agency's dogs are explosives-detecting K-9s."

"Why's that?" she asked.

"There's usually at least one arson K-9 in every district, so the ATF doesn't want to spend budget money on duplicate resources. All it took was for one major arson investigation in the state to pop up when the local arson K-9 team was unavailable. The governor of Colorado pushed to have an ATF arson K-9 team available here twenty-four seven. Blaze and I are it."

"Interesting." But there was one thing he hadn't talked about. "Why did you go into the Marines?"

A dark shadow fell across his face. She likened it to someone yanking down a curtain. He'd shut down on her. Clearly, there was a story behind why he'd joined up. Even more clear was that he wasn't about to discuss it.

"It seemed like the thing to do at the time." He cleared his throat, and she understood the message: personal interrogation of his life was over. "Your turn," he said. "What made your family move here from Brooklyn, and why the NICB?"

"My dad wanted fresh air, wide, open spaces, and above all else better trout fishing." The first of what was to become a long list of her tomboy activities. "Mom wanted safer schools for me and my brothers."

"Understandable. All parents want the best for their kids." Brett looked past her. "It's obvious they love you and your brothers."

She followed his gaze to where her mother and father had their heads together, watching them. "They can be meddlesome, but yeah. They do. And they still love to tell everyone we'll always be New Yawkers and diehard Yankees fans."

"Coloradoans and the Rockies won't hold that against you." Brett smiled.

Her mom brought over their bagels and two strips of crispy bacon on the side. "Here you go. Enjoy."

"Thanks, Mom."

"Thanks, Mrs. S."

When her mother had scurried off, they dug into their warm, toasted bagels.

"Still the best bagels in the state," Brett said between chews. "And the NICB?"

Gemma swallowed and wiped her mouth with a napkin. "I started out as an investigator for an insurance company. When I was sixteen, my best friend's house caught fire. No one was hurt, but there was a fair amount of damage. My friend's dad's high-end electric guitar was burned to a crisp. The insurance company didn't want to make good on the rider, said they couldn't verify the guitar's condition. Luckily, the week before the fire, I'd snapped a shot of my friend breaking her dad's house rules by goofing around with the guitar. The date stamp on the photo was proof, and the insurance company was forced to pay out. From that point on, I was hooked."

"How long did you work for the insurance company?" Brett took another bite of his bagel.

"Five years. But I wanted to dig deeper into hard-core insurance fraud, so I applied to the NICB. Took me four separate applications before they hired me. Ninety percent of the people hired for those spots are retired federal agents *and* mostly men."

"You feel as if you have to work harder. That you have something to prove?"

"Kind of." Actually, he'd nailed that sore spot on the swollen head. Since the moment she'd been hired, she *had* felt like she had to keep proving herself again and again. After getting her case stolen, that feeling had amplified exponentially.

Weird how he'd easily intuited that.

Brett tapped one long finger on the side of his coffee cup. "Guess everyone has something in their past that makes them who and what they are today."

The same dark curtain lowered over his face, again leaving Gemma with the distinct impression there was more to his story than he'd let on. A *lot* more.

Above Brett's head, the TV screen showed two side-by-side images of fire departments battling house fires. Captions beneath each image indicated one fire was in Leadville and the other in Burlington.

Below the fire images, Mimi LaSalle, Denver7's anchorwoman, declared, "Yesterday, fire departments in Lake County and Kit Carson County were battling two separate house fires."

Gemma squeezed what was left of her bagel so tightly a blob of cream cheese fell to the plate. Brett's head whipped around to face the TV.

"Luckily," Mimi continued, "both houses were empty at the time. The cause of the fires isn't yet known. Unfortunately, for the owners, both structures are a total loss."

"Two more houses," Gemma said, her eyes still glued to the TV as she watched fire personnel battle the blaze.

When Brett turned around, his face was hard, a muscle ticking in his sculpted jaw. "Lake County and Kit Carson County are more than four hours from each other. We might have to take a road trip."

CHAPTER SEVEN

Brett parked in front of the courthouse, in Denver this time. Since Colorado Springs had no full-time magistrates, Gavin Aldrich's proceedings had been transferred from Colorado Springs to Denver.

As soon as they'd gotten into Brett's SUV, Blaze devoured the bacon Gemma gave him. During the twenty-minute drive to the courthouse, she'd been on her cell phone and still was, making inquiries with the fire and police departments where the two latest fires had taken place. She might prefer working alone, but judging by what he could hear of the conversation, she was good at getting information out of people.

Just not me.

At the deli, she'd come close. She'd known there was more to his story than he'd told her, but he didn't dare tell her the truth. Not all of it.

Every time her parents had tried hooking Gemma and him up, they'd pointed to her photo on the wall, one he now knew didn't do justice to her natural beauty. Knowing his disastrous relationship history, he'd always politely declined their offers, making up one excuse after another. He liked the Great Scott Bagel Deli, and at the time, he'd worried about alienating the Scott family and missing out on his favorite everything bagel with scallion cream cheese and that amazing coffee.

Now, he'd never consider dating Gemma for a completely different reason.

He liked and respected her too much to risk hurting her, and hurt her he would. Not intentionally, but that was what always happened.

Still, when he'd seen Gemma outside the deli, it had been on the tip of his tongue to tell her how great she looked, all dressed up, even without makeup. When her face flushed, that was all the natural makeup she'd needed. Gemma Scott might not be classically beautiful, but she didn't need fancy finishes like expensive clothes and jewelry or dolled-up hair and makeup. She was like a good pizza. *No toppings needed.* Gemma was the proverbial "girl next door." She took *pretty* to a whole new level.

When down and loose, as it was now, her wavy hair looked like a turbulent red waterfall. Slightly wide-set eyes narrowed, and the tip of her straight, patrician nose twitched, as if she didn't like what she was hearing on the phone.

There was depth to the woman, a core of steel that probably made her aces at her job but would scare a lot of men away. What most women weren't aware of, because it was a well-kept secret, was that most men were insecure. They just hid it behind a lot of macho bravado. Anything threatening that bravado was a hard pass. Ironically, he found Gemma's steel core and competency attractive as hell. That and how easy she was to be with.

He wondered what had happened in her life that she'd needed to erect all that steely armor in the first place. To him, it made her seem more vulnerable, more easily hurt than people who wore their hearts on their sleeves. Stupid thought, but it made him want to protect her. From what, he didn't know. From *him*?

Maybe.

Brett shook it off. Theirs was strictly a working relationship and always would be. Didn't help that he was more attracted to her with every moment they spent together.

He dug into the console and pulled out a navy-blue tie, slipping it under his collar and adjusting the rearview mirror to see what he was doing. Ties were something he avoided more than tofu. He couldn't remember the last time he'd had to torture himself by putting one on. Or eating tofu.

"I'll be there," Gemma said, then slipped her phone into a pocket inside her portfolio.

"*You'll* be there?" He struggled to get the damn tie up and through the bunny hole or however that tie-tying phrase went. "What about *me*?"

"Tomorrow, you'll be going to Leadville, and I'll be going to Burlington."

"Not happening. We're both going to both sites." If she was trying to ditch him, he'd kick her off this case faster than she could say *toasted everything bagel with scallion cream cheese*. He yanked on the tie to start over.

"That's a ridiculous waste of time. It's more efficient if we split up and each take one of the fires."

She unbuckled her seatbelt, then shifted to face him. "Here." She swatted his hands away. "Let me do that or we'll be late. Didn't your father ever teach you how to tie a tie?"

"Yeah, and I try never to wear them. I'm a little rusty." When her fingers grazed his neck, a shiver ran up his spine, and for a brief moment, his brain totally blanked out. Man, he really needed to keep more distance between them. Risking the success of their investigation to satisfy his libido wasn't something he was willing to do.

"Imagine the skinny end of the tie is a tree, and the fox is chasing the rabbit around the tree." He glanced down to see her wrap the fat end of the tie around the other end. "Once around the tree. Twice around the tree." She repeated the same move, then pushed the blade end under the loop and pulled it through. "See that?" She patted his chest, her full lips pressing together as she smirked up at him. "The bunny dove right into the safety of his cool, dark hole. That wasn't so hard, was it?"

Something was. Hard. Getting there, anyway.

Their gazes met and held, their faces only inches apart. Brett couldn't recall a single word she'd said. The only thing penetrating his lizard brain was her warm milk-and-honey scent. Involuntarily, or so he told himself, he glanced down at the tiny blue stone on the gold chain hanging around her neck just above the gentle swell of her breasts. He cleared his throat. "Thanks."

"Um, sure. No problem." She sucked in her lower lip, averting her eyes as she shifted away and reached for her portfolio.

"We'll hit Leadville first," he said when his brain came back online. "We'll go to the site, get copies of reports, and talk to the fire marshal and police department. We'll stay there overnight, then trek east to Burlington."

Pretty hazel eyes widened. "At a hotel?"

"Unless you want to sleep in the kennel with Blaze." At the sound of his name, Blaze snorted and got to his feet, huffing and swinging his head left and right, as if worried he'd missed out on something. "Let's do this."

As he let Blaze out of the kennel and snapped the leash onto his collar, he wondered if staying at a hotel with Gemma was such a stellar idea. Even in separate rooms. Now that it was out in the open that her parents had been trying to set them up, suddenly, that was all he could think about.

"We're taking him inside?" Gemma asked when she'd joined them on the sidewalk.

"Blaze has a side hustle as a therapy dog."

"You never told me that."

"You never asked. We volunteer at the North Metro trauma center and stop in every few weeks to see the kids there. Helps get their minds off their injuries. Physical *and* emotional. This kid's been through a lot. Maybe Blaze can help." A therapy dog had once helped Brett out of a deep, dark place, and he planned on paying it forward for the rest of his life. He slipped into his suit jacket, then locked the Expedition. "I'll put him back up in his kennel before we go into the courtroom."

Before going inside, Brett had Blaze sit in front of the flagpole. He pointed to the American flag whipping back and forth on the pole. "Salute."

Blaze lifted his paw and dropped it on top of his nose in front of his eyes.

Gemma laughed. "That's a neat trick."

"Kids love stuff like that." It was the very sort of thing that had hooked Brett on dogs all those years ago. That and a dog's inherent understanding of when someone was in emotional pain.

While Gemma went through screening, Brett secured his weapon in the security office's lock box.

Blaze's nails clicked on the shiny granite floor as they headed for the pretrial services office to meet with Gavin Aldrich and his attorney. They were buzzed in, then admitted into a small room with a table and four chairs.

Already seated were Gavin Aldrich and the same public defender who'd represented him in court, Anthony Manning. Manning looked the same, but Aldrich looked even skinnier than Brett remembered, and the dark circles under his eyes were bigger, darker. His face was completely devoid of emotion.

Brett knew that look, had seen it too many times in the mirror. Setting aside emotions, hurt, pain, and fear, was easier than facing the demons running around in your head.

Manning stood and held out his hand. "Thank you for meeting with us before court, Agent Tanner." He started to extend his hand to Gemma when she held up her finger.

She tugged out her phone and looked at the screen. "Excuse me. I'll be right back." She left the room, closing the door behind her.

"Gavin." Brett shook hands with the kid. His fingers were long and bony, and he instantly eased up on his grip. "Do you remember me?" He nodded. "This is Blaze." Brett gave Blaze enough slack in the leash to round the table and sit in front of Gavin. "He won't hurt you. I promise. He just wants to say hello."

Blaze held his paw out to Gavin, patiently holding it in the air. Brett understood Gavin's hesitation. Their last meeting hadn't been nearly as pleasant. Gavin was probably remembering eighty-five pounds of Chesapeake Bay Retriever chasing him down.

Cautiously, Gavin took Blaze's paw in his hand. Blaze rested his head in the kid's lap, looking up at him and uttering a high-pitched whine in the back of his throat that sounded like *heroo*. That's when he saw it—the crack in the kid's armor.

The corner of Gavin's mouth that Brett could see tipped up, then he began petting Blaze's head. Blaze uttered a contented groan, then lay down at Gavin's feet. The kid's smile broadened. "What kind of dog is he?"

"A Chesapeake Bay Retriever."

"I never had a dog." When he spoke again, his voice was tinged with anger. "My father wouldn't let us get one."

Brett sat across from Gavin and his attorney. "Maybe someday you can."

"Maybe." Gavin looked over Brett's shoulder. "Who's *she*?"

Brett turned just enough to see Gemma through the small rectangular window, the phone still glued to her ear. "Her name's Gemma. She's an insurance investigator. We're working together."

Still watching her, Gavin made a grunting sound. "She's pretty."

Brett had to give the kid credit for having good taste. "That she is." And she was his partner. *Only* his partner. But yeah…*pretty*.

Gemma returned and sat next to Gavin. "Hi. I'm Gemma Scott."

"I know." Gavin shook hands with her.

"Perhaps," Manning said, looking directly at Brett,

"Gavin might be more comfortable speaking if Ms. Scott wasn't here."

Gemma glared at Manning but kept her cool. Somewhat. Her eyes narrowed a fraction. "And why is that?"

"As I explained to Agent Tanner the other day," Manning continued, "some of the things we need to talk about are of a very...personal nature for my client."

Gemma flicked an accusatory look at Brett. He'd been in possession of information he hadn't shared with her, and she was royally pissed. Time to dig himself out before he disappeared into the quicksand. "The information Mr. Manning shared with me in court *is* personal. It's in the pretrial services report, but even I don't get a copy of that. Bottom line, it's not my place to share it. Even with my partner."

Understanding dawned in her eyes. "I see." She turned back to Gavin, who'd begun squirming in his seat and reached down to pet Blaze again. "You know, Gavin, I grew up with three brothers. There probably isn't anything you could say that would offend me."

"Wanna bet?" Gavin mumbled.

"I volunteer at a place called Hands of Hope. It primarily helps women, but it also helps their kids. Some of those women come to us because their children are being hurt. I've seen the worst of what adults can do to a child. Fathers included."

Gavin wrapped his arms around his stomach and began rocking in his chair.

"I want to help you," she continued, resting a hand on his shoulder. "But it's your decision."

The kid's eyes glistened, and he kept right on

rocking. Seconds ticked by. Tears spilled down his cheeks. With quick, jerky movements, he wiped them away.

Gemma slid the box of tissues sitting on the table in front of Gavin. He snagged one and wiped his nose with it.

Blaze rose and again rested his head on Gavin's lap, doing exactly what Brett had brought him here for in the first place. To give comfort and support in a way no human ever could.

The kid began petting Blaze again, his hand on his dog's head almost frantic as he desperately sought to absorb the calm, quiet understanding Blaze emanated. Gavin took a deep inhale, letting it out on a shaky breath. "You can stay."

Good for you, Gemma Scott. If the kid hadn't wanted her to remain in the room, there would have been nothing Brett could have said or done to justify her staying.

"Thank you." In a show of warmth, similar to what she'd exhibited with Sally Nash, she squeezed Gavin's shoulder, again making Brett wonder what had happened in her past that she normally only showed people her steely, emotional barricade.

Then again, who was he to pass judgment? There were times *he* could be the king of emotional sinkholes. Emotions went in, but they never came out. A major buzzkill for relationships.

Brett tugged a pad and pen from his inside jacket pocket. "For the record," he said, looking first at Manning, then Gavin, "this isn't a 'queen for a day' scenario." Meaning no formal document had been signed giving Gavin immunity. "Anything you say to me can be used against you and as evidence for additional charges."

Manning glanced at his client. "We've already discussed this. We recognize this interview is highly unusual at this juncture, but I believe it's in my client's best interest."

"Then let's get started." Brett flipped open his pad. "Let's talk about the warehouse fire first." That would be the easy part.

"I already told you"—Gavin slammed his fist on the table, making Gemma and his attorney jerk back—"I *didn't* set that fire."

"I know. We believe you." After watching the video from the warehouse feed Brett had sent to the U.S. Attorney's Office, the prosecutor had, too. That didn't mean the kid was completely off the hook, and Manning knew it. "But I still need to ask about it. You may be a witness." Before peppering him with questions, Brett waited for the kid to sit back and the wary calm to return in his eyes. "Did you see who set the warehouse fire?" Witnesses to acts of arson were rare. Even more unusual would be if the only witness was an arsonist himself.

"No." He shook his head, barely meeting Brett's eyes.

The trust wasn't there yet. Maybe never would be. Brett pressed on. "Did you hear anything before the fire started?"

This time, he nodded. "Dooley and I were asleep. I'm a light sleeper. I woke up when I heard a noise, like something metal hitting the floor." Possibly one of the discarded cans of MEK. "Dooley is"—Gavin swallowed—"*was* a heavy sleeper, so he didn't wake up. I smelled smoke and chemicals, so I got up to check it out. The warehouse was on fire. I ran back to wake Dooley up, but I couldn't get to him. I ran out the back door, then stuck around, figuring he'd come out, but he never did. I waited and waited, but he never came out. So I ran. I swear I didn't set that fire, just the dumpsters. I *swear* it."

Gavin started rocking again, and this time he let the tears fall without trying to wipe them away.

Gemma pushed the box of tissues closer. "It's okay, Gavin. We weren't kidding. We do believe you." Again, she touched his shoulder. The contact was minimal, but it did the trick. Almost immediately, Gavin seemed to get hold of himself.

Damn, she's good. Gemma knew precisely when to use that soft, gentle touch. And it was genuine. She really seemed to care about this kid.

After Gavin grabbed a tissue, Brett pressed on. "I'm sorry about your friend. Was Dooley his first name or his last? We'd like to notify his family."

"I think it was Mark Dooley, but he didn't have any family." Gavin shrugged. "None that wanted him."

That explained a lot. According to Manning, Gavin's family hadn't wanted him, either. It would be natural for these two to gravitate to each other.

"How did you and Dooley get into the warehouse? The front and back doors were locked, and there was a security system."

"Only the front door needed a key. The back door had a keypad. We watched once when someone used that door, and we memorized the code. All we had to do was get in before someone set the alarm for the day, then wait until someone showed up in the morning and turned it off. When they did, we either left out the back door or just grabbed our stuff and hid. It was easy."

Blaze nudged Gavin's arm, not letting up until the kid relented and began petting his head again.

Attaboy. Blaze was an awesome therapy dog.

Now for the difficult questions. "By my count, you set at least a dozen dumpsters on fire over the last few months. Why?"

Based on what the public defender had revealed from the pretrial services report, Brett had a pretty good idea why, but he needed to hear it—all of it—if there was any chance he'd consent to being part of the defense's plan.

"I don't know." Gavin stared at the box of tissues, his hand continually stroking Blaze's ears, which were getting a helluva workout today.

"Gavin," Manning interjected, "you need to be completely honest with these people or they can't help you when you go before the judge. Remember? We discussed this. You need to tell them everything you already told me."

"I know this must be hard for you," Gemma said. "Talking about it might help."

"I just—" He broke off and took a deep breath. "I just wanted someone to *see* me. To *hear* me. To know that I was there and needed—" His Adam's apple bobbed as he swallowed repeatedly.

"Needed help?" Gemma asked softly.

"Yeah." He nodded. "But it was too late. Nobody would help me. Nobody would listen. Even if they did, they wouldn't believe me."

Now they were getting to the heart of the matter, and Gavin's explanation had become a jumble of what the kid must be feeling now and what he'd endured as a teenager.

"You're talking about your father," Brett said.

Gavin clenched his jaw. "I killed him. I burned my whole fucking house to the ground. It was the only way out. If I hadn't done it, he would have kept— hurting me." His lips trembled, and his body went rigid. "He'd sneak into my room at night and—" He covered his face with his hands and began to weep openly.

Brett's stomach rolled with disgust and rage for the dead man whose face he couldn't plow his fist into. "Gavin, that's enough. You don't have to say any more." He'd already made a decision to help the kid.

Gavin pounded his fist on the table. "It's *not* enough. I saved Ally—my sister. I *loved* her. I made sure she got out. But now she's gone."

"What do you mean, gone?" Gemma asked.

"I figured they'd send us to a relative's house to live, but they didn't. Nobody wanted anything to do with us. They took her away. I heard she was adopted, but they wouldn't tell me where she went. I asked if the same family would adopt me, but they wouldn't because no one wanted a firestarter in their house. They locked me up in an institution. Then they kicked me out."

"How long have you been living on the street?" Brett asked.

"Two years."

He was twenty now. The second he'd hit eighteen—adult status—they'd kicked him to the curb. *Of all the irresponsible—* Beneath the table, Brett gripped the pen so hard the cover cracked.

For five years, this poor kid had been virtually alone. Brett couldn't help much, but he *could* help some. He glanced at his watch. With the information they'd gotten from Hicks yesterday, AUSA Moran was prepared to drop the felony murder and arson charges for the warehouse fires, but not for the dumpster fires. That was where Brett came in.

He shoved his pad and pen back into his pocket and stood. "We'll see you in the courtroom." He hitched his head to the door, then grabbed Blaze's leash when his dog trotted over.

Gemma followed him out, as did Manning.

"Agent Tanner. What do you think? Will you help?"

He looked through the doorway at Gavin, and again, his stomach twisted with rage over what the kid's father and the system had done to him. "I'll do what I can."

When they'd left pretrial services and were putting Blaze up in the SUV's kennel, Gemma stopped him. "How exactly does Manning expect you to help?"

"You'll see." It might actually work.

And most likely alienate the prosecutor for the rest of his career.

CHAPTER EIGHT

"All rise."

The entire courtroom, including Gemma, stood as Judge Tafoya glided in from her chambers and sat behind the bench. Brett stood beside the prosecutor at the plaintiff's table, while Gavin Aldrich stood next to his lawyer at the defense's table.

The judge wasted no time getting to the point. "Please be seated. This is a continuation of proceedings pertaining to Mr. Gavin Aldrich, charged with arson involving multiple dumpster fires, two warehouse fires, and potentially, felony murder." She picked up a report. "I'm in receipt of a letter to the court provided by the Pine Springs Mental Health Treatment Center. It contains a preliminary psychiatric assessment report on Mr. Aldrich. Ms. Moran, any comments?"

"Yes, Your Honor." AUSA Moran stood, looking to Gemma even more chic in a snug-fitting peacock-blue skirt and jacket suit than the first time she'd seen her. "Based upon information recently supplied to me by the ATF, we'd be amenable to dismissing the charges of arson as it relates to the recent warehouse fires and felony murder, but not for arson as it relates to the multiple dumpster fires."

The prosecutor sat, then, in an intimate gesture, placed her hand on Brett's biceps and whispered something in his ear. Gemma wondered if the woman was attracted to him. Then again, what woman wouldn't be? While she'd been helping him with his tie, she'd gotten a closeup view of his handsome face, his strong neck, that chiseled jaw. And lungfuls of that sexy cologne.

"Mr. Manning?" Judge Tafoya said as she made a few notes.

"Your Honor." Manning stood, holding a document. "I understand the government's position; however, in light of information contained within this report, we request Your Honor recommend treatment at this time, with formal charges deferred pending Mr. Aldrich's final psychiatric assessment."

From her position three rows behind AUSA Moran, Gemma saw the prosecutor shaking her head as she stood. "Your Honor, the government must object. Two years ago, Mr. Aldrich was released from a mental health facility. Since then, he's shown a proclivity for setting fires that could have, had the wind been strong enough on those days, kicked off massive fires. In recent years, the State of Colorado and many other states have been plagued by devastating fires, many of which were started intentionally. For the dumpster fires, the government's position remains the same pertaining to those charges as filed."

"I understand both the defense and the government's positions." Judge Tafoya nodded to both the AUSA and the public defender. "I admit that I'm on the fence about this. I understand there are extenuating circumstances in Mr. Aldrich's past, but even a dumpster fire can get out of control."

The judge flipped through a file, then looked at her laptop. "As Ms. Moran pointed out, in our dry climate, all it takes is one spark blown in the wrong direction.

An entire community can be destroyed, ravaged by fire. We're seeing that all over the country. Arson is a serious matter, no matter what emotional reasons may be at the root cause."

Oh boy. As it had before, Gemma's heart went out to Gavin Aldrich. Unless divine intervention struck, and fast, the judge would accept the government's charges. After that, Gavin would likely wind up incarcerated, rather than be given the help he so obviously and desperately needed.

Manning remained silent, but Gemma didn't miss the meaningful look he threw at the prosecution's table. He was waiting, but for what?

"Your Honor." To Gemma's surprise, Brett stood. She wasn't an expert in court proceedings by any stretch, but even she knew that unless it was a trial with witnesses, the prosecutor was the sole mouthpiece for the government. For an investigator to initiate a statement to the court was well outside normal procedure. "May I address the court?"

The AUSA remained seated, but her neck whipped around as she stared up at Brett. Make that *glared.* A hint of a smile played at Manning's lips.

The judge's brows soared to her immaculately coiffed hairline. "This is highly unusual. Ms. Moran? Any objections?"

AUSA Moran shot to her feet, whispering to Brett, who said something that seemed to mollify the prosecutor.

The AUSA took a deep breath that threatened to pop the buttons off her tight suit jacket. "No, Your Honor." The way she sat in a huff said otherwise.

"Mr. Manning?"

Manning shook his head emphatically. "No, Your Honor. We welcome Agent Tanner's input."

"Very well." Judge Tafoya waved a hand in the air. "Agent Tanner, you may continue."

"Thank you, Your Honor," he began. "I have something to say that I believe is relevant to Mr. Aldrich and may impact your decision as to whether he'll be remanded to jail or receive psychiatric treatment."

"Ms. Moran," the judge interrupted, "why wasn't I made aware of this information in writing and prior to these proceedings?"

The prosecutor stood briefly. "Because *I* wasn't aware of them until precisely sixty seconds ago." This time, there was no mistaking the irritation on the woman's face. She might have the hots for Brett, but she didn't like being overstepped. That, Gemma could relate to.

"Your Honor," Brett continued, "in Ms. Moran's defense, the reason she wasn't aware of what I'm about to share with the court is that it isn't evidentiary in nature."

"Then what exactly is it?" the judge asked.

"It's uh"—he cleared his throat—"personal," Brett answered.

Whoa. This oughta be interesting.

"When I was eleven years old," Brett began, "my friends and I broke into an old, abandoned house for a sleepover. It was my idea, and I convinced my friends to lie to their parents, each of us saying we were staying at the other's house for the night. The place was condemned, but the electricity hadn't been shut off yet. It was winter, so we cranked up the space heater." He paused and took a deep breath, letting it out slowly. "We were telling jokes, doing our best to gross each other out. We accidentally knocked over the heater and started a fire. It spread quickly, blocking the door, and we…couldn't get out."

Gemma's stomach roiled. When they'd been in her office discussing the various causes of all the accidental house fires and she'd mentioned space heaters, she'd detected Brett's reaction. Now she understood the source of it. Whatever he was going to say next wouldn't be good.

"The fire department came. They managed to get me out." Brett's suit jacket tightened across his broad back as he took yet another deep, steadying breath. "My friends didn't make it."

Oh God.

Gemma clapped a hand over her mouth. Hushed whispers came from the other people seated on the benches. She remembered that fire. It was all over the news. She'd been eight years old at the time. Afterward, her parents had sat down with her and her brothers, warning them about the dangers of space heaters. The similarities between this fire and the Torrance Lane fire were eerily similar. No wonder Brett was so vested in this case.

Briefly, he pressed two fingers to the bridge of his nose, then, in a slightly hoarse voice, said, "After that, I became angry and started acting out, got into fights and was suspended from school. I know now that I had PTSD, survivor's guilt, and that my behavior was an unspoken cry for help. Luckily for me, I had people there—my family—who recognized it for what it was. The only things that kept me from landing in jail for one thing or another were their support and good counseling. Gavin Aldrich didn't have the luxury of family support, and judging by what's happened, I'd say he never received adequate counseling."

Just that morning, Gemma had sensed there was something about Brett's backstory he wasn't telling her. Now she understood why. For him to bare his soul and relive that horrible fire in a courtroom must be incredibly difficult. He was doing it for Gavin. Was this what the public defender had been hoping Brett would say? How could Manning have known?

She looked at Gavin's attorney. His brows had lowered, and from the shocked look on his face, he *hadn't* known this was coming. Not all of it, anyway.

"Your Honor is aware of Mr. Aldrich's history?" Brett asked.

"Yes, yes." The judge nodded but kept one eye on her laptop. "I am."

"What you may *not* be aware of," Brett said, his voice taking on an undeniable air of authority, "is that youth arson is more common and more widespread than most people realize. It's a nationwide problem that's gone under the radar for too long. Offenders are often charged with malicious mischief or juvenile delinquency. Forty percent of the people arrested for arson last year were under eighteen."

Brett paused, for effect no doubt, and it was working. The judge had stopped focusing on her laptop and was now giving him the attention his words deserved.

"Some youth arsonists," he continued, "are as young as six years old. Parents often don't seek professional help for fear of having their child on record as an arsonist. Most of these fires are declared as accidental, when really, it's a symptom of a deeper problem, a way to draw attention to a severe stress in their lives. What Gavin Aldrich went through as a teenager was about as stressful as it gets."

"I understand where you're going with this," the judge replied. "But that stressor, Mr. Aldrich's father, has been dead for four years."

"Even though his father is dead, the neglect and abuse Gavin suffered at the hands of that man led to fire as an emotional outlet that still exists today, because no one helped him."

"Agent Tanner," Judge Tafoya said in a sympathetic voice. "Mr. Aldrich was institutionalized for two years. He's *still* setting fires."

Brett's jaw clenched. "And he *still* needs help. Whatever counseling they gave him in that institution didn't work. Incarcerating him in prison won't work, either. It may get him off the streets, but it won't address the problem. It won't get him the help he really needs."

"What makes you think institutionalizing him again will work this time?" the judge asked.

Brett shook his head subtly. "I don't know. Not for sure. But if you give him the chance, this time, I'll be there to help. There's a volunteer program, a companion service. Fire personnel who become friends with youth arsonists can do a lot to bolster a young person's self-image, help them deal with their issues."

He turned to look at Gavin Aldrich. "I didn't go through the horrors of what Gavin did, but I do understand how traumatic experiences can lead to a kid acting out and how that trauma can stay with you years after."

Had it? Stayed with him?

Gemma had to wonder if Brett had really been able to move past the fire all those years ago or whether that trauma still lingered somewhere in his present. It certainly explained why he'd put his life on the line to try and save those kids last year. It must have been devastating when he couldn't. She couldn't imagine ever forgetting something like what Brett *or* Gavin had endured.

Slowly, Judge Tafoya tapped a finger on the edge of her laptop. The judge had sole power over Gavin's future. What she would decide was anyone's guess. Gemma held her breath.

Finally, the judge declared, "Mr. Aldrich, I am directing you to return to the Pine Springs Mental Health Treatment Center for a minimum period of two months, during which time you will submit to additional psychiatric treatment and subsequent evaluation."

Gemma let out the breath she'd been holding. Brett, also, seemed to let out a sigh of relief.

The moment a new date had been set for Gavin to return to her courtroom, Judge Tafoya pounded her gavel and disappeared into her chambers.

Brett grabbed a folder in front of him, then turned brusquely and shoved open the swinging doors. From the determined look on his face, something was brewing behind those dark blue eyes. He strode quickly to the doors in the back of the courtroom. Before Gemma could catch up to him, he was out the door and in the hallway.

"Are you okay?" she asked when she'd finally

caught up to him. He didn't answer. "Talk to me." When he didn't stop, she grabbed his arm, forcing him to stop, but he stared over her shoulder, seeing but *not* seeing.

If it were possible, that lean, sculpted jaw clenched even harder. "Can you hit the road today?" he asked when he finally looked at her.

"To the two fire sites? I thought we planned to go tomorrow."

"I just moved up the timetable. Can you leave today?"

"I guess so. I just have to arrange for my neighbor to feed Jaws, but what's the hurry?"

"I have a gut feeling about those fires."

"So do I, but what's the sense of urgency?" Gemma didn't like the look on Brett's face. A light burned behind his eyes, an unhealthy one that left her with the feeling there was still much she didn't know about what was driving him. "Well?" she prodded when he didn't answer.

"I don't want to see any more people die." He stalked to the exit door and disappeared down the steps.

Gemma gripped her portfolio tighter. Now she had her answer. That trauma she worried about…it was still with him, hanging like an anvil over his head. Maybe hers, too.

CHAPTER NINE

Brett clipped on Blaze's harness, looking forward to the distraction of inspecting the burned-out shell of what had once been 986 Ruby Road in Leadville. Spilling his guts in a federal courtroom had sucked worse than doing it in front of a shrink. He'd done it for Gavin Aldrich, and it had been worth it.

Helping Gavin to stay out of jail, at least for another two months, had left Brett feeling victorious and more determined than ever to nail whoever was burning down these houses. He knew Gemma had wanted to pepper him with questions about his past. Mercifully, she hadn't, and he appreciated her respecting his privacy. Or what was left of it, after his very public, very on-the-record testimony.

The early evening light was still bright and cheery, the air a pleasant seventy degrees. At over ten thousand feet elevation, Leadville was the highest incorporated city in the country, the climate a welcome contrast to the eighty-five-degree heat they'd left behind in Denver.

With the light breeze came the smell of charred wood. Stands of creaking ponderosa pines surrounded the burned structure, along with shrubs and tall grasses. A few birds twittered away in the high branches over their heads. It was a wonder the surrounding property hadn't caught fire, as well. The fire could easily have jumped, then spread to other houses.

Brett looked around. There *were* no other houses.

Not close by. No other property owners who could have witnessed the fire. Convenient.

"Not much left of the place." Gemma snapped a few shots on her phone. "If we don't find something, the fire marshal will have no choice but to declare this fire as being accidental."

"Even a burned-out house has a pattern. Police treat every death as a homicide until proven otherwise. Fire investigation is no different. You know every fire is considered arson until proven otherwise. Sometimes, proving a negative is just as important."

"You and Blaze have your work cut out for you." She tucked her portfolio under her arm, then stroked his dog's ears. "Why the harness this time?"

"The handle." He gripped the rolled vinyl handle on the top of the harness. "If we get into trouble, and I need to get him out of there fast, it's easier hauling out an eighty-five-pound dog with a handle."

"Have you ever had to use it?"

Brett shook his head. "Not yet, but there's a first time for everything." Hopefully not today. He tugged on a pair of leather gloves.

Yellow caution tape surrounded the structure. The remains of the house were completely charred. Only sections of the ground floor walls were still standing. The second floor and roof were gone, most of it having burned away or collapsed onto the first floor.

Any remaining interior support beams were black and sooty. A burned, melted TV and a charred wood table were visible, along with small sections of sheetrock and pink insulation. The only thing that hadn't burned was about five feet of the brick chimney left standing.

Blaze stomped and shook his head, eager to get to work.

Gemma flipped open a folder the Leadville–Lake County fire marshal, Duke Grant, had given them when they'd stopped by his office. "Grant said his preliminary findings indicate the fire was probably caused by a short circuit."

Brett glanced at the open folder. "Any photos backing that up?"

She held out the folder for him to look as she flipped through the fire marshal's photos. "Not that I can see."

"The other houses you've been looking into," Brett said, "how many of them were in isolated parts of town, hidden from the road and with no neighbors close by?" Like this one. The closest house was over half a mile away. A thick stand of trees all but blocked the house from the road. The only reason the fire had been reported by a neighbor was due to wind carrying the smoke across the road and eventually to the next house.

Gemma looked up from the folder. "All of them."

Again, how convenient. If their theory was correct, Brett suspected they'd find a similar scenario at the house in Burlington. "Without physical evidence, we'll have to find another way to prove arson. If it *was* arson."

"Physical evidence is yours and Blaze's specialty. Documentation is mine." She grinned, emphasizing a slight cleft in her chin that he hadn't noticed before. He could well imagine kissing that cleft, then—

Work, Tanner. Back to work.

"Give us a few minutes to work the perimeter."

Knowing Blaze was raring to go, Brett tightened up on the lead, then pointed in the direction he wanted him to go. "Seek."

Blaze put his nose to the dry grass, sniffing, his tail whipping back and forth. For the next twenty minutes, he directed Blaze into ever-tightening circles around the structure, until they arrived at where the front steps used to be.

"Anything?" Gemma asked.

"Nothing." Blaze hadn't alerted outside the house. That didn't mean there wasn't something *inside*. He eyed the remains of the house for structural integrity, then pushed gently on one of the burned timbers on either side of the front doorway. It didn't budge. What was left of the door itself lay in a patch of burned grass, its hardware still intact. For that matter, the door wasn't as burned as he would have expected.

"Hold him for me." He handed Gemma Blaze's lead. "Stay," he said to his dog. Before allowing his dog into the debris, a safety walkthrough was in order.

With the porch and front steps burned away, Brett had to haul himself up the three feet to get inside. His boots crunched on sooty debris as he walked through the house, noting a few pieces of precariously positioned ceiling beams that hadn't burned away or fallen down. Definitely a safety concern.

Minutes later, he held out his hand for Blaze's lead, then pointed into the house. Blaze easily hopped up and in. Brett headed back into the debris and worked Blaze through the house, being careful to avoid any broken glass or other material that could slice open his dog's paws. Minutes later, Blaze hadn't alerted on anything. Whatever had caused this fire, accelerants weren't involved.

A noise had him turn to find Gemma struggling to haul herself into the house. Decades-old images of the house fire that had killed his friends materialized front and center, followed by a searing-hot flash of panic. "Stay out of here! The beams and walls of this house are hanging on by a thread as it is." The last thing he wanted was for her to get hurt, and it was easier for him to concentrate without worrying about someone else.

"I am *not* staying outside." She tossed her portfolio across the threshold and began climbing up.

"Didn't you hear me?" He grabbed the portfolio and tossed it on the grass outside the house. "I said to keep out."

"Damn you, Tanner!" She retrieved the portfolio, looking ready to hurl it at his head. Her brows lowered, and she stomped her foot. "I've been in dozens and dozens of fire scenes in my career. This is no different, and you're not keeping me out. You don't have the authority."

"The hell I don't." He stared down at her from the edge of the foundation. "Unless I can determine that it's safe in here, which it isn't, I have the authority to keep out anyone I want to."

Gemma took a deep breath and shut her eyes. When she opened them, they were shooting daggers, spears, *and* knives. "We're partners in this. Right? Where you go, I go. That was the deal, and there's no way I'm letting you do this without me. I have as much a right to be up there as you do."

"This isn't about *rights*. It's about—" Brett shoved a hand through his hair. What *was* this about?

Fear. Reliving his past would be too painful. He couldn't risk making a mistake again that took someone's life, and certainly not his partner's life. *Definitely* not Gemma's.

"Look," she said, taking another deep breath. "I'm sure you've got this whole 'me man, you helpless woman' thing going on. I get it, it's genetic, and as a man, you can't help yourself. But you have to. If we'd driven to these two houses separately, I would have gone into a fire scene without you, so why is this any different just because you're here?"

Now it was Brett's turn to draw in a calming breath because she was right, and he *didn't* know why this was different. Gemma was just as competent as any agent he'd worked with, so what was this really about? Then it hit him, like a fireball to the chest.

Her.

This time, he didn't want *her* to get hurt. He cared about her, and not just because they were working together. Something else had caused the gut-wrenching fear that she'd get injured. But now wasn't the time to let his personal feelings muddy his brain.

"It's hard to know how much longer these walls will be standing." Reluctantly, he held out his hand. "You can come in, but don't touch anything."

"Duh," she quipped.

Her fingers were slim and soft as she grasped his hand. As it had every time they'd come into physical contact, a tingly warmth shot up his arm. Clenching his jaw, he shook it off. Letting her get to him was a supremely bad idea. Getting involved with her…even worse.

"Thank you," she said when he'd hauled her inside.

While Gemma took photos, Brett meandered through the debris. Piles of sheetrock and roofing shingles lay in the center of the ground floor. "Sit," he told Blaze, then crouched by the sheetrock. He lifted off the shingles to examine the sheetrock beneath. *Interesting.*

Gemma crouched beside him. "Find something?"

"See that hole?" He pointed to where a jagged opening had been cut in a large piece of sheetrock. Broken pieces of thick, curved glass, probably part of a ceiling light-fan fixture, lay nearby. "There aren't any screw holes in that sheetrock."

"So?"

"If that opening was where the ceiling fan was attached, then there'd be holes around it where the fan was screwed on. It probably wouldn't be as jagged, either."

"Then what's the hole for?"

"Good question." He looked up at the clear blue sky. "Fire needs oxygen. By cutting a hole in the ceiling between the first and second floors, you could create a better draft. The front door isn't as burned as I would have expected. They could have intentionally left the door open, along with the second-floor windows, increasing the draft to really get the fire rocking and rolling."

"If not with accelerants, how did they start the fire in the first place?"

"There are lots of possibilities." When Brett stood, Blaze looked up at him eagerly, hoping to go back to work and wind up with another piece of freeze-dried liver. Brett didn't think this was a job for his dog.

He did a slow one-eighty, searching the lower

sections of sheetrock and counting the electrical out-
lets. A gust of wind blew through the house, making
the walls creak. Blaze snorted when one of the bricks
from the chimney fell to the floor with a *thunk*.

Brett's gaze landed on a corner of the floor, where
a large section of shingle-covered roof leaned against
the wall. This was an old house and, as such, wasn't
built to today's electrical code. But he'd bet there was
another outlet hidden by that piece of roof, one the
fire marshal had missed or hadn't gotten to yet behind
all the debris.

He manipulated the piece of roofing away from
the wall, then carefully laid it down on the floor.
Bingo. The roofing had protected the wall from burning, but the discolored, melted outlet cover told a
different story. He crouched, then using a pocketknife
pried off the misshapen cover. Melted copper wires
stared back at him. "See those beads?" He pointed to
the tiny balls of metal on the wires.

Gemma leaned over, and the scoop neck of her
shirt billowed out, exposing the tops of her breasts. "I
see them. Arc beading?"

He dragged his attention back to the outlet, then
nodded. "They could be the result of electrical arcing
that caused the fire, or they could have been caused
by the fire itself." Using an evidence bag, he snapped
off several beads. "Chemical testing can verify that,
but the melted and discolored outlet cover is a good
indication that this fire was electrical when it started
in the wall space behind the sheetrock. The outlet
burns, then the wall studs burn, and the fire spreads
from there."

Gemma took a photo. "If arcing started the fire,

can you tell what caused it?"

"It's an old house. If this is original wiring, it wouldn't be too difficult to overload the circuit. An old lamp, ungrounded... If the wires touch, the circuit breaker should pop, stopping the flow of electricity. But if the breaker panel fails, it could start a fire. An arsonist could have *helped* the circuit breakers to fail."

"How?" Gemma stood to make some notes in her portfolio. "Understanding electrical concepts was never my strong suit."

"It was never mine, either," he admitted. "There are lots of ways. You could remove the spring from the breaker to keep it from popping. You could insert a rusty screw in just the right place. Or you could install the wrong amperage breaker... The list goes on. The next step is to find the breaker box in all this mess."

A stronger gust of wind blew through the house. The walls shuddered. Creaking, louder this time, rent the air. Several long pieces of charred ceiling beams twisted away from where they'd been attached to the wall and began swinging down in a wide arc.

Directly at Gemma's head.

"Move!" he shouted, hurling his body against her and taking her to the floor. He twisted, lunging for the handle on Blaze's harness and yanking him away from the falling beams.

More beams crashed to the floor where Gemma and Blaze had been standing. Brett's heart pounded. Blaze's body shook, and he snugged up tightly to Brett's side. "You okay?" he asked Gemma.

Still partially beneath him, her chest rose and fell

quickly. Her eyes were wide with shock and fear. "I think so." She nodded, and he brushed a few strands of hair from her face. They were even softer, silkier than he'd expected. "But I'm having trouble breathing."

Ah hell. He pushed from the floor and skimmed his fingers over her ribcage through her shirt, searching for signs of pain or swelling.

"Stop it! What are you *doing*?" She batted his hands away.

"I need to check your ribs. You could have landed on something and broken a rib or punctured a lung. You said you couldn't breathe."

"Yeah." A look of exasperation crossed her face. "Because you were lying on top of me, crushing the air from my lungs."

Shit. "Sorry." He stood and held his hand down to her. "How 'bout we get the heck out of here?"

"Good idea."

Outside, Brett ran his hands down her soot-covered back and shoulders to her arms, searching for outward signs of injuries. "Are you sure you're okay?" A few scratches marred the soft, smooth skin on one shoulder, probably where he'd pinned her to the debris on the floor.

Guilt flooded him. *He'd* caused those scratches. "I did that. I'm sorry."

"Forget it," she said shakily. "You probably just saved my life. I saw that piece of wood coming at my head, and I just froze. I concede that you were right about the house, and I feel so stupid."

He snorted. "Stupid is one word I'd *never* use to describe you." And he meant it. Inside that pretty head was more IQ than most people had. Other than his closest friends, Deck and Evan, she had more grit and determination than anyone he'd ever worked with.

"Thanks." An adorable grin curved her lips. Lips he had to stop staring at. If only they weren't so full and lush. *Kissable.* Yep, something about a near-death experience made him want to kiss his partner.

He cleared his throat. "I need to check Blaze."

Standing beside him, Blaze seemed okay, but he was still shaking. Brett knew his dog didn't fully comprehend what had almost just happened, but he understood body language and was taking his cues from Brett. When he'd glimpsed those beams ripping loose, his only thoughts had been for Gemma and Blaze's safety. He might not be shaking on the outside, but inside, he was quaking with terror at what could have happened.

Lifting each of Blaze's paws, he inspected the pads for cuts and abrasions. Next, he ran his hands over his dog's sooty coat. He blew out a relieved breath. His dog was okay. Gemma was okay, but it was his fault she'd nearly been hammered in the head by falling debris. He should have inspected the house better, and he never should have let her convince him to allow her in there with him. He hadn't gone with his gut, and she'd almost been killed.

Brett fisted his hand. That wouldn't happen again. *Couldn't* happen again. He wouldn't let it. From this point forward, he'd never second-guess his instincts.

Gemma tapped into her phone. "I just forwarded the fire marshal our photos."

"Tell him they need to knock down the remaining

timbers before anyone else goes inside." She followed him back to the Expedition, where he dug around for clean cloths they could wipe their hands off with. "Tell him we also want to see that breaker box when he finds it."

The sound of tires crunching on gravel came from the end of the driveway. A large white, unmarked SUV turned in. In a cloud of swirling dust, the SUV braked, then hastily backed onto the road and took off, tires squealing on the asphalt as it sped away.

Gemma's phone dinged, and she looked at the screen. "That can't be the fire marshal. He just texted me that he was still in a meeting."

Blaze uttered a low growl deep in his throat.

"My thoughts exactly, buddy." Brett narrowed his eyes at the receding vehicle.

"What is it?" Gemma followed his gaze.

"C'mon, let's go!" He popped Blaze's door, closing it after his dog had jumped in, then yanked open the driver's side door.

Gemma was already hauling herself into the passenger seat. "Do you know who that was?"

"Nope." Brett cranked the engine, then K-turned the Expedition. "But we're gonna find out. Buckle up." He slammed his foot on the accelerator, sending the SUV flying down the driveway, then cranked a hard right onto the road and took off after the other vehicle.

"You think that was our arsonist?" Gemma clicked on her seat belt.

"Don't know, but I want to find out." He pressed his foot down harder on the accelerator. They'd been too far away to see the tags. He couldn't be certain of the make, only that the vehicle was large. Maybe a Suburban or a Yukon. "You know as well as I do arsonists often return to the scene of their crimes."

"So they can watch the fire and take pride in the destruction they wreak. But that would have been yesterday."

"That only applies to an arsonist coming from a place of passion. Our arsonist is cold, calculated. Everything he does has a purpose." Brett slowed as he came to an intersection.

Gemma leaned forward and pointed. "Look, there! Turn left! I just saw brake lights."

Brett turned left and punched it. Several hundred yards ahead, a white SUV took the twisting road at high speed, forcing Brett to do the same. Behind them in his kennel, Blaze wisely lay down.

"We're gaining on him," Gemma said, her voice filled with excitement.

They *were* gaining ground, and soon, they'd be in town and their quarry would be forced to slow down. It also meant more places to hide.

Sure enough, as they approached the outskirts of Leadville, Brett had cut the distance between them down to a hundred yards, still not close enough to see the tag, and his binoculars were in the back of the SUV and unreachable without stopping.

As they entered the center of Leadville, he eased his foot off the gas. Being a Friday evening, the sidewalks were fairly busy as people searched out the bars and restaurants. A group of runners wearing yellow-and-blue tank tops ran parallel to the road on the sidewalk.

Up ahead, the light at the next intersection

changed from green to yellow. A Colorado Mountain College bus turned onto the main road, squeezing in between Brett and the white SUV and obscuring the tag just when they were getting close enough to read it.

The bus braked to a stop. The light was now red. Brett cranked the gearshift into park, then jumped out into the street. The last he saw of the SUV in front of the bus was its quarter panel as it turned right at the next intersection.

He hopped back in the Expedition.

"Is he still there?" Gemma asked.

"No. He made it through the light." He was about to put the SUV in reverse, then hit the strobes and go around the bus to give chase, but two other cars had lined up behind him, the first of which was practically kissing his rear bumper. He smacked his palm on the wheel. "Dammit."

When the light changed, he followed the bus, then turned right where the other vehicle had turned. No white SUV. He glanced up at the utility poles, searching for city pole cams, but there were none.

"You know," Gemma said, "most fire marshal vehicles are either white or red. It could have been someone else from the fire marshal's office, someone Duke Grant works with."

"If that was a fire marshal vehicle, why didn't he or she drive up and talk to us?"

"Good question," Gemma agreed.

"Because it wasn't the fire marshal." Brett would bet his next paycheck on it.

CHAPTER TEN

An hour later, Brett sat across from Gemma, both of them chowing down on pork tacos at a table in one of the two adjoining hotel rooms they'd gotten at the Rodeway Inn. Gemma had taken the tie from her ponytail. Her long, thick, wavy red hair cascaded gracefully over one shoulder.

As he wolfed down more of his taco, Brett tried not to notice how the late-day sun streaming through the window picked up the highlights in her hair, making the strands shimmer like they were covered with tiny red sparks.

After losing the white SUV, they'd taken a spin through the fire station's parking lot. The fire marshal's vehicles were all red, not white, and with department insignia on the door panels. Duke Grant had not only been in a meeting all day, but he'd confirmed no other fire marshals had been on Ruby Road today.

Brett washed down his second taco with a swig of Two Mile Brewing Company's Leadville Lager. The printer Gemma had dragged in from the Expedition and set on the credenza next to the TV spat out page after page. She wasn't kidding. Documents and data were her thing.

When he'd returned from picking up dinner, her entire bed and half the TV credenza were covered with carefully arranged documents pertaining to the Leadville house fire, including the insurance policy and attached riders, bill of sale, title, deed, home assessment, survey, the fire marshal's preliminary report, and all the photos.

The NICB's access to the ISO database was proving to be just as useful to his case as Brett had hoped it would be.

So was Gemma.

NICB Agent Gemma Scott was not only competent, but he enjoyed her company.

Maybe too much.

She took a bite of her taco, chewing while she scrutinized the title for 986 Ruby Road. The printer took that moment to run out of paper, and she got up to refill the tray. While he'd been getting dinner, she'd changed into shorts, giving him his first look at her legs. Bare, shapely, perfectly proportioned legs.

Gemma glanced over her shoulder, catching him staring at her legs and her backside. He cleared his throat and grabbed his beer, taking another sip, and damn, if he didn't feel like he was back in high school. When he looked up, she'd begun stuffing more paper into the printer tray. He could have been mistaken but could swear she was smiling.

While she refueled her printer with more paper, Brett's tool of the trade also refueled. Crunching came from the corner of the room where Blaze chowed down on grain-free kibble and the special freeze-dried lamb patty Brett occasionally gave him.

"See this?" She handed him a sheet of paper the printer had just spit out. "I'm telling you this house is connected to the others. Guess what the titling company is?"

"Kobuk?" he answered before even looking at the document.

"Ten-four, Special Agent Tanner." She sat and took another bite of taco. When a dribble of meat juices trickled over her lip, she swiped it with the tip of her tongue, then licked her lips. Lips that still—*oh, holy hell*—looked soft and still way too kissable.

He grabbed his beer, chugging a good third of the bottle. Thinking about kissing his partner could lead to all kinds of complications, ones that wouldn't end well. Especially not with his lengthy history of crash-and-burn relationships. That and she'd probably slug him if he tried.

Brett downed the rest of his beer and snagged two more from the mini refrigerator, popping off the tops and handing one to Gemma.

"Thanks," she said, taking the beer and continuing to type one-handed.

Blaze finished eating, let out a loud burp, then lay down on the floor between Brett's and Gemma's feet. She rested a bare foot on Blaze's belly, rubbing it in small circles and making him groan with happiness. Was that—?

Yeah, it was.

Gemma's toenails were painted fire-engine red, her big toes adorned with something that could have been orange flames. God help him. Even her toes were hot. The cargo shorts he'd changed into felt just a bit tighter. "Nice toenails. Are those flames?"

"Yes." She wiggled her toes, then held up her foot for him to examine more closely. On instinct, he caught her calf in his hand. Her skin was warm, smooth, the muscles firm and supple. Their gazes met and held for a moment. "I, um. With the renovation, I'm always breaking my fingernails, but a pedicure lasts longer, so I splurge on a pedi every few weeks."

With their gazes still locked, Brett mumbled, "An excellent investment." He didn't know how long they remained that way. Him holding her slim calf and both their chests rising and falling faster. It was all he could do not to slide his hand to her thigh, just to see if the skin there was equally as soft.

Brett groaned inwardly. If he wasn't careful, whatever this thing was between them could easily get out of control, then blow up in his face the way it usually did. If that happened, he'd undoubtedly lose one of the best partners he'd ever worked with.

Eventually, she tugged her leg from his grasp and began shuffling through a stack of papers on the table.

"Blaze, you want to watch TV?" He reached for the remote. Anything to get his brain back on track.

Blaze scrambled to his feet and sat in front of the TV. Brett turned it on, keeping the volume low, then scrolled through the channels until he found Blaze's favorite. Animal Planet. Blaze uttered low *woofs*, his head bobbing as he tracked the waddling ducks on the screen.

Gemma laughed. "I really did think you were pulling my leg about that." As if realizing her choice of words, she rolled her lips inward and went back to focusing on her laptop.

Yeah, she would have to drag his Neanderthal brain back to him copping a feel of her calf. "Nope." He shook his head. "Like I said, it's his thing." Again, Gemma laughed, a soft, gentle sound he liked.

He opened his laptop and logged in. The screen was barely visible, thanks to the last bit of daylight pouring through the room's west-facing window. Brett stood to pull the shades but stopped. A large white SUV—a Yukon—slowed as it rolled past. The windows were tinted, preventing him from seeing the driver.

Brett bolted to the door and yanked it open. He stared at the tag, committing it to memory while the SUV continued rolling through the lot. He was tempted to give chase, badge the driver, and make him stop, but something wasn't right.

Why, if they'd taken such great pains to evade Gemma and him at the fire scene, would they risk getting caught by trailing them to their hotel? And how would they know where he and Gemma were staying?

The vehicle stopped in the middle of the asphalt running between the two rows of hotel rooms. As soon as Brett started walking, the SUV picked up speed. So did Brett. Just when he was on the verge of kicking into an all-out sprint, the Yukon pulled into a parking spot. A woman got out of the front passenger seat, a man from the driver's side. Seconds later, two small boys jumped from the rear seats.

Brett blew out a breath.

He was getting paranoid. Then again, paranoia had saved many an agent's life.

The boys began tossing a ball back and forth. He watched as they followed their parents into the hotel and disappeared. Other images—twenty-five-year-old memories—flashed before his eyes of two other boys, his childhood friends, Ryan and Cody. But instead of playing ball, they were screaming when the fire blocked their escape. Brett squeezed his eyes shut, trying to push away the horrific memories and failing miserably.

His heart raced, the beat thrumming loudly in his ears. As the firefighter had dragged Brett down the ladder, screaming from inside the house intensified. Then it stopped. The helplessness he'd experienced back then crashed down on him all over again.

Pressure built dead center in Brett's chest. Breathing hard, he dragged a hand down his face. It had been over a decade since he'd had that particular nightmare. The fire a year ago had triggered them again, but this was the first time he'd had one during the day when he was totally awake.

Shit.

When he turned to head back to the hotel room, Gemma stood in the open doorway, watching him with a curious expression. "What was that about?" she asked as they headed inside.

"Nothing." Except that he was on edge. *Too* on edge. He wanted to nail this arsonist so badly he could taste it. He couldn't bring his friends back. He couldn't bring those teenagers back. But he *could* stop it from happening again.

"You sure?" She placed a hand on his arm, eyeing him worriedly. "It didn't look like nothing."

For a moment, he gazed down into her eyes, so full of warmth and genuine caring, he was tempted to tell her everything. How the past could still torture him as if those events had happened only five minutes ago, not two-and-a-half decades ago. Instead, he shook his head, then covered her hand with his and squeezed it gently. "Thanks. I'm good." As much as he wanted to, this wasn't the time or the place for him to spill his guts again.

He gave her hand another squeeze, then closed

the door. They both sat at the table. Gemma started typing, and he reentered the password into his laptop. What he needed to do was get back to the evidence.

An email from the fire marshal caught his attention. "Got an email from Grant. He said he couldn't get in touch with the owners of the house we were at today. Thinks he must have a wrong number."

"Interesting." Gemma stopped typing. "I have a list of all the owners of those twenty-one houses. I've called about a third of them so far and haven't been able to reach a single person. The numbers are either not in service or belong to someone else."

"What about the attorneys handling the closings?"

"Same thing. It's like they don't exist. The owners *or* their attorneys."

Brett sat back. "Suspicious, but it's not anything we can use as evidence." *Yet.* "Who owns the Leadville house?"

"Thomas Williams."

Brett ran a DMV search for Thomas Williams at 986 Ruby Road. *Nada.* Next, he ran Thomas Williams through Accurint and Choice Point, two investigative databases used by law enforcement to ID people, their assets, addresses, phone numbers, businesses, and a host of other records designed to help locate people.

"Well?" Gemma asked a few minutes later.

"Thomas Williams is a common name, but there are no DMV records for any Thomas Williams at Ruby Road. There are a few records in Accurint and Choice Point associating him with that address, but those records all trace back to the title and deed. Other than paperwork, there's no record of him ever having physically been in Leadville." He reread Grant's email, searching for the phone number the fire marshal had called, but it wasn't there. "What's the phone number for Thomas Williams in Grant's file?"

She flipped through a few pages, then handed one to him.

Brett called the number. It had a Chicago area code.

"Vitaglio's," a thickly accented voice answered.

Brett narrowed his eyes. "I'm looking for Thomas Williams."

"*Who*? This is pizza. You wanna order a pizza?"

"No, thanks." Brett ended the call. "It's a pizzeria." Another dead end. "You have that list of the owners you compiled for the other houses?"

She nodded, then stood and leaned over the bed to reach for her portfolio, giving Brett an even better view of her perfect backside. First her lips, then her toenails and calves. Now her ass. On top of everything else, she was a genuinely nice person. Exactly the kind of woman he didn't deserve in his life.

"Here."

When she handed him her list, he scanned it quickly, then grunted. Smith. Jones. Williams. Anderson. Garcia, Wong…

"What is it?" she asked.

"Stand by." For kicks, he did an internet search for the most common surnames in the United States, then compared it to Gemma's list. "Did you know that every one of these last names is one of the most common in the United States?"

"No. That would make it even harder for us to

track these people down. If they even exist."

"Exactly. Even if we can't prove these names are all phony, we can't prove they aren't, which makes it worthless as evidence." They needed more, something to connect all the dots. Otherwise, this was all circumstantial. "Did you bring your spiderweb diagram?"

"Yes." Gemma went to the bed and pulled out the document from an accordion folder. She unfolded the diagram, smoothing it out on the mattress.

Brett went to the bed and looked at the drawing, absorbing every detail, following every line with its possible links to suspects. "We've got a connection between that disgruntled employee, Johnny Nash, and the warehouse fires, and a weak connection between Nash and the Torrance Lane fire, MEK being the common accelerant used at both locations."

"What are you thinking?" Gemma sat next to the drawing, leaning over just enough to give him another glimpse of the tops of her breasts.

Do not *answer that question.* At least, not truthfully.

Brett sat on the other side of the drawing. "How many of your suspicious fires happened in the last twelve months?" She pulled out another folded document, this one an enormous map with Post-its where the colored push pins had been. "Put it on the floor."

She set the map on the floor at their feet. Brett slid the spiderweb diagram to the floor next to it. From their vantage point, they had a slightly distanced view, similar to the one they'd had when the map and diagram were tacked to the wall in Gemma's office.

Gemma rested her forearms on her knees. "Five of the fires happened during the last twelve months."

"Nash was in jail for the last year, so he couldn't have set those fires." Brett's gut told him they were on the right track, but they still didn't have something connecting all those fires to one person.

"He could have had an accomplice," Gemma suggested.

"Possibly." Brett didn't think so. "Nash's motive for the warehouse fires was revenge. Whatever's going on here is calculated, organized, and scattered all over the state."

One of the most useful tools in an arson investigator's toolbox was crime mapping, recording arson cases cartographically. Based on the locations of fires, the likely area where an arsonist lived could be speculated, then a search run through a registry for any previously convicted arsonists living in that area.

But that would never be enough to convict. It merely narrowed down the focus to one area.

"Nash doesn't look good for these, does he?" Gemma asked, although it was really more of a statement.

"No, so let's look at this from a different angle, something we haven't considered before." Brett pointed to the map. "What happened to all these other properties after the houses burned down? Did the owners rebuild?"

"I don't think so." Gemma stroked her chin. "Some of them have been rebuilt by now, but none by the same people who owned the houses when they burned. After all the fires, the property owners filed an insurance claim, then sold the land shortly thereafter."

"Did any of them make a profit?"

"I don't know. I'd have to calculate that based on the original purchase prices. But property values have been skyrocketing over the last few years. That plus the insurance claims…it's conceivable they could make a profit even if the houses were a total loss."

"Can you pull all that data and calculate profit and loss for all these houses? You're better with stats, spreadsheets, and diagrams than I am." He grinned. "I'm more of a hands-on kinda guy."

When he held out his hands, Gemma glanced down, arching a brow. "I'll just bet you are." She sucked her lower lip between her teeth, then slowly let it slide out.

Was that a double entendre, or was she kidding around? *Ah, hell.* The vibes zinging back and forth between them were cranking with energy. *Hot* energy. He could feel it on his skin, in his blood, and in the way his heart revved.

Her lips parted, then her gaze dipped to his mouth, and her nostrils flared. No way was he misinterpreting that body language. She was thinking about the same thing he was and shouldn't be.

Don't do it. Don't. Do. It.

Before he could stop himself, he was leaning in, just a fraction of an inch, waiting to see if she'd split the diff. The moment she did, his lips were on hers. Gently at first, tasting the subtle curves before slipping his tongue inside her mouth.

A soft moan came from the back of her throat as he deepened the kiss, tasting her sweetness mixed with toasty malt and spicy hops. He slid his hand into her thick hair, loving the feel of the silky strands against his rough fingers.

She leaned in closer and put a hand to his chest, hesitantly spreading her fingers wide over his pec. The touch might have been light, but the effect it had on him was hotter than a branding iron, singeing his skin straight through his shirt.

Slipping his hand beneath her thighs, he tugged her onto his lap, right over his erection that was stiffening harder than a cobalt drill bit.

Heat from her body radiated to his. Her warm milk-and-honey fragrance was in his nose and in his lungs. She tasted even better than she smelled, and that was pretty awesome.

With their lips still fused, he rolled them to their sides on the mattress, snugging her petite frame against his, until her breasts pushed at his chest.

She sifted her fingers through his hair, sending sparks across every inch of his scalp. "Mmm."

Yeah. *Mmm. Right there with you, baby.*

He trailed the palm of his hand down the side of her ribcage to her bare upper thigh, just below the hem of her shorts. In slow, teasing movements, he swirled his fingers across her smooth skin, then beneath the hem of her shorts to cup the perfect globe of her ass and pull her against his now fully stiff erection. When she pushed her hips against him, it was his turn to groan.

Her body felt amazing against his and would feel even better when his body was inside hers.

Gemma turned her head away, ending the kiss. "I, um. I don't think this is a good idea."

Maybe not. "Probably not," Brett gritted out. *Definitely not.* He sat up and dragged a hand down his face, trying not to let the *groanus interruptus* escape from his throat.

"I should probably get to work on those money stats you asked for." She practically jumped off the bed, then tugged her shorts down and began smoothing her hair. A moment later, she was back at the table, searching through the stack of files.

He should probably thank her for stopping him before they both did something stupid.

"Blaze." Blaze ignored him, his eyes still glued to the TV. "*Blaze!*" Blaze shot to his feet, panting and snorting. "Let's go for a walk."

Brett snapped on the leash and led his dog outside. Mercifully, the sun had dipped below the horizon. With Leadville's elevation and virtually no humidity, the temperature had to be around fifty. Good thing, because he was burning up.

He could still taste Gemma on his lips and tongue. It was a taste he needed to forget. Kissing her in the first place had been a tactical error, but her sweetness and beauty had overridden his common sense. His priority should be to keep a clear head and keep his brains focused on the arsonist they were chasing. Not to dive into something that was doomed before it had even begun.

Blaze led him through the parking lot, heading for a hedgerow by the hotel office. The white SUV the family of four had gotten out of was still parked in the same space as before. As Blaze lifted his leg on the bushes, another white Yukon approached on the main road in front of the hotel but didn't turn in. Just before rolling past, the driver turned his head.

Dark ball cap. Light colored T-shirt. The vehicle moved on, then changed lanes as it picked up speed.

There had to be hundreds of white SUVs, including Yukons, on the road in Colorado at any given moment. Johnny Nash didn't own a white SUV or any vehicle at the moment. That didn't mean he hadn't procured one.

A vague detail dinged in the back of his head.

Stavros Medukin, one of the three employees Frodo Building Supply had fired, owned a white Yukon. Even if Medukin was out of the hospital, would he really be in any condition to drive?

Someone else could have been driving Medukin's vehicle. Nash? Could they be working together?

Brett tugged on the leash, then headed back to Gemma's room. Not wanting to overfeed his paranoia, he had to consider other, non-nefarious possibilities.

The driver of the vehicle they'd chased after could merely have been using the driveway as a turnaround. But his gut still said otherwise, and right now, it was screaming that they hadn't seen the last of that driver.

CHAPTER ELEVEN

While they descended from the twisting mountain portion of I-70 and finally hit the flat section of highway heading east, Gemma crunched profit-and-loss numbers for the twenty-one houses. By the time they were three hours into the four-hour drive to Burlington, she'd managed to dig up sales numbers on eight of the burned houses and plug them into the new spreadsheet she'd created on her laptop.

She pulled up data for the next house on the list, but her concentration was shot. The fact was she'd spent the last twenty minutes reliving that kiss. Much as she tried otherwise, it was impossible not to. Good old-fashioned chemistry. That's what it had to be.

Because that kiss was… Off. The. Charts.

Sensing Brett's hesitation, she'd met him halfway. Brief though it had been, her body shivered involuntarily as she thought back to his warm lips. Gentle yet demanding. Soft and hard at the same time. How skillfully his tongue had tangled with hers. Not that she had a whole lot of kissing in her personal repertoire to compare it to.

Brett's kisses were exactly how she imagined an awesome, off-the-charts kiss would be.

When he'd pressed her into the mattress and covered her with his big body, it was all she could do not to strip off his shirt and shorts and run her hands over all those powerful muscles. Everywhere she was soft, he was hard, and he *had* been hard. There'd been no disguising how much he'd wanted her. She'd felt how much, right up against the soft cleft between her thighs.

Had she been a fool to stop him? Or, perhaps, an even bigger fool to let them even get to that point. Mostly, it was fear. Fear of the unknown. Fear of the *known*.

In high school, she'd never really had much of a boyfriend. Her college dates had been few and far between. Rather than kissing, those guys had focused more on getting her into bed. Since then, her dating life had been sporadic, at best, and she was okay with that. It was easier working alone and just…*being* alone, rather than wasting her personal and emotional energy on guys who wouldn't stick around after a few weeks.

And then there was her colleague at the NICB. In hindsight, she'd realized the only reason he'd flirted with her and offered his help was so he could learn all about her case, then steal it. Letting him get close to her had been her downfall.

Her mistake and one she wouldn't make again.

Brett struck her as being different, but she would be a fool to let down her guard. That was the real reason she'd slammed the brakes on what could very well have been a night of amazing sex.

Not that I'm thinking about it or anything. Definitely not about all the sensual things a body like Brett's could do to her.

She stole a glance at his hard profile. His lips were pressed together tightly. The creases over the bridge of his nose had deepened in the last twenty minutes. He was stewing about something. Probably not about kissing her. More than likely, he was mulling over the investigation. Occasionally, he frowned, then tapped his finger on the wheel.

Behind them, Blaze snored away in his kennel.

Needing a break, Gemma stared out the window. It never ceased to amaze her how different this part of the state was. Unlike the mountainous region they'd just come from, Burlington sat on the eastern edge of Colorado's arid Central Plains at an elevation of about 4,200 feet and only about fifteen minutes from the Kansas border.

They passed one agricultural field after another, some brown and dry, others lush green from copious irrigation. Occasional windmills dotted the horizon. A quick glance at the dashboard thermometer said the outside air temperature was eighty-four degrees.

"Find anything interesting?" Brett nodded at the laptop propped on her knees.

Confirmation received. Definitely not thinking about kissing. For which she ought to be grateful. After all, she'd been the one to end it.

"Give me a minute." She quickly tapped in the code to tally the new column at the end of the spreadsheet, one that would automatically calculate the profit or loss from the pre-fire purchase price of the homes and the post-fire sale price. She hit enter, then sucked in a breath.

"What?" Brett asked.

"Even with a burned-out shell of a house, between the insurance claims and the riders, eight of the properties I've looked at so far sold for between twenty and forty thousand dollars more than what they were originally purchased for. That's how much property values are skyrocketing."

"No kidding." Brett took the first exit for Burlington, population 3,053, according to the sign they'd just passed. At the end of the ramp, he braked, then turned to face her. His eyes burned with an odd light. "What you're saying is all those homeowners made a nice little profit."

"Pretty much," she agreed.

He turned right onto a local road. "Assuming we're right about this, I'd say the motive is what we expected."

"Money," they both said at the same time.

"Right." Brett nodded. "Except for the Johnny Nash warehouse revenge fires. Those still don't mesh with the arson-for-profit theory."

Only Johnny Nash could explain those.

A few minutes later, they turned onto a heavily rutted dirt road. At the end of the road sat a debris field, the remains of which had once been an eighty-year-old farmhouse. Not a single wall was standing. Littered everywhere were window frames, pieces of sheetrock, and yellow insulation. A large cathode ray tube TV sat twenty feet off to the side of the debris, its glass shattered. Charred beams lay everywhere, crisscrossed over the other debris like a game of Pick-Up Sticks. Luckily, no other houses were situated close by.

Another isolated location.

Brett parked twenty feet from the edge of the debris and left the engine running. "Another common denominator. This house and the one we were at yesterday are so far off the beaten path they're not visible from the road, and there are no neighbors close enough to have witnessed anything."

Yikes. Not only did they have awesome kissing chemistry, if there really was such a thing, but they were so investigatively in sync it wasn't funny. A tiny shiver meandered up her spine. This was the kind of sympatico her parents had. Frankly, she didn't know how she felt about having it with Brett.

The same man who'd had his tongue down her throat and his hand on her ass.

Refocusing, Gemma looked at what was left of the house. Not much more than a few studs and ceiling beams that resembled charred twigs.

The phone Brett had clipped into a dashboard cradle rang. The name on the screen said: Kevin Nungaq.

"This is my buddy in Alaska. He's serving the subpoena for us." Brett put the call on speaker. "Kevin, how was your vacation?" he asked, adding, "Before you give me the gory details, you're on speaker. I'm working with an NICB agent, Gemma Scott."

Kevin laughed. "You have my sincere condolences, Gemma."

"Wiseass," Brett muttered.

"Vacay was awesome," Kevin said. "Good to be back, though. I tried serving your subpoena on Kobuk Titling. The address is a front. It's a packing store. I sweet-talked the manager into forking over some info without another subpoena. Turns out Kobuk's been renting that box for the last four years."

"Who rented the box?" Brett asked. "Someone had to have shown ID and paid for it."

"It was rented by John Smith. The address listed

on the driver's license Smith used to rent the box comes back to another box. This one's a P.O. box in Hawaii. I ran the DL... There's no one by that name connected with that P.O. box number."

Brett's jaw tightened. "How's he been paying for the box?"

"Annually. By postal money order."

"Shit." Brett exhaled loudly. "Any chance they have copies of the money orders or noted the money order numbers?"

Gemma didn't know all the ins and outs of criminal investigations but gathered this was proof the box was a front for a company that didn't really exist. As Brett had said, this guy—or *guys*—had been using common names. John Smith was as common as it got.

"Sorry, man. I already asked. They don't keep those records."

"When's the next payment due on the box?"

"Not for another eight months."

"Damn." Brett narrowed his eyes.

"Anything else I can do to help?" Kevin asked.

"No, but thanks."

"You got it."

Brett ended the call. "Without the money order numbers, we can't find out where they were purchased."

"Another dead end?" Gemma asked.

"For now." He looked up at the rearview mirror. "We've got company."

Gemma glanced at the side mirror to see a Kit Carson County Sheriff's Office patrol car pull up behind them.

While Brett got out and opened Blaze's door,

Gemma grabbed her portfolio. The second she stepped outside, the hot sun and dry air hit her like a slap in the face, as did the faint smell of smoke. Deputy Maws, according to his nametag, met them in front of the patrol car. In one of his hands was a manila folder.

"Agent Tanner?" the deputy asked.

Only now did Gemma realize Brett had called ahead and hadn't bothered to tell her. Was there anything else he was doing on the case that he'd failed to disclose?

A pang of worry stabbed her in the forehead. This was exactly how it had started four years ago. Her colleague had begun making calls and holding meetings on her case without telling her. Before she realized what was happening, her case was no longer hers.

Why she was recalling those awful moments now wasn't clear. Was it really such a big deal that Brett hadn't mentioned he'd called ahead to the sheriff's office? He wasn't anything like her backstabbing colleague. Jacob was the treacherous little prick's name. Perhaps she ought to chill and quit being so suspicious.

Brett shook hands with the other man, who was at least four inches shorter and about forty pounds heavier. "This is Gemma Scott with the NICB."

"The what?" Maws frowned as he took Gemma's hand.

"The National Insurance Crime Bureau," she said, not surprised that the deputy hadn't heard of her organization. Outside of insurance companies and fire investigating agencies, not many people had.

"So do you think this was arson?" Maws asked, getting straight to the point.

"That's what we're here to find out," Brett replied noncommittally.

"In that case"—Maws handed him the folder—"we're glad to have you looking into this. Burlington only has a volunteer fire department, no investigators on staff."

Brett opened the folder, then took a step closer to Gemma so she could review the contents, too. Naturally, a little gust of wind kicked up, and his yummy aftershave made itself known again.

She scanned the first page of the report, noting the person who'd called in the fire. Harold Briggs. Brett flipped through the rest of the folder that only contained a one-page police report and a two-page document from the Burlington FD. With every turn of the page, her attention was inexorably drawn to the rippling play of thick muscles in Brett's forearm.

So he went to the gym a lot. So he could probably bench press a small Chevy. The man's perfect physique was none, zero, and zip of her business.

When he flipped to the last page, the curling tail of his dragon tattoo seemed to flip as well. Everyone who had a tattoo—including her—chose a design that had special meaning. What did the dragon mean to Brett?

"No causation determined," he said.

The deputy shook his head. "Like I said, we don't have a fire investigator anywhere near here. We have a request in with the state, but they haven't been able to make it out here yet from Denver."

Gemma pointed to the report. "Anyone get in

touch with the owners? The Millers?"

Maws nodded. "I've been calling. They never answer, and there's no voicemail."

She and Brett exchanged knowing glances. The pattern of unavailable homeowners was repeating itself.

"Blaze and I should check out the perimeter."

Gemma and the deputy watched Brett and Blaze as they began their perimeter search, spiraling closer and closer to the debris field, pausing to examine the cylindrical propane tank next to the foundation. Not once did Blaze sit. Finally, Brett waved Gemma over to a burned-out stove.

The stove's metal sides were blackened and charred, the front door gone. Three of the four plastic knobs were half melted. "Given their condition, I can't be sure, but one of these knobs *may* be in the open position." Brett pointed to one of the center knobs. "The house could have filled with gas. All it would have taken was a spark to set it off. An explosion followed by a fire."

Gemma took a few closeup shots. "A spark from what?"

Brett looked at Deputy Maws. "Any lightning storms the night of the fire?" Maws shook his head. "Then we may never know what caused it."

Gemma opened the folder. "Was Harold Briggs interviewed?"

Again, the deputy shook his head. "I was on my way to do that right after we finish here."

"Mind if we tag along?" Brett asked.

"No, but be warned. Briggs is ornery and sharp as a tack."

A corner of Brett's mouth lifted. "Noted."

Minutes later, they pulled up in front of another farmhouse, this one a quarter mile down the road and situated on the other side of a thick stand of tall trees. Before they'd even gotten out of their vehicles, the door to the house opened, and a short, elderly man with a full head of gray hair appeared, leaning heavily on a cane.

While Gemma grabbed her portfolio, Brett leashed up Blaze and let him out of the kennel. "Mr. Briggs?" he asked as they met the older man at the front stairs.

"Who's asking?" he snapped, eyeing Blaze warily.

Deputy Maws stepped in. "They're with the ATF, Harold. The Bureau of Alcohol, Tobacco, and Firearms."

"I *know* what the ATF is." When Briggs rolled his eyes, Gemma choked down a laugh. She'd never seen someone pushing eighty roll their eyes before. "Are you here about that danged fire? I've been waiting for someone to come and talk to me."

"We're sorry we took so long." Gemma smiled, walking up the steps to shake hands with the man who so obviously craved attention. "My name's Gemma Scott."

She was rewarded with a lopsided smile. "Aren't you a pretty thing?"

"Thank you." Harold Briggs reminded her of her grandfather, and she knew exactly what he needed. To be the center of attention. "We understand that you reported the fire."

"I sure did." Using his cane, he pointed in the direction of the other farmhouse. "It was hard to miss it. The explosion woke me up. A loud boom. My bed shook. The whole *house* shook."

"And what time was that?" Brett asked.

"2:05 a.m." Briggs began shaking his head. "Those idiots. We don't have municipal gas lines out here. You'd think they'd know how to connect a propane tank before buying a place way out here in the middle of nowhere. It's not the first time that's happened around here, and it won't be the last." He scratched his head. "All that furniture they moved in there is probably blown up or burned to a crisp, right along with the rest of the house."

"How do you know they moved in furniture?" Brett looked in the direction of where the other house had stood. Aside from a few narrow breaks in the tree line, it would have been completely obscured from Briggs's view.

"Spotting scope." Briggs pointed to the far corner of the wraparound porch, where a large camouflage spotting scope perched on a tripod. "I've lived here my whole life, and before the Ashlands sold that farm, they'd been here for over fifty years."

"I see." Gemma nodded, and she *did* see. "You wanted to know who your new neighbors were." And he was a nosy old coot.

"You're darned right, I did." He inched closer to Blaze, squinting. "What kinda dog is that?"

"A Chesapeake Bay Retriever," Brett answered.

Briggs grunted, nodding in approval. "Glad to see you've got a big manly dog, not one of those tiny little yapping things like on those taco commercials."

"Yes, sir." Brett nodded, pressing his lips together, clearly trying not to laugh. "Did you see any moving trucks?"

"Sure did." He nodded. "About two weeks ago, I saw a big white one. Two guys unloaded furniture and brought it into the house."

"Did you see a moving company name on the outside of the truck?"

Briggs shook his head. "No. There weren't any names. I would've seen that, and I would have remembered it."

Of course he would have. Briggs probably didn't miss a thing that happened within a mile of his place. Maybe even the whole town. "What happened after they moved in all that furniture?"

"Nothing. Never saw 'em again. I drove over there five times since, but no one was ever home. Other than the fire department and police, no one's been there since the explosion. Until you showed up."

Gemma eyed the spotting scope. "You were watching us, weren't you?"

Briggs grinned slyly. "Yes, indeed, young lady. It pays to be nosy these days. We wouldn't want any riffraff coming around, now would we?"

"Of course not," she agreed. He and her grandfather could have been brothers, they were so alike.

"Now, Harold," Deputy Maws began. "You can't be—"

"Keep going," Brett interrupted, giving her a quick nod, indicating she should continue. Stupidly, that one little nod of encouragement gave her a serious case of the warm and fuzzies. Most of the other cops she'd interacted with—Deputy Maws being a case in point—would have taken over the interview by now.

"You said they moved in furniture." She pointed to the spotting scope. "Did you happen to see what *kind* of furniture? Were they fancy antiques?"

Last night, after Brett had gone to his room for the night, she could still taste him on her lips, feel his strong body against hers, and smell his residual after-shave that somehow seemed to have transferred to everything in her room. Especially her bed. Sleep hadn't come easily, so she'd pulled up the Burlington house's insurance policy. Not only was the house overly insured for this area, but there was a twenty-thousand-dollar rider in place for expensive antiques.

"Bah!" Briggs slammed his cane on the porch. "What they were was *cheap*. Looked like it all came from a dumpster. Broken legs. Peeling paint. I could swear that old kitchen table was sitting in the used furniture store down on Main Street just last week." He aimed the tip of his cane at Blaze. "I wouldn't have served food to a *dog* at that kitchen table."

Blaze woofed.

As Gemma turned to look at the trees, she saw Brett doing the same. He caught her gaze, arching his brow and urging her to continue. Once again, they were in sync, and once again, her body was overtaken by the warm fuzzies.

"Uh, Mr. Briggs?" She scrunched up her face, feigning confusion. "That house is a quarter mile from here. Even with the spotting scope, could you really see the condition of the furniture?"

"Don't be silly, young lady." His grizzled features twisted. "It's everyone's duty to get to know their neighbors. I snooped. After the truck left, I drove over there and looked in all the windows."

Gemma had a hard time imagining Briggs as a Peeping Tom. Apparently, he was sprier than he looked.

After exchanging contact information with Briggs, she and Brett headed back to Denver. As they hit the ramp for I-70, she typed the addresses of the Leadville and Burlington houses into her spreadsheet.

Now there were twenty-three houses on the list of suspicious fires.

Her cell phone dinged with a text from Duke Grant, the fire marshal in Leadville. He'd taken their suggestion and had the timbers at the fire scene on Ruby Road knocked down, then he'd gone in and retrieved the breaker panel. Grant's next words were short and to the point.

The breaker panel had been tampered with.

The Leadville house was no longer on the list of "suspicious" fires.

Gemma started a new column in her laptop. One for confirmed arson.

CHAPTER TWELVE

By the time Brett pulled into Gemma's driveway, it was nine o'clock. The last vestiges of daylight were quickly disappearing behind the foothills. Gemma's eyes were closed. Her chest rose and fell evenly. It had been a long two days, and he was beat, too.

"Hey," he said softly. Gemma's head lolled toward him. Her eyes didn't open, but when her lips parted, he was tempted to kiss her again.

He shook his head, clearing it of the temptation, but couldn't stop from thinking... What would've happened if she hadn't ended their kiss so quickly?

An all-too-vivid image sprang to mind. The two of them, naked, sweaty, and with him buried deep inside her. One day, she'd realize how close she'd come to making a mistake. If at all possible, he'd be gone from her life before she discovered the truth about just how messed up he really was. How broken and unworthy.

The only thing they should be doing together was working, and it was up to him to keep it that way.

Thanks to the rapport she'd struck up with Harold Briggs, there was now another potential pattern to these fires. They'd stocked the house in Burlington with used furniture. They'd have to provide receipts and assessments proving the furniture was more valuable than it actually was, but if they were already creating phony deeds and titles, what was one more false document?

Still asleep, Gemma sighed. A lock of hair had slipped across her cheek. Unable to resist, he nudged it behind her ear. Her eyelids flickered, then opened.

"Hi," she said.

"Hi," he whispered back. "Home sweet home."

She yawned, then stretched, reaching out to pet Blaze's head as he stuck it through the kennel window.

"Are you up for working tonight?" he asked. With more patterns being established every day, he wanted to help Gemma crunch the rest of those profit-and-loss numbers and start putting it all together in a report.

"Tonight? It's Saturday, and it's" — she looked at the dashboard clock — "after nine."

"We're on a roll. I want to keep going." They were on to something big here, and every day that passed, an arsonist and possible murderer was walking around free.

She sighed, more heavily this time. "Okay, but if you want me to work tonight, you have to feed me. There's nothing in my house."

"What are you in the mood for?"

"Barbecue," she said without hesitation. "From the Piggly Smokehouse on Morrison."

A woman after my own heart.

Figure of speech.

"Piggly's is my favorite place for ribs."

After dropping Gemma off, Brett made the fifteen-minute drive to Piggly's in ten. Only a few cars were in the lot. Before going inside, he grabbed the leash and took Blaze out to relieve himself. Blaze sniffed the gravel, then meandered toward the grass bordering the edge of the parking lot.

Headlights lit up Morrison Road as several vehicles rounded the bend and shot past. One of them slowed but didn't turn in.

Blaze dragged Brett to a spot that must have been particularly interesting. His dog put his nose to the grass, sniffing and snorting. Brett looked at the vehicle that had slowed to a stop on the shoulder just before the entrance to Piggly's. The driver cut the headlights.

A large white SUV.

The front passenger window rolled down. The driver raised his arm. Light from the parking lot and inside the restaurant lit the interior of the car enough for Brett to recognize the dark outline of something in the driver's hand.

A gun.

Brett's heart rate jacked into the stratosphere. "*Blaze, down!*" He threw himself on top of his dog, covering Blaze's body with his own.

Metal pinged as a hailstorm of bullets raked the car they'd just dived behind for cover. Glass shattered, raining shards down on Brett's back and head. More shots rang out, closer this time, hitting the rear quarter panel. Another window exploded, only this time it wasn't in the parking lot. The restaurant's plate glass window had just been shot out.

Keeping his head low, Brett pushed to his knees, still holding tightly onto Blaze's leash as he drew his Glock and peeked out over the hood of the car.

The white SUV's driver's seat was empty. A lone figure disappeared around the back of the SUV and slid behind the wheel. A door slammed. Brett aimed in on the driver and was a hair's breadth from pulling the trigger when another vehicle passed behind the SUV on the road.

He jerked his finger off the trigger. Missing his target and hitting the driver of the other vehicle was a possibility he couldn't risk.

Tires screeched. The white SUV fishtailed as it gained traction and fled west on Morrison Road.

Screaming came from inside Piggly's. As much as Brett wanted to give chase, victims took priority. He raced to the door of the restaurant and yanked it open. Sure enough, one of the restaurant's windows— the one closest to where he and Blaze had been standing—had been taken out. Pieces of glass littered the tile. The few remaining customers had hit the floor, covering the backs of their heads with their hands. The owner, Marty Estevez, and two other employees poked their heads up from behind the counter.

"Everyone okay?" Brett shouted as he holstered. "Is anyone hit?" After the men shook their heads, Brett looked at the customers, gratified to see they also appeared unhurt.

He pulled out his cell phone and called 911. "This is ATF Special Agent Tanner. I'm reporting a drive-by shooting at Piggly's on Morrison Road. No injuries. Suspect vehicle is a white SUV heading west on Morrison. The driver is armed with a handgun." And probably long gone by now. "Everyone stay inside, and stay down," Brett shouted after ending the call.

He went back outside to wait for the Lakewood PD. Already, he could hear sirens in the distance. As he waited, he turned back to face the restaurant.

Had this guy been shooting at Piggly's?

The restaurant's shattered window could certainly be evidence of that.

Then again, the shattered window on the car he and Blaze had been standing in front of when the driver had opened fire could suggest *they* were the targets, and the restaurant window had been hit accidentally.

It wasn't unheard of for a federal agent to be targeted. What were the chances the shooter's vehicle would also be a white SUV?

No charges had been filed yet on the case he and Gemma were working, so it would be virtually impossible for anyone to know they'd even opened an investigation.

Brett rubbed his jaw. He refused to believe there was a leak inside any of the agencies working the case. But what about the witnesses they'd spoken to? Especially Sally Nash.

The woman had been lying about something. She could have called her brother the second he and Gemma had walked out the door. But again, neither he nor Gemma thought Nash had anything to do with the house fires all over the state. Which brought him full circle back to the white SUV.

He didn't have enough evidence to voice it, but if this white SUV was the same one they'd spooked up in Leadville, the driver could have circled around and followed them to the hotel. It wasn't completely inconceivable they'd been tracked from the moment they'd left Leadville. I-70 was a busy highway. He could have missed the tail.

Which meant someone was extremely motivated to take him out of the picture. Permanently.

He went back to his Expedition and tugged the tactical flashlight from his belt. A minute later, he'd confirmed there were no tracking devices attached to the undercarriage.

His stomach hardened as he tried not to let his paranoia take hold and overshadow common sense.

If this *was* about him, and it *was* about the investigation he was working on, Gemma could be a target, too.

Flashing red-and-blue lights flooded the road as patrol cars sped closer. Brett stepped aside, tugging Blaze with him so they wouldn't inadvertently get run down by the good guys. He whipped out his phone and called Gemma.

The first patrol car blew into the parking lot and screeched to a stop. Still waiting for Gemma to answer, Brett unclipped the badge from his belt, tugged out the chain, and slipped it over his head. With his holstered gun exposed, the last thing he wanted was to get drilled by friendly fire.

"C'mon, answer, dammit." Gemma's phone had already rung three times, and he was a microsecond from hauling ass back to her place.

• • •

Gemma went into the bedroom to feed Jaws. She really did enjoy having the little guy around. Okay, so he wasn't warm and furry like Blaze, but she didn't care what Brett had said.

"Don't listen to him." She uncapped the plastic jar and sprinkled food into the tank. "You can too smile."

Jaws sped to the surface, gulping down the flat,

desiccated flakes with the same enthusiasm she'd enjoy chunks of lobster drenched in gobs of butter.

Her stomach growled, and her tastebuds watered at the thought of food. *Any* food at this point. She sat in front of her laptop and yawned. The moment Brett had dropped her off, she'd dug into the assignment he'd given her.

All the boxes in the profit-and-loss chart she'd assembled for the twenty-one houses, now twenty-three, including the Leadville and Burlington homes, were nearly full. There were only a few locations with missing data. Not unexpectedly, the sellers had all made tidy profits by collecting on the insurance, the riders, then selling the land. One such transaction, in an especially trendy section of Aspen, had netted the seller close to a hundred thousand dollars.

That would, hypothetically, mean twenty-three cases of arson-for-profit. Suggestive data and suspicion would never be enough to charge anyone, though, and they still didn't even know who to charge.

Her phone rang. By the time she got to it on the kitchen counter, it had already blared out three bars from "Manly Men," the theme song from *Two and a Half Men* that she'd assigned to Brett's number. Her heart did an awkward little blip at seeing his name on the screen. "Where's my food?" she answered just before the fourth ring. "I'm starving."

"Yeah. About that." Sirens wailing came through the phone.

As Gemma listened to Brett describe the shooting, her jaw dropped. While she'd been sitting in the comfort of her house, working on her laptop, Brett and Blaze had been getting shot at. *Actually shot at.*

Her heart lurched. "Is Blaze okay?" Images of Brett with a bullet hole in his chest was bad enough. If Blaze had been hurt, too...

"He's fine," Brett reassured her, "but we're going to be stuck here for a while working with the police on this. At this point, we can't tell if the shooter was targeting me or the restaurant. Sometimes, people seek retribution on the agent who's investigating them. If that's what's going down here, and it's because of the arson case we're working, you could become a target, too."

She leaned back against the counter. "*Me*?"

"Yeah, you. I need you to lock all the doors and windows in the house, and keep them that way."

"Okay." Grimacing, she looked at the small cardboard box in a corner of the living room—the one containing all the brass window sash locks she hadn't gotten around to installing yet. They'd been delivered over a week ago, but she'd gotten so caught up in the case that work on the house had come to a grinding halt. Luckily, there wasn't much of anything of value inside, other than her power tools.

"I've gotta go, but there's one more thing," Brett continued. "I'm calling a friend of mine to stay with you until I can get there. His name's Evan McGarry. He's an FBI agent."

"An FBI agent?" Did she really need a babysitter? Although it was kinda sweet of Brett to make sure she was safe. *Nah, not sweet.* What agent wouldn't warn his partner that a gun-crazed arsonist might pop in any second?

"Humor me, will you? You'll like him. He's got a dog, too."

"Always a plus." It certainly was with Brett. Blaze had won her over even before Brett had.

"If I'm lucky, I'll see you in a couple of hours."

After Brett ended the call, Gemma set her phone on the counter.

Had he? Won her over?

Well, she certainly didn't dislike him, and she didn't distrust him anymore. In fact, she really *liked* him. Didn't hurt that he was an awesome kisser.

First, she locked the kitchen door, then went to the front door and twisted the deadbolt. Then she went through every room on the ground floor, checking all the windows and closing the few she'd opened to let in fresh air. Luckily, the arid climate was low on bugs. Just about every house in Colorado had air conditioning, but AC cost money. Money that needed to go into the renovation, so she'd spent the summer saving money by opening windows. *And sweating my ass off.*

Next, she headed for the basement. Not many houses in this area had a walk-out basement. That was one of the many things she'd fallen in love with about her little Victorian fixer-upper. *AKA the money pit.*

She opened the door to the basement and flipped on the lights. The old stairs creaked in protest. With every step, musty smells wafted to her nose. It never ceased to amaze her that even in Denver's arid climate, a basement could still be musty.

One wall was stacked high with plastic bins containing personal belongings she'd stashed down here so they wouldn't get covered with sawdust. Only the bare necessities ever made it upstairs.

She checked the basement door to the backyard. Satisfied that it was locked, she headed for the stairs but stopped. A small pile of sawdust sat in the middle of the concrete floor. She squatted next to it and pushed her fingers through the pile. On closer inspection, the pile was fresh. It could have been stuck to the bottom of one of the plastic bins when she'd moved them down here. Prior to purchasing the house, she'd had it inspected, but if her inspector had dropped the ball and the whole house—not just the outside deck—turned out to be infested with termites, she wanted a refund.

Back upstairs, she reluctantly flipped on the ground floor AC. A moment later, the condenser kicked on, and cool air whooshed through the vents. This was the sound of money zooming out of her bank account.

Her stomach growled again. Time for scrambled eggs. Not nearly as good as Piggly's barbecue would have been, but it would have to do.

Being careful not to trip over the portable compressor or the pneumatic nailer cord, she went into the kitchen and pulled out eggs, butter, and cheddar cheese from the fridge, along with utensils from a cabinet. After cracking the eggs into the bowl, she began whisking when a *clunking* sound came from behind her.

Gemma turned, not seeing anything. She began whisking again, and again the same sound. Closer.

Louder.

Hair at her nape prickled, and somehow...she knew.

I'm not alone.

Slowly, she turned, then sucked in a quick breath.

A man stood in the doorway to the kitchen. A ball

cap covered his head. Dark sunglasses concealed his eyes.

She gripped the whisk tighter, vaguely aware of raw, runny eggs dripping down her hand. Her heart hammered, and she sucked in more quick breaths. "Get *out* of my house." Stupid though the words sounded, it was the first thing she'd thought of.

Instead of turning tail and making for the door, he charged her. She threw the whisk at his face, but he easily dodged her culinary weapon.

She lunged for the butcher block of knives but never made it. Strong hands grabbed her waist, spinning her, then wrapping around her neck.

Gemma gasped for air but couldn't even gasp. He'd cut off her airway. She swatted at his hands, then curled her fingers around his to pull them away, but he was too strong. Not that it mattered, what with him on the verge of crushing her trachea, but some part of her brain registered that he wore gloves.

She tried hitting him in the face, but her blows were ineffective. He pressed his body against hers, pinning her back against the counter ledge. She couldn't even knee him in the balls, and with no weapon within reach, she'd soon be unconscious, and after that…dead.

Her vision began to blur. She flung her arms around uselessly. Her fingers contacted something metal. The bowl of eggs. She gripped the edge of the bowl and whaled it against the man's head. Runny egg covered his face, dripping down his forehead behind the glasses.

Mercifully, his hold around her neck loosened, then he let go and took a step back. She drew in a long, wheezing drought of air.

He lifted his glasses and swiped at his eyes. Not enough for her to see his face. She kicked out with her foot, racking his balls. When he doubled over, she raced into the living room, banging her hip against the wood workbench and falling to her knees. On the way down, her forehead grazed the corner of the bench, and she cried out.

She scrambled to her feet. Behind her, booted feet pounded on the bare wood floor. There was no way she'd make it to the door. She grabbed a hammer from the workbench and threw it at him. He dodged the tool and kept coming. Next, she grabbed a screwdriver and hurled that at his face. The thick, plastic handle hit him with a glancing blow, and he grunted, putting his beefy hand to the side of his head.

"Bitch," he growled.

He took another step toward her. She picked up the only other tool on the bench that she hadn't thrown—the framing nail gun. It was still plugged into the compressor and fully charged. This baby shot out three-and-a-half-inch nails.

"You wanna see my *bitch*?" Gemma gritted out. "You ain't seen nothing yet." She raised the nailer and pointed it at him. He froze. "Yeah, that's what I thought." She pulled the trigger and...nothing. Nothing happened.

She pulled it again, then one more time. Still, nothing happened. It took another half a second to understand why.

Pneumatic nailers were designed with an inherent safety sequence. The tip of the gun had to make contact with something, then be fully depressed before firing off a nail.

Shoot. Pardon the pun.

The man laughed.

Gemma gripped the nailer tighter, readying to throw it in his face. *That oughta leave a mark.*

She started to raise her arm when he charged her, slamming her back against the wall and pinning the nailer between their bodies. He rammed his forearm against her neck. Her vision blurred again, and she couldn't breathe.

There was no way she could overpower him. She started to black out, felt her limbs going numb. *I don't want to die.* The man's face looming above her blurred. *There's so much I still want to do. Finish renovating the house. Kiss Brett again.*

Her grip on the nailer loosened.

The nailer.

It was jammed between their bodies. Was there enough pressure for the safety mechanism to disengage? Praying she still had the strength, she canted her wrist, angling the tip of the nailer away from her body and against his. She pushed as hard as she could, hoping to create enough pressure to disengage the safety mechanism...and pulled the trigger.

Ka-tunk.

He roared, then stumbled back, clutching his side. "Fuck!"

Gemma doubled over, sucking in a raspy breath, then lifted her arm and swung the nail gun against him, directly over the wound she'd just inflicted.

Another loud cry, and he fell to his knees.

She let the nailer drop to the floor, then staggered to the door, drawing in painful breaths with each step.

She fumbled with the lock, desperately trying to twist it open, but her hands shook too badly.

Open. Open, dammit!

Breathing hard, she glanced over her shoulder.

The man was pushing from the floor, still holding his side. A vicious sneer curled his upper lip.

Oh God, no.

No way could she let this goon get hold of her again. If she did, he'd re-channel all that cruelty in her direction.

Her heart pounded, and she gripped the lock tighter, managing to twist it open this time. She flung open the door, stumbled onto the porch, and raced down the stairs.

Footsteps pounded behind her. Bile rose in the back of her throat, and her stomach knotted with fear.

He was coming after her.

CHAPTER THIRTEEN

At ten o'clock, the sky looked peaceful, dotted only with stars and the occasional commercial jet headed for Denver International Airport. Piggly's parking lot and Morrison Road heading in either direction were a different story.

There were enough red-and-blue strobes flashing and reflecting off the asphalt to light up Denver for a week. Patrol cars had blocked off the road for a hundred yards east and west of the restaurant. Brett had requested officers cordon off the area so Blaze could search for shell casings while the crime scene team did their thing. Even now, the CSU team was busy photographing the vehicles that had been strafed by gunfire, searching for embedded projectiles.

He gave Blaze his lead, following his dog as he processed scents, his nose to the ground, his tail whipping back and forth. They'd been searching for five minutes. The casings had to be here.

When it came to detecting accelerants, Blaze was a rock star, but he'd essentially flunked out of explosives detection school, which included imprinting on black powder. His dog had shown increased interest in finding spent shell casings but never seemed to exhibit an all-out alert. That didn't mean he couldn't find them.

The first shots had been fired from inside the white SUV. Those shell casings he didn't expect to find. With the gun's ejection port being on the right side of the weapon, those casings would have shot backward and to the right of the shooter, probably ricocheting off the inside of the roof and landing in the back seat.

But the shooter had gotten out of the vehicle. That explained why the second volley had sounded closer. The entire drive-by had lasted only seconds. It was doubtful the shooter had taken the time to stop and collect the casings. *Those* casings had to be here.

Granted, he'd been flinging himself to the ground at the time, but by his count, the shooter had gotten off at least eight rounds in his direction, plus another at the restaurant window. From the sound of the shots, he figured the weapon had been a 9mm. Depending on the make and model, the magazine could have held anywhere from seven to nineteen rounds.

Radios squawked. Distant sirens echoed, but Blaze didn't care. All his senses were finely attuned to scent at the moment, and Brett was hopeful that his dog wouldn't let him down.

Blaze led him back to the road, sniffing and circling on the asphalt before heading back to the gravel-covered lot. It was entirely possible the first patrol cars on scene had crunched the casings down in between the loose stone, but that wouldn't be nearly enough to conceal the scent of a freshly spent shell casing.

His dog's body language changed. His sniffing grew louder. His tail whipped back and forth so quickly he could probably take out a window. Blaze pulled on the leash, leading Brett to the tall grass bordering the edge of the lot near the road. There was no doubting it now. Blaze was on a hot track.

Only five more seconds passed before his dog sat,

a definitive alert. Brett tugged out his flashlight, aiming it at the ground in front of Blaze's paws. Gently, he sifted his hand through the tall blades of grass, swinging the flashlight back and forth until the beam reflected off something.

Brett squatted. A shiny brass shell casing gleamed up at him. Being careful not to trample too heavily with his boots, he searched the area in the immediate vicinity, eventually finding seven more.

"Hey!" he called out to the CSU guys. "I need photos here." The ATF would work with the Lakewood PD on the shooting, but for his own records, he snapped a few shots with his phone.

While a tech made her way over, Brett pulled a small dog treat from his cargo pants pocket and gave it to Blaze. "Good boy, Blaze. Good boy."

Blaze chomped down the treat and wagged his tail enthusiastically, absorbing the verbal praise, which was as much a part of the reward as the food.

"Shell casings?" the tech asked.

"Eight of them." Using his flashlight, Brett lit up the locations.

The tech stuck a numbered orange evidence marker on the ground next to each casing, then snapped multiple shots, each from a different direction and distance. "I'll send over the evidence custodian."

"No need." Brett tugged out a pair of vinyl gloves from one pocket and a plastic evidence bag from another, then began collecting the shells. "I'll send them directly to the ATF lab. It'll speed things up."

The slugs were a different matter entirely. They could be lodged in a tree trunk, embedded in the wall inside Piggly's, or in one of the vehicles parked in the lot. It would take time for the CSU team to find them.

Judging by where Blaze had discovered the casings, Brett could extrapolate the approximate location where the shooter had been standing. The one errant shot that took out the restaurant window probably had, as Brett had suspected, been fired when the shooter was running back to the SUV.

That still didn't tell him whether this was a random drive-by shooting intended to take out anyone...or whether those bullets were specifically meant for *him*. Whether the shooter knew Brett was a federal agent was irrelevant. He could still be charged with attempted murder of a federal officer. In the event he *was* the intended target, the ATF would take point on the investigation, and Brett wanted the quickest ballistic comparison possible. That could only happen at the ATF's National Tracing Center.

Every firearm had unique characteristics. The barrel always left a distinct marking on the projectiles, and the breech mechanism did the same on the cartridge cases. Images of the casings would be entered directly into IBIS—the ATF's Integrated Ballistic Identification System. If this gun had been used in another crime anywhere in the country, and investigators had uploaded images into IBIS, Brett hoped a firearms examiner could make a match. Since one of their own had been shot at, the agency would make this a priority.

"Brett!" a voice called out. His boss, Lori Olyawule, and Tom Willard, the ATF agent who'd investigated the Torrance Lane fire, walked up.

After getting off the phone with the 911 operator,

he'd called his boss, notifying her of the shooting. It hadn't taken her long to get here.

"Are you all right?" Lori rested a hand on his shoulder. "And Blaze?"

At hearing his name, Blaze went to Lori and nuzzled her hand until she obliged with a head scratch.

"Got any holes in you?" Tom asked. His question held humor, but his tone held a note of genuine concern.

"We're both fine," Brett assured them. Although things could easily have gone down differently. He and Blaze could have been peppered with lead.

"Glad to hear it." Lori gave his shoulder a squeeze. "Did you get off any rounds?"

"No." If he had, Lori would have to confiscate his gun, pending the outcome of a shooting review board.

"Good." Lori nodded. "What do we know so far?"

"One shooter in a large white SUV. Blaze found eight shell casings." He held up the evidence bag. "I need to fill out a chain of custody form, then overnight these to the lab. If we're lucky, we'll get a hit."

A Lakewood PD officer Brett had worked with on a case last year, Sergeant Penny Anderson, joined them. She held out her phone for Brett to see. "Marty Estevez, the owner, pulled up footage from the cameras facing the parking lot and the street."

Lori and Tom moved so that they could view the footage.

"This is from the side camera." Penny pointed to the camera on the side of the restaurant, the one facing the parking area. "I've got it cued up to right before the shooting."

They watched as Brett and Blaze walked into the

frame. Blaze lifted his leg and took care of business. Brett watched himself turn to face the road, then the expression on his face changed. That was the moment he'd realized the driver was pointing a gun at him. Half a second before the window directly behind where he'd been standing exploded, he threw himself on top of Blaze, taking them both to the ground. Innocuously soft pops sounded. *Gunfire.*

"Jesus," Lori whispered. "That was close."

More shots peppered the same vehicle, and they watched the other windows shatter and glass rain down on Brett's back.

Penny tapped her phone and opened another file. "This is the camera facing the road."

A white SUV stopped—a GMC Yukon. This time, there was no difficulty in identifying the make and model. The front passenger window rolled down, followed by pops and flashes of light inside the vehicle. The driver's side door opened, and the shooter got out, running around the hood and standing by the edge of the grass, right where Brett had approximated. The shooter opened fire again, aiming in Brett's direction. Seconds later, the driver ran back to the car, firing one more shot over his shoulder before getting back in and speeding west on Morrison Road. Until that moment, the camera angle had been facing the side of the car.

"Replay it." Brett had a bad feeling. "Enlarge it on the shooter and then as the car drives away."

Penny recued the footage, enlarging it with her fingers. In the shadowy dim light, the image of the shooter held no detail, other than that he was wearing dark clothes and a ball cap.

As Brett suspected, the area on the rear bumper where the license plate should have been was empty. "He took the tags off." Even if the cameras at the C-470 interchange a mile down the road picked him up, they'd have nothing to identify. Nothing but the make and model of a vehicle that had to be owned by lots of people in this area, let alone the entire state.

Lori pointed to the phone in Penny's hand. "Was this random or something else? As in, something connected to the case you're working on."

"Don't know." Yet. But his instincts were firing up full blast.

Brett's phone rang. Evan. His friend was probably calling to confirm he'd arrived at Gemma's. "Evan," he began, but his friend cut him off.

"Sorry, man. I'm not at Gemma's yet. I witnessed an accident with injuries on I-70 and had to stop. I called Deck to back me up, but he's tied up with something for another half hour up in Longmont. Just wanted you to know."

"Thanks. Gotta go." He ended the call, immediately cuing up Gemma's number. The need to check up on her, hear her voice, was a repeating drumbeat in his head. He completely understood Evan's moral and ethical obligation to render aid, but he didn't like that Gemma was alone in the house. After the fourth ring, his call went to voicemail. He hung up, then called her again. "C'mon, pick up."

"Something wrong?" Lori asked.

"Don't know." He hoped to hell not. There could be a dozen reasons why she wasn't picking up. She could have fallen asleep and not heard the phone. She could be in the shower. She could be—

Penny's radio crackled. "Two-seven-five, two-four-two, attempted burglary at 146 Field Street, Lakewood."

Brett's heart seemed to stop, then began pounding furiously.

Gemma's address.

"Blaze!" he shouted, already racing back to his Expedition.

He loaded Blaze into the kennel, then jumped in and cranked the engine. Luckily, his SUV hadn't been hit by gunfire.

He hit the strobes, then blasted the airhorn so the officers blocking the entrance would make a hole.

The second there was enough space for him to squeeze through the patrol cars, he punched it onto Morrison Road. Behind him, several other sets of strobes followed—the Lakewood PD cavalry.

"Blaze, down!" He glanced over his shoulder to verify his dog had lain down, then hit the C-470 on-ramp doing eighty, slowing only enough so he didn't tip over in the curve and fly into a ditch. As he merged onto the highway, he flipped on the siren.

Cars pulled over as he shot past, veering into the left lane and slamming his foot down on the accelerator.

His heart beat crazily, and he white-knuckled the wheel. A host of scenarios played in his head, none of them good. The panic rising in his gut made him physically ill.

He and Blaze had just been nearly gunned down, and now there was a report of a burglary at Gemma's house. No way was this a coincidence.

The same person who'd just tried to kill him…

Was trying to kill Gemma.

CHAPTER FOURTEEN

Brett slammed his foot down on the brake pedal, bringing the Expedition to a screeching stop in front of Gemma's house. The units that had followed from Piggly's pulled up behind him. Another patrol car sped in from the opposite direction.

Before opening his door, he took a steadying breath and forced himself to take a quick assessment of his surroundings, verifying no one was lurking in the shadows or behind the bushes edging the driveway.

With his heart jackhammering, he popped Blaze's door, then jumped out and raced to the house. If Gemma had been hurt, or worse—killed—because he'd made the wrong decision… He didn't know what he'd do.

Seemed like every light on the ground floor was on. He pulled his Glock and rushed through the open door.

Gemma sat on the sawdust-covered sofa, holding a towel to her head. Beside her sat a woman he didn't recognize—a very *pregnant* woman.

Penny and another officer piled through the door behind him, weapons out. "Another unit is checking out the backyard," Penny said.

"Is he still inside?" Brett asked Gemma. His body locked with rage as he took in her pale complexion and the bloody towel. The sonofabitch had hurt her, and Brett planned on returning the favor.

"No." She shook her head. "He ran off. I expected him to come after me again, but he didn't."

Blaze went to Gemma, nuzzling her hand and resting his snout on her knee.

"There was no one here but Gemma when I came in," the other woman said.

"Penny." Brett hitched his head to the sergeant. "Check out the rest of the main floor, just to be sure, and have your guys cruise the neighborhood for a white Yukon. I'll take the second floor. Blaze, stay," he ordered his dog, who'd been about to follow.

"You got it." Penny clicked her microphone, issuing orders to search for the Yukon, then went into the kitchen.

He headed up the stairs, keeping the muzzle of his gun at the indoor ready position, aimed at a point in front of his feet. Sounded like the guy had already fled the scene, but Brett wasn't taking any chances.

He flipped on the hallway light, then searched the first two bedrooms and the adjoining bathroom. The rooms were empty of furniture. The floors had all been sanded and were waiting to be re-stained. In the master bedroom, one of the windows was open. He flipped on the lights. The top of a ladder was just visible below the window sash. On the freshly sanded floor were dirty boot prints. About a size thirteen, he estimated. Could have been made by one of Gemma's brothers or a contractor.

Or by whoever attacked her. This could have been how he'd gotten inside.

With his heartbeat gradually returning to normal, he holstered, then went back downstairs to where Penny was also holstering. Brett gave a quick shake of his head, indicating no one was upstairs.

"The house is clear," Penny said into the microphone clipped to her shoulder.

"Backyard's clear," came the response. "Still checking for a white Yukon."

Brett took a deep breath, then knelt beside Blaze, in front of Gemma. Before saying anything, he waited for the icy fury gushing through his veins to ease. Only then did he realize how scared shitless he was that he'd be too late, that he'd bust through the front door to find Gemma lying in a pool of blood.

She watched him from tired, fear-filled eyes. His guts twisted viciously at the stark, cold realization that he could have lost her. Another impulse began as a gentle simmer, quickly boiling inside him until he was powerless to stop it. Not caring how many sets of eyes were on them, he captured her face in his hands and kissed her. On a gasp, she parted her lips, allowing him to deepen the kiss. Her lips were soft, warm, and she was alive.

He didn't know how long they remained kissing. Eventually, his senses returned and he broke off the kiss.

"Well, then," the woman beside Gemma said. She was grinning.

Even Penny Anderson's mouth had curved into a knowing smile.

"Are you okay?" He rested his hand on Gemma's knee. Slowly, she nodded. "Can you let me see your head?" When she pulled the towel away, the rage he'd thought successfully banked came roaring back. The cut that ran from the top of her forehead into her hairline wasn't actively bleeding, but a two-inch-wide splotch of blood had soaked into the towel. And the red marks around her neck were unmistakable.

Hand prints.

His blood heated to the boiling point. The fucker had tried to strangle her. If this really was the same guy who'd tried shooting him at Piggly's, why hadn't he shot Gemma instead of trying to choke her to death?

Could be he didn't want to make that much noise in a residential neighborhood. Or there could be another reason. Choking someone was more personal.

Brett clamped his jaw down hard, then glanced at Penny. "Call an ambulance."

"No." Gemma shook her head, then winced. "I'm not going to the hospital. It's just a cut. When he was chasing me, I fell and hit my head on the workbench."

Penny looked at Brett, her hand poised on the microphone.

"Gemma, please. Don't argue with me." The woman was too stubborn and too accustomed to taking care of herself alone than was for her own good. "I'd feel better if you let a doctor look at you."

"No," she insisted. "I'm not going to change my mind. My vision isn't blurry, and I didn't black out."

"If you haven't noticed," the other woman chimed in, "she's stubborn."

"I noticed," Brett muttered.

"I'm Bonnie, by the way." She stuck out her hand. "Gemma's next-door neighbor and longtime friend, whom she hasn't said a word to about you. Pleased to meet you."

"You, too." Brett shook Bonnie's hand, grateful that Gemma had a good friend living one house away.

Grateful? He sounded like a concerned parent. Or, he reluctantly forced himself to admit, a guy who wanted to be more than just Gemma's partner. "How about a compromise?"

Gemma narrowed her eyes. "What *kind* of compromise?"

Without answering her question, he tugged out his phone and called Tori Sampson, soon to be Tori Decker. "Tori," Brett said when she answered. "Sorry to bother you so late. My partner was hurt tonight, and she's too stubborn to go to the hospital." Gemma wrinkled her nose at him. "Think you could swing by and take a look at her?"

"Of course," Tori answered, and after Brett gave her the address, she added, "I'm just finishing my shift at North Metro. I should be there in ten minutes."

"Thanks, Tor." Brett ended the call and shoved the phone back into his thigh pocket.

"Who was that?" Gemma asked, not bothering to hide the suspicion in her voice.

"A friend. She's an ER doctor."

"Fine," she grumbled, eliciting a snort from Bonnie.

Bonnie gave Gemma a look of exasperation. "Some things never change. You were the same way in college. Always independent, never letting anyone help you."

"Not much has changed," Brett said flatly.

Gemma scowled at him first, then Bonnie. "You're not helping any."

Bonnie threw up her hands. "Just calling things as I see them."

Penny must have been reading Brett's mind and

took out a pad and pen. "Think you're up for telling us what happened?"

"Okay." Gemma cleared her throat, wincing and placing a hand to her neck. "After you called," she began, looking at Brett, "I locked all the doors and made sure all the windows were closed, then went into the kitchen to make eggs for dinner."

Not the upstairs windows. Brett let that slide for now. She'd probably forgotten about the ladder left against the side of the house.

"I heard a noise," she continued, "and when I turned around, he was there. A big guy, wearing a ball cap and sunglasses. He tried to strangle me with his hands."

At hearing the words, Brett compressed his lips, tamping down his anger and holding back a rush of foul language. "How tall?" he asked with a calm he didn't feel in the slightest.

"About your height, but not as muscular."

Penny scribbled on her pad. "Hair color?"

"Brown, I think. Some of it was poking out from under his cap."

"What happened next?" Brett rested his hand on Blaze's back. It was either that or plow his fist through the wall.

"I racked his balls and got away."

"You go, girl." Bonnie wrapped her arm around Gemma's shoulders and gave a little squeeze.

"He followed me into the living room, and that's when I fell and hit the table. I started throwing things at him, anything I could get my hands on. A screwdriver. A hammer. I hit him with the screwdriver, but it didn't stop him. Then I picked up my framing nailer and shot him." She pointed to where a yellow-and-black nailer lay on the floor. The attached compressor took that moment to kick on, filling the air with a whirring sound.

Penny tipped her head to the other officer guarding the front door, who leaned over and unplugged the compressor from the wall outlet.

"You shot him with the *nailer*?" Brett asked. "How did you get it to—"

"Go off? Stupidly, I *did* try shooting it at him from a distance. Of course, it didn't go off. Then he pinned me against the wall while he rammed his arm into my neck."

Brett gritted his teeth. He never should have left her alone. The second he and Blaze had been shot at, he should have hauled ass back to her house. Part of this was his fault. He'd failed her, just like he'd failed the teenagers he tried to save.

"The nailer was stuck between us," Gemma continued, "hard enough that when I pulled the trigger, I made enough contact against his body to set the gun off. I know I hit him, because he screamed and kept holding his hand to his side."

Brett could swear the sound he heard next was the squeaking of his teeth from clenching them so hard.

"Darn, girl," Bonnie exclaimed. "I knew you were good with power tools, but seriously. You're my idol."

"Where were you standing when you shot him?" Brett asked.

Gemma pointed. "Against that wall."

Brett stood and did a circuit of the room, searching for a bloody nail embedded in the sheetrock, but there wasn't one. "It must still be in him."

"Too bad," Penny said. "We could have gotten DNA."

Exactly what Brett had been hoping for. Speaking of which...

Again, he knelt in front of Gemma, taking her by the wrists and turning over her hands so he could look at the undersides of her nails. "Did you scratch him?"

"No." A corner of her mouth lifted. "But like I said, I did get in a solid kick to his family jewels."

Brett couldn't help but smile back. The woman was smart, beautiful, sexy, and a powerhouse. *My little Wonder Woman.*

Don't go there. She's not your woman. She's not your anything.

"How could he get in?" Gemma asked. "I didn't hear a thing until he was three feet behind me. Did he break in through the basement door? Did he come in through a window? I know I haven't installed new window locks yet, but I would have heard him. I'm sure of it. Those windows are old. None of them open quietly."

"He *did* come in through a window," Brett said. "One of the upstairs ones that you left open."

"But how did he get up—" Gemma clapped a hand to her forehead, then winced again. "The ladder. I forgot about the *ladder*. God, I feel stupid. I left it leaning against the side of the house so I could replace some rotten siding right below the window. This is all my fault."

"It's *not* your fault," Brett insisted, meaning every word.

She leaned forward. "How can you say that? Of

course it is."

"It's not, dammit." He took a breath to steady himself. Not only wasn't this the time for an argument, but they still had an audience. "It's not your fault someone climbed that ladder, broke into your house, and tried to kill you. It's *mine*. I should have been here."

A mistake he'd never forgive himself for, and one he planned never to repeat.

CHAPTER FIFTEEN

A muscle in Brett's cheek twitched, and he'd clamped his lips together so tightly the skin at the corners had turned white. He looked ready to explode. But there was something else simmering behind that hardened expression, something that touched Gemma's heart.

Blame.

He blamed himself for what had happened to her. She was the one who'd been attacked, but ironically, it was *she* who had the urge to comfort *him*.

Unable to stop, she touched his face, to stroke his strong jaw and soothe away some of that rage. "There was nothing you could have done," she said softly, well aware that between the Lakewood PD sergeant, the uniform by the door, and Bonnie sitting next to her, they had quite the audience.

"Yeah, there was," Brett growled. "I could have killed him before he hurt you." His jaw went harder.

Gemma let her hand drop, but he caught it. Very gently, he brushed his lips across her knuckles, sending a wave of heat sizzling through her body.

His dark blue gaze met hers and held it. How she wished she could read his mind at that moment. She was no psychiatrist, but the kind of emotion on his face and in his actions surely suggested he cared about her. Didn't it? If so, was she ready to let someone in again, to trust them with her heart?

His brow furrowed. Abruptly, he released her hand, then touched two fingers to her throat. "Was he wearing gloves?"

She thought back to the moment when she'd first seen her attacker standing in the kitchen doorway. Shock was the first thing she remembered. It had taken a moment for it to sink in that someone was inside her house. For a split second, she'd expected it to be Brett, but it wasn't.

Involuntarily, she touched her neck like she could still feel his fingers squeezing, choking her. She'd tried prying his fingers away, and *yes*! "He *was* wearing gloves!" Until now, she hadn't remembered. "Not smooth gloves, something rough. How did you know?"

"There's a mark on your neck — a symbol." He leaned in. "The more discolored and bruised your neck becomes, the more it shows up." He took out his phone. "Do you mind?" She shook her head, and he snapped a few close-up photos. "We can look again in the morning."

Meaning, when her neck was completely discolored and looked like something out of a horror movie. His last statement also implied that he planned to be here in the morning. Did she want him to be?

Gemma watched Brett's handsome face as he examined the images on his phone.

"It looks vaguely familiar," he said. "Could be a work glove with a company brand sewn into the thumb."

He turned his phone toward her, showing her the photos, but she didn't recognize the symbol.

"Sarge." The cop by the door hitched his head to the front yard. "Three people coming up the walk."

Brett's phone dinged, then he looked at it. "Let

them in." He went to the door.

Bonnie leaned in, whispering, "You didn't tell me your new partner was so *hot*. Like ten-out-of-ten hot." Gemma cringed, praying Sergeant Anderson hadn't heard. "If I wasn't already married to the love of my life, eight months pregnant and ready to pop, I'd fight you for him. Ooh, there he goes kicking again." She rubbed her belly. "This is my last one. Trust me, two is plenty."

"I'd settle for one," Gemma mumbled, not really intending to say that out loud, but there it was. She wanted children. Someday.

"It'll happen for you. You just haven't met the right guy yet." Bonnie waggled her eyebrows. "Or maybe you have."

"Who?" *Brett*? No. No way. That was way too big a leap to take at the moment.

"*Yowza*." Bonnie nudged Gemma's shoulder as two men she didn't know came through the front door. "Your house is crawling with hunks. This must be national ten-out-of-ten day, and someone forgot to put it on the calendar!"

Sergeant Anderson made a snorting sound in the back of her throat. "Ma'am, can I get your name?"

As Bonnie gave the sergeant her information, Gemma observed the cluster of alpha males now standing in her living room. The new additions were about the same height as Brett and both equally fit and muscular. They must all suck down the same supplements and work out at the same gym. *The Ten-Out-of-Ten Gym for Hunks*. Where Brett's hair was a light, sandy blond, the other men's were dark brown.

"Step aside, gentlemen." One of the most beautiful

women Gemma had ever seen pushed her way through the crowd of testosterone. Her long, auburn hair, tied up in a ponytail, swayed back and forth as she came to the sofa and set her bag on the floor. *Yay, ponytails.* Whoever this woman was, she rocked it. "You must be Gemma. I'm Tori Sampson. I work in the ER at North Metro." She held out her hand for Gemma to shake first, then did the same for Bonnie.

Blaze all but leaped to his feet, his expression one of obvious recognition as he wagged his tail.

"Hiya, Blaze." Tori gave Blaze a sound petting before turning back to Gemma and sitting next to her on the sofa.

"Sorry about all the sawdust." Gemma's gaze swept the room, taking in the construction chaos first, then the state of her attire. Filthy, sweaty, and every bit as chaotic as her house.

She ran a hand down the back of her hair, which had to be a blood-caked rat's nest by now. Even on her best day, she could never hold a candle to the Tori Sampsons of the world. Tori was the kind of woman she imagined Brett with, not her. Gemma looked like crap, and everyone else in the room knew it. They were only being polite.

"My house looks worse." Tori gave Gemma a smile, one intended to make her feel less self-conscious.

There wasn't a chance in hell that would work.

Tori unclipped her bag, then tore open a package and snapped on tight-fitting examination gloves. While she sifted her fingers gently through Gemma's bloody hair, Gemma looked into the woman's amazingly bright green eyes. Beautiful, successful, composed, and a doctor, no less.

What exactly was Brett's relationship with Tori Sampson? He'd said she was "a friend." One he had on speed dial and who'd come running the second he'd called. What kind of a "friend" did that make her?

Tori clicked on a pen light. "Follow the light with your eyes." She did as Tori directed. Up, then down. Right, then left. When she flicked her eyes left, she caught Brett in deep conversation by the door with the other men. "Good." Tori clicked off the light. "Any blurry vision?"

"No."

"Did you lose consciousness at all after this happened?"

"No."

"Do you feel nauseous, dizzy, or have ringing in your ears?" Gemma shook her head, regretting it when the throbbing in her forehead worsened. "What day is it?"

"Saturday."

"Do you know where you are?"

"Sitting on a sawdust-covered sofa in my money pit of a house."

Tori smiled. "Aside from the cut itself, how do you feel?"

Good question. How *did* she feel?

Angry. Scared. Violated. Confused. How could Brett have kissed her if he had something going with the beautiful doctor? "Just a little headache."

Gently, Tori examined Gemma's bruised neck, then dug into her bag, pulling out several thin white pouches. "The good news is I don't think you have a concussion, and I don't think there's any permanent damage to your neck. But you really should go to the hospital for X-rays." When Gemma opened her mouth to object, Tori held up her hand. "I'm not pushing. Brett already said you don't want to go. Do you have someone who can stay with you tonight?"

"You mean someone who can wake me up every hour on the hour to make sure I'm still breathing?" Gemma asked.

Tori laughed, then unwrapped one of the pouches and began cleaning Gemma's cut. "That's somewhat of a post-concussion myth, although the reason for that is if you *do* have a TBI—traumatic brain injury— and we haven't completely ruled that out with an X-ray, we have no way of knowing whether you're concussed if you're sleeping."

"And you *are* a heavy sleeper," Bonnie said. "Do you want to stay at my place? I'm up just about every hour as it is to use the bathroom anyway."

Ironically, even though she'd been attacked here, she didn't want to leave her house. Not before installing all those window locks. That had just knocked coping all that ceiling molding from the top of her reno list. "I'm staying here," she insisted, wincing as Tori dabbed something antiseptic on the gash.

"Sorry." Tori gave her an apologetic look. "Did I mention this might sting a little?"

Uh, nope.

"So," Tori said as she unwrapped another package, "*do* you have someone who can stay with you?"

Bonnie cleared her throat, then dipped her head in Brett's direction. "*I* might have an idea."

Tori followed the direction of Bonnie's gaze and

smiled. "Well?" She raised her brows suggestively.

Huh? Was Tori offering up Brett to her?

Brett and the two men who'd arrived at the same time as Tori walked over.

"These are my friends," Brett said, "DEA Special Agent Adam Decker and FBI Agent Evan McGarry."

"Call me Deck." One of the men, an extraordinarily good-looking man with chocolate-brown eyes, nodded to Gemma as he rested his hand affectionately on Tori's shoulder.

There was something more than just affectionate about the way Deck was touching the other woman. His hand slipped a fraction lower to gently caress Tori's back. The only word Gemma could think of to describe the man's touch was *intimate*.

"I'm sorry I didn't get here sooner," the other man said, his brow furrowing.

Evan McGarry was as tall and equally as good-looking as Deck, although his hair wasn't brown as Gemma had originally thought. It was jet black, a striking contrast to his apologetic, piercing gray eyes.

"How's she doing, Doc?" Brett asked, concern evident in his expression and the low timbre of his voice.

"I don't think she has a concussion." Tori applied a thin white bandage to Gemma's forehead. "I can close off the gash on her forehead with Steri-Strips, but I need to do something else on her scalp."

"Define 'something else,' please." Stitches? Worse, staples. She'd heard about people having to get their scalps stapled back together. *Yikes*. There was a staple gun somewhere in the house.

"It's called hair apposition." Tori applied another Steri-Strip, then scooted closer on the sofa. "Tip your head down, toward me." Her fingers were gentle as she began doing something with Gemma's hair. "I'm going to use your own hair on either side of the wound. I'll twist the hair together, then secure it with tissue glue. It's a natural form of suture that has fewer cosmetic problems and complication rates than suturing or stapling."

"Lucky me." Gemma looked up at Brett, whose eyes were dark, his hands jammed into his pockets. There might as well be a storm cloud hovering over his head, shooting out lightning bolts. He was angry and still blaming himself for not being here to stop the attack.

She winced at the slight tugging on her scalp. Bonnie grabbed her hand, squeezing it for distraction. Not working. In a timely move, Blaze rested his head on her lap, presenting his ears and giving her something to do with her hands while Tori worked.

"Evan." Brett pulled out his phone. "Can you do me a favor?"

"Name it," the other man said firmly.

While Tori continued twisting Gemma's hair into au naturel sutures and gluing them together, Gemma listened while Brett summarized what had gone down with Gavin Aldrich, starting with the warehouse fire, his arrest, and ending with Gavin's last court appearance.

"I promised I'd help him," Brett continued, emphasizing, "I *want* to help him. That's where you come in. Finding missing kids is your expertise. I want you to try and find his sister, but it won't be easy. Five years ago, Gavin burned down his house, killing his father. He helped his sister, Allison, get out, figuring they'd be taken in by relatives. They weren't. They both went into the system. Allison was twelve at the time, and she was adopted. Gavin never was."

With every bit more of Gavin's story that Brett related, Evan made notes in his phone, and his eyes narrowed more, as did Deck's.

Brett tapped his phone several times. "I'm sending you some files, including my report of investigation, arrest photos and identifiers, and Gavin's history. The kid's got issues, no doubt. I think it would go a long way if you could find his sister."

"Sometimes kids can't be found." Evan's brow furrowed. "No matter how deep I dig."

"I know that," Brett said.

Evan nodded. "I'll do what I can."

Brett rested a hand on his friend's shoulder. "I know that, too."

Gemma flicked her gaze from Brett to Evan, then back again. Something passed between the two men. Something powerful and meaningful. For such a tough-looking guy, there was no missing the fleeting glimpse of sadness and grief in Evan's eyes. Just as quickly, it was gone.

Evan drew in a deep breath, straightening. "I'll get started on this first thing tomorrow."

Brett nodded a silent thank-you.

"All done." Tori tugged off her gloves and stuffed them in her bag. "If you need to, take over-the-counter pain meds for the headache. Don't wash your hair for two days. Eventually, the glue will fall off or wash off on its own. I want to examine the wound again in a week." Tori leaned in, glancing at Brett and whispering, "And remember what I said about tonight. You shouldn't be alone."

"Thank you, Tori." Gemma smiled. "For everything, but I really don't think that Brett—"

"But nothing." Brett's words held a note of annoyance. "If you insist on being so stubborn and staying here tonight, then I'm staying here with you." Blaze barked. "Sorry." He gestured to his dog. "*We're* staying here with you."

Leaning in more, Tori whispered, "Brett wouldn't call me at close to midnight and ask me to drop everything for just anyone." She winked, then clipped her medical bag closed and stood.

Clearly having overheard Tori's suggestive words, Bonnie giggled.

To Brett, Tori added, "Give her some of that aloe vera I gave you. Once the sutures and Steri-Strips come off, it will help minimize scarring."

"Will do, Doc, and thanks. I owe you one."

Tori scoffed. "Don't be silly. You saved my life. I can never repay that." She stood on her toes and kissed him on the cheek.

"Hey," Deck interjected. "I helped save your life, too, and I want some of that kissing, so let's get out of here."

Tori blushed, then sent Deck a look filled with so much love, it took Gemma's breath away. Deck reached for Tori, and they held hands as they walked to the door. Only then did she notice the glittering diamond ring on Tori's left index finger. *They're engaged.*

Her belly flip-flopped. She could only dream of having something like they had.

Sergeant Anderson stood just outside the front

door. "We're heading out," she said to Brett. "Bring her by tomorrow to sign a statement. Negative on the white Yukon, by the way. He could have parked on another street and walked over."

Brett went to the door and shook hands with the sergeant. "Thanks, Penny."

"That would be my cue to leave, too." Bonnie gave Gemma a quick hug. "Something tells me you're going to be in *especially* good hands tonight."

She doubted that. *Safe* hands, perhaps. Brett was probably only staying because they were colleagues, and he knew her windows had no locks. Okay, so they'd kissed and rolled around on a bed for a few minutes. Despite what she thought she'd interpreted as beyond partnerly concern, that didn't mean his offer to babysit went past a professional obligation. More importantly, did she want it to?

Maybe. Kind of. *Um*. It might be a mistake, but yeah. She did.

Brett helped Bonnie to stand, then escorted her to the door. "Blaze, stay," he called over his shoulder. "I'll walk her home, then be right back."

Aside from her and Blaze, her house was empty and quiet. Shortly, she and Brett would be alone. In her house. At night. The realization left her edgy, and she couldn't sit still. Slowly, she stood, then went into the bedroom and looked at the mirror. "Schmear." An appropriate description. Her hair really was a rat's nest, sticking out in more directions than she thought possible. Her eyes were red and with dark circles blooming like caterpillars beneath them. Worse were the bruises on her neck.

The pain wasn't too bad, just a steady throbbing.

She leaned in, turning her head to look closer. As Brett had said, there was some kind of symbol, an emblem, that must have been sewn into the fingertips of the gloves, but she couldn't quite make out what it was. She splashed cold water on her face.

It occurred to her that she hadn't had a man stay over at her place in years. For *any* reason. She closed the bathroom door, then undressed and slipped on the nightshirt she'd draped on a hook. It wasn't much, just an oversize cotton T-shirt. Silk, satin, and lace had never been her thing.

She opened the door in time to see Blaze trotting into the bedroom, going directly to the mattress and circling twice before lying down smack dab in the middle. In the living room, she heard the front door close and the deadbolt being thrown.

When she came from the bathroom, Brett stood just outside her bedroom, holding a bag of dog food. He hitched his head. "I'll sleep on the sofa."

"It's covered in sawdust." Could she sound any more stupid? Of course, he knew it was covered in sawdust.

"I'll wipe it off. C'mon, Blaze. Let's go."

Blaze lifted his head, uttering a snort but making no move to get up.

The next words from her mouth were more shocking than if someone had said she'd just won the Home Renovation Channel sweepstakes. "Sleep with me."

CHAPTER SIXTEEN

"*What*?" The bag of kibble crinkled as Brett gripped it tighter. It was either that or he would have dropped it. He had to have misheard Gemma but could swear she'd just invited him into her bed.

"Sleep with me," she repeated. "In my bed. I mean, my, uh, mattress, since I don't technically have a bed. Just to sleep," she added quickly.

"Uh." Christ, what else did a guy say to that?

Since the day he'd lost his virginity at the ripe old age of sixteen, he couldn't recall *just* sleeping in *any* woman's bed. There'd always been other activities that had taken place before the sleeping part.

"Please?" she asked softly, hanging her head for a moment and calling attention to the fact that all she had on was a white T-shirt. "I just…" She seemed to be struggling to find the words, but he understood.

She'd been attacked and injured in her own home. That would be enough to cut anyone's balance off at the knees. Speaking of knees, hers and the rest of her legs, straight up to her thighs, were bare. Suddenly, the room felt hot. *Blistering* hot. The same way it had that night in Leadville, when her body had been plastered against his.

"Okay." The word had come out rough, scratchy, forcing him to clear his throat. "Just let me feed Blaze and get him some water. Dinnertime, buddy."

All he had to do was give the bag a little shake, and Blaze scrambled to his feet, trotting after Brett as he headed for the kitchen.

Was he really up for this? He'd never slept with his partner before. *Work* partner, that was. Then again, he'd never had a partner that looked like Gemma.

Or one who looks so hot wearing nothing but a T-shirt.

In the kitchen, he poured kibble into a metal bowl he'd brought in, added some water, then watched Blaze chow down.

In his experience, most women liked to wear frilly, silky lingerie to bed. Gemma didn't wear fancy lingerie, nor did she need to. To him, even with her hair sticking out, her throat bruised, and white bandages on her forehead, she was stunning.

On Gemma, that T-shirt was a thousand times sexier than any silky lingerie, but it was more than that. He liked her unexpected sense of humor and her smarts. They were a total turn-on, more than any lingerie ever could be.

He'd always thought of himself as being a strong man, physically *and* mentally, but every man had his limits. Getting into her bed—for *any* reason—might be more than he could handle.

For her, he'd do it, anyway. Because she'd asked. Because she needed him.

Blaze finished his kibble and licked his lips. Brett refilled the same bowl with water, watching as his dog slurped nearly the entire bowl, then about-faced and trotted back in the direction of Gemma's bedroom.

Sweat beaded his forehead, and his polo shirt stuck to his chest. In the hallway, he cranked up the AC. Tonight wasn't a good night to sleep in his usual nighttime garb.

Absolutely nothing.

He stepped quietly into the bedroom, half hoping Gemma had fallen asleep.

No such luck.

Yet he breathed an inward sigh of relief. She'd pulled a sheet over her legs and stuffed one of the two pillows behind her head, using the wall as a headboard. Blaze lay next to her, soaking up her attention as she scratched the underside of his chin and whispered things to his dog that he couldn't quite make out. Whatever sweet nothings she was saying must have been good to Blaze's ears. His tail thumped nonstop, making loud thwacking noises on the mattress.

Color had come back to her face. Unfortunately, the marks on her neck were darkening quickly, sending another hot blast of rage through him. No matter how long it took or what he had to do, he'd find the guy who did this to her and make him pay.

"Can I get you anything?" he said from the doorway. "Pain meds? Water?"

She shook her head. "Thanks. I grabbed some while you were feeding Blaze."

"How about those eggs? You never did eat dinner tonight." Neither did he, but he'd lost his appetite the second he'd seen Gemma's injuries. The only thing he had an appetite for at the moment was to beat the shit out of the guy who'd inflicted them.

She reached behind her head to adjust the pillow and winced. Brett rushed over and knelt on the mattress, reaching over Blaze, who'd planted his big, hairy head on the other pillow.

"I've got this." He did his best to fold the pillow in

half, creating more of a bolster, then reached for the other pillow beneath Blaze's head.

"No, that one's for you." Her cheeks flushed as she averted her gaze.

"Looks like I'll have to fight Blaze for it." His dog looked up at him, his golden eyes daring him to yank the pillow away. Instead, he sat next to Blaze and leaned back against the wall.

Gemma shifted to face him, then began rubbing Blaze's side. His dog groaned with pleasure, rolling onto his back with his legs in the air. Blaze was the biggest ham. Like any experienced government employee, he knew how to work the system.

"Do you always sleep with your gun on?" Gemma dipped her gaze to his holstered Glock.

"Not *on* me," he admitted, then sat forward to unbuckle his belt and slide off the holster.

She continued rubbing Blaze's belly, making him groan louder. "I bet you always sleep with it right next to you. Am I right?"

"Yep." He set the holster on the floor next to the mattress. "Want me to get your nail gun and plug it in over there?" He indicated the outlet next to Gemma's side of the mattress.

She giggled, the first time he'd ever heard such a feminine sound from her. As with the other things about Gemma he was beginning to like more and more, he liked that, too.

The AC might be cranked higher, but his polo shirt still stuck to his chest like a second skin. Using his thumb and forefinger, he tugged it away from his body.

Her hand on Blaze's belly stilled. "I'm not coming

on to you, but if you're hot, you could take off your shirt. It won't, um"—she sucked in her lower lip—"offend me."

Okay.

The second he whipped off his shirt, cool air hit his sweat-dampened chest. The groan he made could have given Blaze's a run for his money. He leaned over and tossed the shirt on the floor. When he turned back, Gemma's eyes had widened, her expression one of sympathy.

Right. My scars.

Over the last year, he'd learned to live with them. At times, he even forgot they were there. His ex had never really been comfortable with them, and from the look on Gemma's face, she found them equally unsettling. The one on his back had been the worst, covering a few square inches.

Her focus shifted to the other burn scar on his forearm. "Do they still hurt?"

"Mostly no. Except when exposed to sun or extreme heat." Like when he'd been standing outside the warehouse fire the other night. "Tori helped me, gave me some of her aloe vera plants. I'll give you one of them to use when your bandages come off."

"Thanks." She looked at his scar again. "Why the dragon tattoo?"

He shrugged. "I just thought it was cool." A partial truth, like so many he'd told her.

The tattoo he'd chosen was a classic black dragon with scales and a long, forked tail that curved around from the underside of his forearm. A dragon had become the bane of his sleeping existence, showing up in his nightmares and killing everyone. The other reason he'd gotten the tattoo was a stupid one.

To show the dragon in his nightmares that he wasn't afraid of it. But he was. More than he cared to admit.

"What did Tori mean when she said you saved her life?" Gemma asked.

"A few months ago, she nearly died in an explosion. It wasn't really me who saved her. Evan was there, too, but it was Deck and his dog, Thor, who nearly died saving her."

Gemma resumed petting Blaze, who'd finally lowered his legs and now lay solidly between them as if he were a chaperone on a date. "Tori and Deck seem made for each other."

Brett couldn't contain the snort that escaped his lips. "Now, yes. It wasn't always that way. In fact, I think it was hate at first sight. It took them a while, but they're in a good place now."

"I see that. They're engaged. What about Evan? What's his story?" she asked on a yawn.

"Evan is complicated." To say the least.

"How so? I saw the look on his face when you two were discussing finding Gavin Aldrich's sister."

"Most of Evan's story isn't mine to tell." Especially the ugly parts. The rest was a matter of public record. "Years ago, Evan's sister was taken. Kidnapped. They never got her back. They didn't even have a body to bury."

Gemma's eyes held sympathy. "That must have been heartbreaking."

"It was." He nodded. "Still is. They never got closure." Evan still hadn't stopped searching for her and probably never would.

"Was he young when this happened?"

Brett nodded. "Twelve."

"So he's dedicated his life to finding other missing kids," Gemma said. "I'm thinking that one day, he still hopes he'll find her."

Again, Brett nodded. "You never know. His track record is the best in the FBI." But every child Evan brought home to their parents was both a triumph and a knife strike to his friend's heart, a deeply painful reminder that his sister hadn't come home. *Dead* or *alive*.

"This happened when he was twelve, so that had to be over twenty years ago."

"Twenty-four." Since then, Evan's personal life had pretty much been on hold.

"What if he never finds her?"

In response, he shook his head. "Don't know." The answer to that question had worried Deck and him since the day they'd learned about Evan's sister—that his friend would never recover and would continue being a shell of a man. It was as if Evan had been living and breathing since the night his sister had been taken, but her abductor had taken Evan's soul with him.

Brett shifted to his side and touched two fingers to Gemma's cheek, not for the first time thinking how sweet she was.

Sleepy eyes looked up at him. "What are you doing?"

Against his better judgment, he cupped her cheek, stroking the pad of his thumb back and forth across her cheekbone. He knew he should let her sleep, but he had to know something. "We both wear body armor, only yours is strictly emotional. You put up a protective wall, so the rest of the world doesn't see how soft and sweet you really are. Why do you do that?"

Eyes that, only a moment ago, had been banked with exhaustion, widened. "I don't put up any walls."

"Yeah. You do," he interrupted, chuckling. "A lot."

"Oh." She clasped his hand, threading their fingers and tugging their hands to between her breasts. "I never really thought about it."

"Is that why you pulled away from me in the hotel room?" Given how hot they'd been for each other, only to have her end things so abruptly, he figured he must have hit a nerve. Or maybe she realized the wisdom of keeping things all business.

"Maybe," she admitted. "That and I haven't shared a bed with a guy in so long I don't remember."

"That's hard to believe." Then again, it would be hard for anyone to get past that thick armor. He knew a dozen guys who'd jump at the chance to be with her, if she'd only let them in.

The thought sent a jolt of jealousy rocketing through his veins.

She frowned. "Why?"

He laughed outright. "Because you're so beautiful."

Her mouth fell open. She looked down at their clasped hands, chewing on her lower lip. "Not having been with anyone in a while was only part of the reason I stopped us the other night. We're partners, and any kind of closeness, let alone intimacy between partners, can get ugly."

"Sounds like you're talking from experience."

Using their joined hands, he tipped up her chin. "What happened?"

She took a deep breath and sighed heavily. "A colleague of mine stole my case. I mean, he literally stole my case file and presented my evidence as his own. I liked him. He knew it and took advantage of it. He, uh…" Her brow creased, then she cleared her throat and swallowed. "He slept with me. He did it to put me off guard, to get close to me and learn all the details of the case first."

"Ouch." No wonder she'd practically kicked him off that hotel bed, and it certainly explained the source of her thick emotional armor. Even though she was making a valiant effort to hide it from him, it was obvious she'd been hurt terribly. Judging by the sadness in her eyes, there was still residual pain at work here, more than she was letting on.

Brett's heart went out to her. Whoever this asshole was, he wished he could pound the guy's face into the ground.

She made a valiant effort at smiling, but it never made it to her eyes. "As long as we're spilling here, it's your turn to divulge one of your worst secrets."

Secrets? He didn't really have any. Everyone knew about the worst parts of his life. Both fires he'd been in had been splashed all over the evening news for weeks. Only the people closest to him—his family, Deck, and Evan—knew what the media didn't.

"I have nightmares." *Fuck*. He couldn't believe the words had just come from his mouth.

"About the fires." The look of genuine concern on Gemma's face touched a cold, dark place in his heart. "I'm sorry. Can you get help, talk to someone about it?"

"I did. When I was eleven." He hadn't talked to a shrink since then. Sitting in a psychiatrist's office twice a week every week for nearly a year had sucked. Somehow, word had gotten out to his entire school, and he'd been ridiculed. "I thought I'd gotten past it. The fire last year triggered them all over again."

She squeezed his hand. "You could go again, you know. Maybe it would help."

"Maybe." *Or not.* A federal agent seeking assistance for PTSD no longer had the same stigma attached to it that it once had, but he had no desire to rehash everything to a psychiatrist.

Gemma yawned, and her eyelids fluttered as she struggled to stay awake.

"Go to sleep," he whispered, then reached over Blaze to tug the sheet to her neck. The bruises around her throat had already deepened more in color. As he released the sheet, Brett curled his hand into a tight fist.

What had gone down tonight at Gemma's house and at Piggly's was a neon light blinking nonstop in his head.

They were being targeted, and if they didn't get a solid lead to follow and fast, sooner or later…

The perpetrator would find his mark.

CHAPTER SEVENTEEN

Gemma woke slowly, though she was still in the hazy stages between sleep and being fully awake. She squinted at the early morning sunlight streaming through the window. At least her head had ceased to pound and her neck had stopped throbbing.

She'd expected to feel Blaze's head snugged against her neck, where it had been when she'd fallen asleep with the dog lying between Brett and her. Only Blaze wasn't there. In fact, there was *nothing* between them, and it was *her* head snugged against *his* neck. The realization had her heart beating just a scooch faster.

How and when had that happened? And where was Blaze?

The last thing she remembered before falling into a deep, dreamless sleep was being way too honest with Brett about her personal baggage. But he'd understood, even called her out on it, something no one ever really had. Somehow, and in such a short time, he knew her better than most people. Then she remembered the rest of their conversation.

His nightmares.

Living that way, night after night, never knowing if you'd wake up in the throes of an awful nightmare... She couldn't imagine what it must be like for him. He was a big, strong guy, but no amount of strength could protect him from a horrible dream. Her heart ached for what he must be going through.

With her head between Brett's chin and his shoulder, she could just make out Blaze's tail on the floor in the living room in front of the TV on the workbench. Brett must have gotten up while she'd been asleep and turned it on for him.

Somehow, her right arm had wound up draped over Brett's gloriously naked, totally buff chest. His skin was smooth, taut, and warm beneath her fingers, with a smattering of light brown, springy hairs. Was that a six-pack or an eight-pack? Did they make a twelve? Either way, there were a lot of undulations in those chiseled abs.

What she ought to do was move, put some space between them. How embarrassing would it be if he woke to find her plastered against him and ogling him like he was a male go-go dancer?

She shifted her head, only enough to look up at his face. Inadvertently, her lips grazed the tawny bristle on his chin. Gemma held her breath, uncertain as to whether she should move away. Did she want to?

Maybe. Possibly. Not really. No. There it was. A definitive *no*.

Continuing to study him felt weird, but she couldn't help it. His body was beautiful. His chest continued to rise and fall, calling attention to his thick pecs, and from there, to the line of hair arrowing down to the waistline of his cargo pants.

She closed her eyes and inhaled, trying to decipher his scent. Not his usual cologne. This was hunky man, yet slightly sweet with a dash of milk and honey. Eerily similar to—

The oatmeal, milk, and honey soap in my bathroom.

While she'd been asleep, he must have gone up-stairs and cleaned up.

Images of Brett standing in her shower, naked, as water rained down on his head, shoulders, chest, and everything else had her snapping open her eyes. She blinked, then blinked again to clear away the erotic images playing out in her head. No need for her mom's high-test coffee to wake her up.

Time to end this.

She felt like a twisted voyeur. Slowly, she began easing away when her hand came into contact with the uneven skin on the side of his lower back. Last night, she hadn't gotten a long look at his burns. She levered on her elbow and leaned over. The part of his lower back just barely visible was slightly pink, raised, and angry-looking.

Gently, she ran the tip of her fingers across the skin, torturing herself by imagining what it must have been like to have hot flames licking at her flesh. Her stomach twisted at the thought.

Suddenly, Brett's abdominals tightened, and a hand shot out, grabbing her wrist.

She gasped.

Dark blue, stormy eyes held her transfixed.

"I, um." She swallowed, and her face heated. This was *so* embarrassing. "I'm sorry. I didn't mean to take advantage of you while you were sleeping, I—"

"I wasn't sleeping." His voice was low, raspy, sexy, and Gemma felt the vibrations from where he held her wrist all the way to her toes. "And you weren't doing anything I didn't want you doing."

"Oh." That sounded dumb, but it was the only thing that popped out of her mouth.

"You can touch me there," he whispered. "Hell, you can touch me *anywhere*."

Her mouth fell open. *Anywhere?* Somehow, she managed to clamp her mouth shut before she uttered another infernally stupid response.

He released her wrist and sat up. "Go ahead. Touch me."

Hesitantly, she skimmed her fingers across his back—*all* of his back—including his burns. As she continued her exploration, powerful muscles rippled and flexed beneath her hands. The burn scars were raised and rough, some still pink.

The more she touched him, the less she wanted to stop. All she could think at that moment was that *she* was the one playing with fire here. The pain and suffering he'd endured trying to save those kids, and she could only imagine the emotional aftermath.

Slowly, Brett began shaking his head. "Don't look at me that way. They don't hurt anymore."

"It's not just that, is it?" she asked.

His brows drew together. "What do you mean?"

"I mean that it's not just the physical pain." She cupped his cheek, his skin beneath the stubble warm to the touch. "Watching those teenagers die and being unable to save them…what it must have done to you, and it wasn't even the first time you were forced to watch children die in a fire."

As his chest expanded on a deep inhale, he closed his eyes and covered her hand with his.

Tears backed up behind Gemma's eyes. "You shared one of the darkest moments of your life in the courtroom that day to help Gavin Aldrich in a way that no one else could." Like Gavin, he'd gone through heart-wrenching experiences. He'd survived, not unscathed, to become a wonderful, sensitive man.

"Don't." He opened his eyes, again shaking his head. "Don't make me into some kind of hero. I'm not. Trust me."

"You are." His words of denial only made her more convinced of it. "All I'm saying is that not everyone is capable of doing what you did. You bared your soul to help someone else. You have a rare strength of character, and it comes from in here." She pressed a hand to his chest. His heart raced beneath her fingers. "I want you to kiss me again."

"Gemma," he whispered. "You're injured, and I don't want to hurt you."

"You won't." Her gaze dipped to his lips, and in that instant she knew. Every bit of caution she'd been harboring where he was concerned sizzled to nothing. "Kiss me," she whispered, barely recognizing the sound of her own voice.

His eyes darkened further. "Is that *all* you want me to do?"

Her heart thudded faster. She shook her head, whispering, "No."

The next thing she knew, his lips were on hers, his tongue seeking hers.

Gemma grasped his shoulders, giving in to the searing heat billowing between them. Kissing between partners was ill advised. Sex between partners would be a monumental mistake.

Right now, she didn't care.

He tugged her to a sitting position, then slipped his hands beneath the hem of her T-shirt and yanked it up and over her head. His hands were big and warm, sliding across her back, then to her breasts and nipples, rubbing them with his rough palms.

His hands stilled, and his face twisted in confusion as he stared at her left hip. "Is that a—"

"Goldfish tattoo?" She grinned. "Yes, it is." Two years ago, right after she'd gotten Jaws, she and Bonnie had been enjoying a girls' night out and had hit a tattoo parlor on the way home. Bonnie had gotten a pink rose on her ankle. Gemma had opted for something a bit more adventurous.

His frown deepened. "It's got teeth."

"Jaws."

Slowly, his lips curved into the sexiest smile she'd ever seen. "I love it." He eased her down onto the mattress, then leaned over and began nibbling at the sensitive skin on her hip, right over her tattoo. Still nibbling and kissing her, he lowered her to the mattress, his hands unexpectedly gentle as they continued exploring her body just like she had done to his.

When he lifted his mouth to look down at her, indecision speared a clear path to her brain. "You know this is probably a mistake, right?" she asked, her mind at war with her body.

"Yeah." He licked his lips, then hooked his fingers around the edge of her panties and began pulling them slowly from her hips. As he followed the progress of her boring white cotton undies down her legs, his throat worked, and he swallowed hard.

"And that it could affect our working relationship?" she added, watching him toss the panties into a corner.

"Uh-huh." He skimmed his hands from her ankles to the juncture of her thighs, then spread her legs, opening her wide. Their gazes met. The look of intense yearning radiating from him sent a ripple of desire that rose to new heights until it was a wave of unquenchable need in her core.

It was a look that said he wanted to devour her.

No matter what happened here, in her bedroom, on her sad excuse for a bed, there'd be no regrets.

Brett struck her as a man who took charge in the bedroom, and she imagined the type of women he'd been with were probably okay with that.

Not her.

In one fluid motion, she sat up, pushed at his chest until *he* was the one lying on his back. She straddled his thighs, then popped open the button of his pants and began pulling down the zipper in slow, teasing increments.

The corners of his mouth lifted as he watched the zipper's progress. When her knuckles grazed the black fabric–covered bulge of his erection, he hissed in a sharp breath. "I should have known a woman who knows how to use power tools would want to take charge."

She hooked her fingers over the waistline of his pants and tight black jockey shorts, tugging both garments down to his ankles before tossing them in the same corner as her panties. His socks came next. "Do you have a problem with that?"

He laughed, a sexy, throaty rumble. "Not a single one."

"Good." She patted his chest. "Wait here."

Gemma practically leaped from the bed, then raced up the stairs and into her bathroom—the one where she had most of her toiletries stored. After rummaging in the tiny closet for a full minute, she found what she was looking for and raced back downstairs.

At the doorway to her bedroom, she stopped short. Her heart sank, and she sighed. Brett still lay on the bed all right. His right arm was flung over his eyes. Snoring, loud enough to rival his dog's, rolled from his parted lips.

Digging out a couple of condoms had seemed like the right thing to do. Safety first, and all. Sadly, frustratingly, it had killed the moment. More like *murdered* it.

After tossing the condoms on the foot of the bed, she lay down next to Brett. How dare he get her all hot and bothered, then pass out on her?

His chest rose and fell evenly. Then again, he'd been faking sleep before.

She leaned down to whisper, "It's just as well. This probably would have been a really, *really* bad mistake. The *worst*," she added for emphasis.

His eyes opened, and he grabbed her, hauling her on top of him and nearly making her scream in surprise. "Did you know that some of the best things in life started out as mistakes?"

"Like what?" she asked, wriggling futilely in his grasp and realizing he'd gone completely hard beneath her.

"Chocolate lava cake. My favorite dessert." He cupped her bottom, then began maneuvering her until she straddled his chest. "A chef mistakenly underbaked a cake, then served it to a customer, who loved the molten, runny center. It became a thing."

He began stroking her spine, up and down, down

and up, sending delicious shivers shooting across her skin. She shut her eyes, savoring the feel of his big hands on her body. "A thing, huh?"

"Yeah. A thing." Again, he cupped her bottom, lifting her up and forward at the same time. His warm breath tickled her thighs, as he slowly, teasingly, lowered her until she was directly over his face. "A very *tasty* thing."

Oh wow. Was he really about to do what she thought he was?

He flicked out his tongue, spearing her core and sending the sharpest, most wonderful zinging sensation to her belly. *Oh yesss.* He was indeed.

As if someone had snapped their fingers, any residual ache from her injuries…gone. All she could feel now was Brett.

His tongue was probing, hot, as he licked and sucked at her sensitive nub, making her writhe against his mouth. Pleasure fanned outward from her core, gradually, at first, like ripples from a stone thrown in the water. As his tongue flicked faster and deeper, those tiny ripples morphed into full-blown waves crashing against the shoreline.

Tension built in her body like an electrical power station on overload. For balance, she smacked her hands on the wall over the mattress. Soon, she could barely keep her eyes open and threw her head back, her chest heaving as she sucked in breaths faster, bucking and writhing.

The sensations were becoming too intense. If she didn't find release, she'd explode one way or the other.

When she tried pulling away, Brett curled his hands over the tops of her thighs, holding her tighter to his mouth. That did it.

The air around them seemed to crackle with energy. A bolt of something lit in her core, right where Brett's mouth was, spiraling upward until it seemed to blast out the top of her head. Gemma cried out, her body shattering again and again until she went limp.

Her breaths came fast, as if she'd just run up the steep hill that led to Green Mountain. Then she was floating. Vaguely, she realized Brett had lowered her to his chest.

She opened her eyes to find him grinning up at her.

"As mistakes go, how was it?" he asked.

"Not bad, G-man." She bit her lip. That was the absolute truth, but she didn't dare speak the rest of what was on her mind.

She didn't *want* to like Brett Tanner, let alone feel something more for him. But she did.

Unfortunately, most of the men she'd liked in her life had never wanted her in the same way. So yeah, not only was this still a mistake, now it was a whole lot bigger.

If she let this—whatever *this* was—continue, she could be in for a whole lot of heartache. He might never steal a case file from her, but she was in desperate danger of him stealing her heart.

CHAPTER EIGHTEEN

As the last tremor of her orgasm had rolled through her, the taste on Brett's tongue was sweeter than anything he'd tasted before. If passion had a flavor, it would taste like Gemma.

"How's your head?" he asked as she scooted off his chest to straddle his hips.

Smooth. Real smooth, Tanner. Here he was in bed, technically, on a mattress, with a beautiful woman, and that was the best he could come up with. Pleasuring her had been his goal, and judging by her body's responses, he'd been successful. He could easily do this—and so much more—all night, but with her injuries, he needed to be gentle.

"My what?" Gemma asked between gasps.

"Your head." Her eyes were bright and clear, but he took his nursing duties seriously. "Does it hurt? Are you dizzy?"

"I feel fine." She touched two fingers to her head, then her neck. "How do I look?"

The skin peeking out from beneath the white strips on her forehead was pink, and the marks on her neck had deepened in color, beginning to turn purple. The protective urges welling up inside him so fiercely astounded him. "Beautiful." To him, she was.

She swatted his shoulder. "You're just saying that."

"I'm not." The more time he spent with her—in *or* out of bed—the more he thought it.

Her grin disappeared, and she arched a brow, her

trademark reaction, he'd come to learn, when she thought someone was full of shit. "All the beautiful women that must fall at your feet...I can't compare to them."

"Then don't. And for the record, *I* don't compare you to them."

"Ahhh." She grinned again. "So you *do* have women falling at your feet."

"I didn't say that." He tugged her hand to his lips, dropping a quick kiss on her knuckles. "Technically, they don't *fall* at my feet. Trip, maybe." She tried yanking her hand away, but he held fast. "I'm kidding. I just like to watch you get all hot and bothered." Yeah, and when had that started? "Seriously, I don't compare you to anyone." Never taking his gaze from hers, Brett wet his lips, brushing them against her knuckles, then running his tongue over them. "You're incomparable."

Oh man. Had he really just said that?

Yep. Because she really was.

Her innate ability to understand what he'd been through... Gemma got him in a way no one else ever had. And when she'd touched his burn scars, she hadn't been repulsed. Rather, she'd somehow managed to put herself in his shoes and feel the same emotions he'd experienced after both fires. Her ability to do that floored him.

Gemma went as still as ice. Slowly, her brows lowered, and the skin over the bridge of her nose crinkled, as if she were gauging his truthfulness. Not that he could blame her. If someone ever told him they thought he was incomparable, he'd know in a heartbeat they were handing him a line of shit. That was the thing. It hadn't been a line at all.

"My god. You're serious."

He nodded. Never in his life had he joked about his feelings for a woman, and he wasn't about to start now. Especially not with Gemma. His feelings for her were as pure as any he'd felt in his life.

"You know." She leaned over until her face was inches from his. "I don't think I've ever seen *you* hot and bothered."

He grinned. "That's because I don't *get* hot and bothered."

One corner of her incredibly kissable lips quirked, then a mischievous glint came to her eyes. "That sounds like a dare if ever I heard one."

Before he could utter a quick retort, she shimmied down his thighs and began stroking him.

Unable to peel his gaze from her hand rising slowly up, then down his shaft, repeating the process a little faster each time, Brett swallowed. "Gemma, I don't think that's a good idea." Because her hand felt so good, he was on the verge of erupting like Mount Vesuvius.

Rational thought fled. The only thing that could possibly have topped this was being inside her warm, wet body.

"Shhh." When she leaned down to place a finger on his lips, her lovely breasts hung low, grazing his chest and sending shock waves to his dick, making it jump in her hand. "I want to do this. You made me feel good. Now it's my chance to return the favor."

"Favor?" Was that what this was about for her? Returning a favor? "You don't owe me anything. And this isn't about me."

"No?" She continued stroking, making him impossibly hard. "It could be, though." She leaned over and licked a pearlescent bead from the tip of his erection.

Brett gritted his teeth. It was either that or he really would explode and launch right off the mattress. Her pretty lips sucked on his head, and the tip of her wicked tongue flicked at him.

He was in heaven. And hell.

The combination of her full lips and tongue, sucking and licking, caressing like a warm wet massage while her hand stroked him was... God, he couldn't find the words. But if she didn't stop soon, he'd never make it inside of her.

In a move so fast she squealed, he flipped their positions so she was lying beneath him, laughing. "I know you like to be on top," he said, kissing her neck just beneath the tip of her earlobe and being careful to avoid the bruised parts of her neck. "To be fair, though, you have to let me win sometimes, or my manly ego will be shattered."

"I'll let you have your way." She laughed softly. "*This* time."

Brett chuckled. He should have known she'd never hand over total control, and he liked that about her. Still kissing her neck, he slipped his hand into her thick hair, being careful not to pull at her sutures. He loved how the silky soft strands felt against his roughened fingers.

As he began working his way south, dropping kisses in the valley between her breasts, and lower, to her belly button, she sighed—a low, throaty sound that made him harder than steel.

Now, where were those condoms he'd seen her toss

somewhere while he'd been pretending to be asleep?

Finding one of the packets at the bottom of the mattress, he tore it open and sheathed himself. He ran his hands up her outer thighs, then around to her buttocks, and pulled her to him until the tip of his dick rubbed against her wet folds. He couldn't wait to get inside her.

Slowly, he eased into her tight, wet warmth, and as he did, she sucked in a breath. Inch by inch, he pushed deeper, uttering a growl so low, so possessively feral, it surprised even himself. He didn't *do* possessive, never had. But there it was.

He hadn't felt this way about being with a woman in so long he couldn't remember. Maybe never.

She gripped his forearms, her blunt nails digging into his skin as she held on tightly, surging her hips to meet his thrusts. With every meeting of their bodies, his pulse rate jacked higher. She was so sexy and desirable, lying beneath him with her eyes half closed, her breasts heaving as she breathed faster. When her tongue darted out to swipe across her lower lip, he couldn't resist.

Resting his forearms on either side of her head, he leaned down and captured her face in his hands. With her hair spread out on the pillow and her face flushed, she was more beautiful than he could have imagined. Softer. And perfect.

Her breasts mounded beneath his chest, and he captured one rosy nipple in his mouth, sucking it and flicking it with his tongue. A tiny little moan escaped her parted lips that was so darned sexy it sent a jolt of current through his body.

Pressure built at the base of his dick. His balls

drew up, tightening to the point of pain, and all he could do was watch the play of emotions on Gemma's face as the orgasm began rumbling through her.

She bit her lower lip. Her brow wrinkled just before she threw back her head and cried out.

Brett thrust once more, exploding inside her and biting back another growl. For a long moment, he remained where he was, absorbing and savoring the last of their orgasms. He rolled to his side, snugging Gemma against him as they both struggled to breathe. Her skin was warm and damp against his.

The urge to stay this way, with her in his arms, was a powerful need, swamping him with all kinds of emotions he didn't dare address. Because she was right. This was going to complicate things.

His growing feelings for her were both welcome and scary as hell. If he was truthful with himself, he cared about her more deeply than he was ready to give voice to. For the first time in his life, he worried that if he fell for her, he still might have to walk away or she still might kick him to the curb where he deserved to be. He'd experienced both those scenarios before, but not with Gemma.

This time, if either of those scenarios played out, *he* could be the one getting hurt the most.

• • •

Outside, the winter winds rolling off the foothills roared like a lion, buffeting the sheets they'd tacked over the broken windows and doorway to keep the heat in.

Brett grinned at the ingeniousness of his plan.

School had let out for Christmas break, and it was time to have some fun. He'd already scoped out the old, condemned house at the end of the road right next to a fire station and found a way for him and his friends to sneak inside. His father would kill him if he ever found out, which made the whole thing *so* much more fun and totally worth the risk.

Through the hole in the roof made by an enormous oak tree that had crashed down during a storm, the moon glowed yellowy-orange. Passing clouds cast shadows on the peeling wallpaper and posters. Despite the hole, the room was dry and pretty warm. The gas company had shut off the gas, but luckily, the power company hadn't cut the electricity yet. The decrepit-looking space heater they'd dragged up from the basement had crackled and sparked when they'd first plugged it in but seemed to be working okay now and was cranked to the max.

Brett aimed the flashlight beneath his chin. Cody and Ryan did the same with theirs, making their faces look creepy. "You guys know why ninja farts are so dangerous?" He shifted on the stack of old furniture cushions and pillows, giving his friends a few seconds to answer. "Because they're silent but deadly."

Ryan and Cody laughed so hard one of them farted, then they all laughed even harder.

Next up was Ryan. "Why was the nose so sad?" Brett and Cody looked at each other and shrugged. "Because it didn't get picked." For effect, Ryan stuck a finger in his nose, then flicked it at them.

"Eww!" Brett yanked the sleeping bag over his head.

"I can beat that," Cody said. "What did one

booger say to the other?"

Brett lowered the sleeping bag, then pointed his flashlight at Ryan. "I don't know. Ask Ryan. He's the nose picker."

"Am not." Ryan hurled a pillow at him.

"Well?" Cody prodded. "What did one booger say to the other?"

"What?" Brett asked.

"You think you're funny, but you're snot." Cody burst out laughing.

Ryan's face twisted. "That sucked." He grabbed another pillow and rocketed it at Cody, who ducked.

The pillow flew over Cody's head. Brett lunged for it but missed. The pillow slammed into the space heater, knocking it over and sending it tumbling onto a stack of sofa cushions they'd piled up for their beds. Crackling and popping came from the heater. Sparks shot from the glowing, red grill plate, landing on more pillows and the sheet they'd tacked across the doorway.

One spark came directly at Brett's head. He ducked under the sleeping bag just in time. More popping sounds. More crackling, then a sudden roar. Cautiously, he peeked out from under the bag.

Sparks continued shooting from the space heater like fireworks. The pillows and sofa cushions were on fire. Flames raced up the sheet they'd hung over the open doorway. Within seconds, the peeling wallpaper caught fire. Posters taped to the wall began to burn, and the space heater continued shooting off sparks, landing on more sheets. Smoke filled the tiny attic, billowing and making them cough. From somewhere overhead came the deafening screech of a smoke alarm.

"We gotta get out of here!" Brett shouted. "C'mon!" Cody and Ryan had their sleeping bags over their heads. "C'mon, you guys!"

Brett could barely see anything through the thickening smoke. Flames blocked their way out. He coughed, covering his mouth with his hand, and raced for the only window that wasn't covered by a burning sheet. He yanked off the sheet and looked down. The drop had to be at least twenty feet.

Another roar, this one louder as flames burst from another pile of pillows.

Still covering his mouth with his hand, Brett coughed. His eyes burned, his throat burned, and his heart pounded. The room was getting hotter by the second. "Ryan! Cody! C'mon!" He waved his arm, but Ryan and Cody were trapped on the other side of the burning pillows.

A glowing spark shot directly toward Brett's face. He twisted away but tripped, whacking his head against the wall by the window. He hit the floor hard. Pain ripped through his skull. He tried getting up, but his vision blurred, and he fell to his knees, resting a forearm on the window ledge.

Cody and Ryan shouted something Brett couldn't make out. He lifted his head. His friends were still trapped on the other side of the room, the fiery blaze blocking their way. They couldn't get to him.

Sirens wailed. Soon, more sounds came from outside. Whatever glass had remained of the broken window shattered, raining shards on his back. Strong hands grabbed him by the waist, hauling him through the window. He struggled, kicking out and flailing his arms. "No!" he screamed. "Get Cody! Ryan!"

As the firefighter pulled him onto the ladder, Brett twisted his neck to look back into the house. Cody and Ryan were there, in a billowing cloud of smoke, watching him with sad, sympathetic looks on their faces. Standing next to them were the two teenagers from the Torrance Lane fire. Behind them, a huge, fire-breathing dragon materialized in the darkness. It opened its jaws, roaring and spewing flames on his friends and the teens. He watched helplessly as they all caught fire, then disappeared in a bright flash of light.

Brett jacked upright on the mattress, his chest heaving as he sucked in heavy breaths. Sweat poured down his face, and he squeezed his eyes shut. *Jesus.* The nightmares had become as much a part of his life as breathing. That sad fact he'd long ago come to accept. Only now, they'd returned with a vengeance, each one worse than the last.

Sunlight streamed through the window. He hadn't meant to fall asleep again, but he had. They both had.

Gemma's chest rose and fell evenly. Like her friend, Bonnie, had said, Gemma really was a heavy sleeper. Blaze, on the other hand, had lifted his head, his golden eyes filled with understanding. He'd been there for Brett so many times right after he'd woken, covered in sweat and sucking in breaths as if there were no more oxygen left in the room.

Brett stroked Blaze's soft ears, letting his dog soothe out the itchy, edgy feeling that made him want to scream.

The outcome of his nightmares was always the same. He still couldn't save his friends, and he couldn't save the two teenagers. He'd failed all of them, and he could never make it right. That hadn't changed, but this was the first time the two fires had crossed boundaries into the same nightmare. His childhood shrink would say there was a message in there somewhere. What it was, he didn't know.

He shifted onto his side to watch Gemma sleep, listening to her breathe. The only recent change in his life was her. And the fact that tonight, both of them could have died.

He let his gaze wander over her face, and the pain in his heart—the fear—was indisputable.

In the space between his heartbeats, the truth crystallized. This new nightmare was a warning.

He was scared of losing Gemma, and he almost had. First at the house in Leadville and again tonight. She'd gotten under his skin and into his thoughts. After all the mistakes he'd made—all the failures—he didn't deserve her, didn't deserve to have anything that good in his life. And yet, if he lost her, he didn't know what he'd do.

Except that he knew he wouldn't be able to live with himself.

CHAPTER NINETEEN

Gemma glanced at Brett's profile as he parked in front of the Pine Springs Mental Health Treatment Center. He'd swung by her house an hour earlier to pick her up on the way to see Gavin Aldrich, and in that hour, the only topic of discussion was the investigation.

No more tender words. No talk of the future, and no talk of them as a couple. Apparently, he'd wiped the slate clean. Maybe they'd only slept together because she'd been attacked, and their emotions had been right at the surface, ready to explode.

Fine. With. Me.

Keep telling yourself that.

Then maybe she'd actually start believing it and quit regretting that she'd dropped her "emotional body armor," as he'd put it, and let him in. A tiny bit, anyway.

Sunday morning after they'd made love—or was it just sex?—they'd driven to the police station where she'd filed a report, then called her boss to fill him in. He'd been appropriately horrified and had wanted to send someone in from another NICB office to work with her. It had taken a full twenty minutes, but she'd finally convinced him she didn't need any help and that she already had a partner.

While she'd been making that call, Brett had not only put out a BOLO on Johnny Nash but the equivalent of a medical BOLO for anyone coming into a hospital with a wound that could have been caused by a three-and-a-half-inch framing nail.

She thought back to their conversation right before making love. Sure, Brett had said some very kind, thoughtful things, but that still didn't mean anything, certainly not coming from a man's brain. Her brothers had taught her that. If only she could flip an emotional switch so easily.

Brett glanced in the rearview mirror. "Evan's here. Let's go." Unexpectedly, he shut off the engine.

"Blaze is coming with us?" Gemma asked as she opened her door.

"I already cleared it with Gavin's doctor." He popped Blaze's door, then got out and clipped on a leash.

Evan met them at the hood of Brett's Expedition. "How's the noggin?"

"Still on top of my neck." Another thing to be thankful for. Some days, it was the little things that counted.

"Let's do this," Brett said, then led the way inside.

Two other men were already waiting in the lobby—Gavin's public defender, Anthony Manning, and another older man with gray hair whose lanyard proclaimed him to be Dr. Gene Franklin.

As introductions were made, Gemma took in the lobby, with its comfortable-looking beige sofas and tall potted plants sporting large white flowers she couldn't identify. The place looked more like a tropical resort than a psychiatric treatment center and smelled more like a flower shop.

That thought amplified as they followed Dr. Franklin down a long, carpeted hallway with light-blue walls and framed photos of lush gardens and tranquil ocean settings. Some of the doors they passed were open. Inside those rooms, Gemma glimpsed double beds, round tables with padded chairs, and more framed photos on the walls.

"Here we are." Dr. Franklin knocked softly on a door that had a brass plaque with the number 12 on it.

Gavin Aldrich opened the door, looking drastically better than when they'd last seen him in court. He wore fresh blue jeans and a white T-shirt. He was clean shaven, his eyes alert but wary.

"Gavin, how are you doing?" Brett shook hands with the kid, making Gemma realize he was trying to treat Gavin with respect and courtesy.

He shrugged. "Two hots and a cot." His gaze remained guarded. Until he caught sight of Blaze sitting behind Brett. "Blaze!" Gavin knelt as Blaze pushed his way past Dr. Franklin and Manning.

Blaze licked Gavin's face, eliciting a grin. Gavin looked up at Brett. "Thanks for bringing him."

"No problem." Brett gave Gavin more time to pet Blaze before asking, "Can we come in?"

Wordlessly, Gavin stood and led the way into his room.

"Hi, Gavin." Gemma rested her hand briefly on the kid's shoulder, taking heart when he bestowed her with a shy smile.

"This is my friend, Evan," Brett said. "He's with the FBI. He specializes in finding missing children."

Gavin's eyes went wide as he shook Evan's hand. "Are you here to find Ally?"

"I'm gonna try. Let's sit down." He indicated the table by the windows. "I want to hear everything about your sister."

Gavin nodded enthusiastically and for the first time showed an emotion other than anger, fear, or wariness. It was hope shining in his eyes now, and Brett and Evan had put it there. Brett was making good on his promise to the court that he would act as a form of "big brother" to Gavin, an authority figure who might be able to help set him on a path to recovery and finding a new life.

Evan unzipped his portfolio and took out a pen. "I need you to tell me everything that happened the night of the fire at your family's house, right after you got out of the house, and then what happened in the days following. Before you were separated from Ally."

At first, Gavin said nothing, chewing on his lower lip as he looked from his attorney to Dr. Franklin.

"It's okay, Gavin," Manning said. "You can't be charged for setting that fire. It's in the past."

Still, Gavin didn't speak. Brett made a barely perceptible gesture, but Gemma caught it, probably because she'd been watching Brett far too much lately.

He looked at Blaze, then tipped his chin in Gavin's direction. Blaze walked unerringly behind Gemma's and Evan's chairs, then sat and rested his head on the kid's lap. How he understood Brett's command and exactly what was expected of him, she didn't know. *Canine ESP.*

Much as he'd done at the pretrial services office, Gavin began petting Blaze's head, stroking his ears, and started to talk.

"I made sure Ally got out," he began. "We were on the sidewalk, watching it burn. Cops came and drove us to my aunt's house. We were there for a few days, then a man and a woman came and took us someplace else." He fisted one of his hands on the table. "Turned out my aunt and uncle didn't want us. I guess I can understand them not wanting me, but Ally was a good girl. She never did anything wrong. It was my fault they didn't want her. They were worried she'd turn out like me and burn *their* house down."

Ever the consummate canine counselor, Blaze nuzzled Gavin's hand, forcing the kid to keep petting his ears.

"Do you know where they took you and your sister?" Evan asked, and when Gavin shook his head, he added, "This place they took you to, was it near your house in Colorado Springs?"

"I think so." Gavin nodded. "It didn't take long to drive there, maybe ten minutes, but I wasn't really paying attention."

"That's okay." Evan jotted something on a pad. "There's a kid's center in Colorado Springs near where you used to live. I know people who work there."

Manning handed Evan a sheet of paper. "This is the name and address of Gavin's aunt and uncle. They still live in the Springs."

"Thanks." Evan tucked the sheet into his portfolio. "It sounds like you and Ally may have gone to Kids Corner. What happened next?"

"Ally was only there for a few weeks before a family took her in. I never saw her again. They took her away when I was playing basketball in the gym with some of the other kids." Gavin blinked rapidly. "They did that on purpose, so I wouldn't be able to stop them. When I asked where she was, they wouldn't tell me. I asked over and over for them to tell me where she was. I *begged* them, but they wouldn't. What happened was all my fault." Tears slipped from his lids and ran down his cheeks.

Gemma put her arm around Gavin's shoulder. From across the table, Brett's gaze met hers. Finding Ally Aldrich was exactly what Gavin needed, and Brett had known that.

Gavin took a deep breath. "No matter how many times I asked where Ally went, all they kept saying was that those records were private and the family who took her in didn't want me."

Evan set down his pen. "I'll start with Kids Corner. I can't make you any guarantees that I can find Ally, but I *can* promise you this: I'll never stop looking. No matter what happens, I'll never stop."

The sincerity in Evan's gray eyes was a palpable thing. She barely knew Evan McGarry, but Gemma had the distinct impression the words he'd just spoken were meant not only for Gavin Aldrich, but for him. About his *own* sister, who'd been kidnapped.

• • •

Thirty minutes later, they said goodbye to Evan, who'd wanted to go directly to Kids Corner and start tracking down Ally Aldrich.

"How did you know?" she asked. "How did you know finding his sister was exactly what he needs?" Because when they'd left Gavin's room, the kid wasn't exactly smiling, but even his doctor had said that his frame of mind was more positive than it had been since he'd begun treatment.

"Because he's fixated. He can't forget what he did, and he can't forgive himself." Brett hooked Blaze's leash around the rearview mirror. "He set the fire that resulted in his sister being taken away. To atone for that, he needs to find her. He needs his family, and she's all he's got. Until that happens, he won't be whole again."

"And you're fixated on finding the arsonist who killed those kids." Not that she could blame him. She wanted that, too. For him, however, it was personal. "What happens if we never catch this guy?"

Brett took a deep inhale. His silence said it all.

If they didn't bring the arsonist to justice, he'd never be whole again. He'd spend the rest of his life trying, though, to the detriment of everything else in his life. Even if she didn't suspect he'd only want to remain friends, could she ever be with someone who was so focused, so driven that they'd set aside all the good things life had to offer? He was punishing himself for his perceived failures, and there was nothing she could do to help.

"I owe you an apology," he began. "We should—"

"Keep things strictly professional," she finished for him, hoping she sounded sincere and adding quickly, "I agree. Like I said, sex between partners makes things complicated."

"Uh, that wasn't what I was going to say, but yeah, it does. I need to stay focused. If I don't catch this guy, other people will die."

Gemma's heart sank at his use of the word *I*. Was he already shutting her out? Okay, so she'd expected their personal relationship had permanently hit a brick wall, but she'd fully expected them to remain partners. Sex between them was majorly screwing things up.

He leaned in, peering at her neck.

"What is it?" Self-consciously, she put her hand to her throat.

"I'll be back in a minute." He got out of the SUV, then went around and lifted the tailgate. With Blaze's kennel blocking her view, she couldn't see what he was doing. He returned with a glove in his hand. "Whoever attacked you wore these. I knew I'd seen that symbol before. It's a shamrock."

Gemma took the outstretched glove, examining the shape embroidered onto the underside of the thumb. She reached up to angle the rearview mirror down so she could look at her neck. The vague shape of a purple, bruise-colored shamrock, identical in size to the one on the glove, was now visible on her neck.

Even she knew this brand of gloves. "I think I've got a pair of these."

"Yeah." He tossed the glove on the dashboard. "They're a dime a dozen. It doesn't give us any new leads to follow. We've still got jack."

His phone rang, and he tugged it from his belt. There was no name on the screen, only letters. *DOL.* Brett's contact with the Colorado Department of Labor and Employment. He put the call on speaker. "Kai, what've you got for me?"

"That information you asked for on John Nash."

"Stand by." He clipped the phone into a cradle attached to the dashboard, then dug into the console for a pad and pen. "Go ahead."

"There's only one entry. During the last pay

period, John Nash worked for two weeks at Hawkin Construction in Denver. You need the address?"

Brett's entire body went as rigid as a two-by-four. "No need. I know it. Can you email me a printout?"

"Just did."

"Thanks, Kai." He ended the call and looked at Gemma. His voice was low, deadly. "Johnny Nash, our suspected warehouse arsonist, worked for Michael Hawkin, the same flipper who owned the Torrance Lane house when it burned down. There's no way that's a coincidence."

Gemma had to agree. As Brett cranked the Expedition and gunned it from the parking lot, she was both excited *and* terrified. Excited at the prospect of nailing this arsonist.

Terrified by the lethal combination of determination and barely banked rage shooting from Brett's eyes.

CHAPTER TWENTY

Brett headed north on I-25. The blood in his veins spiked with so much adrenaline he could barely sit still. This was it. The lead they'd needed. He'd always suspected there was something wrong about the Torrance Lane fire.

That still didn't mean he could prove it in a court of law.

"Brett? You're scaring me." Gemma touched his shoulder, the first time they'd had physical contact since yesterday. On her mattress. As it always did, her touch sent a hot zing of awareness shooting through his body. "Any chance you could slow it down a little? Even Blaze looks worried."

He glanced at his dog, who was standing up in the kennel with his head sticking through the opening and watching him intently. Brett knew that look. Gemma was right. Even Blaze had sensed the change in his demeanor. When his dog licked Brett's cheek, he eased off the gas.

They'd been driving for nearly an hour. The Hawkin Construction office was still ten minutes away.

"Before we talk to Hawkin, let's go over what we know." With the added benefit of keeping his mind occupied with something other than what a shithead he was.

Sunday morning, after they'd had amazing sex, he'd been at a loss for words. As was typical for him, he'd totally choked and shut down on her.

He'd been torn. He no longer wanted to keep their relationship strictly professional, but when she'd offered up the idea, he'd grabbed at it as if it were a lifeline. Involving her more in his effed-up personal life wasn't fair to her. There was no reason why things with Gemma would wind up any differently from all his other relationships that had crashed and burned. This was for the best. For both of them.

But as he refocused on the road and the investigation, he couldn't figure out why it was so much more difficult to accept this decision. Or why it left his heart with an empty, hollow feeling.

From his peripheral vision, he caught Gemma pulling her laptop from the backpack on the floor between her feet. "The Torrance Lane fire is one of the twenty-three on your list, right?"

"Right." She flipped open the laptop. Her fingers flew across the keyboard. "Michael Hawkin was the legal owner when it burned to the ground. Based on the purchase of the house, the insurance, and the sale of the property after the fire, he barely broke even. He may even have taken a loss."

"Any heavy riders on that house?"

"No."

Brett tapped his finger on the wheel as they whizzed through the city of Aurora. "That doesn't fit with the other houses, nor does the fact that MEK was the unintentional cause of the fire."

"I put that house on my list because it was titled by Kobuk," Gemma said, "and because of its proximity to the Frodo warehouse, which was also burned down using MEK."

The stack of questions he had for Hawkin was pil-
ing up fast. "Can you call your contact at Frodo? Ask
him to pull up all invoices for supplies purchased by
or for Hawkin Construction, let's say for three
months prior to the Torrance Lane fire."

"You want to see if Johnny Nash had any part in
those transactions?" Gemma asked as she pulled out
her phone.

"That and it can't hurt to know what supplies were
purchased during that timeframe." As with everything
else they had so far, none of this would be enough to
charge Hawkin. The most he could hope for was to
firm up the link between Hawkin and Nash.

He listened while Gemma spoke to Logan Hicks
and explained their request. "Thank you, Logan," she
said a few minutes later, then ended the call. "He said
he can have that for us in a couple of hours."

By the time they pulled up to the Hawkin
Construction office on the north side of Denver, it
was noon, and the dashboard thermometer indicated
a blistering ninety-five degrees outside.

Gemma grabbed her portfolio.

"Wait." Brett reached for her before she opened
the door. Her gaze flicked to where his hand now
rested on her bare upper arm. He yanked his hand
back. Guess that was how it would be between them
from now on. *Awk-ward.* And his fault. He pointed to
the crew cab pickup and the green Beemer parked in
front of the office door. "I want to run Hawkin and
the company for currently registered vehicles before
we go in."

"For large white SUVs?" Gemma asked.

"Exactly." Now that Hawkin, along with Nash,

were both prime suspects.

Minutes later, he shook his head. "Every vehicle registered to the company is either a pickup truck or a heavy-duty dump truck. His personal vehicle is a brand-new silver Mercedes. That Beemer belongs to his wife, Kelly."

"Business must be good," she said with a sarcastic edge to her voice.

"That pickup in front is one of the company vehicles. Blaze," Brett said over his shoulder. Once he'd slowed the SUV to quasi-legal speed, his dog had finally lain down and gone to sleep, snoring his heart out. Blaze scrambled to his feet, pushing his head through the opening, eyes and ears alert. "Time to go to work."

"What are you going to do?" Gemma asked as she stepped outside. The way the sun was positioned behind her created a halo effect, making her look like she was wearing a crown of fire.

His heart squeezed with so much regret, and for a moment, he was tempted to tell her the truth.

That he wanted her, wanted to see where things might go with them. But again, it wouldn't be fair. Unintentionally hurting people—the women in his life—was what he did. With Gemma, the only thing worse than that would be if she couldn't stand to look at him again, like most of his exes couldn't.

"We don't have a search warrant for the truck." He slipped Blaze's leash from the rearview mirror. "That doesn't mean I can't run Blaze *around* it."

After locking up the Expedition, he let Blaze take care of business on a sidewalk fire hydrant, then led him to the pickup, pointing at the different areas of the vehicle for Blaze to focus on. "Seek."

Blaze's tail whipped back and forth as he sniffed the asphalt by the driver's side door, then rounded the hood and did the same by the passenger door. The back of the pickup was open, but with a tarp covering what appeared to be, based on the size and shape, several fifty-five-gallon drums.

At the tailgate, Blaze's sniffing grew louder, and he swung his head back and forth, taking in whatever scents were coming from under the tarp. Blaze sat in front of the tailgate.

"Is he hitting on something?" Gemma asked.

"Accelerants." Brett leaned over the bed of the pickup. Even he could smell what Blaze had picked up on. "Contractors have legitimate reasons for handling all kinds of chemicals that could constitute an accelerant."

Her brows rose. "Like MEK?"

"Among others." As much as he wanted to whip off the tarp to uncover whatever was beneath it, he didn't have a warrant. "Good boy." He patted Blaze on his side, then tugged a treat from his pants pocket and held it out to his dog.

Again, Brett leaned over the rail, being careful not to actually touch the truck. A set of contractor's gloves sat on top of the tarp near the edge. *Not* the Shamrock brand.

The glass door leading to the office squeaked as it opened. A man about five-ten, wearing jeans, and a T-shirt that said 'Hawkin Construction' on the front, held the door open. "Can I help you?"

The man's gaze took in the embroidered badge on Brett's shirt, then dipped to the badge and gun. He

easily recognized Michael Hawkin from the photo in
the ATF's file. "Michael Hawkin?" Hawkin nodded.
"I'm Special Agent Tanner with the ATF. This is my
partner, Agent Gemma Scott with the National
Insurance Crime Bureau. May we come in and speak
with you for a few minutes?"

He waited a beat, gauging the man's reaction.
Usually, a guilty or concerned person would exhibit
some form of facial gesture or body language at being
approached by a federal agent. Hawkin, however, exhibited nothing. If he remembered Brett was the
agent injured during the Torrance Lane house fire, he
kept it to himself. The man was either innocent and
with nothing to hide, or he was one cool customer.
Brett's instincts were firing on all cylinders, and he
was betting on the latter.

"I guess so." Hawkin looked at his watch. "I don't
have much time, though. My wife and I have an appointment."

"This won't take long." The key was getting their
feet in the door and to get Hawkin talking. "Mind if I
bring my dog inside? It's hot in my vehicle." A partial
truth.

Hawkin didn't have to know Brett regularly left
Blaze in the SUV with the engine running and the AC
blasting. Without waiting for a response, Brett headed
for the door, with Blaze trotting at his side. Before
passing Hawkin, Blaze sniffed the man's boots, then
sat, his body as rigid as a stone.

"What's he doing?" Hawkin took a step back. "He
looks like he wants to take a chunk out of my leg."

Brett and Gemma exchanged knowing looks.
"Nah," Brett said. "He likes you." *The guy's boots*

must stink of accelerant.

"If you say so." Hawkin looked skeptical but held the door open.

As they went inside, Brett slipped Blaze another treat.

Through the open door at the end of a short hallway, a woman was visible sitting at a desk with a cell phone glued to her ear. As she caught sight of them, her brows drew together, and she didn't look happy.

"Have a seat." Hawkin indicated two chairs in the hallway. "I need to talk to my wife for a minute."

Hawkin went into the back office and shut the door. Rather than sit, Brett and Gemma examined the framed photos and certificates hanging on the dark, wood-paneled wall behind the chairs.

"He's quite the pillar of society, isn't he?" Gemma pointed to a Rotary Club service plaque and an award from the Denver Chamber of Commerce.

Brett snorted. Some of the worst serial killers in history hid their inner demon behind a strategically constructed facade, allowing them to wreak havoc without anyone being the wiser.

The next two frames were a college diploma from Prescott College in Arizona and a photo of Hawkin and two other men standing in front of a small airplane inside a hangar. A sign on the wall behind the plane said "Front Range Airport Hangar 8." One of the men had similar features to Hawkin but was several inches taller and wore a visor. Brett recalled from the ATF file that Hawkin had a younger brother, David.

"Do any of these men look familiar to you?" Brett asked quietly. "Could one of them have been the man who attacked you?"

Gemma shook her head. "I don't know. One of them could be the right height. Hawkin and the other man probably aren't tall enough."

Raised voices came from behind the closed door. The door opened, and Hawkin came out, reclosing the door, none too quietly. "We can talk in here." He led them into another office and went around the desk to sit in a large leather armchair. "Have a seat." He indicated the two chairs on the opposite side of the desk. "Please excuse my wife. She's not happy with me today. You know how it is. Can't love 'em, can't leave 'em." He grinned at Brett, as if the two of them shared a secret where women were concerned.

Asshole.

Brett and Gemma sat, while Blaze lay down in the space between the two chairs.

Gemma yanked open the zipper on her portfolio. Hawkin had to be twenty years Robert Hicks's junior, and Brett suspected he was well on his way to being the newest addition to Gemma's list of prehistoric reptiles.

Ignoring the sexist remark, though what he'd like to do was smash his fist into the other man's face, Brett said, "We'd like to ask you a few questions about Johnny Nash."

Hawkin held out his arms. "What about him?"

So Hawkin did know Nash. He'd half expected the man to lie about it. "How long has he been working for you?"

"He worked here for two weeks."

Worked? "Does he still work for you?"

"No." Hawkin shook his head. "He stopped showing up."

"When was the last day he worked for you?"

Hawkin shrugged. "Yesterday or the day before. I don't have time to go to all my sites. My supervisor told me he was a no-show. It happens a lot in this business."

"Did you try calling him?"

Again, Hawkin shook his head. "Not worth my time. If the guys I hire don't show, they don't show. I'll find someone to replace them."

The man still hadn't exhibited any outward signs that he was lying. He'd looked Brett straight in the eye, wasn't fidgeting with his hands, or rocking back and forth in his chair.

"Do you have an address for Nash?" Gemma asked, reading Brett's mind, because that was his very next question.

Hawkin would have basic information on all his employees, including their social security numbers so that he could make the required filings with the DOL.

"I should have." Hawkin glanced at his watch, then opened a file cabinet drawer behind his desk. After searching for a few seconds, he pulled out a folder and opened it. The tab on the folder had Nash's name on it. "Is he in some kind of trouble?"

"We just need to ask him some questions." Like did he set the warehouse fires and was he in cahoots with Hawkin to torch the Torrance Lane house. That question could wait. For the moment, anyway.

"Here it is." Hawkin held out a sheet of paper. "His address is on his employment application form."

Gemma took the document, scanning it for a moment. "He listed his sister's place in Colorado Springs as his home address."

They already knew he wasn't there, so finding him was still an issue. Brett wasn't finished squeezing Hawkin for information. "Did you know Nash before he started working for you?"

"Never met him before. He just showed up here one day looking for work. I needed another hand, so I hired him."

"Nash is from Colorado Springs. You renovated a house down there last year. The one that burned down, killing two kids," Brett added for effect, watching closely for any outward signs of discomfort, but the man's cool-as-a-cucumber demeanor prevailed.

"Shame about those kids," Hawkin said, frowning.

"Yeah, it was." Brett locked eyes with Hawkin for a long moment before continuing, but the man didn't flinch. "Where did you buy your supplies for that job?"

"Frodo. Everyone down there buys from them. They're the biggest contractor supplier in the Springs."

It wasn't much, but at least they'd made another connection between Hawkin and Nash. "Are you sure you never met Nash before he came to Denver? He used to work at Frodo."

Hawkin made a noncommittal shrug. "Frodo's a big place. They've got lots of people working for them, and it's been a while since I did any work down there. I've been buying from suppliers up north, closer to Denver where most of my work is now."

"Did he ever work for you before or *help* you out with anything, such as a *problem* you had?" Brett emphasized the words Sally Nash had used when she'd said that a contractor up north owed her brother a favor.

Hawkin raised his brows. "Help me with what? I already told you I never met the guy until he showed up here looking for work. He could have been working at Frodo when I was buying from them, but I don't remember. Do you want to tell me what all these questions are really about?"

No. Not yet, you sonofabitch. The man was smart; Brett would give him that. "Where were you this past Saturday night between nine and ten p.m.?" As Gemma had pointed out, at five-ten, Hawkin couldn't have been the man who'd attacked Gemma, but he *could* have been the shooter at the Piggly's parking lot. Unfortunately, with Colorado's loose gun laws, Hawkin could own a 9mm and there'd be no record of it.

"At home. With my wife." Hawkin narrowed his eyes, and his voice now held a discerned edge. He nodded to the wall adjoining the other office. "Ask her yourself."

Brett pondered that response. It had seemed like a genuine offer. "I'll do that. I just have one more question. Where were you Friday evening between six and seven p.m.?" When he and Gemma had been chasing after the white SUV. Neither Hawkin nor his wife owned one. That didn't mean he couldn't rent one or borrow one.

"On a job site in Denver. You can ask my foreman."

"What's his name?" Gemma asked.

"Brian Stamos. I'll save you the trouble of calling him." Hawkin took out his cell phone and placed a call, putting it on speaker.

"Hey, boss," a voice answered.

"Brian, you remember the conversation we had at the job site Friday afternoon? What time was that?"

"About five or six. Something like that. It was right before we stopped for the day. Why?"

"And how long was I at that job site?" Hawkin asked.

"Couple hours. You remember. It was a long day. Everything okay, boss?"

"Yeah. No worries." Hawkin ended the call.

"Thank you," Brett said. He exchanged a quick look with Gemma, inquiring wordlessly if she had any questions.

"What do you know about Kobuk Titling Agency?" Gemma asked.

Hawkin shrugged. "Never heard of it."

Gemma's pen poised over her pad. "Are you sure? They titled the Torrance Lane house for you."

Much as he had when questioned about Nash, Hawkin held open his arms. "I buy and sell a lot of houses. We use a lot of different titling companies. I don't keep track of all of them."

Gemma jotted more notes on her pad, then gave Brett a quick shake of her head.

"Thank you for your time. We'll let you get back to work." *For now*.

As a unit, he, Gemma, and Blaze stood. Before going outside, Brett knocked on the adjacent office door.

The door opened, and Hawkin's wife, wearing purple yoga pants and a yellow tank top, stood there. The woman was about five-six, and with sinewy muscles. "Yes?"

"Mrs. Hawkin?" Brett held out his ID. "I'm Special

Agent Tanner with the ATF. I'd just like to ask you a question, if I may." Like her husband had, she glanced at her watch. "This won't take long. I promise."

"Okay." Kelly Hawkin eyed him suspiciously.

Michael Hawkin leaned against the doorjamb of his office, his arms crossed as he made no pretense about listening in.

"Where was your husband this past Saturday night between nine and ten p.m.?"

The woman's lips twisted. "Unfortunately, he was at home." She threw her husband a venomous look.

Interesting. Trouble in paradise. "How do you know? What were you both doing that night?"

She shot her husband a dirty look. "I was on my laptop, and he was sitting on his ass watching *The Fast and the Furious* for the fourth time."

So much for Hawkin shooting at him. His wife seemed genuinely displeased that he'd been home that night. "Thank you for your time."

Blaze led the way outside. As they passed Hawkin's pickup, Blaze lifted his leg, relieving himself.

"Good boy." Gemma snickered. "Did you teach him that?"

Brett grinned. "Some things a good dog just knows."

They continued to the Expedition. When they were all inside with the AC cranking, Gemma tossed her portfolio on the dashboard. "What did you think?"

"He didn't give us anything we can use, and he's alibied for the time we were chasing that white SUV and for the shooting." Brett made a sound of disgust. "But my gut says he's dirty."

They watched Michael and Kelly Hawkin leave the office together. While Michael locked the glass door, Kelly jabbed a finger at her husband and began shouting. Brett rolled down his window but still couldn't make out her words. Whatever they were discussing, she was one PO'd woman. They both got into the BMW, with Kelly driving. A moment later, tires screeched as she punched it from the parking lot.

Gemma sighed. "Quite the loving couple, aren't they?" Her phone dinged, and she looked at the screen. "Logan Hicks sent an email." She began scrolling. "There are at least thirty invoices for materials purchased by Michael Hawkin of Hawkin Construction in the three months prior to the Torrance Lane fire."

"And?" he prompted. From the way the crease on her forehead deepened, she'd found something.

"And," she said, handing him her phone, "most of the purchases were processed by guess who."

Brett stared at the phone. "Johnny Nash." He scrolled through five more invoices. "That fucker was lying. I'd say he definitely knew Nash. It would be hard to forget someone you made thirty or so purchases from in ninety days."

"Begging the question…"

"What else is he lying about?" Brett finished for her.

CHAPTER TWENTY-ONE

The drill whirred as Gemma squeezed the trigger, screwing in the last of the window break sensors on the second floor of the house. She squinted as the sun's rays blared through the window. It had to be after eight.

Last night, she'd gotten a jump on installing her new security system, then, since she couldn't sleep, had risen early, at four a.m. to be precise, and dived right in again.

She stepped back to make sure the two pieces of the sensor aligned properly on the sash. Thoughts of the case—and Brett—had left her tossing and turning last night. Their unstated, silent agreement not to discuss anything besides work was driving her up the wall.

Like him, she'd thought Hawkin had been hiding something, even before they'd spoken with Logan Hicks about the warehouse invoices. There was something about Hawkin she couldn't put her finger on, but no one had ever been convicted on gut instinct. As Brett continually pointed out, they needed more.

She headed downstairs to brew a pot of coffee. At least she'd managed to fend off Brett's insistence on helping her install the security system.

Yesterday, after they'd left the Hawkin Construction office, he'd driven directly to a store that sold residential security systems and helped her pick one out. He'd wanted her to hire the same company to install it, but after being attacked, the idea of total strangers walking around her house sent a spurt of anxiety through her. When Brett had offered to install it for her, she'd politely declined. If she could renovate an old Victorian on her own, installing a security system was a cake walk.

That and she *really* didn't want him in her house again, taking up the same space, breathing the same air. Not after the intimacy they'd shared. The man's presence was too big, too powerful. Just thinking about his big, strong hands stroking her skin, cupping her breasts…the rest of what he could do to her body was too much to handle.

She let her head fall back, chastising herself for being stupid and breaking the proverbial cardinal rule by getting involved with a colleague. Being so attracted to Brett had taken her completely by surprise. What surprised her more was how much she'd come to care about him.

From now on, she'd either meet him at his office, the bagel deli, or at whatever location they were headed to for the day. The last thing he'd said when he'd dropped her off was that he'd call this morning, and they'd figure out their next step. As long as he stayed out of her personal space, and as long as they stuck to business, everything would be fine.

Gemma was reaching for the coffee carafe when a knock came from the front door. She set the carafe on the counter and grabbed her phone to test the new camera. It was probably Bonnie checking in.

As she cued up the door cam, her eyes widened, then her idiotic, incapable-of-sticking-to-its-resolve heart beat faster, because standing on the stoop, holding a Great Scott Bagel Deli bag and a cardboard tray with two large coffees...

Was Brett. Beside him, Blaze cracked his jaws and yawned.

Just when she'd made the decision never to meet him at her house again, here he was, looking showered and clean, and he probably smelled good, too. She, however, hadn't had the chance to shower and probably smelled like a sweaty hippo that'd been rolling around in the dust all day.

Wearing a pressed pair of khaki cargo pants and a black agency polo shirt, he looked every bit the handsome, authoritative federal agent he was. He was so tall that the top of his head practically brushed the bottom of the hanging light fixture. A laptop case was slung over his shoulder.

"You can do this," she whispered, forcing her feet to take her to the door. She reached for the knob. *You can do this*.

When she opened the door, Brett's gaze traveled down her body then up, sending a wave of goose bumps spiking across her skin. So much for doing this. All he had to do was look at her once, and her willpower dipped into single digits.

She mustered a smile. "Good morning."

"Morning." Naturally, the morning sun took that moment to make his eyes appear so clear and so blue, it was like looking at two perfect sapphires.

Until that moment, she hadn't realized just how smitten—God, did people still use that word?—she really was with Brett Tanner.

Blaze's tail whipped faster. Brett's dog she could handle. The dog's handler, not so much.

"You gonna let us in?" His brows rose. "We've got work to do. I want to run a theory by you."

"Uh, sure." She stepped aside, closing the door behind them after allowing him to do precisely what she'd sworn less than five minutes ago never to let happen again: letting him into her home, taking up her personal space, and breathing the same air she did.

Blaze trotted in behind Brett, his body wriggling when she knelt to pet his head and let him lick her chin. "Good morning to you, too, Blaze." At hearing his name, Blaze made an adorable, whimpering sound.

"I see you've been installing the security system." Brett looked around the living room, in particular at each of the windows, before watching her intently, wordlessly for an awkwardly long moment. "That's good." He looked up at the ceiling, then went to the bottom of the stairs and did the same. "You should also install more smoke detectors."

"I have enough to comply with the building code."

He turned and frowned. "You can *never* have enough smoke detectors."

Gemma crossed her arms. She hadn't invited him here again, yet here he was giving her construction advice. "You're annoying. Do you know that?"

"I'm being cautious."

"Overly cautious. And nosy."

"I'm worried."

"Uh, why?" She put a hand to her forehead. *Duh.* Because he'd lived through two fires in which others had died. Could she be just a bit more insensitive?

He cleared his throat. "Did you tack your map and spider diagram back on your office wall?"

"Uh, yeah." Could she possibly start a sentence with anything besides *uh*? Her use of the English language had been fine until she and Brett had made love. Again, was it more accurate to call it sex? A lot of women might refer to what they'd done as *making love*, but a guy's perspective on the matter was totally different, and Brett was a guy.

"Good. Let's eat in there."

Her jaw dropped as he headed directly for the office aka bedroom. "Wait!" He didn't. "We can work out here. All we have to do is clear away the tools from the workbench and bring in some chairs from my garage and—"

"No, in here," he flung over his shoulder, completely ignoring what he had no way of knowing was a desperate plea.

Blaze strolled through the living room, sniffing and scenting every box and bin like he'd never been in her house before.

Her pathetic heart hammered as loudly as if she'd actually picked up a hammer and begun pounding nails into the wall. Somehow, she'd get through this.

In her office, Brett still held the deli bag and coffee. His throat worked as he glanced at the mattress on the floor with the rumpled sheets. He set the coffee and what she assumed were two toasted everything bagels with scallion cream cheese on the table. "Uh, let's get to work." He slipped the laptop bag from his shoulder and put it on one of the two chairs.

Well, good. At least she wasn't the only one starting sentences with the dreaded *uh*.

He popped open the tab on his coffee, then

unwrapped his bagel and took a chunk out of it. Still chewing, he stared thoughtfully at the map on the wall and the spider diagram.

Popping open the other coffee, she stood beside him. Not *too* close beside him.

"These guys are smart," Brett said. "They know enough about house systems to manipulate them into making arson look like accidents. Who would know how to do that?"

"Contractors. Some home renovators," Gemma supplied. "But I wouldn't know how to manipulate the electrical system to do that. That takes an expert."

"Okay, let's go with that, then." Brett sipped his coffee. "No offense, but we're looking for someone who does this for a living, not as a side hustle. Someone like Hawkin."

"No offense taken." She unwrapped her bagel and took a bite.

Brett started pacing back and forth in front of the map. "The only reason the Torrance Lane house came up on your radar was because that house was titled by Kobuk Titling."

Gemma swallowed. "That and the use of MEK to burn it down like the warehouse."

"Right." Brett pointed to the map. "But *unlike* the other houses on your list, plus the two new ones in Leadville and Burlington, we actually *know* who the new owner was at the time of the fire. Hawkin Construction. You said you weren't able to contact a single other homeowner."

He was right, and that wasn't something she'd considered. Yet another reason why the Torrance Lane house didn't quite fit the same pattern as the other houses. "What do you think that means?"

"I think we're on the right track. Maybe Hawkin purchased the Torrance Lane property, intending to do a legitimate flip, but when the house unexpectedly turned out to be a money pit—"

"He had to get rid of it fast," Gemma interrupted. "Otherwise, he'd lose everything."

Brett nodded. "In order to operate out in the open, and to at least give the impression that he was bringing in enough income to purchase his personal residence, a BMW, a Mercedes, and, by the way, the small aircraft he recently bought, he'd need a legitimate business to justify the cash flow. Any other outside income could be comingled. As long as he legitimately flips a house now and then, he could fly under the radar."

"Okay, I'm with you." Gemma stepped closer to Brett, instantly regretting the proximity. Whoever invented that cologne must be a billionaire. "But you said that Hawkin had an alibi for the night of that fire. Is it airtight?"

"Pretty much." Brett frowned. "Remember that award on his office wall from the Denver Chamber of Commerce? At the time that fire was set, Hawkin was receiving that award in front of over two hundred people."

"If he didn't start that fire, then who did?" When Brett raised both brows, the answer hit her. "Johnny Nash. That fire happened right before he went to prison for burglary."

"Hawkin could have ordered Nash to do it at the exact time when he knew he'd have hundreds of witnesses to provide him with an airtight alibi. The other houses on your map were never in his name, so he'd never be connected to them and wouldn't need an alibi for when those fires were set."

"We still need something connecting Hawkin to those other houses," Gemma said, stating the obvious.

"And," Brett added, "we still need to find Johnny Nash. There've been no hits on the BOLO." He sat at the table, then slid his laptop from its case. "I'm going to do a more intensive background check on Hawkin, try and find something we can use to tie him to the other houses. Can you take another look at all the documents for those houses? Could be there's a tie-in to Hawkin buried somewhere in all those transactions."

"Sure." *Ugh*. Because in order to do what he asked, she'd have to sit way too close to him for comfort. Thus far, only one of them was capable of sticking to business, and it wasn't her. "I can try cross-referencing what's in the ISO databases with county land records for the other houses. County records should have scanned copies of all the deeds filed at real estate closings."

After scooting the only other chair as far away as possible from Brett, Gemma sat in front of her laptop. She clicked open the folder containing the property documents on the twenty-two other houses. When she reached for her bagel, her fingers grazed Brett's arm. The only indication that he'd even felt her touch was the flexing of his muscles.

Focus. Focusss!

She picked up the bagel and bit off more than she could chew. *Literally*. Her cheeks must look like a chipmunk's stocking up on nuts for the winter. Finally, she swallowed, washing it down with coffee and an unladylike *gulp*. She'd bet Doctor Tori Sampson never made gulping sounds.

The bagel she normally loved tasted like cardboard, but somehow, she managed to start focusing on the documents on her screen.

• • •

When Gemma had first explained that her home office was in her bedroom while she renovated her house, it had made sense, and Brett hadn't given it another thought. Now, it was *all* he thought about. Sitting less than three feet from the same mattress they'd made love on was seriously screwing with his brain cells and every other cell in his body. Particularly the ones directly behind his zipper.

Rather than show up on her doorstep, he could just as easily have called her to explain what he wanted her to do next. Likewise, he could have worked on his laptop at the ATF office. Numbnut sap that he was, he'd wanted to see her.

Every breath he took brought with it the lingering scent of milk-and-honey soap. As he pulled up the digital copy of the ATF case file on the Torrance Lane fire, memories of what they'd done on that mattress filled his mind.

She'd been so soft, pliant in his arms, so sweet he'd never tasted anything like it. Whatever it was, he wanted more, but he couldn't risk it. Not now, not ever.

With no other outlet for his sexual frustration, he fisted his hands over the keyboard, flexing his fingers repeatedly and praying like hell he could get his shit together. Going into her bedroom again had been another major tactical error.

Blaze came in and lay down at Gemma's feet, not his, leaving him wondering whether she'd been slipping him bacon again behind his back. He began scrolling through the file, reading and rereading what he already knew was on the pages. At this point, he'd practically memorized the entire report.

The only thing new he'd found this morning, when he'd gotten up early to run more background checks, was the tail number on the four-seater Cessna Hawkin had purchased last year, presumably the same one in the photo hanging on his office wall. The first three tail numbers he remembered on the plane in the photo matched the registration he'd dug up.

His phone dinged with a text. The ATF's National Tracing Center had sent him a report on the spent shell casings he'd collected at Piggly's. He opened the report, only a few lines of which were relevant. The technician hadn't found a match in IBIS. Those shell casings didn't come from a gun that had been used at another crime scene known to law enforcement.

Brett let out a heavy breath. He'd been hoping to get a lead on who'd tried to kill him.

Nothing was ever easy.

Gemma clicked the mouse as she pulled up multiple images, side by side, on the screen. He watched her fingers with their practical, short nails fly across the keyboard. Those fingers had known just where to touch him, exactly how to arouse him.

Shit. Those were the same thoughts that had resulted in a measly three hours' sleep last night. That

and being so amped up on adrenaline after talking to
Hawkin and learning about the warehouse invoices
that tied him to Nash.

Ultimately, he'd given up on sleep and gone for a
seven-mile run before the sun had risen. After a quick
shower, he'd worked Blaze through a maze he'd
erected in his backyard, where he'd hidden rags
doused with various accelerants. While Blaze had
been working, so had Brett's mind. He was sure they'd
missed something, and if anyone could find it, it
would be Gemma, so he'd gone to the Great Scott
Bagel Deli.

When he'd ordered two of the same kind of bagel
that was Gemma's and his favorite, Gemma's father
had narrowed his eyes, then asked, "Is that other bagel for anyone I know?"

Not wanting to get into it, he'd grunted in response, then left before her father could launch into
an all-out grilling. Gemma's parents might have been
trying to set them up, but that didn't mean her dad
would take kindly to knowing Brett already had sex
with his only daughter.

About to close out the file, he scrolled to the bot-
tom of the last page but stopped. Beneath the
RELATIVES portion of the report was the name
David Hawkin and several paragraphs regarding
Hawkin's wife, Kelly. The section about David
Hawkin, Michael's brother, contained only one para-
graph.

He'd read all this multiple times since the Torrance
Lane fire. Now that he and Gemma were investigating
other fires Michael Hawkin was suspected of setting
but had alibis for, the scant background on brother

David tweaked Brett's radar. "Can I tap into your wifi?"

"Sure." Gemma nodded, then waited while he clicked on available wifi networks. "I'm sure you can figure out which one is mine."

Several wifis popped up, the strongest signal coming from the network *Jaws*. He clicked on it.

"It's Ilovegoldfish272!"

Brett smiled as he typed in her password. When he'd successfully logged on, he took another bite of his bagel, then typed his own ID and password into CCIC—the Colorado Crime Information Center database—and ran a DMV search on David Hawkin.

David's license had expired about three years ago, as had all the registrations for any vehicles he'd owned in Colorado, none of which were a white SUV. Looked like David was no longer a state resident. But the man was six-three, the same general height as Gemma's attacker.

Brett ran another search in Accurint for prior and current residences, along with employer information. Several residences in Colorado popped up, including his brother Michael's address in Longmont, but David's most recent residence was in New Mexico.

Returning to the national database, he ran David for a driver's license and registrations in New Mexico. This took a bit longer, and as he waited for the system to respond, he glanced at Gemma. Her eyes had narrowed, and her kissable lips pursed and twisted, and he couldn't take his eyes off them.

Forcing himself to do just that, he returned his focus to his laptop to find the system had returned a New Mexico driver's license issued to David Hawkin and a vehicle registration.

Brett leaned back in the chair. David's current registration was for a white GMC Yukon. While he couldn't be certain, he'd initially pegged the white SUV he and Gemma had been following in Leadville as a Yukon. The shooter's vehicle at Piggly's had definitely been a Yukon. Still not a smoking gun, but the circumstantial was stacking up.

"Got something?" Gemma looked at him, brows raised.

"Michael Hawkin's brother, David, lives in New Mexico and owns a white Yukon. Could be coincidence."

"*Another* coincidence. Hmm." Now her lips pursed again, but this time in sarcasm.

It was at that exact moment Brett decided with finality that Gemma's lips were the sexiest he'd ever seen.

When she returned her gaze to her own laptop, he shook his head to clear it of a different image. This one of her sexy lips wrapped around his—

Yeah. Don't go there.

He turned his laptop so that Gemma could view the screen, then he enlarged the driver's license image. "Could this guy be who attacked you?"

After a long moment, she shook her head. "No. Maybe. It *could* be him, but I couldn't pick him out of a lineup and say it was definitely him."

That didn't mean he *wasn't* Gemma's attacker. Not only had the guy been wearing sunglasses and a ball cap, but DMVs everywhere were notorious for issuing licenses with horrendous photos that looked nothing like the actual person.

Further search revealed that, prior to relocating to New Mexico, David had been employed by Hawkin Construction. No shock there. David must have opened his own business, because his employer for the last three years had been DH Construction.

Before closing out the database, Brett scrolled down to the OTHER LICENSES section, searching for any gun licenses. That section was blank.

He must have made another sound because Gemma asked, "Found something else?"

"No." He'd been hoping, though. "Colorado is an open-carry state. You don't have to register guns or get a license to carry openly, but David Hawkin lives in New Mexico. New Mexico is also an open-carry state, but one that requires a license. I was checking to see if David Hawkin owns a 9mm."

Brett queued up a criminal history on David Hawkin. While he waited for the system to kick back a response, he noticed Gemma staring at her laptop screen.

She rubbed her hands together. "Now *this* is interesting." She'd opened up a new window and was in the process of doing an internet search on Charles Pilcher.

The website filling the screen was for Mountain Legal Associates, a law firm in Denver. Gemma clicked on the Meet Our Lawyers tab and from the dropdown clicked Pilcher's name.

"Who is he?" Brett asked. Colorado didn't require a real estate attorney to close on a house, but that didn't mean a buyer or seller couldn't use one.

Gemma gave him a saucy grin that made it increasingly difficult not to kiss it off her pretty face.

"He's a personal injury attorney." She hit a button on her keyboard. A printer on the end of the table fired up and began spitting out pages.

Brett pointed to Pilcher's image on her laptop. "And he's relevant, why?"

"I'll show you why." Gemma closed out the website, then clicked the mouse. The laptop screen again filled with a grid of documents. She clicked on one of the docs, enlarging it and pointing to the notary box. "There. And there," she said after enlarging the adjacent document. "I just looked again at over a dozen of these titles issued by the nonexistent Kobuk Titling Agency in Alaska. I never noticed it before. Each one was notarized by the same person. Charles Pilcher. Right here in Denver."

He leaned in closer to read Pilcher's bio. "If he's notarizing documents for a company that doesn't exist, he's gotta know something. That's good work. *Really* good work." Without thinking, he clasped Gemma's face and planted a quick kiss on her mouth. Her eyes flashed wide.

He dropped his hands. "Shit." *You ass, Tanner.* Great way to send mixed messages. He'd been so amped up on adrenaline he hadn't stopped to think about the consequences of his impulses.

"That's okay." She licked her lips, then averted her gaze. Not before he'd caught the look of pain on her face, making him feel like the bastard he was.

His laptop dinged with an incoming message. HIT CONFIRMATION. Attached to the response was a file. He clicked on it and scanned the essentials. "Two days ago, David Hawkin was arrested by the New Mexico State Police. Recognize him?" Gemma leaned over to look at Hawkin's arrest photo, then shook her head. "Originally, he was pulled over for speeding. He had a concealed, loaded, unlicensed handgun in his possession." As he read the next line to himself, his heart pounded faster. "It was a 9mm."

The same caliber as the gun that nearly killed him and Blaze at Piggly's.

Brett's pulse pounded faster. If the gun had been seized, then sitting in an evidence locker in a New Mexico State Police district office was a gun that could be fired, the spent casings from which could be compared to the ones he'd collected at Piggly's.

If they were a match, he'd know who tried to kill him.

CHAPTER TWENTY-TWO

Why did he have to kiss me again?

Gemma had been doing great until that moment, having successfully hauled herself back onto the no-physical-contact-with-Brett wagon. With what was barely a peck on the lips, he'd yanked her off the wagon, and she'd landed solidly on her ass again. Then, in the time it had taken for him to read the arrest report on Hawkin, Brett had clearly eradicated the moment from his consciousness.

What she ought to have done was stick to her guns, so to speak, and driven her own truck to Denver and met Brett outside Charles Pilcher's office. Instead, here she was, sitting not two feet from a man who set her blood on fire and made her want to jump his bones all over again. He, on the other hand, had deftly avoided discussing that kiss the same way one would avoid stepping on a big, steaming pile of dog poop.

She leaned her arm against the window and sighed. Instead of being angry or frustrated, maybe she should be grateful. Unlike with the colleague she'd gotten involved with, who'd remorselessly stabbed her in the back, things with Brett had ended before she'd been seriously hurt, and with no lingering work complications. With the case, at least, they were still in sync.

The only sounds in the Expedition came from the click of Blaze's nails on the kennel floor behind them and the dog's panting. She rubbed the soft spot behind Blaze's ear. The muscles beneath the warm fur were taut. The dog was so attuned to Brett that he understood something was wrong. She'd once heard from a local K-9 officer that if either the handler or the dog was in distress, the other would know it and feel it the same as if *they* were the one experiencing the symptoms. Emotions traveled up the leash *and* down.

Before leaving the house, Brett had left a message for the New Mexico State Police officer in Raton who'd arrested David Hawkin. As he searched the side streets for a parking spot near Union Station, inside of which was the Mountain Legal Associates office, he glanced continually at his phone. Finally, he snagged a spot half a block away from Union Station.

Two seconds after putting the SUV in park, Brett's phone rang. The letters NMSP lit the screen.

Brett put the call on speaker. "Tanner."

"This is Trooper Sanchez, New Mexico State Police. You left a message wanting information on David Hawkin."

"I did. I see you arrested him less than a week ago. I read what's in NCIC. What else can you tell me about the arrest?"

"I pulled him over for speeding on I-25. He had a concealed handgun, but no license, so I took him in. He said he'd applied for a concealed carry license but hadn't received it yet. He was released, pending verification of the license."

"Did you seize the gun?"

"Yes. He won't get it back until his license is issued."

Brett fisted his hand triumphantly.

Blaze pushed his head farther through the opening, staring at the phone as if he were actually
listening and understanding the conversation. Maybe
he was. Blaze uttered a snort, then rested his chin on
Brett's shoulder.

"David Hawkin is suspected of trying to murder a
federal officer and attacking a woman. I'm sending
another ATF agent to you today to take custody of
that gun."

A loud whistle came through the phone. "I'd be
happy to lock this guy up again for you. You got a
warrant?"

"Not yet. NCIC said he was arrested two days ago.
What time of day, and what was the exact location on
I-25?"

"It was around 1 a.m. I was working the midnight
shift. I pinged him doing ninety-five just south of the
Colorado border between Raton and Springer."

"Did you search his vehicle?"

"I did. No other weapons. No contraband. Mostly
tools and other contractor supplies. The guy owns a
construction company."

"Did you see any work gloves? If so, was it the
Shamrock brand?"

The kind Gemma's attacker had worn.

"I think there was a pair of gloves," Sanchez said.
"I really didn't notice what kind they were."

Brett began massaging his chin. "Anything else
you can tell me about Hawkin? Anything unusual?"

"Not really." A beat of silence, then, "Other than
muddy boots. *Really* muddy boots with some kind of
oily stuff on them. I remember being pissed after I

took him out of the back of my patrol car, because he left a mess on the floorboard. I'll have to take the car out of service and get the back cleaned out."

Brett's eyes narrowed, then he looked at Gemma, brows raised. She shook her head, unable to think of any other questions for the trooper.

"Do me a favor," Brett said. "Can you keep an eye on Hawkin, swing by his house periodically and let me know where he's at?"

"You got it. Happy to assist any way I can."

Brett ended the call and stared through the windshield, unmoving.

Like a bomb about to explode.

He popped the phone from its cradle and placed another call. "Lori, it's Brett."

For the next few minutes, Gemma listened as Brett updated his boss, ending the conversation with an urgent request to have an agent in New Mexico take custody of David Hawkin's 9mm handgun and ship it ASAP to the ATF lab for ballistic comparison to the shell casings he'd collected from the Piggly's Smokehouse parking lot.

If they were a match, Gemma had no doubt Brett would get an arrest warrant for David Hawkin.

• • •

"Brett?"

He could feel it in his bones as surely as if he held the actual report in his hands. The lab *would* confirm a ballistics match.

"Brett?"

When it did, he'd be the first agent in line at the

courthouse to swear out a warrant for the arrest of David Hawkin.

"*Brett*!" Gemma squeezed his arm. "Where *are* you?"

The concerned look in her eyes jerked him back to reality. "Sorry. Just thinking ahead." And wondering if there was any relevance to the muddy, oily boots Hawkin had been wearing when he'd been arrested. He couldn't come up with anything, so he let it go but tucked it away in the back of his mind in a file reserved for weird, unexplainable shit. "Michael and David Hawkin are both contractors, both fluent enough in residential systems to make a house fire seem like an accident. If they're working together, that could explain why Michael always seems to have an alibi."

"Do you really think Michael or David tried to kill us?" Gemma shook her head. "I guess I'm still not seeing why a building contractor would find us so threatening."

"Most wouldn't. Unless they've got something big to cover up—like murder—and they're worried we're getting close enough to find out what it is."

"The Torrance Lane fire. Those kids who died."

"Yeah." They really needed to find Johnny Nash. Brett's gut told him that guy had something on Michael Hawkin, enough to get him hired. But where was Nash now? "Let's go."

Brett locked the Expedition, leaving the engine running and the AC blasting so Blaze wouldn't roast. The second before he closed the driver's side door, Blaze drilled him with a look that told him how disgruntled he was at not going with them.

Nearing lunchtime, the Union Station area was teeming with tourists and people who worked in the LoDo — lower downtown — part of the city. The station itself was not only a rail transport hub, but a one-hundred-year-old historic landmark considered by some to be the crown jewel of the city. Unlike most major cities, Denver had no navigable rivers. Its history had been carved out by the railroad.

The massive light-brick building was situated on the outskirts of Commons Park where Deck, Tori, and Thor had nearly been run down by drug dealers a few months ago. That had been a close one. *Too* close.

Perched above the main doors of the station was an iconic red neon sign that read: "Union Station – Travel by Train." Brett headed for the entrance, glancing at Gemma hustling to keep up with his longer stride. He really did feel like shit about kissing her again.

Bullshit. Truth was he'd never feel badly about kissing her. It felt too darned good doing it. But it was only confusing both of them and taking his brain off-line in ways he couldn't afford.

"Excuse me." She shot him a look so filled with annoyance she could have been sucking a lemon. "Is there a marathon we're running today? Because I forgot my running shoes."

He slowed his pace. "Sorry." Seemed like his favorite word around her.

"Thank you," she said.

He pushed open one of the massive doors and waited for her to enter first. The Mountain Legal Associates law office was located inside the station, along with an eclectic array of trendy shops, bars, and restaurants.

Voices echoed in the cavernous lobby with its high, arched ceiling and rows of arched, leaded-glass windows. Over their heads hung enormous iron-and-glass chandeliers, and beneath their feet were black-and-beige tile, original to the old station, according to something Brett had once read.

Smells of burgers, fries, and garlic made his stomach rumble. With his body operating on massive adrenaline overload, he'd already burned off his bagel and cream cheese.

Charles Pilcher's office was located at the far end of the station. Again, Brett held the door for Gemma as they went inside the office. Large paintings of mountain scenery, the nondescript kind hanging in just about every hotel room in Colorado, adorned pristine white walls. A high, shiny black reception desk stood front and center in the lobby, behind which sat a young woman in her thirties. A microphone headset stuck out from her mass of curly blond hair.

"Can I help you?" she asked with a bright smile that faded as she took in the embroidered badge on his shirt and the gun on his belt.

Brett tugged his creds from his back pocket. "I'm Special Agent Tanner with the ATF. We're here to see Charles Pilcher."

"Do you have an appointment?" she asked with significantly less enthusiasm.

"No. Tell him it's important."

The woman's lips pressed together. Brett had seen that look before on many a law firm receptionist's face when confronted by federal agents. She'd been trained with canned responses to any inquiries made by law enforcement. She looked down at something in front of her, flipping the pages. "I see Mr. Pilcher has an extremely busy schedule today." She handed him a business card. "Perhaps you'd like to call ahead next time for an appointment."

"Oh boy," Gemma muttered.

"Perhaps not." Brett ignored the offered card and rested his forearms on the top of the desk, leaning over it. On the desk was a magazine, not a scheduler or a tablet of any kind. "Perhaps you could tell Mr. Pilcher that federal agents would like to speak with him, that it's important, and that I'm sure he'd prefer speaking to us in the comfort of his own office rather than across town in front of a federal grand jury."

The woman bristled, then tapped her earpiece. "Mr. Pilcher, federal agents are here to see you. Would you like me to—" Her brows lowered. "Yes, sir." With obvious reluctance, Little Miss Sourpuss rounded the desk. "Follow me, please."

Gemma smirked. "What happened to all that Brett Tanner charm?"

He snorted. "It went out the window when she handed me a line of shit."

They were led down a short hallway, where Sourpuss rapped twice on a door before opening it. She stepped aside to let them pass. An unexpectedly smiling man, about five-eleven and forty years old, rose from an ornate, high-backed leather chair that reminded Brett of a throne. On the wall over Pilcher's head were various framed documents, including a diploma.

"Charles Pilcher," the man said, extending his hand first to Brett, then Gemma. "Please, have a seat," he said, still smiling, and Brett failed to detect any insincerity. "I always cooperate with law enforcement whenever I can. So what's this about?"

Gemma unzipped her portfolio and slipped out a pen as she arched a brow at Brett. She, too, understood that Charles Pilcher's attitude didn't jibe with that of his frosty receptionist's.

"Your name came up in an investigation." Brett let his words sink in, watching Pilcher's response. The man looked vaguely familiar.

"An investigation?" One side of Pilcher's mouth lifted, as if Brett's question were a joke and not a calculated salvo across the man's lawyerly bow. "You'll have to be more specific. I'm a personal injury attorney. I get involved in *lots* of investigations."

"I'm sure you do." Brett held the other man's gaze. "This one concerns arson."

Slowly, Pilcher's smile melted away. "I don't believe I have any arson cases on the books."

Now it was Brett's turn to smile. "I didn't say it was one of *your* cases. It's one of mine."

As pre-planned, Gemma whipped out a stack of documents she'd printed before they'd left her house—realty documents Pilcher had notarized for the twenty-three houses on Gemma's list. She handed him the pages. "Please look at these, and tell us if that's your signature and notary stamp."

Pilcher took the papers, then picked up a pair of gold, wire-framed glasses and put them on. Moments later, he tugged off the glasses and handed back the documents. "Yes, that's my signature, and that's my stamp."

"What's a personal injury attorney doing notarizing

documents for realty transactions?" Brett asked.

The man's gaze was rock steady. "It's a quick way to make extremely easy money. Colorado's cap on the fee a notary can charge is five dollars per signature, but the average real estate transaction requires multiple documents to be notarized. By the time a closing takes place, I can make up to a hundred dollars for a single residential purchase or sale in about five minutes of my time, plus the cost of ink. Commercial transactions are even more fruitful."

Brett nodded, pretending he didn't already know that. "So it's a side hustle."

"Exactly." Pilcher nodded in agreement.

Also, as preplanned, Gemma held up one of the deeds Pilcher had notarized. "This is a deed you notarized for a house in Colorado Springs on Torrance Lane. The house was purchased by Hawkin Construction. Do you remember notarizing this document?"

Pilcher shook his head. "Not specifically. But that is my signature and my stamp."

"Do you know anyone at Hawkin Construction? Michael or David Hawkin?"

"I can't say." He glanced at the document. "According to this deed, they were, indirectly, clients of mine, and as an attorney, I can't confirm or deny any knowledge of them."

Nice try, buddy. "You weren't representing them as an attorney for this transaction. You were only acting as a notary."

"True." He nodded. "But I'm still an attorney. It would be unethical for me to discuss this matter with any specifics."

In the long run, Brett didn't think that would pass legal scrutiny, but it was clear the man wasn't about to divulge anything and would keep falling back on attorney-client privilege. "Then let's talk generalities. You notarized Michael Hawkin's signature on that deed. Didn't he have to show ID, then sign the deed in your presence?"

"That is a requirement for notary services, so I'm sure he did."

Again, Brett scrutinized Pilcher's body language, but nothing the man had said so far pinged his bullshit meter.

"Something I'm curious about." Brett leaned back and crossed his arms. "This deed was filed in Colorado, but the title search was done by a company in Alaska. Kobuk Titling Agency. What's your connection to that company?"

Pilcher shrugged. "None really. I'm not even sure how they found me. I think they just wanted a local notary for transactions here in Colorado. I do quick turnarounds for lots of realtors, and they know they can rely on me."

"Have you ever actually met anyone from Kobuk Titling?" Gemma asked.

"No. Our initial conversations were by phone, but that was years ago. Now, all our transactions are by email. That's the way of the world these days, right?"

"I'd like to see one of these emails," Brett said, knowing he was pushing the boundaries of attorney-client privilege and wondering where the extent of Pilcher's cooperation would end.

Pilcher steepled his hands beneath his chin, looking thoughtful for a moment. "As much as I'd like to

cooperate fully, unfortunately, I'm unable to comply
with your request. All the documents emailed to me
by Kobuk Titling are for legal transactions, and I have
a duty as an attorney to protect the attorney-client
privilege. You understand."

Actually, Brett did. There were ways around that,
but any investigative proceedings involving an attorney would take him down a slippery slope and would
take time. He'd need a grand jury subpoena for
Pilcher's records and a long list of ATF and DOJ ap-
provals to obtain one.

"Can you at least provide a name, email address,
and a contact number for someone at Kobuk?"

Pilcher made a *hmph*ing sound. "I'm not certain
what this is all about, and you obviously don't want to
provide me with much information. While I do understand the federal government's need for discretion,
under these circumstances, I'd be more comfortable if
you reached out to Kobuk directly on your own. Since
I do work for Kobuk, I think that would be best."

Brett gave an answering *hmph*, intentionally mim-
icking Pilcher's tone. The man had deftly avoided
stepping into that patch of quicksand. He and
Gemma already had the listed address and phone
number for Kobuk Titling. Names and email addresses could be verified later. As for the email, another
subpoena might nail down the account holder and an
IP address.

"How do you get paid for your services?" Brett
asked. Another avenue to unmasking whoever was
behind Kobuk Titling was to follow the money trail.

"PayPal."

"Who do the payments come from?"

"A Kobuk account."

Brett went with a Hail Mary. He already knew what the response to his next question would be, but he had to ask. "Would you mind sharing one of those PayPal invoices or receipts?"

Pilcher's hands once again steepled beneath his chin, and his eyes narrowed. "Unfortunately, I can't provide that information, either. That document contains private account information that I'm not at liberty to divulge."

It had been worth a shot. Federal grand jury subpoena it was, then. "Gemma, anything else?"

She shook her head and began tucking the documents back into her portfolio.

"Thank you for your time, Mr. Pilcher." Brett stood, extending his hand across the desk.

"It's always a pleasure to help law enforcement." Pilcher took Brett's hand, shaking it enthusiastically. Above the man's head, Brett eyed the diploma on the wall. Prescott College—the same college Michael Hawkin had attended.

Sonofabitch.

"Thank you," Gemma said.

As they left Pilcher's office, steam built steadily between Brett's ears. "I know I've seen that guy somewhere before."

"You sure?" Gemma asked.

"Yeah." Brett nodded. "I just can't remember where." Not yet. The answer hovered somewhere in his head, just out of reach. And he couldn't be certain the graduation years were the same, but what were the chances that Michael Hawkin and Charles Pilcher had both graduated from the same college?

Slim to fucking none.

The man was lying. And he was a damned good actor.

CHAPTER TWENTY-THREE

"Well, what did you think?" Gemma asked.

During the walk back to the Expedition, Brett hadn't said a word. The only indication that he'd heard her question at all was the ticking of a muscle in his cheek. Even Blaze, who strolled between them, kept looking up at Brett, as if he, too, were inquiring about what was going on inside Brett's head.

They continued into Commons Park so Blaze could stretch his legs and do his stuff. The air was hot but dry, and a light breeze moderated the impact of the sun's rays. The park was busy, with people sitting on benches in the shade while they ate lunch, others running, biking, or strolling along the concrete trails bordering the South Platte River.

Brett stared across the grass field, deep in thought. This was turning into a repeat of their not-conversation in the SUV earlier. She knew he was driven by some inner demon to catch the arsonist, and she understood it. He wanted to nail whoever had torched the Torrance Lane house and killed those kids. But this silent treatment was getting to her. "Brett, I thought we were a team. This isn't what I signed up for, so don't shut me out."

"He's lying."

Blaze sat between them, his golden eyes riveted on Brett.

"Who's lying? Pilcher?" She hadn't detected so much as a whisper of untruth from the man's responses.

"Did you see the diploma on the wall?" Finally, Brett turned to face her. "It's from Prescott College. He and Hawkin went to the *same* college."

"I didn't notice." She gave herself a mental slap. Brett's trained investigator's eye had picked up on that, but she hadn't and felt stupid for the oversight. "But Arizona's a border state with Colorado. That still could be nothing more than a coincidence." The moment she'd said the word—*coincidence*—she realized how silly that sounded. Before interviewing Pilcher, there'd already been more than enough coincidences on this case to fill a roll-off dumpster, and now this. "I see what you mean. But where do we go from here? If we approach Pilcher again, he'll only keep playing the attorney-client privilege card."

"I agree. What we need is a subpoena for his records for something that will tie all this together." Relief shot through her at Brett's use of the word *we* again. "If I'm right, Charles Pilcher is doing more than just notarizing deeds. As an attorney, he can provide legal coverage and keep spewing attorney-client privilege to protect not only himself but the Hawkin brothers."

Gemma thought back to all the evidence they had and all they *didn't* have. If she inserted Pilcher and the Hawkin brothers into all the blanks in her charts and spider diagram, all their theories about Hawkin began taking better shape.

"What I'd like to get," Brett continued, "is a search warrant for his office and his computer, but that won't happen based on coincidence. We need probable cause, and we still don't have it. Getting a subpoena for an attorney is going to be a bitch."

He led them into the shade where Blaze plopped down on the grass, then rolled onto his back, kicking his legs in the air. Brett pulled out his cell phone. When his boss answered, he lowered the volume. "Lori, I'm here with Gemma Scott. We just interviewed an attorney we think is up to his eyeballs in all of this. As an attorney, he's in a position to provide legal coverage for the entire fraudulent scheme of buying houses, burning them down, then collecting on the insurance."

After Brett had provided a rundown on the details, including the subpoenas he wanted for Pilcher's records and both Pilcher's and Kobuk Titling's PayPal accounts, Lori said, "You know that going after an attorney requires HQ and DOJ approval. Write it up. Fill out the forms, cite all your evidence, cross every *t*, and dot every *i*."

"Will do," Brett said, nodding.

"This will take a while," Lori added. "If we're lucky, we can have those subpoenas in a couple of weeks."

Brett frowned. "A couple of *weeks*?"

Gemma understood his frustration. Every day that passed was more time for critical evidence to take a walk.

A sigh came through the phone. "I hear where you're coming from, but we need to do this the right way. Don't go near this attorney again until you have that subpoena in your back pocket."

Brett shoved a hand through his hair. "Yes, ma'am."

"And by the way," Lori said. "DNA from that cigarette stub you collected at the warehouse came back with a match. It belongs to John Nash. Do you have enough to arrest him for that fire?"

"Not sure. He has a history of arson, but no convictions. His DNA puts him at the scene. It *should* be enough, but the U.S. Attorney's Office always wants more. For all we know, he could be just a witness. I need to talk to Nash first."

To do that, they'd have to find him.

"Keep me posted."

"Will do." Brett ended the call.

Blaze finished rolling around and leaped to his feet, shaking off a few blades of dried grass. Brett reached down, unerringly finding his dog's head. The look of exasperation on his face echoed her own thoughts. He wanted to nail these people so badly. What would happen if he didn't? The answer was obvious.

His determination would turn into an unhealthy obsession. Maybe it already had.

Brett's phone rang again. This time, he didn't put it on speaker, and she couldn't see who the caller was.

Nearly a full minute passed, and with every second, his eyes narrowed more. "What's the exact location?" Another few seconds ticked by. "We're on our way."

Brett shoved the phone back onto his belt, then dragged a hand down his face. "We finally got a hit on that BOLO I put out on Johnny Nash. That was the Colorado State Patrol in Briggsdale. Nash's body was found in an oil field. Three gunshots to the chest."

CHAPTER TWENTY-FOUR

Brett slowed as he turned onto Weld County Road 68, heading for Briggsdale and into the heartland of Colorado's oil and gas production. His jaw was starting to ache from clenching it so hard. A big missing piece of the puzzle had just been blown away. Literally.

Gemma sipped quietly on a coffee they'd grabbed before leaving Denver and picking up lunch. Blaze stared out the kennel window, his nose pressed to the glass, as if he were watching the scenery whiz by.

They'd been on the road for over an hour, heading to the northeast part of the state near the Wyoming border. Ten miles ago, they'd left the green, irrigated, and circular-shaped fields behind. The single lane road they were on now was surrounded on both sides by dry-as-a-bone irrigation ditches and fields. In the distance, oil derricks loomed tall and proud.

With Weld County spewing out 85 percent of the state's crude oil and around 50 percent of the state's natural gas production, it was no wonder. Farmers and ranchers had long ago figured out that selling or leasing their fields to the oil and gas companies was far more lucrative than ranching or agriculture.

Gemma yawned, holding her hand over her mouth. This had already been a long day and was fixing to be even longer. Through it all, she hadn't complained once, and he admired her for that. Even though this was the job—long hours and many a night away from home—half the agents he worked with would already have been whining about getting home for dinner and a cold beer.

Following specific mile-marker directions given to him by the CSP trooper, Brett turned onto an unmarked, unpaved, rutted dirt road, one of many in this area used by trucking companies to access the derricks and above-ground holding tanks.

Brett hadn't had a reason to be in this part of the state in a long time, and he'd forgotten just how rustic and isolated it was.

Dust clouds billowed around them. The Expedition rocked and rolled, the front bumper occasionally hitting the road as the SUV dipped low into one of the deep ruts created by heavy tanker trucks.

"Wow." Gemma reached for the grab handle above the door. "I've never been out here. My job takes me to where there are houses, not where there's nothing."

Brett eased his foot off the gas, maneuvering around a particularly deep pothole. "Good place to dump a body."

They drove for what seemed like another half mile but was probably only a few hundred feet. The road was still rutted but had turned muddy from a recent rainstorm. Up ahead, a police barricade had been set up. Beyond that was a cluster of CSP and Weld County Sheriff's Office vehicles. A state trooper in a sky-blue shirt, gray slacks, and Smokey Bear hat came around the barricade.

Brett rolled down the window and held up his ID. "Special Agent Tanner, ATF. Trooper Rollins here?"

"She's over there." The trooper pointed to the cluster of official vehicles, then began moving the barricade.

"Thanks," Brett called out as they drove past. He parked next to a gray van—the Weld County Coroner's Office vehicle. He grabbed a notepad and stuck it in the thigh pocket of his pants. "Let's do this." The moment he stepped outside, his boots sunk a full inch into the mud. Just before closing the door, Blaze let out a sad little whine. Unlike many human agents Brett had worked with over the years, if his dog wasn't working, he wasn't happy.

"Bye, Blaze." Gemma scratched Blaze's ears, then closed her door and walked with Brett to where a group of officers stood off to the side of the road, staring into the adjacent field.

One of the CSP troopers, a tall woman with a long brown braid hanging down her back, turned. She glanced at his shirt. "Agent Tanner?" When he nodded, she held out her hand. "Trooper Rollins."

"This is my partner." He indicated Gemma. "Agent Scott with the NICB."

Rollins's brows rose, but she didn't question what an NICB agent was doing out in the middle of an oil field. As Gemma had said, this wasn't her usual turf.

While the two women shook hands, Brett eyed the crime scene about fifty feet into the field, near an old, rusty oil derrick. An irregularly shaped area had been staked out with yellow tape, inside of which a tech snapped photos and another made notes on a clipboard. A path leading from the road to the scene was taped off, leading Brett to believe it was also part of the crime scene.

"The coroner's investigator is still working the scene." Rollins tipped her head to the field. "He's been in there for hours. Said he'd be out soon to give us an update. What does the victim have to do with your case?"

"He's a suspect in an arson investigation."

"Then I think your case is closed," Rollins said drily.

Maybe not. "Do you have an approximate TOD?"

"Maybe a couple of days. We're waiting on the investigator." She grimaced. "It's pretty gruesome. The body's been chewed up by foxes, coyotes, and magpies gnawing on it. I was first on scene and could barely make out the bullet holes in the guy's chest."

He and Gemma exchanged glances. If Nash had only been dead for two days, he could have set the warehouse fires, and they still couldn't completely rule out the possibility he had something to do with the Leadville and Burlington fires. But he doubted Nash had been the shooter at Piggly's or was Gemma's attacker. Nash's description didn't fit those suspects.

In Brett's estimation, David Hawkin was still looking good for those crimes.

"Who found the body?" Brett asked.

"Some oil workers. They came here to service the derrick. This one's old and off the beaten path. That's why they didn't find it sooner. They didn't see the body at first." The trooper wrinkled her nose. "But they smelled it."

"Why is this section here taped off?" Gemma pointed to the path leading from the road, through the field, and right up to the crime scene that had been taped off on either side. The short grass was slightly more tamped down than the surrounding area. "Was the body dragged into the field?"

Rollins nodded. "That's what we think."

Good observation, not that Brett was surprised. Gemma had excellent investigative instincts.

"He could have been killed on the side of the road," Brett suggested. "Or anywhere else, for that matter, then dragged through the field, so the body wouldn't be discovered quickly."

"Exactly," Rollins said. "If workers hadn't shown up to service the derrick, it could have been months before he was found."

With all the predators out there, by then, there would have been nothing left but a pile of bones.

A stocky man wearing khakis, a blue polo shirt, and tight-fitting blue gloves walked toward them from the crime scene, skirting the taped-off drag trail.

"These people are with the ATF," Rollins said. "This is Investigator Peter Chu with the coroner's office."

"What can we do for the feds today?" Chu asked.

"I had a BOLO out on the deceased," Brett said. "He was wanted for questioning in an arson investigation. What can you tell us?"

"Despite the condition of the body, I estimate he was killed approximately two days ago, but I need about a week's worth of testing to confirm that. We can just barely make out GSWs to the chest, three of them. Animals have been feeding on the body. If it weren't for the driver's license in his wallet, we would have had a hard time ID'ing him without dental records. Most of the tips of his fingers have been chewed off."

"We'd like to see the body," Brett said.

"Follow me."

Before they'd gotten within twenty feet of the crime scene, a whisper of a breeze brought with it the putrid odor of decaying flesh. Chu lifted the yellow tape for them to walk under. Cameras clicked as two CSU guys took close-up shots.

Nash had been thirty years old, five-nine, and weighed one-sixty, according to his rap sheet. What remained of the man was every bit as gruesome as both Rollins and Chu had described.

Nash lay on his back. Half the man's face was gone, revealing most of his teeth in a gruesome, macabre smile. As Chu had said, the tips of his fingers were all but gone. In the upper right portion of his chest were small holes in the once-white T-shirt Nash wore. What remained of skin was covered with dirt and black residue Brett surmised was dried blood.

Other than funeral service viewings, for which a mortician had cleaned, prepped, and dressed the deceased to look the same as he or she had been prior to death, most people never saw a dead body. Gemma's face had paled considerably, but he saw no signs of imminent puking. She'd seen the charred body in the Frodo warehouse, but this was different, even more gruesome, and she was still holding it together.

Several orange evidence markers had been set by boot prints in the mud, but no shell casings, giving more credence to the theory that Nash had been killed elsewhere, or the shooter may have picked up the shells. "Any slugs in or under the body?" If there were, they could be compared to the casings Blaze

had found at Piggly's, and both the casings and projectiles the ATF lab would collect after firing David
Hawkin's seized 9mm.

"We were just about to check." Chu signaled to
one of the CSU guys. "Let's roll him over."

Chu and the other man took position at Nash's
shoulders and legs, carefully rolling the body onto its
side. Gemma gulped. Masses of squirming maggots
spilled from three holes in Nash's back onto the
ground.

That answered one question. The GSWs were
through-and-throughs. There'd be no slugs found in
the body. Even if this was the kill location, which
Brett doubted, the slugs could have penetrated as far
as twelve inches into the ground.

Chu frowned. "I can't tell if there are any holes in
the soil. We think he was dragged here from the road.
Either way, I'd have to go back to the office for a
metal detector."

"No need," Brett said. "I may have something better. Are you just about done documenting the scene?"
Rollins had already told him the deputy coroner investigator and his team had been here for hours.

"Boys?" Chu looked at his CSU team, both of
whom nodded. "Aside from bagging the body, yes."

"We'll be back in five." He touched his hand to the
small of Gemma's back, urging her ahead of him. At
the back of his SUV, he lifted the tailgate and grabbed
a bottle of water that he handed to her. She uncapped
it, then gulped down half the bottle.

"Better?" he asked.

She nodded and gave him a grateful smile. "Poor
Sally," she said after taking another sip. "I wonder if

they've notified her yet. She'll be devastated. Her brother wasn't exactly a pillar of society, but he was still her family. I'll call her in a day or two, see if there's anything I can do to help."

He watched her take another sip of water, amazed that, despite what she'd just seen, Gemma had the empathy to think of Nash's sister and how this would affect her.

"I think she'd appreciate that." He flipped open the lid of his evidence kit and tugged out a fresh pair of gloves and several evidence bags that he stuffed in his pocket. He snagged Blaze's leash, then popped open the kennel. "Come with me," he called out. "You can take photos if Blaze finds anything."

"Blaze? I thought he was an accelerant-detecting dog."

"He is. Blaze, sit." His dog was so excited about going to work that his body wriggled so hard and fast Brett couldn't snap on the leash. Finally, Blaze sat, his tail whipping back and forth with such exuberance, bits of mud flew in every direction, one landing on Brett's leg. A bath was definitely in both their futures. "Blaze flunked out of explosives detection school. That doesn't mean he can't find shell casings. He found the ones at Piggly's."

Brett led Blaze back to where Chu and his team were busy bagging up Nash's body. Most of the maggots had dispersed, wriggling away in search of their next meal. Brett pointed to where the body had lain. "Seek."

Blaze put his snout close to the ground, his nostrils flaring. He circled several times, trying to pick up a scent. From his body language, Brett doubted there was anything there. Even twelve-inch-deep slugs would leave a scent trail from where they entered the surface. Then again, finding black powder wasn't his dog's forte.

He let Blaze off the leash, allowing him to search a broader area in less time. If the shots that entered Nash's body had been fired in the vicinity while Nash had been standing up, the slugs could have traveled a great distance.

Brett used arm signals to send Blaze farther into the field. They watched him traverse a broad area, occasionally circling back, his head down and his tail whipping in the air.

"How long does this take?" Gemma asked.

In truth, he and Blaze could spend an entire day out here searching. But with the drag trail, he really didn't think Nash had been killed here. "We'll try something else."

He whistled, and Blaze loped over, eagerly awaiting Brett's next command. Brett pointed ahead to the taped-off drag trail. "Seek." Blaze trotted under the tape. As he reached the edge of the road, his gait increased.

Brett gestured to Gemma. "Follow me. He might be on to something."

By the time they caught up, Blaze's circles had become tighter. He'd walked past the entrance to the drag trail and sniffed a particularly muddy patch on the edge of the road, then sat.

Trooper Rollins and several others who'd been watching joined them. Every cop knew the signs.

Blaze had just alerted on something.

Brett tugged the gloves from his pocket and snapped them on. "Take a few shots before I dig in."

He waited while Gemma used her cell phone to take several pictures, then he crouched in front of Blaze and began sifting his fingers through the mud. A couple of inches down, his fingers contacted something hard. A cylindrical object.

A shell casing.

He tugged it from the mud and held it up for Gemma to snap another shot.

"Holy cow," Rollins said. "So he was shot right here on the edge of the road, then dragged into the field. We never would have found that."

"Not without a metal detector," Chu chimed in as he and the CSU guys carried out the black bag containing Nash's body.

True that. But it would have taken you longer. Blaze had probably saved the locals at least a day of searching.

Brett dug around for a few more minutes in the same general area before coming up with two more casings. More hushed expletives came from the other officers. After Gemma photographed the additional casings, Brett deposited them in an evidence bag.

He whipped off his gloves, then dug out a liver treat for Blaze, who scarfed it down the way Brett would have hoovered the brisket at Piggly's Smokehouse. He thumped his hand on his chest, and Blaze rose on his hind legs, resting them on Brett's shirt and leaving behind muddy paw prints. Brett didn't care. Blaze had more than earned the praise. "Good boy. *Good boy!*"

Gemma started clapping. The other cops joined in.

When Blaze had lowered down to all fours, Brett did his best to wipe off his shirt. The muddy residue felt oily to the touch. Not surprising, given they were

in an oil field. He stared at his fingers, rubbing them
together and recalling something he'd deposited in
that folder for weird, inexplicable shit.

"What is it?" Gemma asked.

"This mud," he answered, putting the pieces together. "It's oily."

She gasped, and her eyes went wide. "That New
Mexico state trooper said Hawkin left *oily* mud in the
back of his patrol car."

"Yeah, and oil can be fingerprinted." He'd never
worked that kind of case, but he'd heard from a Coast
Guard agent that it could be done.

"What do you mean, it can be fingerprinted?"

"The Coast Guard has a lab that can compare oil
samples. It's similar to human fingerprint comparison." He whipped out another evidence bag and
scooped up a mud sample, one with a discernible
sheen on the surface. "Wait here."

He headed back into the field where the body had
been dumped and grabbed another oily mud sample.
Back at the road, he held up both plastic evidence
bags, turning them until the sunlight hit on the oil's
iridescence.

"If these spent shell casings match the ones from
Piggly's, that puts the same gun at both locations. If
this oily *mud* matches what's in the back of Trooper
Sanchez's patrol car, that would put David Hawkin at
this location, too." And push them way past coinci-
dental and into the solid, indictable evidence zone.

That was, if Trooper Sanchez hadn't had his patrol
car cleaned yet. Maybe they'd get lucky.

CHAPTER TWENTY-FIVE

At seven a.m., the Denver Special Ops Task Force office was quiet. Only a few agents working heavy cases were in at this hour, Brett being one of them.

The other two desks in the office reserved for the K-9 squad were empty. Not even Deck or Evan had come in yet. The only sounds came from the hole puncher as Brett punched holes in the copies of the chains of custody and packing slips.

He slid the pages over the metal fasteners in his official case file and pressed down on the metal tabs. With any luck, the express carrier he'd just relinquished the spent shell casings to would arrive at the ATF lab in Walnut Creek, California, by the end of the day. The mud samples, having been shipped to the Coast Guard laboratory in New London, Connecticut, probably wouldn't arrive there until tomorrow morning.

Blaze slurped water from a bowl in the corner of the office, then settled on his bolster bed.

Heavy boots echoed in the hallway. A moment later, Deck sauntered in.

"Heard you guys had a busy day yesterday." Deck leaned down to give Blaze a pat on his head. "Heard *you* did *real* good, buddy."

Blaze gave a throaty sigh, as if discovering critical evidence in a homicide investigation was all in a day's work.

Deck sat on a corner of another desk. "Rumor has

it the dead guy up north was a person of interest in your arson case."

More boots sounded in the hallway, then Evan stalked in, carrying a stack of files. "Morning, ladies."

"Thor and Blue in their kennels?" Their dogs all knew each other, but sometimes three alpha canines in one room was too much dog for one small office.

Both men nodded.

Evan dropped the files on his desk. "What's with the dead guy?"

"Johnny Nash was our best lead." Brett stood to open a file cabinet and tucked his case file in the top drawer. "We're pretty sure he torched a warehouse down in the Springs, but he could have confirmed that Michael Hawkin paid him to set the Torrance Lane fire."

Deck whistled. "Didn't realize all this was connected to that case."

Evan sat behind his desk. "What's the connection?"

"Johnny Nash is—or, rather, *was*—the connection." Conveniently, the man was dead. Yet another in a long list of coincidences and convenient aspects of the case that was getting longer every day. "Gemma found a common thread between that fire and more than twenty others over the last few years. That's what convinced me to work with her on this."

For the next ten minutes, Brett brought his friends up to speed on Gemma's research and their recent findings, including David Hawkin getting arrested in New Mexico.

"Could David Hawkin or Charles Pilcher have hired Nash?" Deck asked.

"For that matter," Evan suggested, "could Pilcher or David Hawkin have set the Torrance Lane fire?"

"I don't see Pilcher getting his hands dirty, but I do see him as the brains behind Kobuk Titling and all the phony documents." Brett rested his arm on top of the file cabinet. "I suppose it's possible that David Hawkin could have done it, but he'd already moved to New Mexico and started his own business by then. He was never a suspect, and nobody ever interviewed him. But what Sally Nash said about a contractor up north owing her brother a favor for a problem Nash took care of for him points to Michael Hawkin right here in Denver."

"What about Nash?" Deck asked. "Are either of the Hawkin brothers good for his murder?"

"Maybe." Brett nodded. "I just sent out some mud samples that may put David Hawkin at the scene of Nash's murder. If we go with the approximate TOD the coroner's investigator gave us, David Hawkin could have killed Nash in the oil field, then driven south, back to New Mexico the same night. The timing is about right. That New Mexico state trooper said he pulled Hawkin over in Raton two nights ago."

"With oily, muddy boots and an unlicensed 9mm," Deck added.

"Close to a slam dunk," Evan said.

Nothing in law enforcement ever was, but that was about as close as it could get.

"You said you already made a run at Michael Hawkin," Deck said. "Any chance of talking to David Hawkin?"

"That's the plan," Brett said. "If ballistics confirms all the shell casings came from the gun the New

Mexico State Police seized, I'll get an arrest warrant.
If the mud samples match, that will be the icing on the
cake. I have a trooper down there keeping an eye on
the guy."

The first call he'd made yesterday after leaving the
oil field was to Trooper Sanchez, who'd been working
a midnight tour and hadn't come on shift yet. Brett
had left a message requesting Sanchez to *not* clean
out the back of his patrol car until he'd grabbed a
mud sample.

"So"—Deck grinned slyly—"all this came from
Gemma approaching you with her evidence and her
theories?"

Deck and Evan exchanged looks, Evan's equally
amused. In Brett's experience, Evan was rarely
amused to the point where he actually smiled. His
friend was sporting one now.

"She's quite a woman," Evan said.

"She's an outstanding *investigator*," Brett said,
ignoring Evan's implication, even though his friend
was right. Gemma *was* quite a woman. Unfortunately, not *his* woman. Much as he was beginning to
wish otherwise. When his friends continued smirk-
ing, Brett changed the subject. "Any luck finding
Gavin Aldrich's sister?"

The smirk on Evan's face disappeared faster than
a rainbow. "I've got a solid lead. I should have something soon."

"Thanks, man. I'll stop by to see Gavin later today.
I'll let him know."

"Good morning, gentleman." Lori Olywule came
in holding a steaming mug of coffee.

His boss was a hard worker, usually in the office

long before the rest of her staff.

Lori blew on her coffee. "I coordinated your sub-poena requests with the U.S. Attorney's Office and HQ. We're in a holding pattern."

"Thanks." Lori's investigative experience and effi-ciency were legendary, something Brett appreciated. It allowed him to concentrate his efforts in the field, rather than getting stifled by government red tape.

Brett's cell phone rang. *NMSP* lit the screen. "Tanner," Brett said.

"This is Trooper Sanchez. I got your message, and you're in luck. I didn't get around to cleaning my car yet, so I took a sample of the mud. It's dry, but it's still there. What do you want me to do with it?"

Hot damn.

"I'll give you an address to ship it to. It's the U.S. Coast Guard lab in Connecticut." Brett forwarded the lab's contact info to Sanchez, along with his own email address. "Treat this as evidence. Do a chain of custody and send me a copy of the chain and the packing slip."

"Will do," Sanchez said. "And I'm not sure where David Hawkin is. No vehicle in the carport for the last twenty-four hours, and his house was dark last night. I'll keep you posted."

Did David Hawkin know they were looking for him? That was something he had to consider. In the last few days, they'd interviewed Michael Hawkin and Charles Pilcher. One of those interviews had set something in motion.

"What is it?" Lori asked when Brett had ended the call.

"David Hawkin may be in the wind. I think the

second we walked out of Michael Hawkin's and Charles Pilcher's offices, one or both of them called David to warn him."

"That's a possibility," Lori agreed. "But you need to wait for the lab results to come back and for the subpoenas. Understood?"

"Understood," Brett said reluctantly. Every minute that passed was another opportunity for evidence to disappear and for co-conspirators to get their stories straight.

. . .

Two hours later, Brett left the Pine Springs Mental Health Treatment Center. He'd wanted to make good on his promise to Gavin Aldrich and the court about being a big brother and mentor to the kid.

Aside from petting Blaze and throwing a ball for him in the center's recreational area, Gavin hadn't said much. Until Brett had notified him that Evan was making headway on finding his sister. The hesitant smile on Gavin's face had more than made up for his boss ramming her stand-down order down Brett's throat again.

He put Blaze up in the kennel, then headed from the lot. As he took the ramp for I-25, he began tapping a finger on the wheel.

The attorney was the key to everything. Brett might not be able to prove it yet, but Charles Pilcher was full of shit. With his acting skills, the man could have been a Broadway star.

Images of the framed Prescott College diploma on the wall over Pilcher's desk sprang to mind, as did the one on Michael Hawkin's office wall, the one right next to the photo of Hawkin and two other men standing in front of an airplane.

Something started meshing in Brett's memory.

He flipped on the turn signal and slowed, pulling onto the shoulder. Traffic whizzed by, rocking the SUV. Blaze stuck his head through the kennel window, snorting and blowing warm breath on Brett's neck.

Holy shit.

Now he knew why Pilcher looked familiar. And from what he remembered of the DMV photo, one of the other men in the photo *could* have been David Hawkin.

The other was Charles Pilcher. He'd been wearing a visor, concealing part of his face, but it was definitely him. He'd said he didn't know Michael Hawkin.

Pilcher had been lying. About *everything*, Brett now guessed, and he also assumed that the second he and Gemma had walked out of Pilcher's office, the man had been on the phone with *both* Hawkin brothers.

Lori's orders screamed so loudly they might as well have been tattooed on his brain, but so were the faces of those two kids who died last year. He owed it to them and to every other future victim of this conspiracy to put a stop to it. And he owed it to Ryan and Cody.

Battling the guilt over surviving that fire when he was a kid might be a war he'd be stuck waging for the rest of his life. The only thing that could possibly ease it and help him atone for surviving when Ryan and Cody hadn't was to nail the Hawkin brothers and Charles Pilcher.

Brett pulled back onto the highway. He knew what

he had to do. It could very well cost him his job, but it was the *right* thing to do. In his mind, it was the *only* thing to do.

He punched it, rocketing the Expedition up to ninety as he headed north, back to Denver. Gemma would be pissed, but he had to leave her out of this. He could be walking into a career-ending shitstorm, and he didn't want her caught in the fallout. He cared about her too much. Hell, it was more than that.

He was falling for her. He didn't know when that had happened, but it had.

In the week since he'd known her, he'd come to understand many things about Gemma, things he hadn't expected.

The tough facade she showed the world wasn't a facade at all. She *was* tough as nails, but behind those steel walls was a soft spot for dogs and struggling, unwed mothers with newborns. For abused and abandoned young men like Gavin Aldrich.

And for *him*. When they'd talked about his burns, what he'd glimpsed in her eyes was pain. *His* pain, for what he'd been through and was *still* going through.

That tough shell would protect Gemma from many things, but the tender side of her could still be hurt professionally *and* personally.

Brett pounded the wheel with his fist. Shithead that he was, he'd already done one of those and was about to do the other.

· · ·

The same receptionist greeted Brett. "Good morning. May I help you?"

"Is he in?" Brett hitched his head in the direction of Pilcher's office.

"Yes, but do you have—"

"An appointment? I do now." Brett blew past the receptionist, heading toward the back office. He flung open the door with enough force to intentionally cause it to smack against the wall.

Pilcher shot up from his chair as if he'd been goosed. Surprise and fear lit the man's face. "What are you doing? You can't just barge in here."

"Mr. Pilcher!" the receptionist shouted behind Brett. "Do you want me to call the police?"

"First of all," Brett threw over his shoulder, never taking his eyes off Pilcher, "I *am* the police. Secondly, I have a feeling that when Mr. Pilcher hears what I have to say, he won't want anyone else around."

Unlike the first time they'd met, Pilcher's bravado slipped, a sliver of worry evident in his eyes. "That's all right, Mina."

Brett all but slammed the door in Mina's face. "Have a seat, Pilcher. I have a story to tell you. Most of it you already know."

Slowly, Pilcher sank onto his chair, the steaming mug of coffee and half-eaten pastry wisely forgotten. "What do you want?"

"Answers." Rather than sit, Brett rested his hands on Pilcher's desk and leaned in. "You lied to us. You *do* know Michael Hawkin. You not only went to the same college"—he flicked his gaze to the diploma—"but he took you flying. You're in a photo on the wall in his office."

Pilcher sneered. "So what?"

Brett sneered back. "So making a false statement

to a federal officer is a felony. You can get up to five years in prison for that alone." Unlikely, but it was in the Federal Criminal Code and Rules, and even a personal injury attorney would know it. "Why did you lie to us?"

As expected, Pilcher clammed up. Any half-assed attorney would be smart enough not to make incriminating statements. But Brett was patient.

"That's all right." Brett straightened, crossing his arms. "I *know* why. You, Michael Hawkin, and David Hawkin are behind at least twenty-three fires in Colorado over the past four years. You created phony documents: titles, deeds, insurance policies, all with the names of people who don't exist. Then you burned down the houses, collected on the insurance and pricy riders, sold the land, and moved on to the next property."

Pilcher fisted his manicured hands on the desk, his knuckles as white as his shirt. "I assure you I haven't burned down *any* houses."

"Of course not." Brett snorted. "You'd never get your hands dirty. You're the brains behind Kobuk Titling Agency and all the phony documents in this conspiracy. I'm getting subpoenas as we speak to track down every bit of information on Kobuk Titling and your PayPal accounts. The money trail never lies." He'd have to add bank subpoenas to the list, but Pilcher didn't need to know that.

Pilcher's eyes widened a fraction, but he remained silent. The man needed a little push.

"You're an attorney, so you know that every co-conspirator can be charged with the same crimes committed by others in the conspiracy, even if *he* didn't physically commit them." Now for the coup de grace. "Including murder."

Pilcher's eyes flared wider. The fear that had been mostly banked until now screamed from the man's face. "What the hell are you talking about?"

"For starters, did you know that someone tried to shoot me and strangle my partner in her own home? That's one count of attempted murder and one count of attempted murder of a federal officer." Pilcher swallowed. "Did you know that Johnny Nash's body was found in an oil field? He was shot to death. That's another murder I'll tack on to your rap sheet."

"*What*?" Beneath his suit jacket, Pilcher's chest rose and fell faster. He began shaking his head, and his complexion had turned whiter than milk, telling Brett one thing.

Pilcher's reaction had been too severe. He'd bet Pilcher hadn't known Nash was dead.

"Johnny Nash set the Torrance Lane fire, didn't he? *Didn't* he?" Brett slammed the heels of his hands onto the desk, making Pilcher flinch violently and sending coffee sloshing over the top of the mug. "You're in this up to your eyeballs, and it doesn't matter if you didn't pull the trigger."

Again, Pilcher swallowed and began sucking in shallow breaths. "I don't know anything about Nash getting shot, and I don't know anything about what happened at the Torrance Lane house. Michael owned that house outright. Anything that happened there after he bought that property is on him. *Not* me."

"Wanna bet?" Brett snarled. "You're a part of this conspiracy, and that fire was intentionally set. That makes it murder. Do you have any idea what it's like to be burned alive?" He didn't wait for a response. "I'll tell you." He leaned down, getting in Pilcher's face. The man's gaze fixated on the disfigured flesh on Brett's arm. "At first, it stings, and you try to get away from the flames, but you can't. Then you experience the most unimaginable, excruciating pain as the fire feasts on your skin. If you're lucky, you'll die of suffocation before that ever happens. If not, eventually the fire will burn away your nerve endings and you'll feel nothing at all. When your body temperature rises above one hundred five degrees, enzymes can't function. You'll go into organ failure and shock. It can take as long as two or three hours for your body to fully burn. If your skeleton is still on fire, your bones will turn to ash."

Pilcher's white complexion had turned a grotesque shade of Wicked Witch of the West–green. He covered his mouth with his hand. A gurgling sound came from his throat as he leaned over and puked into a garbage can.

When the retching had subsided to dry heaves, Pilcher plucked several tissues from a box on his desk and wiped his mouth. "What happened to those kids was an accident. I had nothing to do with it. It was a legitimate purchase made by Hawkin Construction. All I did was create the title and the deed."

"Did you and Michael discuss the house being a money pit and that he needed to get rid of it fast?"

"Y-yes."

"So he paid Nash to torch it for him on a specific day and at a specific time. That way, he could set up an airtight alibi. Say it." Every admission had to be verbal, or it was worthless.

"I don't know anything about that."

"You're lying."

"I'm *not*." Pilcher's lips compressed into a tight line. "Michael didn't discuss burning down that house with me."

"But you knew all those other houses would be burned down. Didn't you?" Pilcher nodded. "Say it. Yes or no."

"Yes. I knew, but *I* didn't burn down *anything*. That was all Michael and David. All I did was create documents and insurance policies."

"Did David Hawkin shoot Nash?" They'd still need the labs' analyses on the mud and shell casings, but Pilcher's statements would corroborate the findings.

"I don't know." Pilcher wiped his mouth again with a clean tissue. "I didn't know they were going to kill him."

"But you knew something." That much was evident.

He nodded. "Nash went to prison for burglary right after the Torrance Lane fire. When he got out, nobody would hire him. Michael did, then Nash started blackmailing him. That's all I know."

"What did Nash have on Michael Hawkin?" Brett knew the answer to that question, but still had no proof. *The Torrance Lane fire.*

"I don't know, I swear it. I asked Michael about it, but he wouldn't say what. Only that Nash was a punk and a pain in the ass."

Still not enough to charge Hawkin. "Did Michael's wife have anything to do with this?"

"No, she doesn't know a thing. Their marriage is on the rocks, and she's getting ready to leave him."

That explained the frosty vibes he and Gemma had gotten when they'd interviewed Michael at his office. The wife's eyes had been shooting daggers at her husband.

Brett straightened, a mixture of excitement *and* disappointment shooting through his system. He might be in a world of shit when this was over, but at least Pilcher had cracked half the case wide open. They still didn't have anything solid on who set the Torrance Lane fire and who was really behind it. That part of the case was still circumstantial. Without something more, an AUSA would never charge Michael Hawkin for killing those kids. The wheels of justice had been set in motion, but they still weren't rolling smoothly down the track.

Pilcher sagged in his chair, then lowered his face into his hands. "What will you do next?" he mumbled.

"Sit tight. Do nothing. Say nothing. If you contact the Hawkin brothers in any way, shape, or form, I'll add obstruction to the list of charges you're facing. If you're a good boy, I'll let the prosecutor know you cooperated." Some, at least.

Back in the Expedition, Blaze wagged his tail and wriggled his body at the prospect of finally seeing some action. "Sorry, buddy." He gave his dog a good scrubbing beneath the chin, then tugged the hem of his polo shirt from his pants and peeled off the slim digital recorder taped to his chest, relishing the sting as a few chest hairs came with it.

A federal agent wearing a wire without preapproval wasn't illegal in Colorado, but it *did* violate agency and DOJ policy in this judicial district to record a conversation without someone's knowledge, particularly an attorney.

He took his phone off mute and noticed a missed call and a text from Gemma. *Where are you?*

His boss first, then Gemma. Both the women in his life would be royally pissed at him. The only question was who would be *more* pissed.

"Lori," Brett said when his boss answered. "I've got everything we need to get search and arrest warrants. I just came from Charles Pilcher's office. He confessed and gave up the Hawkin brothers."

His boss's next words made Brett's gut clench to the point where, if he'd been standing, he would have doubled over in agony.

CHAPTER TWENTY-SIX

"I've been suspended. I'm off the case." Brett shoved a hand through his hair.

"*What*?" Gemma took in Brett's appearance. He looked like hell. One side of his short hair stuck out in several different directions like he'd run a rake through it a dozen times. "Come inside."

Instead of Blaze stopping to give his usual greeting, he began following Brett as he paced around the living room.

"It's my own fault." Absently, he stopped and rested his hand on Blaze's head, as if unconsciously absorbing some kind of much needed canine support.

"Come here and sit down. Tell me what happened." Using a rag, she swept sawdust off the sofa, then sat. Worry parked itself dead center in her head. It was nearly six o'clock. While she'd been typing up NICB reports, she'd been wondering where he'd been all day. Now, she wasn't sure she wanted to know. The suspicious part of her brain told her he'd ditched her and gone off on his own. The woman in her couldn't believe he'd do that. Especially after everything that had passed between them.

Brett sat, and Blaze lay down at their feet. The dog watched him with big, sad eyes. Brett leaned back and pinched the bridge of his nose. Whatever had gone down had been bad. No words were needed to tell her that much. She sat on the opposite side of the sofa and waited.

The sigh Brett made was more of a groan. "You'll hate me when I tell you what I did."

"Maybe." God, she hoped not. "But you won't know for sure until you do."

"Do you remember when we were leaving Pilcher's office? I said I thought I'd seen him somewhere before. I did. On the wall in the Hawkin Construction office. There was a photo of the two of them standing in front of an airplane."

Gemma sat up straighter. "That lying sonofabitch. That was him?" The bad feeling she had worsened tenfold. "What did you do?"

"My boss told me to stand down until we got the subpoenas and the lab results back from both labs. She wants to have it all tied up neatly in a perfect bow on a shiny silver platter for the U.S. Attorney's Office, because that's the way they like it. I didn't want to wait for more evidence to take a walk, so I broke orders."

"You confronted Pilcher," she whispered. And he'd done it without her. He'd intentionally conducted a critical interview without his partner. *Without me.* She dug her fingers into the back of the sofa cushion. "You could have called me. I should have been there with you."

"No. I couldn't, and you shouldn't have. The last thing I want is for you to get involved in whatever shitstorm I created for myself."

Gemma pressed her lips together, trying to maintain a professional calm she didn't feel. It had taken a giant leap of faith to partner with him in the first place. *Please don't make me regret it.*

"Pilcher admitted to conspiring with Michael and

David Hawkin to burn down all those houses for profit, but he denied knowing anything about the Torrance Lane fire. The only other thing he did say was that Nash was blackmailing Michael Hawkin for something."

Gemma gasped. "That's why they killed him."

Brett nodded. "I think David pulled the trigger on Nash, and I also think he tried to shoot me and attacked you. That all happened after we interviewed Michael at his office."

"Are we getting warrants for all of them?" She'd thrown in *we* to see if she was still part of the team. Then again, with Brett on suspension, there might not be a team.

"No. At least not yet." Brett made a disgusted sound. "My RAIC ordered me to turn over the tape I made of Pilcher's confession. She's reassigning the case to another agent, probably Tom Willard, the agent who investigated the Torrance fire. I spent the rest of the day getting my ass reamed out for violating a direct order and for insubordination."

So that was it. Brett had gone all Lone Ranger on her, and now they were both, essentially, off the case, because she had no intention of working with Willard.

This partnership had spiraled down the toilet faster than a tornado, and the last thing she would do was partner with anyone else. Maybe she should have gone with her gut, should have found a way to get around the fact that she'd need subpoenas to move forward with her own NICB case.

Perhaps it wasn't too late. Maybe she still *could* move forward.

"The decision to go with you to Pilcher's office

wasn't yours alone to make," she gritted out. "We're partners. We should have talked about it first. And let's get something clear." She pointed a finger at him. "You might have been suspended, but *I* wasn't, and I don't answer to the ATF. Thanks for getting us this far, but I still have all my evidence, and I plan to keep going. With or without the federal government."

Brett leveled her a cold, hard look. "Do that, and you could be charged with obstruction."

"Based on what?"

"Based on the fact that this is an active federal investigation. If you go off on your own, without a federal agent, and withhold critical information, it could be considered as interference."

No way would she let him tell her what to do. "That's a chance I'm willing to take."

"And I'm not willing to let you take it. It's too dangerous." He stood, then knelt on the floor in front of her, taking her hands in his. She tried pulling them away, but he wouldn't let her. "I know you're used to working alone, but you can't do this by yourself. Let me make a call in the morning to my boss and to Tom Willard. This was your case to begin with. My RAIC knows you brought me and the ATF into it. I'll make sure Tom does, too. They won't push you out. I won't let them."

There were so many personal stakes at play here, he could never understand. This case was an opportunity to re-earn the respect that had been stolen from her four years ago. Despite Brett's reassurance, she didn't completely trust the ATF not to push her out. Mainly because *he'd* already pushed her out when he'd gone after Pilcher without her, and that was what mattered most. Not the rest of the ATF. Only Special Agent Brett Tanner, because *he* mattered to her. Somehow in the middle of all her caution and skepticism, she'd started having strong feelings for him. Or dare she say it...

She'd fallen for him.

A storm of emotions whirred around in her head and in her heart. Anger. Sadness. Disappointment. She took a deep breath, struggling not to lose control. "I understand why you believe you did the right thing, but you did, in fact, push me out because this was *our* case." Or so she'd thought. "You getting kicked off the case affects me, too." In ways he would never know, and she could never tell him. Not now. Maybe never.

Remorseful eyes leveled on her, and she was reminded of how her mother and father looked at each other after they'd had a big, raucous argument. But her parents had a closeness, a loving partnership. They shared everything, good or bad, with no secrets between them. She, on the other hand, had never had that with anyone, and she'd stupidly begun to think maybe Brett could have been that person.

Apparently, her parents had thought so, too, or they wouldn't have been planning to set her up with him. They saw what she'd seen. A handsome, intelligent, perfect man. Everything a woman could want.

Only he wasn't perfect. His singlemindedness, the intense determination that drove him, was all there was to his life. There might never be room for anyone else, including her. That was why he was alone and perhaps always would be.

"I'm sorry, Gemma." Brett's eyes clouded with guilt.

Guilt. That was the key to what drove this strong-as-iron, yet vulnerable, man. Survivor's guilt was a powerful emotion, one that could have horrible and lasting effects on people.

Her anger was instantly tempered by the knowledge of how desperately he needed to assuage the guilt that still ate him up inside after all this time. That guilt had been compounding daily since the Torrance Lane fire, when Brett hadn't been able to save those teens.

The virtual balloon filled with Gemma's anger didn't exactly pop. It was more like someone slowly letting the air out of a tire with a resounding *hiss*. What would happen to him if Charles Pilcher and the Hawkin brothers somehow managed to evade justice?

Would Brett forever remain in the past, held down by memories he could never escape? He'd once told her that people who hung on to the past were afraid of the future. *And doomed to extinction.*

As long as he remained on this destructive path, this destructive *destiny*, she'd be a fool to let him take her with him. But she couldn't help it. Her emotional body armor not only lowered, it dropped to the floor and stayed there. With nothing to protect it, her heart went out to him, fully.

Where he was concerned, she was weak. Gemma cupped his face with both hands, then let him break her rules again.

He slipped his hand to her nape, pulling her toward him, then knotting his fingers in her ponytail and tugging the band from her hair.

His lips were hard and hot. There was no teasing, no gentle foreplay. His tongue was devastating as it swept her mouth.

She sifted her fingers through his short hair, then down to the corded muscles of his neck and back. His kiss tasted of need, pain, and desperation.

When he hauled her to the edge of the sofa, she wrapped her legs around his waist. Heat bloomed in her core. His big body trembled beneath her touch. Then their hands were everywhere, tearing off clothes, stroking bare skin, white hot with desire.

The trail his fingers made as he skimmed his hands over her breasts lit a fire in her soul, a craving only he could satisfy, one that left her flushed and writhing in his arms.

Brett gathered her naked body and carried her into the bedroom. "Blaze, stay," he called out over his shoulder. The dog made a soft *woof* but remained in front of the sofa.

As Brett laid her gently on the mattress, he buried his hands in her hair, still being careful of her sutures, controlling her head, the angle of the kiss, demanding more. And she gave it. Willingly.

He gazed down at her with raw emotions flaring in his eyes. Emotions she couldn't name, couldn't identify. Except for the fierce, desperate need that echoed her own. His body melded to hers, his kisses leaving her breathless and aching for him.

Uncontrollable shivers rippled through her as his big hands again skimmed down her breasts, rubbing against her nipples, then down her belly to between her legs. His fingers slipped inside, and she groaned.

"I need to be inside you. Now." He flicked his finger at her sensitive nub, and she trembled.

She wanted to be there for him, to give him the

physical release he so obviously needed and that only she could provide.

Brett reached for the second condom she'd tossed on the mattress the other day, tore off the wrapper, and rolled it on. He nudged her legs apart with his knees, pushing inside, stretching her, filling her with every emotion he couldn't voice. She clung to him, trying to absorb his pain into her body and knowing she never could.

He clasped her hips, holding her steady as he slid in and out, rocking into her until her entire body was a jumble of sensations. He captured her mouth, thrusting his tongue inside as he pistoned faster.

Tremors ripped through her. Sparks flashed behind her eyes. Tearing her mouth from his, she arched her back, her breasts pressing against his chest as a loud, throaty cry tore from her mouth.

His chest heaved as he watched her from hooded eyes, searching her face and leaving her feeling bare, exposed, and wondering if he could read her mind. Then his body stiffened, and he threw his head back and groaned.

The force of what they'd just done, the implications, left her shaking. She was in love with him, but Brett was a wounded warrior, inside *and* out. Much as she wished otherwise, she could never be enough to heal him. Only he could do that.

He rested his forehead against hers, as if he could no longer bear the look in her eyes or he didn't want her to see the one in his.

Gemma's heart began cracking right down the center. It started slowly, as a thin fissure at first, then it tore into two jagged, painful pieces. She hoped she was wrong, because their lovemaking had felt like goodbye.

"I know you," Brett said as he lifted his head and opened his eyes. Gone was the raw emotion, the desperation she'd glimpsed earlier. In its place was a warning. "If you do this, call in backup. If not the ATF, call your people. The police. Anybody. But don't try to do this alone."

Gemma didn't answer. *Couldn't* answer. She'd continue to operate the way she always had pre–Brett Tanner.

Alone.

• • •

The teenagers on the second floor screamed. Brett's heart pounded faster. One more second and he could reach them. He was so close.

A thick coil of flame snaked up the banister like a giant boa constrictor. The snake opened its mouth, roaring as it morphed into his nemesis—a giant black dragon, screeching, then spreading its wings and spewing flames onto the walls, the ceiling, and everything else in its path.

Coughing, Brett hit the stairs at a dead run. Smoke curled all around him, clouding his vision until he could barely see. An ear-splitting crack rent the air. Pounds of sheetrock and burning timbers slammed onto his back, pinning him to the stairs. Pain blasted his entire upper body.

He tried hauling himself from beneath the burning timbers but couldn't move. That was when it started. Sharp stinging, then intense burning as flames licked at his arm and back. He twisted to shove the debris away, only to find the black dragon sitting on his back, shrieking louder as it brought more searing pain to his burning flesh.

Through the thickening smoke, the figures barely visible at the top of the stairs weren't the two teens. It was Ryan and Cody. Their faces twisted with fear. Smoke billowed around them, then they screamed. Their faces rippled, morphing back into the two teenagers. One of them—Tammy had been her name—reached for him. Only it wasn't Tammy. The tortured face staring down at him...

Was Gemma.

No!

His heart beat faster than he thought possible. He gritted his teeth as he tried pushing up from the stairs. Every muscle in his body screamed in agony, but he couldn't free himself of the debris pinning him down.

He looked up. With every passing second, the flames licked closer to Gemma. He had to get to her before it was too late.

Again, he opened his mouth, screaming her name: *Gemma! Gemma!* But no words came.

Powerless to move, he watched in horror as her thick, beautiful hair caught fire. She threw back her head and cried out.

Brett woke, his chest heaving and his heart pounding, as he searched the darkened bedroom. Gemma lay on her side, facing away from him and breathing softly. Apparently, she really was a heavy sleeper. His dog wasn't.

At some point after he and Gemma had fallen asleep, Blaze had come into the room and lain down at the foot of the mattress. His dog watched him, moonlight reflecting off his eyes, making them glitter like gold.

As they did every time he woke from the same perpetual nightmare, the scars on Brett's arm and back stung as if he'd been burned only moments ago. He wiped the sweat from his brow, then dragged his hand down his face.

When he'd been a child, nightmares had nearly destroyed him. Tonight's nightmare trumped them all, because this time, he hadn't been able to save Gemma.

He gazed down at her, resisting the urge to skim his hand over her bare shoulder and the gentle curve of her waist. Making love to her again hadn't been in the ops plan, but he'd needed to show her in ways he could never verbalize just how important she was to him. She was like a drug to his system, one he needed, or he'd go crazy.

He loved the way she arched her brow when someone was lying, how she slipped his dog bacon at every opportunity, and even sharing an everything bagel with scallion cream cheese with her. And who could forget her goldfish tattoo? Bottom line was she made him happy.

Brett leaned over, glimpsing the tiny, fanged orange fish on her hip. He eased away, then shook his head. The room might be dark, but he'd just had the clearest, brightest glimpse into the self-destructive recesses of his life.

He hadn't been avoiding happiness because it was his penance or because he didn't deserve it. His biggest fear was falling in love.

What if he couldn't protect her?

It was better to avoid love than to lose it. And so the vicious cycle had begun turning again, and he'd shut down. The difference this time was he didn't want to lose the happiness he'd found with her. This time, he wanted to keep it.

His gut twisted painfully at the memories of Ryan and Cody's funerals. He couldn't bear going to Gemma's, couldn't handle watching her coffin being lowered into the ground.

He stared out the window at the moon glowing in the early morning sky. In the dim light, he could just make out Gemma's map on the wall and the spider diagram she'd taped next to it. She'd done a lot of hard work on this investigation, including uncovering criminal patterns no one else could have.

More than once, it had nearly gotten her killed.

Keeping her safe and nailing the Hawkin brothers was his prime directive now.

He had to keep her out of this. Otherwise, he had no doubt that she'd go off alone, half-cocked, and put herself in danger again.

Twice before, he hadn't trusted his instincts, once at the Leadville fire scene, and again outside Piggly's after he and Blaze had been shot at. Both times, he'd second-guessed himself, and both times, Gemma had nearly been killed. He couldn't take that, couldn't lose someone he loved. He would *not* fail her again.

Brett gazed down at Gemma one last time, his heart heavier than he thought possible. That elusive happiness he craved so deeply with her was about to crash and burn. For what he was about to do, she'd hate him for all eternity.

At least she'd be alive to do it.

CHAPTER TWENTY-SEVEN

In typical fashion, Gemma woke slowly, groggily, craving a good strong cup of her mother's coffee. She lifted her head from the pillow, not surprised to find that Brett and Blaze weren't there.

She grabbed her phone from the floor and clicked the home button. It was after eight o'clock. With a groan, she pushed from the mattress and shoved a hand through her hair, sweeping it from her face.

Her body ached in all the right places. She closed her eyes, involuntarily conjuring up Brett's face and the low, sexy timbre of his voice.

He'd known how badly he'd hurt her, and while she was still annoyed at him ditching her for the Pilcher interview, she sympathized with his rationale. After everything he'd been through in his life, she understood, and the soul-deep remorse in his eyes had touched her heart.

Pushing to her feet, Gemma headed for the stairs, not bothering to even throw on a robe. First on tap this morning was a long, hot shower to ease her body and clear her mind. She put her foot on the bottom step and froze.

Oh. My. God. She raced back to the bedroom, hoping and praying that in her groggy state she was wrong. One look at her bedroom walls, and her blood ran cold.

"Oh no," she whispered, still not quite believing what she was seeing. More accurately, what she *wasn't* seeing.

Gone was her map, with the locations of all the fires. Gone were the fire scene photos and the spider-web diagram. All that stared back at her were bare white walls.

Not caring that one of her neighbors might catch a glimpse of her completely naked through one of the curtain-less windows, she spun, her heart beating furiously. *Furiously* being the pivotal word.

Her stacks of documents and manila folders— gone, too. In fact, the only thing left on the desk was her printer.

No. It wasn't possible. *He didn't. He wouldn't!*

But he had.

Brett had taken total advantage of the fact that when she slept, she slept like the dead. The worst part was that he'd stolen her laptop.

Gemma fisted her hands in her hair, straining the sutures in her scalp and trying not to scream. She snatched her cell phone from the floor and cued up Brett's number. After four rings, it went to voicemail. "Brett, you bastard. I want my files back. I can't believe you would do this to me."

Her voice cracked, and the lump in the back of her throat choked off anything she might have said next. She ended the call and threw the phone on the mattress. Tears stung the backs of her eyes, and she blinked rapidly, refusing to let herself cry over him. *Too late.*

Hot tears trickled down her face faster than she could wipe them away.

She could probably recreate most of her evidence, but that would take time. Everything had been meticulously organized and catalogued. It would take days, if not weeks or a month, to recreate everything.

She let her head fall back and took a deep breath, trying to steady her swiftly disintegrating control.

It didn't matter what his reasons were for doing this. This was unforgivable.

How could she have been so wrong about him?

She'd once thought they were in sync, professionally *and* personally. The personal pain was worse. *Much* worse.

Last night, she'd given him the physical comfort he so obviously needed, but she'd given him so much more than that.

She'd fallen in love...and he'd betrayed her.

Crushed didn't begin to explain how she felt. The hurt she'd experienced yesterday seemed trivial compared to this.

Where once she'd stupidly thought he understood why she worked as hard as she did, now she realized he'd never respected her, never really *seen* her. Now she knew that had to have been an act.

He was just like everyone else, like all the other men she'd ever worked with who constantly overlooked her.

"Oh God."

Her ugly history was repeating itself. What Brett planned to do with all their evidence wasn't clear. He'd been removed from the case, but he could be planning to hand it over to his own agency. Since he took everything, whoever wound up with the case would probably run it to the finish line without her.

Or he could have something else up his sleeve. Like taking this to the finish line alone, which was what she should have done in the first place.

"Fine," she gritted out. It didn't matter what his plan was. He'd shown his true colors, and she should be glad he'd been exposed before their personal relationship went any further.

"Two can play this game, and I can do it just as well as you can, Special Agent Tanner."

Gemma shoved her arms into a thin cotton robe, then began charging up the stairs. She'd gotten halfway up when the doorbell rang. "What *now*?"

Turning, she headed back downstairs and peered out one of the front windows. Bonnie stood on the other side, dressed for work and massaging her back.

Still in the throes of a complete and utter meltdown, Gemma yanked open the door with more force than necessary. Only her friend's perfectly positioned head prevented the blaring sun from burning her retinas.

"Good morning, sleepyhead." Bonnie's gaze dipped down then up. "Rough night? Or should I say, *good* night?" She sent Gemma a suggestive look. "You've got that post-sex look about you, and I caught your partner leaving your house about an hour ago."

"Yeah, well." Gemma stepped aside. "You might as well come in and get off your feet. And for the record," she added, closing the door, "that was the walk of shame, and I don't mean about sex. This was a *real* walk of shame."

After they'd sat on the sofa, Gemma told Bonnie everything that had gone down between her and Brett since the moment they'd met, including his recent absconding with her entire case file. By the time she was done, she'd practically gouged five slits in one of the sofa cushions from where she'd been digging her fingers in deeper and deeper.

"Hmm." Bonnie pursed her lips. "Okay, you're pissed off."

Gemma held out her arms. "Duh, Mrs. Obvious."

"Let me finish," she said in a soothing tone, one Gemma had witnessed her use many times on clients at Hands of Hope. "Have you considered there may be another perspective on this? Another reason other than ditching you that drove Brett to take your case file?"

"No." Gemma sat back with a huff and crossed her arms. There was no redeeming reason she could come up with to vindicate his actions.

"For someone so smart and so observant, you're missing some very critical things. You're looking at this from a strictly professional perspective and completely ignoring the personal side of things."

"I am *not* ignoring the personal side of things," Gemma countered, squeezing her arms tighter across her chest. Point of fact, she'd stared them in the face last night, which had led to sex, and look where that had gotten her.

Bonnie shook her head, much as Gemma had also witnessed her friend doing to her daughter. Who was thirteen years old. Then again, she *was* acting like a recalcitrant child.

Bonnie smiled calmly, another reason she was such a good counselor. She'd not only been through her own personal hell during college, but she had an innate skill for helping others to help themselves. "You are the smartest woman I know, and you work harder than any *five* people I know. I know you do that, because you think you have to in order to earn re-spect. You don't. People will see you for the intelligent, sensitive, and successful person you are. Brett does."

Gemma shook her head in disbelief. "Haven't you been listening to anything I said?"

"You have eyes, but sometimes you don't see. You have ears, but sometimes you don't hear." Again, Bonnie smiled. "From what I saw and heard the other night after you were attacked, that man cares for you. A lot, and not just as a partner. What you described is an alpha male in full-on protective mode. He's doing this to protect you, not to hurt you. It's clear to me," Bonnie continued, putting a hand on her chest, "that Brett has his own demons to slay in more ways than one. He's trying to distance you from whatever's com-ing next so you don't get hurt again. I also think he's doing this because he *does* respect you." She winked. "And maybe more than that."

"I really don't think what he did has anything per-sonal to do with me." Again, she shook her head, more forcefully this time. "Or to protect me. I think he used me to get what he needed, and now that he's got it, he's leaving me behind in the dust." Just like what had happened to her four years ago.

"I know you." Bonnie sent her a look filled with compassion. "You're thinking about what your col-league at the NICB did to you. He stole your case and took full credit for it."

"How could I have been so stupid?" Gemma un-crossed her arms and began massaging her forehead with both hands. Freaking history was repeating itself, and it was her fault for falling prey to it again. Hadn't she learned her lesson?

Apparently not.

"You know what makes me feel even more stupidly pathetic about this?" She let her hands fall to her lap. "I told Brett about that incident. He knew how much it bothered me, and he obviously didn't give a crap, because he just did the very same thing to me."

Gemma twisted the belt on her robe around her fist. Brett had hurt her, more than anyone ever had.

The bitter taste of disappointment filled her mouth. She really was weak where he was concerned. Because she loved him. Damn her treacherous, foolish heart.

Bonnie's brows drew together. "My impression of Brett is that he isn't that kind of man."

"I know you mean well," Gemma said, grateful for her friend's input, even if she was dead wrong. "But that's where we'll just have to agree to disagree."

"Okay, okay." Bonnie sighed, holding up her hands in defeat. "So what's your next move? I mean about the case."

"I don't know." Normally, case-related decisions came easily to her. For the first time in her career, she didn't know which direction to go in.

"Please promise me something." Bonnie reached as far as her belly allowed to clasp Gemma's hand. "Take a step back. The people you and Brett have been investigating are dangerous. There must be someone else who can help you. Baby Tucker here"—she gently rubbed her belly—"needs his aunt Gemma around to whip up her famous grapefruit margaritas when his mama can finally have one again."

That drew a reluctant smile from Gemma. She really had missed drinking those with Bonnie. "Okay, I promise."

"Good." She gave Gemma's hand a quick squeeze, then released it and began massaging her lower back. "Now for the reason I came over here in the first place. You gave Sally Nash a business card for Hands of Hope, and she's actually been in to see me twice to get some help managing her situation."

Gemma smiled grimly. "I'm glad she reached out to you. I wasn't sure she would, and you might as well know that her brother died recently. She's going to need your help even more now."

Bonnie nodded. "She did mention that when I spoke to her this morning. She actually called the main number looking for *you*. Apparently, she lost your business card and was hoping I'd know how to get in touch with you."

"Why?" Something about Bonnie's delivery made the hackles on Gemma's neck stand straight up.

"She was very upset and said that she had something really important to tell you and *only* you and that it's urgent. It concerns her brother."

• • •

"Are you sure she said ten thirty?" Gemma rechecked the time on her phone as she paced around the modestly furnished Hands of Hope lobby. Sally was already ten minutes late.

Several wood chairs with brightly colored cushions lined one wall, while an emerald-green sofa sat against another. A few framed prints of flowers and gardens hung on the walls. The atmosphere had been designed to be calm and soothing. Right now, it wasn't doing anything to calm her nerves.

"She'll be here," Bonnie said from where she sat on one edge of the sofa with her feet up. "You should have heard her over the phone. She'll *be* here."

Gemma made another circuit, passing the receptionist desk, manned, or rather *womanned*, by another counselor named Maddie, whose kind expression was just the sort needed for a job like this.

She couldn't imagine what Sally had to say that was so important and so urgent, yet when she and Brett had first interviewed her, they'd both gotten the impression she'd been holding something back.

A small, beat-up sedan drove into the lot and parked. Gemma recognized Sally as she got out of the car, then gathered the baby in her arms. "She's here." Gemma held the door open for Sally, noting the woman's red-rimmed eyes.

Sally swallowed, and it was obvious she was on the verge of tears. "I'm sorry I'm late. I was at the Weld County Coroner's Office." She took a deep, shuddering breath. "Identifying my brother's body."

"Oh, Sally." Gemma draped an arm over the woman's shoulder. "I'm so sorry about Johnny."

Bonnie wriggled to the edge of the sofa and stood. "Let's go to my office. It's quiet, and no one will disturb us there."

The moment Bonnie closed her office door, Sally burst into tears. Picking up on her mother's anguish, little Paige began fussing.

"Why don't you let me hold Paige?" Bonnie held out her arms, taking the baby and settling on a cushioned chair, crooning to the infant, who cried louder at first, then began to settle. "You two take the sofa."

Gemma grabbed a box of tissues from Bonnie's desk and indicated Sally should sit. As much as she wanted to get to the point of the meeting, the woman's grief took priority.

"Thank you." Sally dabbed at her eyes, sniffling. "I need to tell you some things, and I'm not proud of it. When you came to see me last week, I-I lied to you. I'm sorry, but Johnny is—oh god, *was*—my brother. He wasn't always a bad person."

"I'm sure he wasn't." In her heart, Gemma believed that was true. "Circumstances often dictate the path a person takes in life. Some paths lead to the darker side." Brett's life had definitely taken him down a dark path, yet she couldn't help but feel he was at a crossroads. The question was whether he'd continue down the same path he was on or change directions.

Sally nodded. "I believe that's what happened to Johnny. He used to be a good person, a good brother, but then things changed." She began shaking her head. "He did some bad things, I know that, but he was still my brother. Until Paige came along, he was all I had for my entire life. He always protected me. I felt that I had to protect him back. Can you understand that?"

Actually, Gemma could. "I have three brothers. They were always getting into trouble. I lost count of how many times I covered for them."

"Not like this." Again, Sally shook her head, more emphatically this time. "But now that he's gone, I don't have to protect him any longer. It's important to the families of those dead kids that they know the truth."

Gemma tensed, trying not to let her excitement show. The woman's brother had been murdered, after all. Whatever Sally said next could be pivotal.

Sally took a deep breath, staring at her clenched hands. "When he got out of prison, he told me that he set the fire that killed those kids. He was very upset and angry about it. They told him the house was empty. The kids weren't supposed to be there."

Gemma inched to the edge of the sofa. A hundred questions were on the tip of her tongue, but the best thing to do was let Sally tell Johnny's story in her own time and in her own way. The woman was grieving and felt bad enough as it was about lying to her and Brett in the first place.

Sally took another shaky breath before continuing. "It was a builder, a flipper, like on those TV shows. They were buying things at the warehouse where Johnny worked. That's how they met. They'd just purchased a big house that needed a lot of work, so they were at the warehouse a lot. They told Johnny the house had so many problems they were going to lose money on it."

Gemma could barely sit still. "What else did he say to Johnny?"

"That it would be a godsend if the house just disappeared. Johnny was given money to take care of it on a certain day."

Gemma couldn't believe what she was hearing. Sally had to be talking about Michael Hawkin, not David Hawkin, since Michael had been the one to purchase supplies at the Frodo warehouse. By hiring Johnny Nash to burn down the house on the same night that he received the award from the Denver Chamber of Commerce, he had a rock-solid alibi. "Do you know how much Johnny was paid for setting fire to the house?"

"No." Sally shook her head. "Right after the fire, Johnny was arrested for breaking into some other houses. I only spoke with him a few times when he was in prison, but he didn't say anything about the fire back then. When he got released a few weeks ago is when he told me what he'd done. He said the least this flipper could do was give him a job."

Now for the most important question. "Sally, I need you to think carefully. It's very important. Do you know the name of the guy who paid Johnny to do this?"

When Sally nodded, Gemma's heart beat faster.

The name Sally spoke next sent a shock wave through Gemma. At first, she'd thought she'd misheard Sally, but no. She hadn't.

Oh. My. God. She'd thought her heart was beating fast before. Now it was thundering.

She caught the equally surprised look on Bonnie's face.

Tears began streaming down Sally's face. "I know I should have come forward sooner, but it wouldn't have brought those kids back, and Johnny was my brother. I couldn't do anything to hurt him, but now that he's dead, it doesn't matter anymore. Does it?"

Willing her hand not to tremble, she squeezed Sally's hand. "You did the right thing telling us."

"Wait. There's more." Sally reached into her

pocket and pulled out a folded piece of paper. She unfolded it and handed it to Gemma. "Before Johnny went north to see that flipper, he gave me this and told me to hide it for him."

Gemma's heart slowed as she stared at the paper. Scrawled in black ink was an address. *18 Torrance Lane*. "Did Johnny write this?"

Sally shook her head. "No. He said they slipped him this note one day, so he'd know which house to burn down."

"May I keep this?" Gemma asked.

Sally nodded.

With slightly trembling fingers, Gemma refolded the note. Now, she had a decision to make. This was too important to keep to herself. She had to make sure this information got to the right place.

Bonnie and Brett were right. These people *were* dangerous, and she couldn't do this alone.

"Excuse me for a minute. I'll be right back." She stepped outside Bonnie's office and closed the door. After tugging her phone from her pocket, she stared at it. Asking for help sucked, but she couldn't be stupid about this.

Brett was off the case, and he probably wouldn't take her call, not after the way she'd railed at him in her voicemail message. Part of her still didn't want to talk to him, either. Phoning this in to the ATF's main number was an option. She could ask for Brett's boss. Ironically, doing so would be like betraying Brett. Given how *he'd* betrayed *her*, she shouldn't care about that. But she did.

The NICB's resources were spread thinly around the country. She was the only NICB agent stationed in Colorado. By the time any of her colleagues were close enough to actually do something, it would be too late. Besides, she'd still need law enforcement assistance.

There were only two other people she trusted enough to call, one in particular. She cued up his number, and when he answered, she took a deep breath. "It's Gemma. I need your help."

CHAPTER TWENTY-EIGHT

No vehicles were in Michael Hawkin's driveway, not the Mercedes, the Beemer, or the pickup truck, although Brett wasn't sure the pickup would have fit in the garage. That left the Mercedes and the Beemer.

Absently, he stroked Blaze's ear as the two of them watched the house. Blaze hadn't been too happy about leaving Gemma's place that morning. When Brett had used hand signals to get his dog off the mattress, he'd gotten up, albeit reluctantly, telling Brett precisely what was on his dog's mind: bacon for breakfast.

After leaving Gemma's house, he'd driven to the Hawkin Construction office. The pickup wasn't there, either, and the office door had been locked. No one had answered Hawkin Construction's main phone line when Brett had called, so he'd driven to the man's residence. Hawkin could be at a job site, but that didn't stop the warning flags from whipping around in his head.

Trooper Sanchez hadn't reached out again about locating David Hawkin. If Michael suspected the walls were closing in on him, he might also disappear.

Movement through one of the windows caught his attention. Someone was inside. If it was Hawkin, he planned on confronting the man and recording anything he said. That would, of course, piss off his boss again and get him into even more hot water. Seemed like all he'd been doing lately was pissing off all the women in his life.

Gemma's short voicemail message had said it all. It had killed him to steal her work, and he'd known how angry she'd be when she woke up. Some asshole had stolen one of her case files in the past. Now *he* was the asshole, but it had to be done, because no way did he want her pursuing this on her own. Gemma was tenacious and too smart for her own good. She'd never back down, one of the many things he admired about her.

He looked at her laptop and the stacks of files on the passenger seat. Ultimately, she could recreate everything, but that would take time, especially with no laptop. The plan was to finish this long before that ever happened.

Kelly Hawkin came down the steps, wearing yoga pants, a white tank top, and with a small gym bag slung over her shoulder. The garage door opened, revealing the Beemer and the Mercedes. Kelly headed for the Beemer. As she'd been the first time they'd met, she didn't look happy.

Brett bolted from the Expedition and jogged across the street. "Mrs. Hawkin," he called out as she opened the Beemer's door. "I'm Special Agent Tanner with the ATF. We met last week at your husband's office. Do you know where your husband is?"

The frown she gave him was more of a sneer. "He left town on a buying trip."

"A trip?" Those warning flags whipped faster. "To where?"

She shrugged. "I don't know, and I don't care. He said something about buying tile for a big order."

David Hawkin's whereabouts were unknown, and

now Michael was MIA. The more Brett thought about it, he'd bet his ass the guy wasn't planning on coming back anytime soon. If ever. Either David Hawkin had warned him, or that snake attorney had reached out to him, despite Brett's warning not to.

"How long ago did he leave?"

"At least an hour ago. With any luck, he won't come back."

"Thanks," he shouted over his shoulder, then jogged back to the SUV.

Picking up on whatever vibe Brett was giving off, Blaze pranced in the kennel, his nails clicking on the hard floor.

"Soon, buddy." He hoped.

Kelly's Beemer backed out of the driveway, then sped off down the street. Her parting shot about her husband struck a logical chord. From what Pilcher had said and what Brett had witnessed the other day, Hawkin and his wife were a stone's throw from divorcing, and they had no children. The man had no personal ties here anymore.

By plane, the Mexico border was about six hundred miles as the crow flies. If Hawkin had gotten wind that he was about to be arrested, he could try to flee the country. Once he made it across the border, he could disappear and find a way to a country without an extradition treaty with the U.S.

And gee, go figure, New Mexico was on a direct course from Colorado to the border. The reason Trooper Sanchez couldn't find David Hawkin *could* be that he was hiding out somewhere until his brother Michael swung by to pick him up so they could *both* flee.

Brett tapped his fingers on the wheel, staring up at the sky and the thick cloud cover obscuring the sun. It was only a theory, but it made sense. He and Gemma had ruffled some big, homicidal feathers that were about to flap away.

He rested his hand on the gear shift, about to crank it into drive, but stopped, shaking his head. "What the hell am I doing?" Blaze gave a gruff snort. "Yeah, exactly."

When he told his RAIC what he was up to, she'd blow a gasket. As long as he kept her in the loop, maybe he could still salvage his career. To shore up his theory, he called Trooper Sanchez. Working midnights, the guy might be sleeping, but this was too critical to wait.

"Sanchez," a sleepy voice said.

"It's Brett Tanner with the ATF. Sorry to wake you. Any word on David Hawkin?"

"No. Neighbors say they haven't seen him in days, and he hasn't shown up for work, either. His crew is looking to jump ship and find work somewhere else."

"Thanks, man." Now David Hawkin was officially MIA, too. Not that Brett was surprised.

Before calling Lori, he pulled up the report he'd downloaded on Michael Hawkin. He scrolled to the section on registered vehicles, memorizing the Cessna's tail number. N98986.

No matter what his boss said, he was going to the airport.

"Lori," he said when she answered.

"Brett, I know why you're calling. Before you ask, I reassigned your case to Tom Willard. We're still waiting on those subpoenas and the lab results for the shell casings and the mud, but with the attorney's admissions, Tom is working with an AUSA to get arrest warrants for Charles Pilcher and the Hawkin brothers. We should have them in a few hours, then we'll send a team down to New Mexico to grab David Hawkin, one to Denver to arrest Pilcher, and another to Michael Hawkin's office to grab him there."

"Hawkin isn't there."

A beat of silence, then, "And how do *you* know that?"

"Because I just came from the Hawkin Construction office, and it's locked down tight. I'm sitting outside Michael Hawkin's house." He braced for impact.

"You're *where*?" Lori shouted, forcing Brett to pull the phone from his ear. "You're on suspension! You're supposed to be home with your feet up, eating bon-bons, goddammit."

Brett grimaced. Lori never cursed. That told him he was in even deeper shit than he'd anticipated, which was already pretty deep. "Lori, just listen. I think Michael and David Hawkin may be trying to leave the country, and I don't think they're coming back. Once they hit the border, they're gone."

Muffled cursing came through the phone, followed by a loud exhalation. "This better be good, Tanner."

Brett fisted his hand on the wheel. At least she was listening.

"I think Pilcher squealed. The second Gemma and I walked out of his office, I think he called Michael and David Hawkin to warn them."

"In that case," Lori said, "we'll add Pilcher's phone records to the subpoena and obstruction to the charges. What else?"

"A state trooper in New Mexico's been looking for David Hawkin. No one down there's seen him, not his neighbors or his employees. Now Michael is MIA, too. His wife said he left town an hour ago on a business trip. I don't buy it. To cover all the bases, we should alert Denver PD at Denver International to see if he's booked on any international flights, but I don't think that's how he'll leave the country."

"Why's that?" Lori asked.

"He keeps a small Cessna at Front Range Airport." Brett gave Lori the tail number. "He and his wife are on the verge of divorcing. There's nothing keeping him here. If he stays, he'll go to prison, and he knows it. I'm guessing he'll make a pit stop in New Mexico for his brother, then they'll fly to Mexico."

Another call lit Brett's cell phone. *Evan.* Brett sent the call to voicemail, along with a quick text message that, if he and Deck were able, to meet him at Front Range Airport.

"Is there a tower at that airport?" Lori asked.

Evan kicked back with a brief response. *Ten-four. Call me.*

"Yes." Brett pulled onto the road. He knew that airport. Not well, but he'd been there once before. It was about twenty minutes east of Denver International and off the beaten path. From where he was now, it was at least a forty-minute drive, and Hawkin had an hour's head start. "There's also a small CSP station on airport grounds."

"Good," Lori said. "Assuming that's where Hawkin is, I'll notify the tower to not let him take off, and I'll see if the troopers there can find him and hold him for us until the teams arrive. And Brett, if I know you, and I do, you're en route to the airport. Wait for Tom Willard and his team. They're at the U.S. Attorney's Office getting the warrants. I'm ordering you, do *not* take this guy down alone. Wait for backup. You got it?"

Brett hit the on-ramp for I-70. Yep, his boss did know him well. "Copy that."

• • •

Forty minutes later, Brett parked out of sight at the end of East 51st Avenue, one of the narrow roads running between the hangars. From his vantage point, he had a clear view of Hangar 8, where Michael Hawkin kept his Cessna.

During the drive from Hawkin's house to the airport, Lori had called to notify him she'd spoken with Front Range air traffic control, who'd confirmed Michael Hawkin had filed an instrument flight plan to Mexico, with a short stop at Vaughn Municipal Airport in Vaughn, New Mexico. The manager of the airport had also told Lori that Hawkin shared a hangar with an aircraft stripping and painting company that had recently been shut down by the EPA for unlawfully storing and using toxic chemicals.

Hawkin's pickup was nowhere in sight. Now it was a waiting game. Brett might never have the evidence to charge Hawkin with setting the Torrance Lane fire, but at least they'd nail him with an arson-for-profit conspiracy and, possibly, the murder of Johnny Nash.

His phone lit with Deck's name. "I'm pulling into the airport now," Deck said. "What's your twenty?"

"East 51st. It's the third right turn off the main road. Park behind me." Since Tom Willard and his team hadn't arrived yet, and the state patrol based at the airport were out on other calls, he was grateful for the backup. Despite Lori's orders, if Hawkin's plane so much as twitched, he had no intention of waiting.

"Ten-four."

Less than a minute later, Deck pulled up behind him. "Stay here, buddy," he said to Blaze, then met Deck outside. "Thanks for coming." Deck and Evan always had his back, and he'd always have theirs. It was part of the bond they'd forged over the years, one just as solid as those he shared with his own siblings.

"Anytime. You know that. What's the plan?"

"I have a strong hunch that Michael Hawkin is planning on fleeing the country with his brother. He's got a plane in that hangar." He pointed to Hangar 8. "No signs of movement. Tom Willard and his team are bringing an arrest warrant for Hawkin in case he shows up here."

"We hanging tight until they get here?"

"Yep." Brett nodded. "Evan coming?"

Deck looked at his phone. "Yeah, he was with Gemma. She asked him for help with something. Whatever they were doing, they finished, and he's on his way. Should be here any minute now."

She what?

After what Brett had done to her, he would have bet a shit-ton of money she'd never call a federal agent for help again. But she had, and she'd called Evan. Not him. At least she'd heeded his warning and called somebody instead of charging off gangbusters on her own.

Evan's SUV turned the corner and parked behind Deck's. As Evan jogged over, his expression was unexpectedly upbeat. "You won't believe what just happened."

Loud whirring came from behind them. The door to Hangar 8 started opening. Inside the hangar was a pickup truck. Beside the truck was a Cessna. Large plastic and metal fifty-five-gallon drums lined the wall of the hangar behind the plane.

The hangar door continued to rise steadily. A man Brett thought was Michael Hawkin threw a duffel bag through the open left side door of the aircraft. The plane's tail number solidified it.

N98986. Hawkin's plane.

"Dammit." He'd been parked inside the hangar the entire time.

Waiting for Tom Willard wasn't an option. Regardless of whether the FAA issued him a ground stop, Hawkin could be airborne within minutes. "Hold that thought," he said to Evan. "Let's go get him." Brett sprinted back to his Expedition.

He slammed his foot on the accelerator, gunning the SUV to the end of the road and onto the grass separating the dead end of 51st Avenue and Hangar 8. The vehicle shimmied and rocked as he pushed it harder. Letting this fucker get away...not gonna happen.

As he neared the hangar, he glimpsed another plane, a Beechcraft, behind the Cessna on the other side of the hangar. Brown paper covered the plane's windows, the silver body of the aircraft completely stripped of paint.

Hawkin bent to pull the chocks from the plane's

nosewheel, then lifted his head. At this point, Brett was close enough to catch the momentary surprise on the man's face. Hawkin hurled the chocks aside and hopped into the plane. The propellor began spinning.

Brett slammed his foot down harder on the gas pedal. If he didn't make it in time, Hawkin could roll out of there onto a taxiway before Brett could stop him.

He drove onto the pavement in front of the hangar, only slamming on the brake when he was within a few feet of the now-fully spinning prop. Deck and Evan parked on either side, preventing Hawkin from skirting around Brett's Expedition.

As Brett jumped from the SUV, he popped Blaze's door. Between three armed federal agents and Blaze, Hawkin wouldn't get away.

With Blaze at his side, he charged to the airplane and yanked open the pilot's door. He'd love nothing more than to haul Hawkin out and throw him to the ground, but if the man's foot on the brake was the only thing holding the plane in place, doing that would send it on a collision course with their SUVs.

"Federal agents!" he shouted over the noise. "Shut off the engine, and get out!"

The air smelled of chemicals. Blaze snorted. Like a hunting dog, he "pointed" to the plastic drums stacked neatly against the nearest wall. *MEK*. The aircraft stripping and painting company must have been using it as a paint stripper before they were shut down.

Hawkin's face twisted with malice as he reluctantly turned off the engine. The plane's propellors slowly ground to a stop.

"Put the hand brake on." Brett waited for Hawkin to pull the brake handle before hauling him out of the cockpit and spinning him around. "Hands on the plane." Not waiting, Brett shoved the man against the fuselage and started patting him down for weapons.

Over the plane's nose cone, he caught sight of another pickup—*Gemma's?*—driving down the narrow road in between the row of hangars. She hopped out and speed-walked toward them.

A spurt of anger rose in his throat. He hadn't wanted her anywhere near this, yet here she was. "What the hell are you doing here?" he growled when she'd come to within a few feet. "And keep back." A runway of cover models could parade in front of him, and he'd still be capable of focusing on his job. For him, Gemma Scott was *the* most distracting woman on the planet.

Because I'm in love with her.

She was one of the most headstrong, stubborn women he'd ever known, but he loved her. From the top of her head, to her goldfish tattoo, right down to her flame-and-fire-engine-red toenails.

Gemma pointed a finger at him. "Listen, you dumbass. I have something important to tell you, and you're going to want to hear it." She jutted her chin at Hawkin. "*He* needs to hear it, too."

Evan nodded subtly. "I'd listen to what the lady has to say."

"Don't move, asshole," he ordered Hawkin, who kept his hands plastered to the side of the plane. He'd grill Evan later as to how Gemma even knew where they were. "You're under arrest for arson, and someday, I swear to God, I'll arrest you for killing those kids."

"I did *not* burn down that house," Hawkin shot back over his shoulder. "And I didn't kill those kids."

"He's telling the truth." Gemma parked her hands on her hips. "Partly, anyway."

Brett flicked his gaze to Hawkin. "If he didn't do it, then who did?"

Hawkin looked over his shoulder. "My—" His eyes widened, then he snapped his mouth shut.

"Shut up, Michael," came a female voice from behind them. "Don't say another word. I'll get you a lawyer."

Kelly Hawkin, still wearing her yoga outfit, charged toward them from the hangar door. With every angry stride, the gym bag Brett had seen her with at the house slapped against her hip.

Guess she hadn't been headed to the gym after all. She must have sped directly to the airport, beating Brett by only minutes, then parked her Beemer somewhere else and walked over.

He narrowed his eyes. What was she even doing here?

"In that case," Gemma said to Kelly, glaring at the other woman, "you might as well get one for yourself, too."

Brett looked from Gemma to Kelly, narrowing his eyes even more. "What are you talking about?"

"I met with Sally Nash today," Gemma said. "She *did* lie to us. Johnny told her Kelly Hawkin paid him to burn down the Torrance Lane house because it had turned into a money pit. She gave him a note with a handwritten address on it. After the fire, Johnny was upset because Kelly had assured him the house was empty. Johnny had no idea those kids were inside.

When he got out of prison for burglary, he gave the note to his sister and told her to hide it. Then he went to Hawkin Construction, figuring they owed him something more to keep quiet."

Kelly huffed. "That's ridiculous."

"It's not," Gemma insisted.

Brett's blood started to boil as he absorbed Gemma's revelation. He didn't doubt anything she'd just said.

Kelly Hawkin had completely snowed him. *She'd* had 18 Torrance Lane burned down. Never once had he pegged her for this. Leaving him wondering what other part she'd been playing in the Hawkins' arson-for-profit scheme.

Sally's statements about what her brother said to her would be inadmissible in court as hearsay, but the note could be admitted as evidence, and she could testify about where it came from. The fact Nash asked his sister to hide the note could show consciousness of guilt on Nash's part. All they'd have to do was authenticate Kelly Hawkin's handwriting.

He didn't know whether to shake Gemma for showing up here or haul her into his arms and kiss her. He pointed to Michael Hawkin, who'd been watching over his shoulder, his hands still plastered to the side of the plane. "Stay right where you are, Hawkin."

Brett tugged a set of cuffs from his belt. "Kelly Hawkin, you're under arrest for arson and felony murder."

She jerked back, pivoting as she shoved her hand into the gym bag. "Oh, hell, no."

Blaze barked. Brett and Evan were closer, and

lunged for Kelly.

Not fast enough.

She grabbed Gemma's arm and hauled her backward.

The barrel of a mini-Glock pressed against the side of Gemma's head.

Shock emanated from Gemma's eyes. Brett's stomach went rock hard, then his heart started beating faster than he thought possible. Fear and panic nearly obliterated his vision *and* his ability to think clearly.

Because the barrel of that gun was not only jammed against Gemma's temple, but Kelly Hawkin's finger was wrapped firmly around the trigger. One wrong move or decision by any of them...

Gemma would be dead in less than a heartbeat.

CHAPTER TWENTY-NINE

Cold sweat broke out on Gemma's forehead. Brett was talking, his lips moving, but the only sound she heard was the pounding of her racing heartbeat in her ears.

Brett, Deck, and Evan had pulled their weapons, but the way Kelly was positioned behind her, bent low and ducking her head down, none of them had a clear shot. The more she tried angling away from the barrel of the gun, the harder Kelly jammed it against her skull. What she wouldn't give to have her framing nailer right about now. She'd empty the entire clip of nails into the woman's chest.

"Get on the ground," Brett ordered Hawkin. "Face down and with your hands behind your head."

Hawkin started to comply, dropping to his knees.

"He goes free," Kelly said in a high-pitched voice, shoving the mini-Glock's barrel harder against Gemma's head. "Or she dies."

Hawkin's gaze darted back and forth between Brett and his wife. Gemma wasn't certain which one of them he was more afraid of. Hawkin's eyes rounded on his wife. "What in God's name are you doing?"

"Cleaning up your mess." She hauled Gemma tighter to her chest, still using her body as a shield. Hot breath washed against the side of Gemma's head, mixing with the nasty chemical odor in the air. "I knew you'd fuck this up. I told you not to buy that house, but you just *had* to keep it for yourself.

Burning down that dump was the easiest way to get rid of it and recoup at least some of our money."

"Nash was blackmailing you, wasn't he?" Brett asked, inching closer, and Gemma recognized the tactic for what it was. A distraction. Behind Brett, Deck and Evan fanned out laterally. "That's why you killed him."

She made a scoffing sound. "Nash was a greedy, stupid little shit. He had to go. When you two started piecing it all together, you became another problem I had to get rid of."

Gemma gasped. *Kelly* Hawkin had ordered the hits on her and Brett, *not* Michael, like they'd wrongly suspected.

Brett took another step closer. Blaze followed, uttering a low growl.

Without batting an eyelash, Kelly aimed her gun at Brett's chest, stopping him. "Don't move. I have no qualms about killing her *or* a federal agent. That goes for the rest of you." She glanced at Deck and Evan.

From the rigid stance of both men and the way their jaws were clamped tighter than a vise grip, like Brett, they were waiting for the right moment to disarm the woman.

"Are you crazy?" Michael shouted. "Put the gun away. You're only making this worse."

"Nothing's changed," Kelly snapped, repositioning the gun's barrel against Gemma's temple. "The plan is still the same. We're getting out of here, and they can't stop us." She edged closer to the plane, dragging Gemma with her. "Move!" she shouted in Gemma's ear, making her flinch.

"You'll never get clearance for takeoff." Brett's

low, deadly voice filtered through to Gemma's fear-laced brain. "Let her go." He aimed his gun at the ground in front of Gemma's feet. His narrowed eyes glittered like blue glass. Evan and Deck had also aimed in, but she knew none of them would shoot while Kelly had the gun mashed against her face. She had to do something, had to give them an opening.

"Clearance?" Kelly laughed. "You think I give a shit about *clearance*?"

Slowly, Brett shook his head. "There's no way out of here. Even if you do take off, there's no place you can land where I won't hunt you down. The FAA will track you. Wherever you go, I'll never stop coming for you." A look of rage, so pure and unadulterated, shone from his eyes. "Let. Her. Go."

Blaze's big head lowered, the hair on his spine at full attention. The dog might not speak English, but he knew whatever was happening was bad.

"I don't think so." Kelly tightened her hold around Gemma's waist and backed up to the Cessna's open door.

Brett took another step toward them, clenching his jaw.

"Don't!" Kelly dragged the barrel from Gemma's temple to her cheek. "What do you think a bullet will do to this pretty face? She won't so look so pretty, will she?"

Maintaining a position of safety, hunkered down behind Gemma, Kelly shoved the pilot's seat forward. Grunting, she hauled herself up and onto the rear seat. The barrel of the gun now pressed firmly against the back of Gemma's head. "Get in!"

Moving backward slowly, and half expecting her

skull to be blasted into smithereens any second, Gemma climbed inside the plane and onto the rear seat. Again, Kelly wrapped her arm around Gemma's waist, tucking in tightly behind her.

"Michael, let's go," Kelly shouted, then pulled the pilot's seat back into place. When he hesitated, Kelly screamed louder, "Come on!"

Michael shot to his feet, then jumped into the pilot's seat and yanked the door closed.

The plane's motor sputtered to life. The prop began turning, gathering speed until Gemma could no longer make out the individual propellers.

Through the side window, she locked gazes with Brett. His jaw was so tight, every muscle and bone stood out starkly, but it was the look of fear on his face that sent a chill down her spine. There was nothing he could do. He wouldn't risk taking a kill shot and accidentally killing *her*.

Blaze began running in circles around the plane, barking and trying to get to her.

"Try to escape, and I *will* shoot you. Do you understand?" When she didn't respond immediately, Kelly shouted, "*Do you understand?*"

"Y-yes." Gemma gulped. Kelly Hawkin was a ruthless, merciless woman. There was no way she'd let her live. As soon as they took off, Gemma was a dead woman. Kelly would either shoot her and dump her out of the plane in mid-air, or they'd land somewhere, then blast her in the head.

The engine roared, and the nose of the plane swung in a tight arc, turning toward the other side of the hangar. Michael reached up to the visor and clicked what looked like a garage door opener.

The door on the other side of the hangar rose. The plane continued turning in a one-eighty. When the door had fully opened, Gemma's heart thumped faster. A paved road—a taxiway—just outside the hangar led directly to the airport's one and only runway.

She twisted her neck to look behind the plane to where Brett, Deck, and Evan stood. Time was running out. In fact, it *was* out.

This was no different from being attacked in a parking lot and dragged into a vehicle. Hadn't her father and brothers taught her that? Once they rolled out of here, it was all over. She might die trying to escape, but at least she'd go out knowing she'd tried.

The plane completed its arc. Hawkin nudged the power, and the plane picked up speed, rolling faster toward the open door. The voice in her head echoed louder: *Now, now, now!*

She took a deep breath, bent her head forward as far as it would go, then slammed it backward, ramming it into Kelly's head.

"Fuck!" she bellowed.

Ouch. Pain shot to the back of Gemma's skull. White flashes obscured her vision.

Kelly's hold around her loosened. The muzzle of the gun lowered, scraping along her cheek.

Gemma grabbed Kelly's wrist, jerking the gun away from her head.

"You bitch!" She pounded on Gemma's head with her other fist.

Gemma's shoulder muscles screamed as she grappled for control of the gun. She was in relatively good shape, but Kelly was bigger, and she was strong. If she managed to regain control of the gun, Gemma had no doubt the woman wouldn't hesitate to shoot her in the head.

The plane roared toward the open door. Ten more feet and they'd be outside the hangar.

Drawing on every bit of strength she could muster, Gemma slammed Kelly's hand—the one with the gun—against the back of the pilot's seat. A gunshot blasted inside the cockpit.

Michael screamed. Blood spattered the inside of the front window. "You shot me!" He released the controls and grabbed his shoulder.

The plane's nose abruptly changed course, then dipped as they rolled over a long metal drain running the width of the hangar. The plane veered off at an angle.

Heading directly for the wall.

"Do something!" Kelly shoved Gemma, slamming her against the opposite bulkhead, then leaned over her husband's shoulder to grab the control wheel, which did nothing to change the plane's direction.

Gemma looked up to see the wall of drums rushing at them.

A second before impact, she flung her hands in front of her face and screamed.

• • •

The plane picked up speed, veering on a collision course with the wall.

No! Gemma's scream ripped through Brett. They'd all heard the gunshot. His guts twisted with terror that she'd been hit.

As a unit, Brett, Deck, Evan, and Blaze took off

running, racing across the hangar. Fear threatened to burn a hole in Brett's chest.

The nose cone impacted first. Dull thumping came next, as the propeller blades hit the plastic drums, slicing through them like butter before scraping against the wall with a high-pitched screech.

Clear liquid gushed from two of the drums, spilling onto the hangar floor beneath the plane. The harsh chemical odor was strong enough to burn Brett's nose. Blaze snorted, the smell affecting his dog's super-sensitive nose even more.

With every spin of the prop, the plane rocked sideways. Brett and Evan ran past the tail, heading for the door. Sparks shot from beneath the cowling. An instant later, the nose cone erupted in a ball of flames.

If the fire hit the vapor coming off the MEK, the entire hangar could go up, along with all the chemicals stored in those drums.

"Extinguishers!" Brett shouted.

"On it!" Deck spun and ran for the nearest fire extinguisher.

"Got your back," Evan yelled.

The prop kept turning, scraping paint off the wall and sending more sparks in the spilled MEK. He had to get Gemma out of the plane. Fast.

Brett raced for the pilot's door. Before he got there, the door opened. Michael Hawkin jumped from the cockpit, clutching his bleeding shoulder as he hauled ass from the plane. Brett let him go. He wouldn't get far.

On the opposite side of the plane, Gemma and Kelly fell through the other door in a heap of flailing arms and legs, right into a puddle of MEK. The liquid splashed in all directions, soaking their clothes.

The prop continued turning, shooting more sparks as it scraped in a slow arc against the wall. A steady stream of sparks hit the MEK, setting the vapors ablaze with a loud *whoosh*. The fire's track shot toward the women.

Brett raced back around the tail of the aircraft, splashing through the puddle. He grabbed Gemma's arm and hauled her to her feet. A few feet away, Kelly pushed to her knees, then stood.

"Gun!" Deck shouted, dropping the extinguisher.

Brett released Gemma, shoving her behind him as he drew his weapon. Three Glock 9mms echoed in the hangar. Kelly staggered backward. Blood seeped from the half-dozen holes in her torso, soaking her white tank top. She fell to her knees, then onto her face.

"Brett!" Gemma yelled. The lower portion of her jeans was on fire.

Brett yanked off his shirt. She had to be soaked with MEK. If he didn't get the fire out immediately, she'd go up in flames and burn to death before his very eyes.

He tamped his shirt against her leg, snuffing out the flames before they could shoot past her knee.

Smoke continued filling the hangar.

Deck hitched his head to the door. "Time to leave, boys."

Evan covered his mouth and coughed. "I second that."

Gemma swayed on her feet, and Brett picked her up in his arms. Her head lolled to the side, but her eyelids flickered.

"Brett!" Deck shouted.

Both Deck and Evan raised their weapons, aiming in on something behind him.

Blaze barked, and Brett spun to see Kelly rushing them. Her shoes had caught fire, but she didn't stop coming. Blaze took off, charging at her.

"No!" Brett shouted, coughing. He could only watch in horror as Blaze leaped on Kelly, his front paws landing on her chest and sending her flying backward into the burning MEK.

Her entire body ignited like the tip of a match. In less than a second, she was a living, breathing fireball. She screamed once, then windmilled her arms, spinning and turning, sightless, as she fell on her back, then stopped moving.

Blaze backed off, coughing and spitting.

"We've gotta get outta here," Evan shouted. "That plane could blow sky high and into the next county."

"Blaze!" Brett yelled, and his dog bounded after them as they ran outside into the fresh air.

Fire engines roared down the road, their air brakes hissing as they came to a stop. Firefighters with SCBAs jumped out and dragged hoses from the trucks. Behind the trucks, an ambulance came to a grinding halt.

Michael Hawkin hadn't gotten far. Brett glimpsed him hauling ass around the outside of the hangar, trying to flee down the road between all the emergency vehicles.

Evan hitched his head in the direction of the receding figure. "We've got him."

Deck and Evan raced after Hawkin.

Brett carried Gemma to the nearest fire truck. "Get a hose on her!" he ordered a firefighter, then began stripping off her clothes. In addition to being an eyes, nose, and throat irritant, MEK could also cause skin burns. At high concentrations, it could even cause damage to the nervous system.

"I'm okay." She coughed. "I'm okay."

A paramedic rushed over, then slipped an oxygen mask over her face.

Brett gripped her hand tightly. She was shaking but breathing. The adrenaline that had been pumping through his system finally began to ebb. He'd almost lost her. Again.

Over the top of the mask, Gemma's red-rimmed eyes met his, and in that one moment he had a flash of clarity like he'd never experienced.

I can't live without this woman in my life.

Even though Kelly Hawkin was dead, knowing he had the evidence to charge her for the Torrance Lane fire had the effect of yanking away the blinders that had been giving Brett tunnel vision. Other things in his peripheral vision came into focus.

He wanted Gemma and had no intention of letting her go. Ever.

A firefighter had begun washing off her legs with water. While a paramedic started an IV and took her vitals, the epiphanies kept barreling down the track.

What Gemma didn't—and *couldn't*—know was that he'd do whatever it took to make up for what he'd done.

Even if it took the rest of his life.

CHAPTER THIRTY

Early Saturday evening, Gemma stood on her porch, looking into the backyard and maintaining a watchful eye on her brother, Chris, as he hooked up the gas line to her brand-new—of all things—firepit.

She shuddered. A week and a half had passed since nearly getting burned alive. Maybe a firepit wasn't such a good idea after all. Last winter, she'd cemented the round base with natural stone. It had seemed like a good idea at the time. Now, maybe not so much.

Her other brother, Ben, pushed a button on the side of the pit. She heard a click, followed by a soft *whoosh*. Stepping closer, she peered over the edge of the deck. In between the shiny black stones she'd set in the firepit's basin, blue-and-orange flames flickered as if they were alive.

Chris waved her over. "Come down here and check this out!"

Not a chance. Not today. Maybe next week. Or next month, when the weather started changing. "Thanks, Chris. It's perfect. I'd better check on Dad and Rory."

She went back inside to where her father and Rory were putting the finishing touches on the living room's baseboard molding. The smell of fresh paint wafted into the kitchen. The *ka-tunk* of pneumatic nailers echoed in the air.

After working on her house alone for nearly a

year, she'd made headway, but ever since her near-death experience, she'd become impatient to finish the renovation quickly and really start *living* in the house, not just subsisting in it. So she'd finally accepted what her family had been offering since the day she'd signed the deed.

Their help.

But there was so much more to it than that. In the end, trying to do everything alone hadn't proved a thing. All it had proven was that she *couldn't* do it alone. She had to admit even her time working with Brett had shown her two heads were better than one.

It was becoming a thing now, this asking for help and working with other people. Between her father and brothers, plus the contractor she'd hired and paid extra to install the new deck, she'd have the place whipped into shape in no time. True, she'd be watching her bank balance dwindle and eating ramen noodles for the rest of the year, but it would be worth it in the end.

"Come over and hold this for me, will ya?" Rory said.

Gemma crouched so she could hold the end of the molding while her brother nailed it into place.

Her father positioned another piece of trim on the chop saw. "How are your burns?" He nodded to her lower legs. Wearing shorts for comfort left her slightly pink ankles and shins exposed.

"They're fine, Dad." Thanks to Brett. Given how soaked with MEK her clothes had been, if he hadn't acted so swiftly...

A wave of nausea rolled through her at the thought of what could have happened. She'd have been toast. For real.

As it was, her throat hadn't been permanently affected by the vapors, and her mild burns would heal. Brett, Deck, and Evan were also fine, although Blaze had suffered some burns to the pads of his feet. Blaze had probably saved *all* their lives.

She scooted along the floor so Rory could continue punching nails into the baseboard.

"Have you seen him lately?" her dad asked.

"Him" could only be one person. *Brett*. She shook her head. "No, but it's okay. He just wasn't the one. Sorry, Dad."

He paused with his hand on the chop saw. "I don't understand how we could have been so wrong about him. Your mother and I were certain he'd be a good fit for you."

Emptiness and resignation filled her heart.

Bonnie's words of wisdom may have been spot on, but it didn't matter. Even if he'd stolen her case files and shut her out of the investigation because he cared for her, Brett's survivor's guilt and PTSD were still calling the shots in his life.

Given the complexity of the investigation, she'd understood perfectly when she hadn't heard from him a day or two after the hangar fire. Though Kelly Hawkin was dead, what Gemma had been hoping was that since Brett finally had proof Kelly was behind the Torrance Lane fire, he could move on with his life. But then two days turned into three, then three into four, and by the time a full week had passed, she'd given up all hope of seeing him again.

"I can finish this, Gem." Rory glanced at her legs. "You should get off your feet."

"Thanks." She climbed the stairs to her brand-new attic office.

Her dad and brothers had taken apart her work-table, hauled it to the attic, then set it back up for her. A fresh coat of creamy yellow paint brightened the small space, as did the new ceiling light fixture, but it could never take the place of natural lighting.

She sat at the table and stared at the triangular-shaped section of wall beneath the house's front dormer. That was where the special-order eyebrow window would have gone. If only she could afford it.

If only it didn't cost five thousand dollars.

She flipped open her laptop. A few days after getting out of the hospital, Tom Willard had stopped by to interview her about the events at the hangar and to return her laptop. She'd given consent for the ATF to copy all the relevant files. Tom had been fairly tight-lipped about the investigation, saying only that the U.S. Attorney's Office was still reviewing evidence but was inordinately pleased and had complimented Gemma on her thoroughness and especially for her little chat with Sally Nash.

Gemma had also been visited by her bosses from the NICB's main office. Other agents from around the country had sent flowers and get-well emails. Gemma hadn't expected that. Maybe she ought to give them another chance.

Speaking of other chances, her parents had already begun screening new deli customers for her next pro-spective date. Deli dating was something she had no intention of living through again. If she ever dove back into the dating pool again, *she'd* be the one in charge. *Not* her parents. Though she knew they meant well. They wanted her to have the same once-in-a-lifetime kind of love they'd found.

She tilted her head back and stared at the ceiling.

What if Brett Tanner was her once-in-a-lifetime love? And what if that was all some people got? One love. And when it was gone, that was it. Game over.

At least she still had her job. Maybe that would be enough to make her happy in life.

The moment she'd thought those last words, her gut squeezed with undeniable sadness, because…what if it wasn't?

• • •

Evan was waiting for Brett when he pulled up to the Pine Springs Mental Health Treatment Center. The facility Brett had started going to a week ago for his PTSD issues wasn't nearly as nice, but the shrink who'd been dissecting his brain wasn't half bad.

In the passenger seat of the Audi parked next to Evan's SUV, a young woman in the front passenger seat ran a hand down her long brown hair. Evan had been successful in his quest. Brett could only hope *he'd* be successful in his *own* quest. For peace and sanity.

His determination to bring down Michael Hawkin had morphed into an ugly and twisted obsession, one that had begun ruling his head, to the detriment of everything else in his life. He hadn't wanted Kelly Hawkin to die, but he *had* wanted to bring the Torrance Lane arsonist to justice. It had taken a shooting review board less than a day to clear Brett and his friends.

Lab results on the shell casings had confirmed David Hawkin's gun had fired the rounds he'd collected from the Piggly's Smokehouse parking lot and the oil field where Johnny Nash had been murdered. The U.S. Coast Guard lab had also fingerprinted and matched the oily mud from the same field to the mud left in the back of Trooper Sanchez's patrol car. Sanchez had been only too happy to assist ATF agents in New Mexico in putting the *habeas grabus* on David Hawkin and locking him up.

As of a week ago, it was official. Michael and David Hawkin, along with Charles Pilcher, had been charged with an arson-for-profit conspiracy. Now that Kelly Hawkin was dead, none of them had any qualms about throwing her under the bus, and their stories were consistent.

Hawkin Construction had been in the red for some time. They could barely pay the mortgage on their own home, so Kelly came up with a way to make more money. She'd been the brains behind the entire scheme, fine-tuning the details with Pilcher, who'd lied about her involvement. Michael and David had been the ones to torch all the houses on Gemma's list.

David was also charged with Nash's murder and for attempting to kill Brett and Gemma. As it turned out, David Hawkin had moved to New Mexico so they could start burning down houses for profit there, as well.

Lastly, a handwriting expert had, indeed, confirmed Kelly Hawkin had written the note Johnny Nash asked his sister to hide for him. Knowing her husband would be a suspect, she'd arranged for Nash to burn down the house at the exact moment Michael was receiving an award from the Denver Chamber of Commerce. Michael hadn't known his wife was behind it until months after the fact. That was why he'd been so convincing when the local police and the ATF interviewed him and he'd denied any involvement in the fire.

In the end, justice had been served, and it was turning out to be the first step in Brett's healing process. The ATF ruling that Brett would keep his job also helped.

Thirty days on the beach without pay was his penance, which gave him ample time to get his personal affairs in order. Spilling his guts to a shrink again after all these years wasn't something he wanted to do. It was more like a necessary evil. If there was any chance he could finally break free of the shitstorm in his head and convince Gemma that he was worthy of her, it had to be done.

He slipped Blaze's leash from the rearview mirror. The moment his hand touched the leash, Blaze was on his feet. He got out and opened the rear door of his personal pickup, a red Dodge Ram, then clipped on the leash.

Brett hadn't talked to Gemma since the hangar fire. After meetings at his office, he'd stopped by her hospital room once, but she'd been asleep. The next day, he'd swung by again, but she'd already been released, and it was just as well. Before talking to her again, he needed to be sure he was making headway with the shrink. He was beyond grateful to a god he hadn't sworn allegiance to in years that she hadn't died.

"Ready, buddy?"

Blaze barked, then hopped from the truck. Another wave of relief washed over him as he looked at the felt booties Blaze wore. When he'd tackled Kelly Hawkin in the hangar, Blaze had suffered chemical burns on the pads of both feet from landing in an inch-deep puddle of MEK. In typical canine fashion, Blaze had suffered in silence. Ten days had passed since the fire, during which time Brett had applied special ointment to the dry and cracked pads. One more day and the booties could come off.

"Let's do this."

Allison Aldrich Brady, now seventeen, and her adopted mother, Diane Brady, joined them on the sidewalk.

"Thank you for allowing this meeting to take place," Brett said to Mrs. Brady. "This will mean a lot to Gavin."

"It means a lot to Ally, too," she replied. "I've come to realize over the last few years that she needs her brother as much as he needs her."

Evan rested his hand on Ally's shoulder. "Are you ready?"

Ally gave a quick nod. "I've been waiting five years for this moment. Does he know I'm coming?"

"No," Brett said. "It's a surprise."

"C'mon, then." Evan's lips curved into a genuine smile. "Let's make his day."

Once in a while, Brett had seen Evan smile, but the only times he'd ever seen his friend truly happy was when he'd been successful in finding a missing child. Alive, that was. Unfortunately, that wasn't always the case.

Outside Gavin's room, Brett knocked on the door.

"Go away!" came the shouted response.

Dr. Franklin, who'd met them in the lobby, cleared his throat. "He's had a rough couple of days."

"Then it's time to cheer him up." Brett knocked again, harder. "It's Brett Tanner. I brought Blaze. Open the door."

"No. Go away," Gavin repeated.

"May I?" Ally asked.

"Be my guest." Brett winked.

Ally knocked again. "Gavin? It's Ally. Please open the door."

Seconds of silence passed. When the door opened, Gavin peered through the crack, then his eyes widened. Eventually, his mouth fell open, but no words came out.

Ally began wringing her hands. "Aren't you going to say something?"

"Ally?" he whispered, opening the door wider. "Is it really you?"

She nodded, rolling her lips inward as tears trickled down her face. "It's me." She threw herself at Gavin, wrapping her arms around him.

"Oh god." Gavin squeezed his eyes shut, returning the embrace. He opened his eyes, looking at Brett, then Evan. "Thank you," he choked out.

Brett couldn't stop grinning as he watched the tearful reunion. He didn't harbor any false hope that he and Gemma would have a similar one, but he was sure gonna try. "Catch ya later, kid."

"Gavin, Ally?" Evan said. "Whatever you do, don't lose each other again." Without another word, Evan turned and walked away.

Brett watched Evan's receding back. He knew his

friend felt good about Ally Aldrich, but with every missing child he found, a little part of Evan died inside. He'd just accomplished something remarkable, because he was the best at what he did, but he still hadn't managed to find his own sister. And it was killing him, slowly and by painful degrees.

"Blaze, let's go." With obvious reluctance, Blaze followed him and Evan back outside. Brett rested a hand on Evan's shoulder. "Thanks, man. You did good."

"Yeah." Evan nodded. The smile was gone, replaced by the ever-present expression of sadness and loss Brett had become accustomed to over the years.

"You'll find her. If anyone can, *you* will." He prayed it wasn't six feet under in an unmarked grave. "Let's get out of here. I need backup, in case Gemma decides to shoot me with her framing nailer."

CHAPTER THIRTY-ONE

"That's it." Gemma pressed the last of the new cooktop's blue backsplash tile into the mastic, then stepped back to admire the zigzag pattern she and her mom had designed together.

"Oh, honey." Her mother clapped her hands together. "It's beautiful. You really do have exquisite taste in tile, sweetheart."

"Thanks, Mom. It was a team effort." She draped an arm over her mother's shoulder. She'd been delighted when Gemma had asked for help with the design. It was the first time she'd asked her mother for input on the house.

Her mother's arm tightened around Gemma's waist. "I'm so glad you finally asked us all to help."

"Me, too, Mom. Me, too." In the last week, they'd accomplished what would have taken her six months, maybe more, to complete on her own. And she'd loved having them here.

Shouting from the front lawn filtered into the kitchen. The shouting turned to laughter. Gemma and her mother rushed out the front door and onto the lawn. Parked on the street in front of her house were three more vehicles, none of which she recognized.

But she did recognize the big golden-brown head in the back seat of the red Dodge pickup. Blaze. Wherever Blaze was, Brett was, too. They were a team. They shared an unbreakable bond she'd once stupidly hoped to have with Brett. She gave a quick shake of her head to clear it of what she now realized was a naive, unrealistic thought.

When Brett rounded the hood of the truck and let Blaze out, Gemma swallowed. Wearing khaki shorts that showed off his long, powerful thighs and calves, and a blue T-shirt that molded to every cut muscle in his shoulders, chest, and abs, he could still make her heart beat faster. Okay, so he was still hot. That didn't mean she'd forgiven him, or ever would.

"Brett! How nice." To her dismay, her mother went right up and drew him in for a tight hug.

"Gee, thanks, Mom," Gemma mumbled. He'd broken her heart, but her mother still adored him. Worse, her brothers shook hands with him as if they were best buds. Only her father stood back, eyeing Brett speculatively, then throwing Gemma a concerned look.

Cautiously, Brett approached her father. Reluctantly, her dad shook Brett's hand.

Deck and Evan joined what was now a small crowd on her front lawn. Spotting her, Blaze loped over and barked until she leaned down to pet his head and let him lick her chin.

"Hello, Blaze. I've missed you." He barked again, pressing his big body against her legs. When she straightened, eight pairs of eyes were on her. Why Brett and his friends were here, she didn't know. Maybe they'd come to update her on the U.S. Attorney's Office investigation.

Brett's smile faded as he looked at her. "Hi," he said.

All other conversation around them ceased. Even the birds seemed to have stopped chirping, and the squirrels stopped chattering.

"Hi?" He had to be kidding. "That's all you have to say after ghosting me?" *And not only breaking my heart, but crushing it into sawdust.*

"Uh-oh," Chris said.

"Someone's in the doghouse," Rory whispered.

Ben chuckled. "And it's *not* his dog."

Brett shoved his hands in his pockets. "I had some things I needed to take care of."

"Such as?" Not that she cared, not really. What he did with his life from now on was his business, not hers. Clearly, he'd come here to tell her something, so the sooner he did it and left again, the easier it would be for her treacherous heart to resume beating at a normal rhythm. As opposed to the way it was ricocheting around in her chest at the moment.

He glanced at Evan. "Evan found Gavin's sister. This morning, we brought them back together."

"That's wonderful." Gemma smiled. "I'm happy for him. For both of them." Hopefully, being reunited with his sister would help Gavin in ways no amount of psychiatric therapy ever could.

Brett nodded. "And Judge Tafoya signed off on extending Gavin's psychiatric care for another six months before making her final decision, but things look promising."

"That's good news." It really was. *Stick to your guns, girl.* "But that didn't take you ten days."

"No, it didn't. I, uh, had some other things to take care of."

"Let's give them a little space, shall we?" Her mother hitched her head at her brothers and her dad, including Deck and Evan in her not-too-subtle hint.

The others walked off, but not too far, and she could tell her entire family was eavesdropping.

"Let me get this straight. You thought you would just show up with good news and all would be forgiven?" *Not.* Not by a long shot.

He grimaced. "Definitely not that."

"What, then?" Because she really wanted to get this over with. Whatever *this* was.

"I brought you something. A peace offering." He went to the back of the pickup, in the bed of which was a large, rectangular object covered by a blanket. Brett lowered the tailgate, vaulted up, then whipped off the blanket.

Gemma's jaw dropped. Numbly, she went to the tailgate, still not believing what she was looking at. Covered in shrink wrap and secured in a wood frame was an enormous eyebrow window. Vaguely, she heard the hushed exclamations from her family.

"Wow."

"Holy shit."

"That had to have cost a bundle."

It had. Vividly, she recalled the moment when she'd priced one out, then nearly had a coronary.

She ran her gaze over the stunning, arched window, the expertly crafted frame. "It's beautiful," she choked out.

Brett grinned. "I was hoping you'd like it."

"Of course I like it, but-but…" She couldn't finish the sentence. Why had he done something so thoughtful, so monumentally generous? Tears leaked from her eyes. She swiped them away, but they just kept coming.

"Is she *crying*?" Ben asked in an incredulous tone.

"Nobody's made her cry in, well, so long I can't remember," Chris said. "We might have to take Brett out back and beat him up for that."

Her mother giggled. Her dad laughed, and her brothers began snickering like a bunch of little boys.

"Well?" Brett watched her intently. "Do you really like it?"

"Like it?" She *loved* it, but that wasn't the point. This was an incredibly wonderful gesture, one he clearly hoped would mend fences between them. But no way would she make it that easy on him. He'd hurt her terribly. She needed to be strong, and there were things she had to get off her chest before ever considering forgiving him.

Not that forgiveness was on the table.

Nope. No way, no how.

Not yet, anyway.

She swallowed, wiping away the last of her tears. "Come with me," she ordered. "We need to talk."

Without looking back, she stormed into the house.

• • •

"Somebody's in trouble."

"He's gonna get it."

"Yup, she's about to ream him a new one."

"You guys are hysterical." And they were right. Brett was about to get his ass reamed out by a five-foot-one powerhouse of a woman.

He hopped out of the pickup. Blaze had abandoned him in favor of Gemma and had followed her inside.

Evan slapped him on the back. "Good luck."

Deck grinned. "You're gonna need it. And take this." He handed Brett a potted aloe vera. "It's from Tori for Gemma's legs."

"I'll tell her." As Brett went through the living room, he noted the newly installed floor and ceiling molding and, in the kitchen, the new tile backsplash and fresh paint. He found Gemma in the backyard, sitting in a chair with her legs propped on the edge of a firepit. Blaze busied himself by trotting around the yard, sniffing the grass, then laying down and rolling around on his back.

Since she didn't invite him to sit in one of the other chairs, he waited. And waited.

And it was killing him.

Finally, after what seemed like minutes but was probably only seconds, she let out a huff. "You can sit down, if you want to."

He held back the breath of relief threatening to whoosh loudly from his lungs, then took the chair next to Gemma's. Her toenails were white with little orange fish on the big nails.

"Nice toenails."

"Thanks. With my burns, I had to forego the usual foot bath and calf massage." She sighed. "Too bad. That's the best part about getting a pedi."

"I'll have to take your word for that. And speaking of burns…" He set the aloe plant on the ledge of the firepit. "This is from Tori. For your legs."

"Tell her I said thanks." From the determined set of her jaw and the fact that she wouldn't look at him, he had a lot of sucking up to do. Groveling *and* sucking up. He was just as determined as she was. More so, but he understood her anger. He'd certainly earned it.

For someone unaccustomed to working with others, let alone asking for help, trusting and partnering with him hadn't come easily for her. When it finally had, he'd yanked the rug out from under her.

As he stared into the flickering blue-and-orange flames in the firepit, it occurred to him that she'd broken new ground by asking Evan for help, then by recruiting her family to help with all the new work he'd seen. They were both making life changes.

Still, she said nothing, preferring to stare at the firepit.

"Don't you want to know what I've been doing over the last week and a half?" he asked, breaking the silence.

"Aside from reuniting Gavin with his sister, I don't care what you were doing." Her lips trembled, and she shifted in the chair.

Brett grinned. It was killing her that he wasn't telling her. It was the oldest rule in the federal agent interviewing handbook. Human beings had an inherent need to fill in the pregnant pauses, so if you wanted a person to say something, you clammed up. Frankly, he wanted to confirm that she still cared enough to know what he'd been up to. "Are you *sure* you don't want to know?"

She shifted again, recrossing her legs. "Yes. I'm sure. Of course I'm sure."

Wait for it.

She made a sound of exasperation. "Okay, what?"

Brett's grin broadened. *Gotcha.* "Besides helping Evan with Gavin and his sister, I've been working with Tom Willard to put the finishing touches on the case for the U.S. Attorney's Office." He recapped everything that had happened in the last week, including the indictments.

"How nice for you." She smiled, that same sarcastic, vinegar-sweet smile he'd seen on her before. "It sounds like you wrapped up the case with a bow."

"Don't you mean *we* wrapped up the case with a bow?"

"No." She looked at him as if she wanted to gut him. Which she probably did. "*We* didn't. Because *you* went off without me."

"It was your rapport with Sally Nash," he countered, "that solved the Torrance Lane fire." Something so unimaginably important to him, he could never repay her. "So yeah. *We* wrapped up the case. Together."

"There *is* no together," she hissed. "Not anymore. Not since you went around me. The only reason I was able to find you at the airport was because I followed Evan."

Ah. They'd all been wondering how she'd managed that. Evan had assured him that he hadn't told her where he'd been going after taking Sally Nash's statement.

He waited a few moments for some of the steam to stop shooting from her ears. "I'm sorry for what I did, but I'd do it again in a heartbeat. I never meant to hurt you. I went around you to protect you."

"I don't *need* protecting. What I *need* is to be part of a team again. *Our* team."

"Not a chance." He stood and began pacing around the firepit. "I can't work with you anymore."

"Why not?" She stood and fisted her hands at her hips, something he'd come to realize she did when she was about to stand her ground, and damn did she look hot doing it. "You waltz in here, bearing gifts, yet you don't want to work with me again?"

Color rose to her cheeks, and her eyes burned with a passion he'd come to love. Neanderthal that he was, no small amount of pride tickled him that he was the one who'd made her look that way.

"Well?" she prodded. "Why can't you work with me anymore?"

The memory of her face staring back at him from the cockpit of Hawkin's Cessna rammed him in the solar plexus. "Because I failed you. You're too much of a distraction to me, and because of that, I didn't see any of it coming. I should have, and I can't let that happen again." He'd die first. Because of his mistake, again, *she* almost had.

"Why am I such a distraction?" Her voice had softened.

Before he told her why, she needed to know everything. "I've been seeing a shrink." He let that sink in before continuing, wanting to gauge her reaction.

Her brows rose slightly. "That's good."

"I'm a work in progress and probably will be for the rest of my life." A life he prayed she'd want to live *with* him. "I've been living with survivor's guilt and PTSD for so long now that I've forgotten what life's like without it. But I have to find out, or there'll be no room for anything else in my life."

"Like what?" she asked, inching closer.

"Like happiness, brightness, and beauty. Like you." He closed the distance between them. "You're the light in my life. You're all the brightness and beauty a guy could ever wish for. Do you think you could ever love a guy like me—a work in progress?"

"Wait." She waved her finger at him. "Let's not jump the gun here. Let's get back to that distraction thing. Why exactly am I such a distraction to you?"

"Because you're so damn beautiful." More so right at this minute than ever before.

"Not that I agree with you, but that's superficial." She cocked her head, eyeing him oddly. "What else?"

Brett's heart was in his throat. Was he making progress? He couldn't be sure, not with Gemma. She always kept him on his toes. "You're kind, caring, and when you believe strongly about something, you never back down. You're the most amazing woman I've ever met." No truer words had ever crossed his lips.

"And?" Her voice had softened again, more this time.

"And mostly," he replied, swallowing the giant lump in his throat, "because I love you. You're all I think about. Whenever you're around, I can't see straight. Hell, I can't see *anything* but you."

She took a step back, and his heart squeezed. The love of his life was about to walk away forever. Then she stopped. Her eyes shimmered, and she began blinking rapidly. "Oh."

Oh? What had that meant? She still hadn't said she loved him back. The rest of his life depended on her answer to his next question.

"So could you ever love a guy like me—a work in progress?"

She rolled her lips inward, then nodded. "Yes."

"Are you sure?" If she wasn't, it only meant he had more work to do. More groveling and sucking up. "Because if you aren't, I'll—"

"I'm sure." She stepped closer, then threw her arms around his neck, smiling up at him. "I love you, too," she whispered on a sob. "We both have a lot of learning and healing to do. We can do anything. *Together*."

Thank God. He wrapped his arms around her, lifting her off the ground and hugging her tightly. He kissed her deeply, sweetly, savoring her taste, her smell, the feel of her body snugged against his, and everything else about her.

Especially her love.

He didn't know what he'd done to deserve her, but he was looking forward to spending the rest of his life earning the privilege.

ACKNOWLEDGMENTS

ATF Special Agent Canine Handler Rennie Mora, and ATF Supervisory Special Agent Rebecca Sauerhaft, for those lengthy phone conversations in which you shared your complex world with me. Rockland County Sheriff's Office Detective Robert Moger and his accelerant detection K9 Peyton, for graciously sharing your time and expertise. NICB Supervisory Special Agent Jon Hersely, for the marathon brainstorming session that led to the plot of this book. To my friends at the U.S. Attorney's Office, thank you for the refresher course in the Federal Rules of Criminal Procedure. Kayla Gray and Cheyenne McCray, for being steadfast friends and the most awesome critique partners for so many years I've lost count. My editors, Robin Haseltine—Robin, so glad you're on my team!—and Heather Howland, and the entire Entangled staff. Last, to my readers. Without your support, none of this is possible.

AUTHOR'S NOTE

K-9s are a highly specialized component of law enforcement few officers are blessed to experience and pose challenges most of us never encounter on the job. I've done my best to accurately reflect this unique aspect of law enforcement. Any mistakes contained within this book are entirely my own.

AMARA
an imprint of Entangled Publishing LLC